The Observer

The Observer

Natalie Wexler

KP
KALORAMA
PRESS
Washington D.C.

This book incorporates a number of historical documents, but it is essentially a work of fiction. Although most of the characters are based on real people, and many of the events described actually transpired, much of the plot and virtually all of the dialogue are invented. Spelling and punctuation in the documents have been modernized, and some have been edited for length and clarity.

ISBN: 978-0-615-99149-8

Library of Congress Control Number: 2014905064

Book design by Ray Rhamey

Author photograph by Sophie Feldman

Cover art: Francis Guy, *View of Baltimore from Chapel Hill,* 1802-1803, Brooklyn Museum; John Vanderlyn, *Eye of Theodosia Burr,* Senate House State Historic Site, New York State Office of Parks, Recreation and Historic Preservation

For Sam

who knows what it's like to found and edit a magazine

A note to the reader

All passages that appear in italics are taken from actual publications. Although some have been edited for greater clarity and readability, they are essentially what appeared in print in 1806 and 1807.

September, 1806

Baltimore, Maryland

Chapter One: Eliza

This morning we ate our breakfast as usual, the three of us: Father, Polly, and myself. Mrs. Morris arrived at her accustomed time with the provisions she had acquired at the market: a limp chicken, some yellowish cabbage, a few dented apples. At eight, as always, Father left for the Dispensary, eager to tend to whatever victims of disease the night might have washed up. And Polly and I settled in the library with a slate and some chalk, for the realization has struck me that next month she will be turning six, and I am determined that she'll learn her letters without further ado. All in all, it was an unremarkable morning, offering no clue of what the afternoon would bring.

Alas, my efforts at instilling some learning in Polly soon foundered. After a mere ten minutes, she began to whine and pout and rub her eyes, complaining of fatigue, and at last she threw the slate upon the floor. Had this same scene not transpired a dozen times or more in the last month, I might have relented; I might have put her on my knee and pressed my cheek to hers and called her my own little Moggie, as she perhaps expected. But, I reminded myself, the girl must learn, it was time: no child of mine, male or female, will make her way in the world unlettered and untutored. I suppose at that moment I may have thought of that lout her father, wherever he may be, so feckless and lacking in ambition. And so I told her that if it was only amusement she sought in life, she would suffer for it; and that a life of idleness would surely lead to misery and wickedness.

It was no more than what my own father had said to me, or more often to my brother, many times in my childhood, but it had an effect on Polly all out of proportion to what I'd intended. She stared at me, her eyes wide, and then her features drew themselves together, giving her the aspect of a small pink prune. A moment later she burst into a loud sob and ran from the room. I had an impulse to follow the child and tell her I hadn't intended to cause her such distress. But no, I told myself, you must be firm. Give her time to consider her mistake, and she will return, chastened and ready to learn.

And so instead I picked up the latest submissions that Mr. Cork had sent for me to read and evaluate for publication in the Companion, and within a few minutes I was sufficiently absorbed in attempting to peruse them that I had entirely forgotten Polly's lessons.

The first offering on the pile was a long poem, written in heroic couplets, concerning some romance that had gone awry. The initial stanzas appeared to have some merit, but the author soon proved himself neither a Pope nor a Dryden, and certainly no Johnson. The heroic couplet, I considered, is a form to be closely guarded; when it falls into the wrong hands it is tiresome in the extreme. Perhaps one should be required to obtain a license before attempting to employ it. "No!" I wrote on the first page.

Next was a tale, no doubt meant to be amusing, of a bachelor pursued by three young coquettes, sent by a correspondent styling himself "Cloanthus." But the subject was such a tired one, and the writing generally so puerile, that I soon cast it aside. I had just begun the third, an essay on the decline of the Holy Roman Empire that appeared more promising, when a messenger arrived with a missive from none other than Mr. Cork himself.

I sighed as I broke the seal, expecting some peremptory chastisement for not having returned the submissions to him yet — for I have become accustomed to such messages. Either he is a much faster reader than I, or he does not invest the care that I do in reading what arrives in our letter-box — or perhaps, as I suspect, it has been so long since he himself has read a submission (though he currently bears the title of Editor) that he no longer has any understanding of how much time the task requires. But as I unfolded the paper and read the words he had scrawled there — once, then twice, and then a third time to ensure that I had comprehended them rightly — I felt my breath catch and my heart beat faster. "Yes, yes," I heard myself whisper aloud. "Yes, yes, I will!"

I had just settled down at the desk to write my reply when someone was again at the door. "My dear Mr. Cork," I began to write, heedless, expecting that it was some tradesman or prospective patient seeking my father, and that if I let the knocking continue Mrs. Morris might be induced to extract herself from the bowels of the kitchen and send whomever it was away. But apparently Mrs. Morris could not see fit to separate herself from her chicken and her cabbage, and the knocking began afresh. I glanced out the window and spied a handsome red carriage and four horses that I immediately recognized, with a start, as belonging to Mr. Patterson.

"Betsy!" I murmured in alarm, and raced to the door.

She swept past me impatiently into the sitting room, no doubt put out about being kept waiting on the doorstep. "I can't imagine where Mrs. Morris has got to," I called after her.

She removed her hat and looked around for a clear surface on which to place it, with no success; at last she settled for a spot atop a stack of medical volumes that Father had been consulting the evening before.

"If the woman can't be bothered to answer the door, I shouldn't bother to keep her on, if I were you," she said, removing her lavender kid gloves and placing them in the interior of her upturned bonnet.

"Or perhaps ..." She glanced around, as she always does on her infrequent visits to our humble cot, with an expression of distaste. And as always, I suddenly saw the room through her eyes: the cloudlets of dust at the corners, the piles of books and papers on the floor and tables, the submissions I'd been reading scattered about. Polly's slate still on the floor where she'd flung it. "Or *perhaps*," Betsy continued, "what you need is another servant."

"Perhaps," I countered, "but the unfortunate problem is that if we hired another servant we would have to find a way to pay her."

Betsy looked at me sharply, perhaps interpreting my remark as a jab at the small army of slaves that maintain her father's various houses in a state of pristine order.

"But I'm so glad you've come," I said quickly. "I've just received a letter, the most extraordinary letter—"

"Indeed? What a coincidence. So have I." She extracted a folded paper from the beaded black reticule that dangled at her wrist and extended it to me.

"From Mr. Bonaparte?" I asked, taking it.

It has been months since any word has come from her supposed husband—not that I would ever apply that limiting adjective in her presence, but when a marriage has been declared null and void by the Emperor of France, and when the husband in question has the spine of an earthworm, one must perforce entertain some doubts as to the marriage's continued existence. I of course had my reservations about Jerome Bonaparte from the moment he set foot in Baltimore, some three years ago now. I know all too well that when marriage is entered into impulsively, it is entered into at one's peril. And Betsy then only eighteen, a full year younger than myself when I contracted a similar, if far less celebrated, misalliance! I tried to warn her against it, but she was more determined than I have ever seen her, which is saying a great deal. Not even the imperious Mr. Patterson, before whom strong men routinely quake, could exercise his paternal authority to force a breach between the besotted couple. It remains to be seen if the Emperor will succeed where he has failed.

I opened the letter with some eagerness—not having forgotten my own letter, but recognizing that there could be no discussion of it until this other matter had received my attention. After a long silence, no doubt enforced by his brother Napoleon, there has in recent weeks been a small flurry of communications from Jerome. Some months ago he was sent on a naval mission to the West Indies—which, as compared to France or Italy, is but a mere trot down the lane from Baltimore. What cared he, he'd written from Cayenne in May, for wealth and title; he would throw all his prospects over to be with his *bien aimée femme* and his *cher fils*. He'd promised to come to them as soon as he could—or at least used words that raised that expectation in Betsy's breast.

The letter in my hand was only a few lines, written July 17th aboard a French ship—it carried an engraving at the top of a galley apparently manned by heroic classical personages and escorted by a large winged creature from whose mouth there streamed a banner emblazoned with the words *Liberté des Mers*. There was no salutation, and the signature at the end consisted merely of the initials "J.B." I scanned the page: He had only time for a word; he was well; and he had *"bien du regrêt"* at being only 150 leagues (these last words underlined) from her without being able to enjoy the happiness of seeing her. He embraced her with all his heart, he sent *"une caresse"* to little Jerome Napoleon, and his compliments to her family. And that was all.

"So," I said, looking up, "he will not come?"

Betsy stiffened her chin. "It would seem not. He's probably back in France by now." She looked away for a moment, towards the bookcases, and when she turned back all the hurt and disappointment she was trying to keep at bay seemed to rush to her eyes — her lovely hazel eyes, usually so cool and languid, now soft and moist. "What a stupid fool I was to think ..." She stopped and raised her small white hands to cover her face.

"Oh my dear girl," I soothed, wrapping her in my arms as though she were a child of thirteen again and I the wise and worldly eighteen-year-old she had so admired. "It's not so easy to defy the wishes of an emperor, you know. He does love you, you must never doubt it. The way he looked at you, when he left us in Lisbon, as though he were engraving your image on his soul? I saw it myself, and there was no doubting his sincerity." Here I spoke nothing less than the truth; whatever else Jerome was, he clearly worshipped at Betsy's delicate feet. "And all the lovely things he sent you?" Indeed, my eye was only an inch or two from one of the pearl and garnet earrings salvaged from the poor waterlogged box of treasures that had arrived a few months ago. "You have a husband who adores you, and who will never stop adoring you. You must remember that."

She pressed her head against my shoulder, and I wondered for a moment if her thoughts ran parallel to mine. I could not banish from my mind the self-pitying consideration that I too have an errant husband — a husband who has certainly stopped adoring me, if he ever did, and whose prolonged absence lacks the excuse of an emperor's wrath, or indeed any excuse, excepting that of poverty. Five long years, and I have received no expressions of *regrêt*, no missives containing *une caresse* for Polly. I fancied that the pressure of Betsy's head signified a recognition that I understood something of her distress. But then she suddenly drew back from my embrace, her grief and bewilderment having given way to vexation.

"But what good will his adoration do me," she spat at me, "if he keeps himself at a distance of thousands of miles, reveling in the trappings of royalty, while I'm condemned to live in this dreadful place, surrounded by those who despise and mock me? I would prefer a husband who was less adoring and more *present.*

Allow me to remind you that it has been well over a year since that day in Lisbon. Bo is now more than a year old and has yet to meet his father!"

It had vanished, it seemed, that moment of sympathy between us, if indeed it had existed. She was again the hard, disdainful woman I have watched her become these last twelve months, and I no more than the lady-in-waiting she sometimes condescends to grace with her attention. Still, I knew the lines it was my duty to repeat.

"You mustn't abandon hope," I told her. "He may yet prove himself a hero in battle, as he promised, and ask for you and Bo as his reward."

"Jerome a hero?" She raised a sly eyebrow. "Do you really think so?"

I had to laugh, and as I laughed I felt the distance between us shrink once more. It was indeed no easy thing to picture. Jerome surely looked the part of the dashing young naval adventurer, but alas, he lacked the character — and the stomach, as we discovered during our Atlantic crossing, when he was just as seasick as the rest of us.

"But of course I will appear unconcerned, in public," Betsy continued, her manner now brusque. "We must all behave as though we have the greatest confidence in him and his intentions." She adjusted her shawl, a rose and green Indian pattern shot through with threads of gold, arranged herself on the settee, and regarded me coolly. "But you said that you'd received a letter too?"

"Oh yes ..." It seemed so trivial now, compared to the events on the world's stage that touched her life. "From Mr. Cork."

"Mr. Cork of the Companion?"

I nodded and took a breath, then my words came out in a rush. "You'll never guess. He's asked if I would take on the position of Editor!"

She frowned. "Are you sure?"

"I'll show you!" I looked about the room. "I know it's here somewhere, I just had it in my hand." It took me a minute or two, I confess, lifting this book and that, before I found the letter — under the pile of submissions I'd been reading, of course. I seated myself across from her on Father's old yellow armchair to await her verdict.

"What this says," Betsy sniffed when she'd finished perusing it, "is that he wants you to take on the *duties* of Editor."

"But clearly, he means that I would *be* the Editor. If it were only the duties he wanted me to carry out, we could simply continue on as we are now. He has the title, and I have all the work." I plucked up the pile of submissions and let them fall again to the table with a small slap. "Oh, well," I added, as several sheets escaped from the pile and floated down onto the carpet like large square snowflakes, "I imagine some of these offerings would be greatly improved by having their pages rearranged at random."

Betsy allowed her rosy lips to curl upwards at the edges. "But you're always complaining so about them — Cork and Mr. Harmer and my brother Charles and the rest. I thought they were all hopeless idiots who blocked your superior ideas at every turn. Ill-behaved boys, you've called them."

It was difficult to tell whether she was mocking me or endorsing my view of the situation. If there was hostility beneath her smile, no doubt it was due to her unaccountable fondness for her rake of a younger brother.

"We've had some disagreements, it's true," I said carefully. "And some of them weren't entirely welcoming of a female presence at their meetings, at the beginning — they were convening at one of those filthy taverns near the harbor until I insisted we meet here instead. But they needed me, you see, as they hadn't the time to go through all the submissions or write much themselves, once they'd finished their studies at St. Mary's. They've all taken up business, or the law, or what have you. And as I told them, it was only fitting that a lady, who doesn't have such demands on her time, should make herself useful by devoting herself to the sorts of cultural endeavors they could no longer manage. And it seems they've at last come to respect my views, and my greater experience of life. Or at least Mr. Cork has. Why else would he offer me the post of Editor?"

Betsy tapped her lip with a finger, thinking. "And who pays for this undertaking? Does the paper have enough subscribers to cover its expenses?"

I shrugged. Betsy has always been far more interested than I am in the commercial aspects of life. "I believe there's some arrangement with Mr. Cork's uncle — he has a shipping concern, I imagine your father knows him. It seems he's been underwriting some of the costs."

Betsy continued to look thoughtful. "Are the correspondents paid for their articles?"

"Of course not! Nor have any of the editors ever received a penny for their labors. It's in the nature of a civic duty, undertaken by gentlemen — and the few ladies who have submitted essays or poems — for the amusement and edification of their fellow citizens."

"So that leaves only the costs of printing, and paying the carriers," Betsy went on. "How much do you charge for a subscription?"

"Heavens, I don't know! I only concern myself with the editorial side of things." I glanced at the tower of manuscripts beside me. "Which is quite enough, in my opinion."

Betsy followed my gaze and shook her head. "Why you should want to undertake all that work I can't begin to fathom. Although I'll admit your articles do have a certain flair. That one you wrote about playing loo, a few weeks ago, the 'Biddy Fidget' one — it seemed the whole town was talking of it."

I fear an immodest grin spread across my face as a pleasurable warmth suffused my veins.

"It's a great deal of work, it's true," I said, in as sober a tone as I could manage. "But as I told those boys — I mean, *gentlemen* — I feel I must do what I can to raise the level of culture in this city, which we both know is in desperate need of improvement. What's needed, and what the other periodicals here fail to supply, is the judicious use of praise to encourage the few worthy artistic efforts amongst us. And, of course, the occasional satirical sally to gently prod the inhabitants of this place to a better understanding of their own follies. I sometimes wonder if any city on earth has seen such an abundance of material wealth coupled with so complete an absence of taste. That new bank on Market Street, for instance, the one at the corner of Calvert. Have you seen it?"

Betsy rolled her eyes. "The one with the pillars that support nothing? How could I miss it?"

"And it's not only that they lack any function! It's that they're set off in little niches, as though they were *objets d'art*. Except, of course, that you can't really see them."

"Yes, because they're walled off in sentry boxes, like watchmen." We were both in the throes of merriment now. "I suppose the idea is to ward off any thieves who should take it into their heads to approach. Surely any thief in his right mind will be intimidated by a column in a niche! Now, *there*'s a subject for satire." She leaned forward from her perch on the settee and placed her hand on mine, her eyebrows drawn together in concern. "But you must be discreet," she warned.

"Well, I hadn't intended to use my own name, of course. What do you think of 'Tabitha Simple'? I fancy it has a disarming ring to it."

Betsy shook her head, sending her dark curls dancing. "*Timothy* Simple perhaps."

"Oh ..." I waved my hand in the direction of the side table, accidentally sending a pewter candlestick clattering to the floor. "I fail to see why my sex should be of any concern to the public," I said, picking it up. "There were no objections to 'Biddy Fidget' expressing her opinions in print."

"Half the town probably assumed old Miss Fidget was actually a man. But even if they didn't, there's quite a difference between a female correspondent and a female *editor*. Have you ever even heard of such a thing?"

I paused. "No, I suppose not. But why should it matter?"

"Eliza, really, you needn't look any further than the pages of the Companion itself. Wasn't it the Companion that published that article saying women were incapable of true learning—that they were only fit to be 'smatterers in knowledge,' or something of the sort? And that educating them only resulted in their becoming intolerably puffed up with vanity?"

"Yes, but that was months ago. And we published a refutation by another correspondent the following week." But the memory of the incident still burned. I had argued against accepting the first piece for publication, but at the time I had only recently been allowed to start attending editorial meetings—which are now a thing of the past, as the gentlemen no longer have time for them—and my remonstrances only produced some rolling eyes and half-stifled laughter.

"The fact remains," Betsy continued in a lecturing tone, "that we are in Baltimore, not Paris." There was a slight catch in her voice on that last word, with its evocation of the place she longed to be. "And Baltimore may tolerate the occasional piece of writing by a woman—a witty tirade against loo, or a few lines of poetry—but it's simply not ready for a woman editor, and perhaps never will be. Baltimore ladies are considered fit only to listen with rapt attention to Baltimore gentlemen—to their grubby little stories of counting houses and the rise and fall in wheat prices, as though they were fascinating tales of adventure and derring-do. No doubt it's only to escape such stifling ennui that the females here are so eager to conceive the brats of these men, and then devote themselves to the even more enervating task of nursing and raising them! If the men in this town were able to say anything of even the remotest interest, I'm quite sure that the number of births would decline by half."

I couldn't quite stifle a smile; it's always amusing to hear such venom spew from one who wears the face of an angel. I certainly sympathized with her sentiments. And yet it seemed to me that as usual, in her bitterness and flippancy, she had lost sight of what was truly important. Yes, the town and its inhabitants are dull—but we must try to improve and enliven the situation, not merely ridicule it. "Then you would advise me to reject the offer," I said, with perhaps a touch of acid in my voice. "Because, as you point out, we are not in Paris?"

She stood and began to put on her gloves. "If you're determined to undertake it, I would simply caution you to be on your guard. I shouldn't want you to suffer as I have. People can be quite cruel."

"Oh, I won't care what people say, so long as they take out subscriptions!" Then I considered that she might interpret this remark as a belittling of her own feelings—and it's true the town has been vicious towards Betsy of late, seeming to gloat in her exceedingly public humiliation. "Perhaps you're right, though. There's no need to adopt any name at all—I can simply be the nameless, sexless 'Editor.'"

But Betsy's attention had wandered. She was at the window now, rubbing away at a spot on the glass to peer at old Pompey outside, asleep on the bench of her carriage, the horses twitching and the reins slack. "Look at him." She sighed and shook her head. "Lounging as though he were in his bed. What will people think? They all know who his mistress is. Really, I should tell my father to sell the wretch down South and replace him with someone more suitable. In my position I must be extremely careful about appearances, you know, Jerome was quite clear on that score … Oh, but there's *your* father now." She peered more closely through the thick, and, I admit, rather dusty pane. "And he seems to have some sort of street urchin with him."

"Oh dear, what now?" I tried to laugh lightly. If Father had brought home another lost soul, some orphan who had turned up at the Dispensary with yellow fever or cholera, that would be problem enough. But to have the poor wretch, whoever or whatever it was, cross paths with the grand Madame Bonaparte ... that was to be avoided at all costs. No doubt, I thought, he would escort this person right in through the front door. Betsy—indeed all the Pattersons—are already dubious enough about Father's scarcely concealed reverence for the poor and disdain for the wealthy. And given that they are the wealthiest family in town, with the exception of the Carroll-Caton clan, one may well understand their sentiments. I sometimes think that were it not for our kinship, distant as it is—and were Father not a skilled doctor whose ministrations have more than once restored the health of a Patterson child—they would hardly tolerate us.

I hurried Betsy into the hall, anxious to avoid an encounter, but I proved too late.

"Why, if it isn't Betsy Patterson!" Father cried jovially as he flung open the front door. "Or rather—my apologies ..." He extended a thin stockinged leg, splattered with what appeared to be the contents of a slop bucket at the Dispensary, and bent at the waist with a flourish of his hat. "*Madame Bonaparte.*"

"Dr. Crawford," said Betsy in clipped tones. Perhaps, given her circumstances, she imagined an element of mockery in his elaborate salute. But she allowed her hand to be kissed and regarded the creature who stood behind Father with remote and uncertain curiosity.

"Ah," said Father as I winced, "allow me to present Miss Margaret McKenzie." He stepped aside and revealed a girl who appeared to be about sixteen, her copper-colored hair escaping from its pins, her tattered clothes hanging from an undernourished frame, and her expression one of sullen wariness tempered by surprise and awe. News of the notorious Madame Bonaparte's adventures and travails had penetrated even the walls of the almshouse, I surmised.

Betsy nodded coldly and almost imperceptibly, promised to convey Father's respects to her parents, and exited with apparent relief, eager to awaken the delinquent Pompey. No one but Father would have deemed it proper to present a pauper wench to Betsy Bonaparte. But he seemed oblivious to the outrage he had occasioned.

"Now, Eliza," he said as he put a hand on his charge's bony shoulder, "you must see to Margaret. She'll need a place to sleep and some warmer clothes—perhaps you have something that would be suitable?"

I sighed and tried not to look directly at the girl lest my exasperation show too clearly. "A place to sleep? Here? How long is she to stay?"

"Well, that is something we must discuss. But I think she can be of great service to us. To you, in fact."

"Really?" I allowed myself a glance at the girl, who had crossed her arms before her chest and now appeared to be studying the floor with great intensity. "Well, I'll just bring her downstairs to Mrs. Morris in the kitchen, and she can attend to her." I addressed myself to the top of the girl's head, which I noted could use some washing; the vermin that might be frolicking there, their number and variety, was a topic I preferred not to consider. "Come, follow me."

Margaret, wearing ill-fitting boots, nearly tripped on the uneven stairs as we descended to the cellar; no doubt she will need new footwear as well, I thought with a sigh.

Mrs. Morris was standing at the table in the center of the kitchen, plucking the chicken she had arrived with this morning, which would presumably find its way to the dinner table in some more palatable form. Polly was there as well, I noted, sitting under the table and playing with some old cups and spoons that Mrs. Morris must have supplied. She dropped her playthings and regarded me with some trepidation as I entered the room. Almost the way her father used to look at me, I realized, when he'd committed some transgression—arriving home at dawn, for example, still reeking of alcohol and some other woman's scent. I shuddered internally, regretting this morning's scene. I have no desire to be the sort of mother who inspires fear in her child. And yet, I told myself, the girl must learn to attend.

"What's this, then?" Mrs. Morris said with a distinct lack of enthusiasm as Margaret appeared, her eyes still downcast.

I gave Mrs. Morris Margaret's particulars. "Perhaps she could sleep on a pallet in here?" I glanced around. "Or in the storeroom?"

"I suppose," Mrs. Morris said dubiously, wiping the perspiration from her brow. "But I'll need some linen, and a coverlet for her. And I won't have time to do it now, ma'am, not if you want your dinner before midnight."

"That's all right, the pallet can wait until later." The girl was now looking down at Polly and scratching the back of her neck. "But see to her bathing now, at least. Heat her a basin of water, and find her something clean to wear. She can have something out of my clothes press. Something old. A chemise and that dark green frock, perhaps, the one that's been patched." Noticing that Mrs. Morris had sighed wearily and was now plucking the chicken with increased ferocity, I added brightly, "And then she can help you with dinner. Can't you, Margaret?"

But Margaret was no longer standing beside me; she had crouched down to Polly's level and was examining the small collection of kitchenware under the table with interest.

"What's that?" Margaret said, pointing to an inverted teacup with a chip in its rim. It was the first I'd heard her speak; her voice was low and a little hoarse. Good Lord, I thought, has she never seen a teacup before?

"It's a house," said Polly softly, but with a note of pride.

"And who lives there?"

She pronounced the word *thar*, using a hard "r" — a country "r," I thought.

Polly picked up the teacup to reveal a walnut and a hazelnut. "This is the mother," she said solemnly, pointing to the walnut, "and that one's the baby."

"Is there no father?"

I gasped inwardly. It was no question to ask a fatherless child. I saw Polly slowly shake her head.

"Well then," Margaret said, "we must find one, mustn't we?"

This was presumption itself, to encourage unhealthy fantasies in my daughter's imagination, longings that must ever remain unfulfilled.

"Now Margaret," I said briskly, "you must get out of those things and make yourself clean. Mrs. Morris will help you."

I had intended, of course, to tell Father the news about my new position at once. But now I raced back up the stairs to interrogate him as to what precisely his plans were for this Margaret McKenzie.

From the Companion, September 20, 1806:

TO READERS AND CORRESPONDENTS.

Assistance should really be given by those who wish for the continuance of the Companion; however trifling the few pages it contains may appear, the labor and anxiety of preparing it, when left entirely to one person, make it so oppressive a burthen that we sometimes feel our spirits bend beneath the task.

But we recommend CLOANTHUS to practice composition, and improve his style and judgment, before he appears in print . . .

Chapter Two: Margaret

I had a scare today, but I reckon I'm safe enough, at least for now. The lady of this house, Mrs. Anderson, she had a gentleman call on her this afternoon. It seems the two of them are engaged in publishing a newspaper or some such thing. They'd scattered sheets of paper all about the sitting room (I had tidied it up this morning at Mrs. Morris's bidding, but it never stays the way I leave it for more than five minutes, so I don't know why I should bother) and they were deep in an argument about something. Mrs. A had ordered tea and Mrs. Morris couldn't be disturbed, and Polly was amusing herself with some charcoal and paper I had given her, so I was elected to bring it in.

"He simply won't stand for it," the gentleman was saying. "He says it's too sharp, too pointed. In fact what he said was that it was mean-spirited."

"Mean-spirited!" Mrs. A said, rising and pacing the way she does when something has upset her, all angles and bones, waving her arms about. "Has your uncle never heard of satire, Mr. Cork? One can't write effective satire without casting a few stones, you know."

"But that's just it. He says he has no interest in financing the publication of satire, or at least not the acid variety you practice. But I suspect his opposition in this instance has something to do with the fact that he's on quite good terms with Mr. Sullivan."

Mrs. A paused. "Sullivan?"

"The builder of that bank. The one with the pillars that you found so amusing?"

"Ah. I see." Mrs. A stopped pacing, but you could tell that she was still riled. She crossed her arms, closed her eyes, and shook her head. "Just put the tray on the table," she said to me, but of course I couldn't, as there were several piles of books there. "Oh," she said, and moved them off onto the floor, so that later I can have the privilege of putting them back on the table, because she gets upset if you put them on the shelves where she says she can't find them, and there's barely any more room there anyway. "You may go, Margaret," she said. "I'll pour."

But then, as I turned my back to leave, I heard her cry out and I saw that she'd spilled tea all over the table and some on the floor. Maybe because she was agitated, but as I've learned in the two weeks I've been here, it's quite usual for her to spill things and knock things off tables and break things. It's a wonder anything in the house is still in one piece.

I turned back and told her I would fetch a rag in the kitchen and return to clean up the mess. And I was just as glad to be able to come back, for I was curious as to what they were on about. And the name she'd called the man by, Cork, sounded familiar.

"But how was *I* supposed to know that 'Cloanthus' was Charles Patterson?" Mrs. A was saying, pacing about the room now, when I came back in with the rag. "And even if I had known, why should it have made a difference? I won't publish rubbish simply to flatter the powerful, nor will I suppress my opinions to avoid offending your uncle. 'A Safe Companion and an Easy Friend,' indeed! With a motto like that, it's no wonder people expect nothing but insipid praise from the Companion."

"No one is saying you must confine yourself to praise, but must you express yourself quite so strongly?" Mr. Cork said as I sopped up the tea. "If you softened your opinions a bit, or made your criticism less specific —"

"No, this is simply intolerable!" Mrs. A cried. "It's difficult enough to get the Companion out week after week, all on my own, with no help." Here she shot a dark look at Mr. Cork, as though he was the one who was meant to be helping her, which I suppose he is. "But to have my editorial judgments questioned, my writing suppressed, for reasons that are entirely illegitimate … I simply cannot, *cannot* — "

"Now, now, calm yourself," Mr. Cork said. I stole a good look at him for the first time since I'd come in. I did recall him from somewhere: a young man, maybe twenty, with golden hair and a few curls at his forehead, full lips, a nose that hooked a bit but was not unpleasant to look at. "I may have an idea."

"Excuse me," I said, "but I've cleaned up the tea now. Do you want me to pour?"

Mrs. A looked at me for a moment as though I were a mosquito buzzing at her ear. I don't know if she was irritated because of what they were talking about, or because she'd spilled the tea, or because I hadn't called her "ma'am," which I've decided I won't do, and it's all right with the Doctor so she shall have to make her peace with it.

"Yes, fine, Margaret. Go ahead and pour." She turned back to Mr. Cork. "What is it, then? Your idea?"

"Just a moment." I could feel his eyes on me, and I tried to turn my face away, because I began to have a notion concerning where I might have seen him before. "Margaret? Is that your name?"

I nodded, but kept my eyes on the teapot and the cups.

"Didn't you used to work for the Legrands? On Pratt Street?"

"No, sir," I said, trying to keep my voice steady, and my hand, for I didn't want another spill. I thought it best to call him sir. "Never heard of the family. It must have been another girl there who looked like me."

"Very like then, very like indeed." He frowned—I didn't dare look at him again, but I could hear the frown in his voice. I imagined he put a hand to his chin, which stuck out just a bit, in a sort of balance to the nose, and that he was stroking it. "I could have sworn it was you."

"Well, never mind that," said Mrs. A impatiently, and I was grateful to her for once. "You may go now, Margaret."

"Thank you, ma'am," I said, even though I had nothing to thank *her* for, as it was I that had brought the tea and her that had spilled it, but then again, I was thankful to be allowed to go, very thankful, even if she hadn't the slightest idea she'd done me a favor. So I called her ma'am and even gave her a curtsy, which I thought would please her.

I shut the sitting room door behind me and raced to the backstairs, and when I got there I sank down on the top step and put my head in my hands, hoping that no one would call my name anytime soon. I was shaking now, like a dead leaf in a high wind, and I could feel the sweat soaking through my chemise. I swallowed hard and breathed and closed my eyes, but my heart was still galloping away.

I should have known better, I scolded myself. I should never have agreed to come to work here, where I might run up against someone who had been at the Legrands'. Service doesn't agree with me anyway. I don't much care for rich people, and I don't much care for being ordered about as though I'm a trained dog. Fetch this, carry that. That's not what this country is supposed to be about, that's what Papa always said. You're as good as they are, Maggie, and don't you forget it, he would tell me. We've no kings here, and no damned aristocrats.

But then, the Doctor was so kind to me, after Papa and Fanny had breathed their last, that I let myself be persuaded. And what choice did I have? Mrs. Brooks would never have let me stay in our room at the Point, as we owed her at least three weeks' rent. And even if she did, I could never have earned enough to pay for the room by going back to slop work. Twelve and a half cents for a pair of trousers that takes two days of hard work to finish? Six cents a day was enough to keep us in bread and ale while Papa was alive, or at least when he was working, but it wouldn't cover a room and whatever else I'd need to keep body and soul together.

I know girls, of course, who have taken to the streets, and who appear to make a nice living off the sailors and the men who work the docks. Alice, for instance, who had the room across from us at Mrs. Brooks'—she made more in one night, I warrant, than I did in two weeks. But the noises coming from Alice's room sometimes gave me a fright. And I know Papa didn't want that life for me, he'd most likely rather have seen me starve. Nor Mama either, though I was young enough when she died that I imagine the thought never entered her mind.

"We'll give you a nice warm place to sleep," the Doctor said that day after he had come round to look in on Papa and Fanny and found only myself still breathing. "My daughter will give you some clothes, and you can eat as much as you like. And I have a granddaughter, almost six, who you can tend to."

He said the girl needed some attention, that her mother—his daughter, Mrs. Anderson—was occupied with a great many things, and in any event hadn't the patience to spend long hours with a child. I suppose that was what hooked me, like a silly wriggling fish, the thought of the little girl. And I guess Dr. Crawford knew it would, because he knew Fanny had been no more than eight, and I suppose he'd seen what I felt for her.

So then I started to want to work in his house, more than anything, and I began to tell him I knew something about cooking, and that I was pretty handy with a needle, which is nothing more than the truth, and I was sure I could make myself useful to him.

"I have no doubt, my dear," he told me, and squeezed my hand. "No doubt at all."

He had that trace of Ireland in his speech that put me in mind of Papa.

"But I suppose," I said softly, "that you'll be wanting references." I forced myself to say it, before my hopes were lifted too far.

He squeezed my hand again. "I saw the way you cared for your father and your sister, for five days running," he said. "All the patience and the tenderness you showed them. Why should I want references when I have the evidence of my eyes?"

I felt some tears coming at that, though I did my best to halt them, and told him it was very good of him. It surely sounded better than the almshouse, where we spent a few weeks last winter after Papa was let go from the mud machine, and I was kept awake every night by the screams of the lunatics and the coughs and moans of the ill.

Of course, when I saw the Doctor's house, I was something disappointed. It looks decent enough from the outside, though nowhere near as large as the Legrands', but the inside is quite a different picture. When I first came in and saw that Madame Bonaparte in the hall—every bit the beauty they say she is, although when she saw me she looked as though she'd just been handed a slab of maggoty meat—I fancied the family must have wealth and connections. But then I saw the shabby furniture and carpets worn nearly through, not to mention the layer of coal dust coating everything and the piles of books and papers on every surface and many places on the floor. And just a pallet in the storeroom for me to sleep on, and, to wear, an old frock so badly patched I took the stitches out and redid them myself. And yet, I reflected, it was just as well they were poor, as it lessened the chances they were acquainted with the Legrands, and that I should encounter anyone who knew them.

And then today, that Mr. Cork, right there in the sitting room. He was at the Legrands' only two or three times, perhaps, while I was there, in the company of other young gentlemen and ladies, friends of Miss Legrand. I can only pray that he's no longer on good terms with her, or at least won't think to mention that he came across a girl who looked remarkably like their old maidservant Maggie.

"MAH-gret! MAH-gret!" I suddenly heard from the cellar. It was Polly's high little voice. The Doctor knew what he was about, bringing me here to care for her. The moment I saw her, playing in the kitchen that day — as pale and thin and breakable as the china cup she was playing with — every bit of me, from the hair on my head down to the nails on my toes, wanted nothing more than to keep her safe and make her happy. Mrs. A seems to think her a nuisance, or no more than a little head that must be stuffed with lessons. But she's only a child, and a child needs room to play and dream. It was what Fanny should have had, by rights. Even before she took sick, she was hired out to Mrs. Brooks all day, gathering wood chips where she could and helping with the washing, too exhausted by the end of the day to do more than fall asleep.

I stood and straightened my frock and apron and then walked down a couple of steps and called back to Polly.

"Look at what I made!" Polly said, appearing at the bottom of the steps and picking her way up them as fast as her small legs would allow, a scrap of paper in her hand.

"Oh, my," I said, seeing what she'd done with the charcoal, "that's very good, very good indeed, my girl."

"It's Mrs. Morris," she explained, her round brown eyes serious, "and that's her spoon, and that's a bowl, on the table. But she kept moving about, and she didn't like it when I asked her to keep still."

I smiled. "No, she wouldn't like that. But never mind, you've done a very good job. That's her nose, I'd know it anywhere." Fanny used to be tolerably good at drawing, whenever we could come by a bit of paper, but she always had trouble with noses. "But now," I told her, "you see the table, the way it looks as though it's all tipped forward instead of being flat? I can show you how to make it look more like a real table, if you like."

Polly nodded eagerly, and we sat back down on the steps. I took the charcoal from her hand and, turning the paper to its blank side, began to show her the trick Mama taught me when I was only a little older than Polly, angling the lines of the table top and drawing the back legs higher up and smaller, so that the whole thing seemed to be traveling into the distance.

Polly opened her mouth in amazement. "Can I try?" she said, reaching for the charcoal.

She bit her lower lip and set herself to copying what I had done as best she could, leaning on the stair below me. "Careful," I told her, "you don't want those lines to tilt quite that much, do you?"

She frowned and began to smudge what she had done, then drew over it quite nicely. Just then I heard the sitting room door open and Mrs. A and Mr. Cork come out.

"So you'll speak to Mr. Patterson as soon as can be arranged?" he was saying.

"Indeed, I will!" Her voice was excited. I didn't dare look out into the hall — I had to hush Polly and shake my head to keep her quiet — but I knew that Mrs. A's cheeks were flushed and those green eyes of hers were shining, for I had seen her excited before. She often becomes excited, for one reason or another. "This is a splendid idea, Mr. Cork, truly splendid. I never imagined that I should have such an opportunity, I really never allowed myself even to dream" —

"Yes, yes, well, we shall have to see how things transpire. Do let me know if I can be of any assistance with Patterson. And if we are successful of course you can rely on me for the weekly column, which should run right on the front page, so as to set the proper tone."

"Of course — satirical, but general and temperate. And I shall be happy to contribute criticism of the fine arts."

"Oh, I think we'll need someone knowledgeable in that line, an expert of some sort. There's that Frenchman who's come to teach drawing at St. Mary's. Perhaps —"

Before I could stop her, Polly stood and bolted past me, apparently unable to contain herself any longer.

"Mama, Mama," she cried, running down the hall, "look what I drawed!"

"*Drew*," she chided, but gently, as she was in good spirits. "Now Polly, first you must say hello to Mr. Cork. This is my daughter Eliza. But we call her Polly."

I heard Polly say "how d'ye do, Mr. Cork," just like a little lady, and Mr. Cork say that he was highly pleased to make her acquaintance.

"Now then, Polly," Mrs. A. said, "what have you got there?"

There followed some expressions of admiration for her drawings from the two of them, Mrs. A quite extravagant in her praise. She's a fond mother when she's in good spirits.

"Do you know," Mrs. A. was saying, "that it took the great artists of Italy hundreds of years to learn how to draw a table like that? And you only five years old, and you figured it out all by yourself!"

"But *Margaret* showed me," I heard Polly protest, to my dismay.

"Did she now?" said Mr. Cork. "Well then, she's the clever girl."

"Goodness," Mrs. A exclaimed, laughing, "an artistic housemaid! What next? Are there no end of wonders in this shining new democracy of ours?"

"And why not?" Mr. Cork replied. "Talent is no respecter of wealth and position. An artist can spring as well from the stable yard as the palace." And then he began saying things I wasn't sure I understood entirely, about what he called an Italian artist whose name sounded like Georgie Oney. I knew a Francis Oney once, though, and he was no more Italian than I am. But Mr. Cork said some other Italian had written about the life of this Oney, and about his humble origins, as he expected Mrs. A must be aware.

"Well, of course, but ... but ...," Mrs. A replied, sputtering a bit, "artistic training, surely, is necessary. Education, exposure to the masters of the past. A *true* artist" —

"My dear Mrs. Anderson." I heard the door creak open. "You must excuse me, I'm afraid I have an urgent appointment. These are weighty and important questions that we must save for another occasion—perhaps, indeed, for the pages of ... our new publication. We must think of a name for it, mustn't we?"

A few more words were exchanged before Mr. Cork at last departed, and while I was relieved to hear him go, I could not help but think on what he had said about artists and stable yards, which I thought had a great deal of sense to it. And if an artist can spring from a stable yard, I thought, why not a kitchen? If it could happen in Italy, where they still have kings and princes, why not in this country, as it's a democracy where we all have our rights? And I felt my body begin to tingle at the idea.

From the Companion, October 4, 1806:

TO READERS AND CORRESPONDENTS.

We have many apologies to make for frequent instances of incorrectness. But the entire arrangement of the Companion depends on one alone, and whether the editor is grave or gay, whether visions of hope and pleasure play before her imagination, or she is sunk into despondence and beset with a whole legion of blue *devils, the printer, like her evil genius, still pursues her at the stated period, and the selections must be made, and the proofs corrected, and of consequence, "The Safe Companion and Easy Friend," must sometimes as well as* safe *and easy* be sad *and* soporific.

However, we propose shortly making some alterations in our plan. We have assurances of ample assistance. From a multitude of counselors we hope to derive wisdom, and from a bright constellation of belles esprits *that have promised to lend us their aid we shall certainly often derive wit.*

Chapter Three: Eliza

Today was the appointed day for our *tête-à-tête* with Mr. Patterson—Father and I—and I was so anxious and fretful last night that I'm sure I slept no more than an hour or two. I don't know that I've ever wanted anything so much as this: to begin my own publication, free of the trammels imposed by others, at liberty to shape it as I see fit. What the reading public craves is not safety and ease but wit and provocation, and that is what I intend to serve up. And once there is a paper with some life to it in Baltimore, I'm certain that writers of talent and discernment will be clamoring to have their work inserted in its pages. I've already had numerous offers of assistance from some extremely promising corners—although the drawing master at St. Mary's, Mr. Godefroy, has declined to contribute articles on the fine arts, he has offered up his friend, the eminent Mr. Latrobe! Quite the coup, that, to snare the nation's most celebrated architect as our resident critic.

But first we are in need of some sympathetic philanthropist to provide the necessary funds. Hence today's meeting with Mr. Patterson—whose name I proposed to Mr. Cork not so much because I imagine him to be a devotee of finely wrought satire, but rather because I believe he might consider himself as being somewhat in my debt. For I trusted that the passage of two years had not entirely erased the memory of the perils I had subjected myself to as traveling companion to his eldest daughter.

Still, Betsy had warned me against presenting myself as the paper's editor, urging that my father and Mr. Cork be portrayed as sharing that role, with myself functioning merely as their assistant. To this I reluctantly agreed, knowing the tenor of Mr. Patterson's views on the proper place of females. But as soon as we entered the front hall Betsy took me aside, scowling as though I had committed some mortal sin.

"How *could* you be so careless?" she hissed at me.

I knew at once what she meant: in Saturday's number, I had employed the feminine pronoun in regard to myself as editor. Father had brought the lapse to my attention Saturday evening, but by then of course it was too late.

"With all the work that has fallen on my shoulders," I protested, "I can't be expected to attend to every tiny detail! When one is writing about oneself, one uses the pronoun one has become accustomed to. But I'll be more careful in the future, I promise."

"If there is a future."

Suddenly I felt myself all atremble; Mr. Patterson had been sent for from his counting house next door and was liable to arrive on the scene at any moment.

"Do you think he saw it—your father?" I clutched Betsy's arm, which was bare, as she was wearing one of those flimsy French gowns of hers that cause all the Baltimore matrons to avert their eyes—and all the Baltimore gentlemen to fasten theirs upon her. "Oh, dear God!"

"I don't know. I certainly didn't bring it to his attention, and he's said nothing. But it has been quite the topic of conversation. I heard it mentioned yesterday evening at the Browns'. Your name was brought up as a suspect, of course."

"Really?" I confess that for a moment I forgot my alarm, so pleased was I to think that my little lament had reached the public ear.

"Here he comes." Betsy was squinting out the window. "Just remember what I advised." She turned to me, cocked her head, and sighed. I expect she was thinking that it would have been best had I not come and rather left the business to Father alone, as she had urged. After all, it would be Father who would need to sign any note for repayment of a loan, since I, as a married woman, am legally barred from any such undertaking. But I could no more allow another to plead for the funds to launch my new publication than I could have assigned someone else to birth my own child.

Betsy now ushered us both into the sitting room, all rose-colored silk and gleaming silver objects, never a snuffbox out of place. One would scarcely surmise that some eight children reside in that house—the younger Patterson offspring and little Bo. Within a minute or two Mr. Patterson joined us, his air distracted, as though eager to return to counting his coins—or whatever it is one counts in a counting house.

"What's this, then, that Betsy tells me about a paper?" He barked this more in the direction of Father than myself, peering down over his aquiline nose.

"It's called the Companion, Father, remember?" Betsy prompted. "The one Charles has written a few articles for?"

"Yes, yes. Yet another way he's found to waste his time."

"In point of fact, this is to be a new publication," I put in quickly, hoping to change the tenor of the conversation, "one that will undertake to elevate the taste and morals of our fellow citizens through the use of satire. You see, the former editor of the Companion, Mr. James Cork—"

"Richard Cork's son, is that?" Mr. Patterson squinted and jutted out his lower lip in a gesture of faint recognition.

"His nephew, sir." I almost added that Richard Cork had been providing the Companion with a subvention, but as that information might lead to some inquiry concerning the elder Mr. Cork's decision to discontinue his support, I held my tongue. "But this new publication," I continued, "will be far livelier, and will attract more subscribers, than the Companion, which if truth be told has suffered from—"

"And this young Cork is to be the editor?"

I glanced at Father, who displayed no apparent inclination to speak, and then at Betsy, who gave me a look of veiled warning. "Mr. Cork will certainly take a large role in the management of the publication, and will supply a humorous essay every week under the *nom de plume* of Benjamin Bickerstaff. But he has recently taken a position as a clerk at Mr. Bennett's law office, and to his regret he's found that his duties there preclude—"

"So who *is* to be the editor, then?"

"I believe it is to be something of a committee, is it not?" Betsy interjected before I had a chance to answer. "Mr. Cork and Dr. Crawford and perhaps one or two others."

Father and I nodded obediently.

"Crawford, do you have the leisure to take up this sort of thing? You mean to tell me you can find the time, what with your practice, and your various charitable endeavors? That place you've opened down at Fell's Point?"

"Yes, the Dispensary," Father replied. "It's going very well, very well indeed, and yes, I am quite occupied. But with my daughter's assistance—"

"You don't mean to say she's going to assist you in taking care of those diseased paupers?"

"Oh no, no!" I thought I detected a hint of regret in Father's voice—not because he had ever hoped for *my* assistance in the medical line, but because of what had transpired with Thomas. His intention in shipping his only son off to England had been to train up an assistant and eventual successor, but of course it had resulted only in the sorest of disappointments. "I meant," Father continued, "with the publication."

"Ah." Mr. Patterson extended his legs from the armchair in which he sat, crossed his arms, and fixed me with his gray eyes. "Mrs. Anderson, what, pray tell, is the exact nature of your affiliation with this proposed paper?"

I swallowed and reminded myself of the need for circumspection. "I have written the occasional article for the Companion, and I expect I shall do something similar for the Observer. Did I mention that we have chosen that name—the Observer? We intend it to reflect what we hope to accomplish with this paper, to hold a mirror up to Baltimore society, to chronicle its virtues and its follies, and to honestly set forth our observations. Indeed, I think we shall choose as our motto—"

"You appear to be quite intimately familiar with the plans for this paper, for one who intends to be only an occasional contributor." With his right hand he took up a silver letter opener that lay on the table next to him and began to tap it idly against his left thigh, as though whetting a small dagger. "It's all very well for a lady to take up her pen once in a while, I suppose, if the fancy strikes her, and set down her thoughts, but I don't see why she should feel compelled to share those thoughts with the general public." He sniffed and paused in his tapping, the corners of his mouth turning down in distaste. "It's a bit unseemly, isn't it? Write a letter to a friend if you want to write, that's what I say."

"But sir, you know, the ladies in France—" I began.

"Do you think I care two figs for what they do in France?" His voice was quiet and cold, and the letter opener was now pointed directly at me. With the word "France" evoking painful thoughts that no doubt occupied us all for the ensuing silent seconds, I stole a glance at Betsy, sitting beside me on the sofa. She was gazing at her hands in her lap with apparent calm, but I knew that her thoughts must be roiling.

"But write away, if that's what you want to do," he continued, leaning back and waving the letter opener away from its apparent proposed trajectory towards my breast. "I shouldn't like to think, though, that you were neglecting your duties to your father and your daughter because of your connection with this publication." He lowered his abundant eyebrows slightly, and deposited the letter opener firmly on the table. "They are, one need hardly remind you, your primary responsibilities. And I'll have nothing to do with an endeavor that would distract you from them. That would scarcely be a good example to set for others." With this he transferred his gaze to Betsy.

It was with great difficulty that I restrained myself from pointing out that I had, at his own behest, absented myself entirely from my beloved father and precious daughter for a period of eight months last year, to cross the Atlantic with Betsy, and that as a result I came very close to never having the happiness of seeing either of them again. How dare he warn that my devotion of a few hours a day to an endeavor I could enjoy in the safety of my own house, within easy reach of my family, would amount to neglect of them?

Father, perhaps discerning my brewing fury, cleared his throat. "Oh, I assure you, Patterson, Eliza would never think of neglecting us! She is the great comfort of my declining years— I'm afraid they are indeed upon me, and perhaps have been for some time now. And no one could ask for a more tender, a more devoted mother."

I winced internally, wishing his praise were truer to the mark. And yet, I try, I try. God knows I love the child.

"Indeed," Father continued, "it is my belief that the few hours she will devote to this paper every week will in fact render her an even better helpmeet. For the tedium—the *ennui*, as the French say—of pursuits that are entirely domestic will be relieved by an exercise of the mind that will no doubt buoy her spirits and strengthen her constitution, both mentally and physically."

Yes, yes, I thought, grateful that I had a father whose perceptions were so acute, who knew even better than I what a being like myself requires for happiness. Since my childhood he has delighted in my hunger for learning, throwing open to me the treasures stored in his library and his own brain, and never discouraging me on the grounds that I was a mere female. But Mr. Patterson only reared his head back in a gesture of derision and emitted a sort of snort.

"So that is your prescription, Doctor? Women who are dissatisfied with their lot in life should shut themselves up in rooms, neglect their duties, and write nonsense for periodicals?" He shook his head and curled his lips. "I'll thank you not to foist that remedy on any of the womenfolk in *my* family."

"But Father," I said quickly, seizing on an idea that had just come to me, "perhaps Mr. Patterson would be interested in your plan to use the pages of the Observer to disseminate your views on the practice of quarantine."

"Quarantine?" Mr. Patterson, leaning forward again, quickly replaced his sardonic smile with an expression of keen interest. "A most pernicious practice that, holding goods out in that lazaretto in the harbor for days, letting them rot there, and then at last allowing them to be unloaded when they're no longer of any use to anyone. Why, just last week they detained an entire shipment of mine, coffee they suspected of contamination! Of course, by the time the authorities released it, it was good for nothing but dumping to the bottom of the sea."

"Exactly!" said Father, as I felt my muscles begin to relax; out of the corner of my eye I saw Betsy give me an almost imperceptible smile and nod. Father began to warm to his new theme. "A tremendous waste of goods and money, and for no defensible reason. It's an old and useless practice, and it is my intention, through a series of articles, to evince its total inefficacy. You know, I had extensive experience of treating tropical illness during my years in the West Indies, and observing the course of its progress, and the idea that disease is carried by these goods is simply —"

"And you propose to put forward this argument in the ... whatever it's called ... this paper?" Mr. Patterson demanded.

"Why, yes. I envisage a series of articles which would demonstrate that quarantine can have no effect on the prevention of disease." Father paused, at last seeming to grasp the direction of Mr. Patterson's interrogation. He smiled. "I should think the topic would be of great interest to merchants like yourself, as it's a practice that is so unnecessarily burdensome to the commerce of this country."

"Indeed." Mr. Patterson rested his elbows on the arms of his chair, brought his hands together beneath his chin in a kind of prayerful posture, and pursed his lips for a moment. "And how much money did you say you needed to begin this publication?"

Father hesitated and glanced at me.

"I believe Mr. Cork estimated that the cost of producing a prospectus would not exceed fifty dollars," I said quickly, "which would allow us to print about fifteen hundred copies, to be distributed as widely as possible. The prospectus is intended to be a sample of the proposed publication, with the first installment of what is to be Mr. Cork's series of humorous articles. And we shall have a variety of other essays, perhaps a poem or two. And an essay on the encouragement of the fine arts by none other than Mr. Benjamin Latrobe!"

"Latrobe? The one who's engaged in building Bishop Carroll's cathedral?"

"The very same!"

"And what then?" Mr. Patterson said, his eyes narrowing. "Suppose I give you the fifty dollars and you produce a prospectus. What next?"

My heart began to beat rather faster than I would have liked, and I took in air in an effort to slow it. "Why, then we would have subscribers, of course. The subscriptions are to be five dollars yearly, payable half-yearly in advance."

At my urging, Father handed Mr. Patterson the estimate of costs that Mr. Robinson had produced for us.

Mr. Patterson glanced at it for a minute and then turned to Father. "And your article on quarantines ... that would appear in this prospectus?"

Father knitted his brows. "I have a good many notes on the subject, but of course it will take some time to put those in the proper form for an article. And I shouldn't want to go off half-cocked."

"But you'll have it done soon?"

Father nodded solemnly. "As soon as is humanly possible."

Mr. Patterson crossed his arms and closed his eyes for what seemed like several minutes; I felt scarcely able to breathe.

Betsy broke the silence. "I'm sure I need hardly remind you, Father, that Dr. Crawford was kind enough to allow Mrs. Anderson to accompany me on my journey to Europe, which I have no doubt was an exceedingly difficult sacrifice for him. And that Mrs. Anderson was at my side when the cannons were trained upon us at Amsterdam."

I couldn't help but shudder. I do my best never to recall that incident, but Betsy's discreet allusion seemed to be having its desired effect.

"Yes, yes," Mr. Patterson said, opening his eyes at last. "I'm well aware of all that." He uncrossed his arms and leaned forward towards Father, his elbows resting on his thighs. "All right then, Crawford," he continued, as though Father were the one who had described the plans for the publication. "I'll give you the fifty dollars for the prospectus, but on this condition: you won't undertake publication unless you obtain five hundred subscribers in advance. I can see the usefulness of this paper, but I don't intend to operate it as a charitable endeavor. And I expect that should the paper begin to turn a profit, which I rather doubt, I shall be repaid the fifty dollars with interest of five percent. Are those terms agreeable to you?"

"Yes! Yes indeed." Father glanced in my direction and smiled. "That's most generous of you."

Mr. Patterson then extracted himself from the scene as quickly as possible, trailed by Father's and my effusions of gratitude. As soon as the Pattersons' grand front door had closed behind him, I began to twirl through the sitting room as though on a dance floor, quite as though I were a child of six instead of a woman twenty years past that. My joyous circuit was halted by an unfortunate collision with a card table, which sent a silver tray clattering to the floor. No harm was done, but the commotion apparently roused Mrs. Patterson from the nursery, for she soon appeared in the doorway of the parlor with little Bo on her hip.

I embraced the dear lady, who then engaged Father in a brief conversation concerning a bout of the flux that was afflicting little Octavius, at which juncture I turned my embrace upon Betsy.

"I cannot thank you enough," I whispered. "I don't know that he would have agreed if you hadn't brought up Amsterdam."

She drew away from me and, placing her arms upon my shoulders, fixed me with a level gaze. "If you believe yourself in my debt, repay me by doing what you promise. Hold up a mirror to these citizens of Baltimore and show them what fools they be."

I laughed and exclaimed that it would be my pleasure, and we took our leave — me fairly skipping the few blocks down Market Street from the Patterson manse to our far humbler abode, and Father straining to keep pace with me. There is much to be done, and not a minute to lose. And I have already composed a motto, which is to be emblazoned prominently at the front of every issue: *The friend of Socrates, the friend of Plato, But above all, the friend of truth.*

From the Journals of Benjamin H. Latrobe, October 28, 1806:

No. 1. Ideas on the encouragement of Fine arts in America

Written at the instance of several friends in Baltimore for the paper edited by Mrs. Anderson.

In the flourishing city of Baltimore, which in the short period of less than half a century has risen from nothing to the rank of the third city in the union, there is not yet heard a whisper which indicates that the fine arts – the arts of architecture, sculpture, and painting – should be nurtured among us. And yet we only wait the nod of our great men.

With very little leisure from the pursuits of a profession which occupies the principal part of my thoughts and time, I shall therefore venture to offer to my fellow citizens what occurs to me as worthy of consideration on the subject of the arts. My communications will probably be very irregular both to method and importance. With you, Mr. Editor, it rests to judge whether you will even admit into your paper this first missive of one on whose contributions you cannot depend.

Chapter Four: Margaret

What a day it was today, with a sky so brilliant and blue it almost hurt your eyes to look at it, and a gentle breeze that smelled more of September than November—the warmth all the sweeter because it was the last you might feel for many months. This morning nearly my first thought was what misery it would be to spend a day like this inside the house, sweeping up coal dust or chopping cabbage, or whatever Mrs. Morris takes it into her head that I should do. It was a day that put me in mind of my childhood on the farm, before Papa lost everything and we had to remove ourselves to the city—a day to be spent running through tall grass or climbing up apple trees. And there's nothing of either description anywhere near us on Hanover Street, just bricks and stones and horse droppings, until the street scrapers come along. Even the public square a few blocks away is little more than dust and dirt.

So it was a welcome surprise when the Doctor declared this morning that Polly must take some exercise at the estate of an acquaintance of his in the countryside, for the sake of her health, and that I should be the one to escort her there—Mrs. A having decided she was so overburdened with work she couldn't possibly spare the time to ramble about in the muck, as she phrased it. The Doctor even hired a coach and driver to take us there and back, for it would have been a tiresome journey for Polly's short legs.

And what a fine feeling it was, parading through the streets in a carriage like a fine lady, even if it was only a battered old double chair with a single mangy horse. Polly and I made the most of the journey, pretending for a while that we were royalty, and then singing foolish nonsense songs that made it quite clear to anyone who might overhear us that we were nothing of the sort. I couldn't say where we traveled to, other than that we headed north from town. The crowded, clustered houses soon grew sparser, with brick replaced by wood, and then these in turn replaced by stretches of green fields, bordered by white picket fences, and stands of trees. Off in the distance you might see a fine house, all on its own, so big you could fit three of the Doctor's houses inside it. Sheep were grazing on small hills, and cows were lowing and flicking their tails about, and I began to feel lighter than I had in years, as though I were a child myself again with scarcely a care in the world.

After a while the driver stopped by a wooden gate leading to a field and said he would come to fetch us in two hours, as the Doctor had instructed. We took our basket with us, which I had packed with bread and cheese, and the paper and charcoal I had brought in case Polly grew tired of walking and wanted to draw, and promised the driver we would return at one o'clock.

At first Polly ran ahead through the field like a little filly, jumping and prancing on her stick-like legs. It seems, from things the Doctor and Mrs. A have said, that the poor child is prone to illness, although she has only had one bout of fever in the two months I've been at the house. Down at the Point we'd have deemed that healthy, but of course they're not accustomed to so much sickness in other parts of town.

After some minutes of gaiety and frolic Polly began to cough and grow tired, so we looked about for a likely spot to settle and soon found a smooth stretch of grass and a few small trees we might lean our backs against. Polly wanted to have our bread and cheese then and there, but I thought it too early and distracted her with the paper and charcoal.

"Do you see that house over there?" I said, pointing to a grand structure of three stories on a hill at the other side of the field that I might have thought was a public building but for its being so far out in the country. "Do you think you could draw it?"

She told me yes, she thought she could, but she wanted to know if *I* could draw it as well. So we both set to drawing the house, as well as the two chestnut horses that stood in the foreground, and some sheep in the distance that looked like small clouds fallen to earth. So intent were we at this task that we failed to hear the footsteps behind us, and were quite startled to hear a man's voice calling out, "Ho, ho, what have we here? The artistic housemaid and her charge, is it?"

It was, I knew as soon as I heard the voice, that Mr. Cork again, the very person I would most have liked to avoid. He has been at the house several times these past weeks, often in company with some other gentlemen, discussing that paper he and Mrs. A are working on. That paper is all Mrs. A has a care for of late—she's hardly spoken more than a word to poor Polly in days. Indeed, Mr. Cork was in the parlor just two days ago, and through the door I heard Mrs. A telling him he must give her something he was supposed to write—something about bickering, I think—as it was almost time to send it to the printer. And then he told *her* that she must change something she'd written, about how the ladies of Baltimore were foolish and badly educated. Well, if Mr. Cork is to write about bickering, all he need do, really, is recount what goes on between him and Mrs. A.

I stood up as quick as I could from the grass and bobbed my head and said good day to him. Polly got up on her knees and extended her drawing by way of greeting.

"A fine rendition!" he said to her heartily. "Look at all those windows. But ..." He turned to me. "I saw that you were sketching as well. May I see your version ... Maggie? Is that the name?"

"It's *Margaret*, sir," I corrected him, shivering inside, wondering again what he knew about what happened at the Legrands'. I have tried my best not to wait on him in the sitting room since that first visit—once I even pretended to have fallen suddenly ill when Mrs. Morris asked me to bring in the tea.

"Quite an accomplished sketch," he said, nodding appreciatively. "If you finish it, I should think my uncle might even buy it from you and display it in the house."

"Your uncle?" I glanced at the great house. "Is that his house, then?"

"Indeed it is. And he tolerates my circumnavigations about the property, on fine days such as today." He sighed and his eyes took in the gleaming sky, the trees that still held a few orange and crimson leaves, the green hillocks spotted with sheep. "I should be at Mr. Bennett's law office right now, copying out some dull writ, but to spend a day such as this indoors is an absolute crime. Don't you agree?"

"Oh, that I do," I said with feeling. Did he have powers to see inside my own head? "I consider myself very fortunate not to be shut up in the kitchen today."

"I should think so. You're much too pretty to be shut up in a kitchen on any day."

I blushed at that and made my thanks for the compliment. He was smiling and leaning against a tree, and I could see that his teeth were white and even, and the sun was making his fair hair glint. He did look nicer than just about any man I've ever met. But I knew I must be on my guard.

"Oh, but I'm not shut up there all the time," I told him, bending down and brushing back Polly's hair with my hand, thinking a reminder of the child's presence might keep Mr. Cork's attentions to me on this side of proper. "We go out for walks, and we go down to the square sometimes, don't we, Polly?"

She nodded vigorously, but then turned her attention back to her drawing, biting her lower lip with the effort. She's very determined about her drawing, which generally I find admirable, but at that moment I rather wished she would tire of it and tell me we must keep on walking.

"Dr. Crawford is a great believer in exercise," I said, more to have something to say than because I was interested in imparting the information. "That's the reason he sent us here today, so that Polly could take some exercise." I nodded towards where she sat, hunched over her sketch. "He must be right about that. I haven't seen her look this well in weeks."

"You're looking quite healthy yourself, if I may say so. Much pinker and plumper than when I first saw you there. I suppose the good Doctor is treating you well?"

I blushed again. "He's been very good to me, the Doctor."

"And your mistress? Has she been good to you too?"

"I can't complain." My mistress! Never would I call Mrs. A that, as though I were no better than a slave. Papa used to call the man he worked for on the mud machine his boss, so that's what I would call Mrs. A, if I had to call her something.

"Oh, but you could complain to *me*," he said. Then he put on a sad face, like someone acting out a part. "The way she orders me around, I can only imagine how she treats a real servant."

I had to laugh a bit at that, and had to remember to cover my mouth because my teeth are nowhere near as nice as his, but all I said was that she had paid me little mind of late. "Because she's so occupied, as you know," I told him. "With the paper."

"Ah yes, the paper, the paper," he sighed. "And what do you know of the paper?" He crossed his arms before his chest and looked down at me from his height, almost father-like. "Perhaps you know that I write for it under the name of Bickerstaff?"

"Oh, it's no affair of mine." I shouldn't want him to think I've been listening at the sitting room door, although the truth is I have.

Polly stood up just then and announced that she had finished her drawing, and so Mr. Cork and I proceeded to admire it.

"But what's this?" said Mr. Cork, taking the drawing and pointing to one of the horses. Polly had decided to give it wings, and it was flying up to the roof of the house. "Horses can't fly, you know."

Polly regarded him solemnly. "That one can," she said.

He shook his head and looked at me. "If you're to be her drawing mistress, shouldn't you instruct her to draw what she sees before her, and not whatever fantasy comes into her head?"

I took the drawing from him. "Why shouldn't she draw whatever she likes? It's a lovely thought, a horse with wings."

He began to laugh, and said so it was, and that in fact the Greeks had thought of such a thing long ago, and that seemed to reassure him it was all right, for some reason. Then Polly said she wanted the drawing back, as she had decided she wasn't finished yet after all.

"And how is it that you've come to know so much about drawing?" Mr. Cork asked me once he'd helped Polly fix the paper to the small board I had brought.

"You mean someone like me? A serving wench?" I heard the insolence in my tone, but I couldn't help it.

He didn't seem to take offense, and only shrugged. "It isn't the sort of accomplishment one usually finds in a girl of your kind."

I started to say something saucy back, about how perhaps he didn't really know what girls of my kind were capable of. But his face was open and curious, not mocking at all, and I reflected that what he said was only the truth. Then I remembered what he had said that day in the front hall of the house, about how even stable boys could be great artists.

And so I told him it was my mother that had taught me, that she had come from a family of some means—means enough to hire a drawing teacher for her, at any rate. That she had been quite good at drawing, and that before she died she had taught me everything she knew.

Mr. Cork picked up my sketch of the house again from where it lay on the ground and studied it. "She taught you well, your mother." He looked at me and smiled, and it was a gentle smile. "I suppose it must remind you of your mother, when you draw."

I felt tears spring to my eyes and swallowed to keep them back. I nodded and looked at the ground. Again I felt he had a strange power to see into my mind. Except that—as he couldn't know—drawing reminded me not just of my mother, but of Fanny as well. And Papa, who told me more than once I was as talented as those painters whose works hung in the great houses. Not that I'd believed him, of course, but it was sweet to hear him say it.

"I finished!" Polly announced. It was a lovely drawing, although of course she hadn't been able to capture any of the colors with her charcoal. How I should like to use paints and copy the colors of things someday, instead of always reducing the world to gray and black, and then teach Polly how to do it. But I can't see that I shall ever find the money to buy paints, and even if I could, there's no one to teach me how to use them.

Mr. Cork admired Polly's drawing again, and then said he must be on his way. "Alas," he said, bowing to us as though we were fine ladies, "I fear my employer doesn't share my views on the criminality of spending such a day as this indoors."

And so he set off. By rights I should have been relieved to see the back of him, before he started asking me about the Legrands once more. And yet, as Polly and I ate our bread and cheese, I found myself looking over my shoulder, watching his tall frame grow smaller as he neared the road, and wishing that we might meet again.

From the Observer, January 17, 1807:

The Lucubrations of BENJAMIN BICKERSTAFF, ESQUIRE.

No. III

The dignity of Baltimore, already distinguished by her commercial enterprise, begins to manifest a taste for the arts and sciences, which must soon rescue her from the contemptuous sneers of her rival sisters and make her a powerful competitor in the paths of literature, as she already is in those of trade.

Our female seminaries are numerous and respectable, and many of their conductors are eminently qualified to give to the sex those accomplishments which dignify and adorn their minds and prepare them to move in the high rank which nature has designed. Indeed an observer of our city would be ignorant of one of the sweetest attractions it possesses if he were not acquainted with the character of our fair. Their manners are such as are calculated to give that polish to the amenities of social intercourse which render society agreeable. Such is the province of woman: to delight and be amused, to restrain and be controlled, to improve and be instructed. While they maintain their proper dignity in society, they must always force a correspondent degree of respect.

Chapter Five: Eliza

Whet a day, what a disagreeable, harried day—as are so
many of my days of late, with all the work that has fallen
to me, and all of the frustrations. And yet, for all that, it has ended
well, I think.

I spent the morning up to my elbows in submissions and papers, choosing this one, rejecting that, hastily correcting an in-
felicitous phrase here or a grammatical solecism there. I should
not complain, I scolded myself, as I do so often these days, for I
have achieved my heart's desire. And to be sure, sometimes I am
happy, sublimely happy, so caught up in my reading and editing
and decision-making that I lose all sense of the passage of time.

And so it was today, when Margaret brought Polly in and
simply stood there at the library door holding the child's hand
and saying nothing, like a beast of the field. "What is it, then?" I
said at last, looking up. I suppose I might have sounded a trifle
impatient, as I was struggling with a particularly recalcitrant sentence in the second installment of a biographical sketch of Lord
Mansfield.

"I didn't mean to interrupt," Margaret said, sounding out of
sorts as usual, and as usual not addressing me by any term of
respect. "But it's time for Polly's lessons. That's what you said
yesterday evening, that you wanted her to come for her lessons."

"Oh, heavens, is it 11 o'clock already?" I looked at the clock
on the wall, which mutely provided an affirmative answer. What
had I been thinking yesterday evening? With Mr. Robinson
readying his press to receive the material for our next number
in only a few hours, I could scarcely afford to devote even ten

minutes to anything other than the task before me. And yet it has been days, perhaps weeks, since I last endeavored to provide Polly with some instruction. Father has gently chided me, asking how I expect her to be ready to attend Madame Lacombe's two years hence if she hasn't the faintest idea how to read or write or do sums. And he's right, of course. To think that I, who once taught in that very school and bemoaned the neglect of mothers who sent their daughters there without any preparation whatsoever, should be guilty of the very same sin! And yet, it won't do to delay our next number and disappoint our subscribers (not quite the five hundred we had said we required, but no doubt their ranks will soon increase) simply to drill a child in the letters of the alphabet.

"Oh Polly dear, Mamma is so sorry," I said, resting my pen in its stand and going over to where she stood. I knelt down so that our eyes might meet and placed my hands on her birdlike shoulders. "I'm afraid I'm much too busy to teach you today, but I promise we shall have a lesson tomorrow. You can wait till tomorrow, can't you?"

"Oh, I don't mind, Mamma!" Polly said gaily, wriggling away from me and taking Margaret's hand again and pulling on it. Then she said to Margaret in a sort of stage whisper, "Now we can *draw*!" The child was biting her lip and nearly jumping up and down with eagerness. "You said I could try to draw *you* next, remember?"

I saw Margaret's sullen expression melt into a smile that mirrored Polly's own, and I heard her say with a gentleness she never uses with me, "All right then, you can try." And the two of them stood there for a moment, the one gazing up and the other gazing down, all fondness and unconcern. And off they went.

It's all very well for the child to learn to draw, I suppose, and I know I should be thankful that Margaret has somehow acquired the skill to teach her the rudiments of the art. But drawing is all Polly seems to think about since Margaret arrived! And to receive instruction in drawing before one learns to read the simplest sentence or calculate the sum of two plus two—that, to me, is indeed putting the cart before the horse. Polly must have more than the smattering of inane "accomplishments" that is deemed sufficient for young ladies to consider themselves educated in this town. It's just as I wrote in the Companion only a few months ago:

they merely learn to strum some wretched tunes on the piano, acquire a smattering of French that is entirely abandoned with their school books, and become acquainted with the latest styles of dancing and dress—all at grievous expense to their parents.

Of course, if Polly continues to exhibit inclination and talent, drawing lessons may well enhance her appreciation both of the natural world and the works of the great masters. But when the time comes, I'll have her instructed, not by a housemaid, but by some person who is qualified to do so—someone like Mr. Godefroy, an exceedingly accomplished artist who has been forced to offer private drawing lessons to supplement the paltry income from his teaching duties at St. Mary's.

Well, I shall take matters in hand concerning Polly tomorrow, I told myself as I turned back to the sketch of Lord Mansfield, in which I was soon immersed. I then moved on to the second installment of Mr. Allen's essay on how the European powers laid the seeds for their own destruction by Bonaparte—an admirable article, indeed. As I have received several communications complaining that the subject has little to do with our affairs here in Baltimore, I thought it suitable to pen a short introduction to the piece, explaining its importance. But I had scarcely written two sentences when there came a knock at the door.

I immediately put down my pen, hoping that it might be a messenger from Mr. Cork (alias Bickerstaff), whose "Lucubrations" for the next number I am still awaiting—although without much eagerness, as they're bound to be as insipid as his previous installments. So much for biting satire! But I saw, with a mixture of emotions, that the visitor was in fact Betsy, whom I haven't seen in weeks. She's been spending a great deal of time in Washington City, where she is determined to discover whatever news she can about her husband—or ex-husband, perhaps I should say, now that Bonaparte has induced the French ecclesiastical authorities to declare her marriage invalid. That news, along with the rumor that Jerome is soon to be forced into a second marriage with a German princess, has understandably plunged Betsy into a state of some distress, although I warrant she cloaks it well enough when charming the gentlemen at the French and British legations.

"I can't stay long," she said distractedly, to my relief, as she swept past me. "We're having the Catons to dinner, and Father of course insists that I be there." She sighed. "I haven't even chosen a frock yet. But ..." She looked around for a seat and at last settled on Father's armchair, which she first dusted with one of her gloves. "I've just perused the last few numbers of the Observer, and I feel you should know my thoughts."

"Of course." I felt some rising apprehension, but her expression was inscrutable. "I trust you've noticed there's been no indication of my sex?"

"Oh, yes—it's all 'Mr. Editor,' and 'Sir.' I'm not concerned about that." She removed her bonnet and set it on the table. "And Father doesn't seem interested in reading the paper himself. He only wanted to know if there's anything about quarantines in it yet, and I told him there wasn't."

"No, Father is still composing his thoughts on the subject." I doubt that my father has thought twice about the subject since our conversation with Mr. Patterson—he's been far too busy at the Dispensary and attending to his patients—but I promised myself to raise it with him at once. "But I trust that you've found other articles that have served, perhaps, to divert, to amuse, to edify?" I smiled encouragingly. Betsy can be quite a sharp critic, and if our offerings fail to find favor with her, we may well lose the benefit of Mr. Patterson's generosity—which I fear we may need to call upon in the future.

"A little too much edification, I'd say," she sniffed, "and not nearly enough amusement or diversion. A biography of Lord Mansfield?"

"I believe some of our leading figures at the bar are finding the series of great interest. One must have a little something to suit all tastes, you know!"

"But what of your plan to hold up a mirror to the follies and vices that surround us? There were those excellent articles on the fine arts in the prospectus and the first number—by Mr. Latrobe, I suppose."

I smiled and nodded, but refrained from mentioning that Mr. Latrobe—either because of the press of other business or, as he wrote in his second and last essay, because he despaired of ever fostering an appreciation of the arts amongst the members of the commercial classes—has decided to discontinue his contributions.

"But in this last number," Betsy continued, "your Mr. Bickerstaff—or Cork, or whatever you choose to call him—fairly ran out of adoring adjectives with which to praise the young ladies of this town. Really, I scarcely recognized them from his description!"

I closed my eyes and shook my head. Betsy knew nothing of my continual arguments with Mr. Cork and my exertions to steer the paper in the direction I thought we'd agreed on. My words now came flowing out, tumbling over themselves, as I endeavored to explain what I have been suffering at Mr. Cork's hands: his objections to what he considered Mr. Latrobe's overly severe criticism, his opposition to my own attempts to decry vulgarity and folly, his insistence that I make no alterations whatsoever to the perfection of his own prose. Far from reforming Baltimore, he seems to want to do nothing but sing its praises.

Betsy folded her hands in her lap and allowed herself a self-satisfied smile. "Didn't I warn you?" she said. "He may have conferred the title of editor upon you, but he never expected that a female would dare to act as one."

"It's true," I said, pleased to have someone with whom to share my indignation. "He's insufferable!"

"Ah, well," she continued with a little sigh. "I suppose it was worth the experiment, you trying to edit this paper. But you see? It can't be done. Not in *this* city."

"Of course it can!" I exploded. "It's only Cork who's making it impossible. His essays are pure rubbish. *And* he's always impossibly late getting them to me — no doubt in an effort to prevent my having the time to make any improvements to them, or try to. If I don't get his wretched 'Lucubrations' within the next hour, we may not have the number printed in time for delivery to our subscribers on Saturday!"

I'd begun pacing about the room, coming to rest at last near the window, where I leant my head against the glass. Betsy was silent for a moment.

"Well, then," she said at last, "*are* you the editor or aren't you?"

I swallowed and tried to keep my voice steady. "I am! But what can I do?"

"You could simply write something yourself."

I turned to face her, my mouth open in amazement. "In the place reserved for his 'Lucubrations'? Why, I suppose I could, couldn't I?" I laughed at the audacity of the suggestion. "But I need a subject. Immediately."

"If I were you I'd write some response to that ridiculous paean of his to the females of Baltimore! What of their foolishness, their ridiculous affectations? The way they twist themselves this way and that, desperately trying to attract the attention of the bucks?" Betsy's color deepened as she warmed to her theme. "Why, only two evenings ago I saw Louisa Caton at a ball at the assembly room, writhing about like a reluctant eel in the grip of the cook, trying to show off the *blue veins* adorning her *marble skin*."

Betsy struck what looked to be a painful pose, her neck all askew and her limbs at unnatural angles—which did, I must admit, put me in mind of the coquettish contortions all four Caton girls have been trained by their Mamma to engage in. Even Bess, dear Bess, who has more heart and more head than the rest of the family combined. And Marianne, despite the fact that she's a married woman now—married, in fact, to Betsy's brother Robert, much to Betsy's chagrin, for she's always had a raging antipathy towards the lot of them.

I began to laugh, giddy at the thought of committing these observations to prose and placing them on the front page of the Observer. Then I paused. "But I shouldn't want to hurt Louisa's feelings. Or the rest of the family."

"Don't be ridiculous. You won't mention her by name, of course. She'll never deduce that you're talking about *her*. She can't possibly realize how absurd she appears—if she did, she wouldn't behave that way. And there were a dozen girls doing the same thing, more or less. Just think of the public service you'll be performing."

"It's true. I won't really be speaking of Louisa—the young lady I describe will be no more than a fiction, a satirical device." But then another cloud arose to obscure the sunny vista that had begun to stretch before me. "I imagine, though, that Mr. Cork will be rather put out about being displaced from the front page."

Betsy rolled her eyes impatiently and began putting on her gloves. "Surely it's no more than he deserves. And it will teach him a lesson. If you're truly the editor, then it's your right to decide what to publish—especially as he's been so remiss in fulfilling his obligations." She stood and retrieved her bonnet. "Go to it, then—the printer is waiting, is he not? And I'm eager to see the result of your labors. It will cause quite the sensation, I have no doubt."

I kissed her cheek and thanked her, and we said a hurried goodbye. And with a burst of energy that came from I know not where, I seated myself at the desk and began to write as fast as I could—now very much hoping that Mr. Cork's lucubrations would not arrive until after I had finished.

From the Observer, January 24, 1807:

The Lucubrations of BENJAMIN BICKERSTAFF, ESQUIRE.

To Benjamin Bickerstaff, Esq.

I cannot tell you how much I am delighted, dear Mr. Bickerstaff, with your lucubrations, because you appear to stand forth disposed to be the champion and advocate of the fair. Nevertheless, I would not have you too indulgent to their vanities and their errors; for it is just such a pen as yours that is best calculated to laugh them out of their follies, and while you amuse, improve them.

There is not one of the whole catalogue of follies attributed to women which is more justly deserved than that of affectation. I saw a lovely creature the other evening at the assembly, who, if contented with what nature had done for her, would have been grace and captivation personified. But no; she was resolved to owe the number of her conquests to the ingenuity of her machinations. She turned and twisted her head like a Chinese Mandarin, by way of not suffering a blue vein or a contour to escape her victims; and for the purpose of displaying the perfect symmetry of her form, she writhed her person about like an eel in the ruthless grip of a cook.

Now, Mr. Bickerstaff, if you will only prevail on these ladies to re-assume their natural characters, you will serve the cause of grace and beauty; but if you find the sex incorrigible, I do entreat you will use your influence to have a teacher of affectation added to every female academy, so that if this qualification is indispensable to ladies, they may at least attain it in such a degree of perfection as to know how to conceal art under the appearance of nature.

I am yours,

TABITHA SIMPLE.

From the Observer, January 31, 1807:

The Lucubrations of BENJAMIN BICKERSTAFF, ESQUIRE.

My first emotions upon seeing the last number of the Observer were those of pleasure when I found myself unexpectedly *honored by an address apparently from the pen of a female.*

My correspondent has "a charter as free as air" to direct all the artillery of her wit *against affectation, an object of implacable disgust. But she must learn that satire to be useful must be general, and to be respected must be just. To me it appears that this Achilles in petticoats, for I am satisfied that no woman could have written such a letter as that of Mistress Tabitha Simple, was not well employed when he endeavored to wound the feelings of an amiable, a lovely, and unoffending female.*

I did not see this letter until it had passed the hands of the printer. To a friend I immediately complained of the impropriety of inserting such a letter under a title which belonged exclusively to another, without his consent. The subject of this lucubration may probably be unpleasant to the Editor of this miscellany, but I am compelled to declare that I have suffered more pain than she can possibly experience. To avoid all future misunderstandings, it is now distinctly stated that nothing shall hereafter appear in the Observer, EITHER FROM THE PEN OR UNDER THE NAME OF BENJAMIN BICKERSTAFF.

Chapter Six: Margaret

I set out this morning with my basket, as Mrs. Morris bade me, and with instructions to purchase the cheapest cabbages and potatoes that could be had, if they weren't yet entirely rotten. But I had no sooner turned onto Market Street than I heard my name being called. It was a voice I was certain I recognized.

"Good day to you, Mr. Cork," I said briskly, pausing only slightly in my forward progress. I didn't like to appear unfriendly, but I had no wish to be engaged in conversation, if that was his intention. The more time I spent with him, the more likely he'd be to remember that he really had seen me at the Legrands', if he hadn't realized that already.

But he fell into step with me, and what could I do? First he went on for a while about the weather, and how cold it's been this week, and what were the chances it might snow again, subjects on which I had little to say. Indeed, I was frozen enough, the cloak provided by Mrs. Morris being scarcely thicker than a shawl, and discussing such matters only made things worse, reminding me of my numb fingers and toes.

"Not like that day we met at my uncle's, is it?" he said. "That perfect day?"

"No, not half," I said shortly. But I felt a bit of warmth creeping through me, remembering that day, and how we met, and how he'd said just what I'd been thinking myself about it being too beautiful to stay indoors. And how he'd told me I was pretty. The truth is I've thought about that day many times in the past two months.

"And what about your drawing?" he asked. "Still making your sketches?"

I glanced at him sideways, to see if there was any mockery on his face. But his expression appeared only to match the friendly interest I heard in his voice. He does have a nice face, with those full lips of his, and his fair hair hanging in little curls down his brow, which is quite broad.

"I draw when I can find the time, and I can get my hands on some paper." I saw the vegetable stalls up ahead, and slowed my pace a bit. It had been a while since anyone asked me questions about myself. Dr. Crawford does on occasion, but he's so occupied with the Dispensary, I scarcely see him. "Sometimes I draw with the child, to amuse her, but I don't think Mrs. Anderson likes her to spend time drawing."

"No?" He looked at me more intently, his eyebrows raised in surprise. "Why ever not?"

I only shrugged. It won't do to go telling tales on my boss, no matter how much I'd like to. And indeed, I don't honestly know why Mrs. A objects to Polly's drawing, except that she wants her to spend the time learning her letters and numbers. But she doesn't expect me to teach such things to her, although I could, and she never can find the time to do it herself.

"She's an odd woman, your mistress," Mr. Cork continued, almost as though he were talking to himself—and fortunately not looking for me to agree with him, although I would certainly be inclined to. "Bitter, cruel. Perhaps one could say that it's understandable, given her misfortunes. But one might as easily say that she's brought her misfortunes on herself. That no husband could bear to live with a woman like her."

So there was a *Mr. A* somewhere, who'd run off! I'd assumed her husband was dead."Do you know, Margaret, who Miss Louisa Caton is?" Mr. Cork had shifted his gaze from the distance and was now looking directly at me.

I had to think a minute. The eldest Miss Caton is now Mrs. Patterson, so he couldn't have meant her. Then there were the three younger sisters. Which of them was Louisa? I recalled having heard the next eldest addressed as Bess, when I was at the Legrands', where they were frequent visitors—and she was the one who came to take tea with Mrs. A one day last month. I thought Louisa was the next one after that, not the youngest. That's Emily, I'm pretty certain—the homely one. But all I did was shake my head no. The bosses don't like us knowing too much of their affairs.

51

"Louisa Caton is the most amiable, the most unoffending of young ladies. And yet for some reason your mistress saw fit to launch a blistering attack against her in the pages of our paper. Or *her* paper, I should say."

"It's not yours anymore, then?"

"Not after that attack. I could no longer associate myself with a publication that would stoop so low." He shook his head and touched the long fingers of his right hand to the point on his forehead between his eyes, as though his thoughts were causing him pain. "If you had only seen the distress, the incomprehension, in the poor girl's eyes when I showed her that article. Indeed, she refused to believe that another female — and one she called a friend, no less — could have spewed such venom at her. I pretended to agree, to spare her feelings. But I knew the truth, of course."

I wondered if he was in love with Louisa Caton, he seemed so put out about it.

"I'm sorry to hear the lady's so unhappy, but sir, if you'll excuse me, I must get to the market before all the decent cabbages are taken." I gestured with my basket in the direction of the stalls. "Mrs. Morris will have my head if I come back with nothing."

"Ah yes, of course," he said, smiling. "We wouldn't want you to lose that pretty head."

I blushed at that, and began to move past him.

"But Margaret." He put his hand on my arm, the one with the basket, and my stomach did a small leap. His voice was lower now, urgent. "Just a moment more. I need your help."

"*My* help?" What could I possibly do for him, I wondered? His hand was still on my arm.

"With Mrs. Anderson. I know her, I know what she has in mind for the Observer. She intends to mount more of these cruel, mean-spirited attacks on innocent people. She simply despises Baltimore and everyone in it. Perhaps because of her own misfortunes, I don't know." He took his hand away and began to run his fingers through his curls. "Satire, she calls it! It's monstrous, and it must be stopped."

"But what is it you want *me* to do about it?"

He smiled again, his eyes smiling right along with his mouth; I wondered if I could draw eyes that smiled like that. "Merely observe," he said. "Observe the Observer, you might say."

His eyes were light brown, but with little flecks of green and gold. I don't know that I've ever seen eyes that color before. I wanted to paint them, to try to capture those colors.

Just then, an older gentleman came by, one I didn't know but who was obviously acquainted with Mr. Cork, for he called a greeting to him. For a minute or so they exchanged some little chatter, and I nearly walked off. I could see a fair number of people at the market, all of them intent on buying my cabbage and potatoes, or so I imagined. But just as I had resolved to continue on my way, I heard Mr. Cork making some excuse to the other gentleman, tipping his hat, saying farewell. He motioned me into an alley, and I had no choice but to follow.

"Now then, Margaret," he continued. "All I want you to do is meet with me occasionally and tell me what you've seen, whether your mistress has said or done anything that might interest me."

"Like what?"

"Oh, if she's planning to publish another one of her so-called satires, for example. So that I might at least warn the victim." He paused. "Or if she says or does anything indiscreet. If she's intent on exposing what she considers the follies and foibles of others, it's only fair to bring *her* defects to light, is it not?"

"Bring them to light? How?"

"Ah, excellent question. Through another publication, one that I intend to begin in the coming weeks, with some associates of mine."

"And you would put them in there, these ... observations of mine."

"Perhaps, if it's the only way to protect the reputations and safeguard the feelings of innocent people. And there are greater considerations as well." He glanced behind him for a moment, then leaned closer, his voice urgent. "I tell you, that woman doesn't only have contempt for Baltimore, she's one of those who have contempt for America — for democracy itself. We're all vulgar and tawdry in her eyes. Not *European* enough. She'd have us all return to the days of monarchy and lords and ladies. And she intends to use the paper to put forward that nonsense." He folded his arms across his chest and once again seemed to be talking more to himself than to me. "I should have known ... Give a woman like that a passing acquaintance with Latin, a little dabbling in moral philosophy, and she starts to fancy herself a reincarnation of the goddess Athena." He made a little snorting noise and returned his attention to me. "So what do you say, Margaret? Will you help me?"

I didn't know what to answer. I could believe what he said about Mrs. A being no democrat, with her fine airs. I could just see her at some royal court, sashaying about like that French queen who lost her head. It would be no more than she deserved, having me spy on her—for it seemed that was what he was asking me to do. And if I said no, would he go to the Legrands and tell them he'd stumbled upon their old maid Maggie? It didn't seem as though he remembered me, but how could I be sure?

Still, I felt that prickling in my belly that tells me when something isn't right, just like I felt that day at the Legrands'. This time, I told myself, I must heed it. What if Mrs. A found out, or even began to suspect, what I was doing?

"I'm sorry, sir, but I'm afraid I can't help you. I don't really know much of what goes on above stairs. Most of the time I'm in the cellar with Mrs. Morris and Polly."

He smiled and again put his hand on my arm. "I understand. There's some risk for you, of course. But I'd make it worth your while."

Money, then. Dr. Crawford pays me a dollar and a half a week, which I'm sure is all he can afford, and I get my meals and a bed, but what I would give for a bit of cole, to buy a new frock or a warm cloak. But no, I told myself. What use would a few dollars be to me if I were tossed out onto the street, with nowhere to go but the almshouse?

"Not just money," Mr. Cork said, as though he could see right through my skin to my thoughts. "I happen to be acquainted with an artist, a most accomplished man who has taught himself all he needs to know about the making of art. He's a tailor and dyer by trade, but true genius such as his will flourish no matter how rocky the soil in which it is planted."

I nodded, and I remembered again what he'd said about that artist from the stable yard that day at Mrs. A's.

"This man—Mr. Francis Guy—gives lessons on occasion, imparting to certain fortunate students all that he has laboriously discovered for himself. Not only how to use a pencil for drawing, but also how to use watercolors and pastels, even oils. And his own ingenious techniques for capturing a scene."

I swallowed hard and bit my lip, felt my heart beating.

"Margaret," Mr. Cork said, "would you like to take lessons from Mr. Guy?"

"Yes sir!" If I'd thought longer, perhaps I would have said no, but it was my feelings that were pushing the words out, not my brain. "Yes, please. I would."

"I would of course bear the costs not only of the lessons themselves, but of any materials you might require."

"Thank you, sir." My voice was little more than a whisper.

"And I," he said with a slight bow, "thank *you*. Can you meet me here again next Friday, at this same time?"

I nodded and made my way at last to the cabbages and potatoes. There were scarce pickings by the time I got there, and I was sure Mrs. Morris would scold me for not finding better, or at least getting a better price, which indeed she did. But all I could think of was how I might paint them, all their greens and browns, with watercolors and pastels and oils.

From the Observer, February 21, 1807:

THE OBSERVER.
By Beatrice Ironside.
The Friend of Socrates, the Friend of Plato,
But Above All, the Friend of Truth.

BEATRICE IRONSIDE'S BUDGET.

"Speak of Me as I Am."

Nothing doubting that much curiosity has been excited to know what manner of woman our female editor may be, we shall proceed without further delay to satisfy our readers on this important question.

Mistress Beatrice is neither ugly enough to frighten a fiery courser from his repast, nor handsome enough for the Parson to turn aside from his discourse while he admires her beauty. She is old enough to have set aside some of the levities of youth, and young enough to remember that she has had her share of them; for the sun has not yet revolved thirty times around his orbit since she began her journey through this nether world.

Accident having thrown her much more in the busy throng than generally falls to the lot of woman, she has acquired a knowledge of human nature which will assist her much in prosecuting her work. The chief object of these speculations will be to exhibit virtue and good sense in their most pleasing colors, and to lash with the utmost force of satire she can command the vices and follies that fall beneath her notice. If she should touch a picture with such lively strokes that folly perceives its likeness and is enraged at the dexterity of the artist, Mistress Beatrice must forgive the anger so excited when she remembers how often the conscious blush of shame mantles her own cheek.

Mistress Beatrice therefore now gives notice that her lucubrations will not be directed against individuals, and she will steadily pursue her course, unmindful of the frowns of great or small. She happens to have been so constructed that she can turn an iron-side to the "proud man's contumely" (or woman's either), and insolence and neglect she knows how to endure with the happiest indifference. She will therefore always take the liberty of laughing at the affected, the ridiculous, and the vain, whenever it pleaseth her good fancy to do so.

Chapter Seven: Eliza

A most delightful day today, a welcome respite from my incessant editorial duties, and spent in most delightful company. Mr. Godefroy, who in addition to his responsibilities as drawing master at St. Mary's has taken on the challenge of designing the school's new chapel, graciously offered to escort me on a tour of the construction—inspired, I surmise, by the letter I published in the Observer last week which commented upon it favorably.

I hesitated, but as the proposed date of our excursion was a Monday, and the printer does not demand the pages for the week's number of the paper until Thursday, I was bold enough to abandon my desk, scarcely visible beneath its stacks of submissions, for a few hours. True, I had promised Polly we would at last commence her lessons in arithmetic, but the poor child is still recovering from a fever, and no doubt would have been even more unwilling and out of sorts than usual. And how could I resist an invitation to view a building that has occasioned the most excited commentary, not only in our city but in others as well? The prospect of seeing with my own eyes what has been described as a structure in the Gothic style—the first to be built on these shores—was too alluring to be denied.

And I was not disappointed despite the high March winds, which I'm afraid forced a rather abrupt end to our tour—for it appeared at one point that the gusts were about to bring down a part of the tall front façade, causing Mr. Godefroy to enter into a heated exchange with the builder about the need for additional buttresses. It was thrilling to be in the midst of all those workmen, shouting orders to one another and carting piles of bricks about.

We at last took refuge from the wind and dust and noise in a classroom where Mr. Godefroy gives his lessons and stores his materials, and where it was scarcely warmer than outside. While we shivered there—with, I'm afraid, my nose red and my eyes streaming—Mr. Godefroy showed me the most exquisite drawings, sketches he had made of columns and capitals and spires, with exacting precision and the finest detail. It was charming to see the blush that came to his ordinarily pale cheek as I exclaimed over his work.

"But Madame," he said to me (in French, as he is far more at home in his native tongue, and delighted to discover that, thanks to my childhood years in Martinique, I am able to converse in it with ease), "if one wants to see the chapel as I hope it will someday be, one must look at this."

And then he unveiled a large drawing of the most enchanting church I have ever seen, its pointed arches and towering spires rising heavenward as sublimely as those of Notre Dame in Paris—or, I should say, as the drawings I have seen of Notre Dame. At the bottom right was the artist's signature, "Maxim. Godefroy." We held the sketch gently, Mr. Godefroy's hand at one end and mine at the other, to protect it from the dusty table.

I confess I felt tears come to my eyes and had to swallow hard, so swept was I by strong emotion. I scarcely trusted myself to speak, but I feared Mr. Godefroy would take my silence for disapproval rather than its opposite. "It is Baltimore's great good fortune," I managed to say at last, in a small, strained voice, keeping my eyes on the drawing, "to have so gifted an architect in our midst, for we're so desperately in need of beauty."

There was a pause, and I stole a glance at him. His face is that of a true artist, long and lean, with a high forehead and dark eyebrows over burning orbs that meet the world without flinching. But now I saw in those same orbs a deep and noble melancholy. "Madame Anderson," he said, "I cannot tell you what it means to hear such kind words. Indeed, it is my dream that this church will establish my reputation as an architect and bring me further commissions. But not everyone in this place has expressed such appreciation for my presence here."

I knew whereof he must be speaking, for he has told me the Sulpician fathers pay him a mere pittance, and that the families who have hired him for private drawing instruction provide him little more. They're more than willing to spend freely for china plates with invented family crests, or carriages with gilded trim, but ask them to spend a few pennies in support of the arts and their purses snap shut before the words have fully escaped one's mouth.

"Oh, my dear Monsieur Godefroy, you mustn't let them discourage you!" I told him, my words rushing out in a flood of sympathy. "The people of Baltimore simply don't know any better. At least not yet. It's such a young city, you know—not like Paris, not even like Philadelphia, or New York. Why, thirty years ago, there was nothing here, nothing at all! It takes time for standards of taste to develop. People require examples to assist them in distinguishing what is beautiful and good from what is cheap and abhorrent. And this church!" I turned to the drawing again. "When they see this church, and they compare it to the brick boxes they call buildings, thrown together willy-nilly, then they will begin to understand."

Mr. Godefroy ducked his head in a gesture of gratitude. "My dear Madame," he continued, "whether you are right or not in your predictions, it does my heart good to hear you voice them. And you, with your paper you are helping the people too. Is that not right?" He began to carefully roll up the drawing and return it to the shelf whence it had come.

"I'm doing my best, to be sure. But, like you, I've found my efforts aren't always appreciated."

I felt a little shudder, thinking of all that has transpired these past weeks, since Mr. Cork took it into his head that I had slandered his beloved Louisa Caton and announced his indignant departure from the pages of the Observer. I had begun to draft a plea begging him to reconsider, but halfway through I realized, with a laugh, that my life would in fact be far easier without having to wrestle with him and his tiresome lucubrations, and I gleefully crumpled the letter and threw it into the fire. Still, thinking of Louisa's feelings, I tried to refute his accusations in an editor's note, saying that if I'd had any female in mind, it was one who'd long been in a cold and silent grave, the victim of her own vanity.

I thought matters would end there. But when I saw the Catons at the assembly a few evenings later Louisa distinctly snubbed me, turning her head aside when I offered a greeting and pretending to be searching for something in her reticule. I confess I was wounded, for I've known her since she was a small child.

It was Bess who came to confront me, a half an hour or so later — perhaps chosen by the others as an envoy, as they know she's my favorite. Thus far, at least, Mrs. Caton's heroic efforts have failed to dull the natural sharpness of Bess's wit, or to supplant her undulating grace with a fashionable mince.

"Eliza," Bess chided, her usually gentle eyes boring sharply into me, "you must know that Louisa is seriously distressed. We all are, Mamma especially. She's quite beside herself. How could you have written such a thing?"

I protested as strongly as I could that it wasn't meant to be about Louisa, but Bess would have none of it. She slapped her fan shut and tapped it against one hand. "You must have known people would think it was Louisa, whatever you had in mind. It's true, of course, she does twist herself about rather too much. But there's no reason to point it out so savagely in public. Comparing her to an eel!"

I glanced around and lowered my voice. Fortunately we were standing in a somewhat secluded alcove by a window, partly hidden by the draperies. "I'll tell you something in confidence," I said. "You may repeat it to Louisa, and the rest of your family, but I beg you to reveal this to no one else."

Bess leaned closer, her eyes inquiring.

"It was Betsy," I whispered in her ear, shielding my lips with my fan, lest anyone should be watching. Betsy wasn't in attendance at the assembly herself, but at least one of her brothers was, and I thought I had spotted her sister as well.

"Mrs. Bonaparte?" Bess's eyes widened. The musicians had just finished a polonaise, and I had to press my finger to my lips to warn her to lower her voice. "*Betsy* is Tabitha Simple?" she whispered.

I hadn't meant to give that impression, exactly, but what could I say? I was now inwardly writhing with remorse, much like that cursed metaphorical eel. The idea that I might lose Bess's friendship was too distressing to contemplate. And it was true that Betsy had planted the seed in my mind.

"You know how she feels about all of you, your entire family," I said, which was nothing less than the truth. "It's unaccountable and entirely unjustified of course, but she simply can't control her jealousy. And it's only grown worse now, with the city gloating over Mr. Bonaparte's abandonment of her. Or," I added quickly, "so it feels to her." For, at least in Betsy's mind, it's the Catons themselves who have led the gloating.

"I suppose I should have known." Bess rested a hand on my arm. "I told Mamma it couldn't have been you who wrote it. But …" She took her hand away and shook her head, sending the brown curls that peeked out from her turban to bouncing. "Isn't it true that you're the editor? That's what Mr. Cork told us. Surely you could have refused to print such venom."

I could feel the blood rushing to my head, hear my heart pounding. I needed to think quickly. "I'll tell you something else, but again, in strictest confidence." I took a breath. "It's Mr. Patterson who has provided us with the money to publish. We'll have enough money from subscribers to support ourselves, of course, eventually — soon, I hope. But we needed money at the beginning, and the fact is, we still do. And so …"

Bess's eyes widened again, and then she nodded, understanding — or what she believed to be understanding — spreading across her handsome face. "So Betsy threatened to withdraw her father's support unless you published her letter," she said slowly.

I said nothing to confirm or deny this conclusion, but only promised Bess I should never again publish anything that could possibly be construed to cast opprobrium on any member of her family, and that I was profoundly sorry for any distress I had caused them. Bess squeezed my hand and gave me a smile. But the smile was a troubled one, and I haven't heard a word from her since.

As if that weren't enough, Mr. Brown accosted me at church last Sunday and stated, in the chilliest of tones, that he knew full well it had been *his* new house I had mocked in my comments published in the previous day's number of the Observer, and turned a resolutely deaf ear to my protestations that I hadn't had him in mind at all. In fact, it was Mr. Chase's house I'd been thinking of, but I couldn't very well reveal that, and so I insisted that the house had been a creature of my own invention, meant to stand in for all constructions that, however well-meaning, exhibited a lack of style and taste — not, I added with feeling, at all like his own well-appointed and pleasingly proportioned abode (this last being more diplomatic than honest).

"Well, never mind," he said, raising his chin and looking down the length of his broad, ruddy nose at me. "It's really of no importance to *me* what you put in that paper of yours. I don't subscribe, mind you. The whole thing was only brought to my attention by a neighbor of mine, but it's truly beneath my notice."

Of course, I couldn't divulge any of this to Mr. Godefroy at the chapel this morning, although his kindness—and what I was beginning to perceive as a kinship in our spirits—induced me to believe that he would receive such a confession with the utmost sympathy. Instead I told him about the other controversy that has erupted in recent weeks. It began with Mr. Cork's parting salvo in the Observer, in which he used the feminine pronoun to refer to the editor. I confess I failed to spot the telltale "her," having weightier concerns on my mind at that moment. But that three-letter word produced a near avalanche of inquiries, betraying the public's burning curiosity to know who, or what, this female editor might be. As my secret was now out, and seemingly attracting more readers, I thought to make the most of it and introduce myself to the public in the guise of "Beatrice Ironside"—the name "Tabitha Simple" having been irredeemably tainted, and "Ironside" being in any event a more suitable descriptor of my temperament.

But while a few have applauded the entry of a female into the journalistic fray, it seems a greater number are appalled by my audacity—not least among them Mr. Patterson, who has expressed the view that he was duped into lending his support to the enterprise under false pretenses. No doubt his indignation was stoked by his son Charles, still fuming from my refusal months ago to publish a submission of his that was both puerile and execrably written. And Cork, of course, has taken up a perch at a new periodical, preening his ruffled feathers and chirping songs that generally have my presumed failings as their theme.

"But I don't understand," Mr. Godefroy said when I'd unburdened myself of this information. "What is the harm in a lady editing a publication? Why do these gentlemen not appreciate what you are trying to do?"

It was so clear, so simple, the way he put it: why not, indeed? I smiled at him, sadly. "Alas, my dear Mr. Godefroy, I fear the French are far more enlightened in their views on the proper role of women. Here we are expected only to charm men and then to bear and raise their children, all the while never presuming to challenge their authority on even the most trivial matters. But—"

I felt my spirits brighten. "Whether they appreciate my efforts or not, the number of our subscribers has increased. I suppose they're curious to see if I fall on my face—but what care I, as long as they subscribe!"

And pay their bills, I might have added—for the bulk of our new subscriptions have arrived without a remittance enclosed, despite our notice stating quite clearly that the fee is payable in advance.

I left Mr. Godefroy with my profuse and heartfelt thanks for the tour of his chapel and an invitation to come take tea with Father and myself next week, for I should like to cultivate him as a correspondent for the Observer. Mr. Godefroy protested that his English is far from adequate to the task of writing for publication, an assessment with which I'm inclined to agree, but I assured him that I should happily translate whatever he produced. Indeed, once we began to converse in French it was as though an entirely different person revealed himself, one who, far from being tongue-tied and reticent, was fairly bursting with astute and gracefully expressed observations.

I confess that my interest in the gentleman is not solely of the editorial variety, for I am curious to know more of the circumstances that have produced such a remarkable individual. I asked him in passing what had led to his departure from France, but he only shook his head and said it was a long and sad story that must be left for another day. I should like that day to come. I should like to call Mr. Godefroy my friend, and I believe that he would welcome such a connection. We shall each of us need a friend, perhaps, in the days to come.

From the Observer, April 4, 1807:

BEATRICE IRONSIDE'S BUDGET.

In a community like this, where the nobler sex are almost entirely engrossed by parchments, pulses, or price currents, the attempt of a female to promote the cause of taste, literature, and morals by undertaking the arduous employment of editor to a weekly paper would it seem have been forwarded with assistance and encouragement. Such were the expectations of Beatrice, such the flattering prospect with which she entered on her new avocation. But alas! luckless dame, not long were the illusions of thy fancy to deceive thee, not long ere the futility of thy hopes was demonstrated, and vexation usurped their empire in thy spirit.

If the sheets of this Miscellany contain only dissertations on morality and selections from the best authors, everyone exclaims: how dull, how insupportable! And the Observer might apply to the legislature for the liquidation of its debts. On the other hand, if Beatrice endeavors to enliven the page by using the arm of ridicule to combat folly, a thousand divinities suppose themselves pointed at and condemn her, like Actaeon, to be torn in pieces *by merciless hounds.*

Benjamin Bickerstaff, Esq., the gravest satirist, the brightest star of literature of the age, gave up his post in the Observer ... sic transit gloria mundi. *Beatrice lived over the shock; but not content with depriving her of his glorious emanations, Benjamin – the gallant, the benevolent, the* magnanimous *Benjamin, the oracle of half the little Misses of the city – proclaims aloud that the sun of* the Observer *has set forever. In his last solemn finale he pronounced its doom – for what, when not irradiated by his beams, can flourish!!!*

Chapter Eight: Margaret

It has been a month now since I started my lessons with Mr. Guy, on my Saturday afternoons off, and I'd thought to have made more progress by now. It's just sketch this, sketch that—a hard-boiled egg the first week, a sad little flower plucked from the side of the road the next. Today the task was to copy a sketch Mr. Guy himself had done of a country house, standing in the midst of some hills, with a few tiny ladies and gentlemen strolling in the foreground.

I don't mean to complain, I'm very grateful for the lessons. The two hours I spend at Mr. Guy's room in Old Town—his studio, he calls it—are the pleasantest of my entire week, leaving aside some of the time I spend with Polly, and as soon as I leave I begin counting the hours until I can return. But I still haven't used anything but charcoal, and I'd hoped to be learning to use colors by now. Mr. Guy says I show some promise, but he insists I'm not ready for such things. So I can only gaze longingly at the bladder colors—that's what he calls the pigs' bladders filled with oil paints so bright they seem to be alive. Or the pastels, which are softer but still lovely to look at, laid side by side in their box like sleeping families of reds and greens and blues and yellows. But Mr. Guy has his rules, and apparently one of them is that any pupil—no matter how long she's been sketching in charcoal—must wait at least three months before attempting to use colors.

"But can't I at least use the charcoal to sketch a portrait?" I asked him today. The truth is I have little interest in drawing eggs and flowers, and even something so large as a house isn't near as exciting to draw as a human face.

"A *portrait*?" Mr. Guy scoffed. "Why, a face is the hardest thing of all to draw! Excepting a hand. No, you must practice a good while before you attempt a portrait."

So I went back to copying the house, using little feathery strokes as Mr. Guy has instructed, while he worked nearby on decorating the side of a small table with a painting of a ship at sea, blending greens and blues and black until the color of the water was something very close to what one sees down at the Basin. It's quite amusing to watch Mr. Guy paint, for he'll stand far back to study what he's done and then advance again with his pencil or brush in the air as though meeting an enemy in battle, sometimes pausing on the way to take a mammoth pinch from his snuff jar. Sometimes he talks to himself while he works ("No, you fool, wrong again!" he'll scold), and sometimes he sings, so that even if it's just the two of us it can be quite merry. And in spite of his rules, I'm becoming fond of him. He's an odd-looking man, with yellowish skin and fierce black eyes that put me in mind of one of the lunatics I used to see at the almshouse. But he's given me paper and charcoal to bring home with me, so I can practice between lessons, if I can find the time. And I'll allow he's taught me a thing or two about drawing.

Then, after an hour or so, there came a knock at the door: Mr. Cork! He had brought me to the first lesson, to show me the way, meeting me at the foot of the bridge over the Falls. For it wouldn't have done for him to come anywhere near the Doctor's house and risk being spotted by Mrs. A. I had hoped he might appear at Mr. Guy's the next Saturday, but I hadn't seen him since then, and I felt a little jump in my stomach when the door opened to reveal him standing there. And then when he came up close behind me and admired my sketch I couldn't keep myself from a smile that stretched the width of my face.

"Well then, Guy," he said, draping his long body across an arm-chair by the window, "what do you think of our Miss McKenzie? Does the young lady show some talent?"

I felt myself go red, hearing him call me Miss McKenzie—and a lady—and not being able to breathe until I heard Mr. Guy's answer.

"Aye, that she does," Mr. Guy said mildly, putting aside his brush and wiping his hands on a cloth as he made his way over to the table where I sat. I let out my breath and went redder and tried to keep my mouth from spreading into a smile again. "But she's an impatient one. Wants to use the bladder colors! Wants to paint portraits! Everything all at once, she wants."

"I'd say that shows a fine ambition." I looked over at Mr. Cork and saw the way the sun was catching the gold in his hair, and all the colors in his eyes — the brown and green and bits of yellow — and I thought that of all the people I'd ever seen, his was the portrait I'd want to paint, putting together dabs of colors the way Mr. Guy was doing with his sea water.

Mr. Guy sniffed as he examined my drawing. "Well, perhaps next week I'll allow her the use of the red and black chalk."

"The very soul of generosity, you are!" Mr. Cork crossed his legs, and I could see the outlines of his muscles in the britches that stretched tight against his thighs. "Have you told her how you got your start as an artist?"

It appeared the two of them knew one another fairly well, although you can tell Mr. Guy isn't a gentleman like Mr. Cork. He speaks with an English accent, but it's a country kind of accent, and while his clothes are well made, his manners are rough. He doesn't smile and say please and thank you, the way Mr. Cork does.

"No, you tell her, Cork," Mr. Guy said distractedly. He took a dusty piece of bread from the table and rubbed it across the short cross-hatch of lines I'd drawn to indicate the house's shadow, so that they were smudged. "I'm sure you'll make a much better story of it."

So Mr. Cork commenced telling me that Mr. Guy had been apprenticed to a tailor and dyer in England, and had met with some success in that field. ("Appointed dyer to Her Majesty," Mr. Guy put in. "*And* the Royal Princesses.") Nevertheless, continued Mr. Cork with a shrug, he had unfortunately suffered some business reverses ("Through no fault of my own," Mr. Guy called out, taking my paper off the board and beginning to fasten it again, though I had done it just as he told me). Mr. Guy had then fled to this country ("Emigrated!") and made his way to Baltimore, where he set up a dye works, which unfortunately caught fire and burned to the ground (here Mr. Guy released a heartfelt sigh). Nothing daunted, he set up his wife in a shop whilst he undertook to become an artist, although, said Mr. Cork, he hadn't the first idea how to draw.

"Now that's an outright lie!" Mr. Guy interjected, letting the board fall to the table, and turning on Mr. Cork with his black eyes burning and his hands planted on his hips.

"I meant no offense," Mr. Cork protested. "But you told me you'd had no lessons, no training. So naturally I assumed—"

"But I'd been drawing since I was a child!" He began to walk up and down the room, waving his right arm above his head as he talked. "My grandfather, who I'll have you know was one of the finest glass stainers in all of England, used to take me out to Derwent Water, and we'd sit there together and sketch what I assure you is the grandest landscape in all creation."

"Me, too," I started to say. "I used to draw when I was a child." I wanted to add that I could remember sitting with my mother out under a tree sometimes when the weather was fine and she could spare a few minutes, sketching the hills we could see from our farm. But Mr. Guy seemed not to have heard me.

"I've been drawing and painting all my life, sir, lessons or no," he went on. "I've been my own teacher, and I could ask for no better. And I'll have you know I made paintings long before I came to Baltimore." With that he strode over to the opposite wall, away from the windows, and removed a drape from a large canvas that was leaning against it. "Just look at *that!*" he said as he removed the cloth and waved it above him, like one of those street conjurers that can make a dove appear where before there was only an empty hat.

And indeed, it did seem a conjurer's trick, for suddenly there in front of us was a city street, full of bustle and life, workers busy in the foreground, and ladies and gentlemen talking to one another further back, buildings going off to the right down to a harbor full of the masts of ships. It was as though he'd thrown open a window, but I couldn't place the scene in Baltimore. The building on the left was much grander than any I've seen here. What was it?

"The Tontine coffee house," said Mr. Guy as he turned to me, as though I'd spoken. "At the corner of Wall and Water Streets in New York." He turned back to the painting and looked at it fondly but sadly. "My mistake was to paint it after I'd moved to Philadelphia. Couldn't even raffle the thing off there! Not even after President Adams himself came by and pronounced it a fine work. People in Philadelphia don't want paintings of New York, no more than people in Baltimore do."

"I have to agree with that old royalist Adams, for once," said Mr. Cork, squinting at the painting and leaning forward in his chair. "It's remarkable. Why not paint something like that of Baltimore?"

I was thinking the same thing. None of the other half-finished paintings I'd seen in Mr. Guy's studio, on easels or leaning against walls, were anything like this one of New York. Mostly they were like the sketch I was copying: a single house in the countryside, with just a few tiny people in fine clothes standing about as though they had nothing better to do than pose for a painting. Which they probably didn't.

"No, landscapes and houses, that's where the money is." Mr. Guy patted the drape back into place over the painting as though tucking a small child into bed. "People don't want paintings of buildings that don't belong to them, even ones in their own city. They want a record of the fine house they've built themselves, the green land that's theirs." He stuck out a hand towards a painting leaning against the far wall. "Like your uncle."

I took in my breath as I realized that the painting he was pointing to was of the very house where Mr. Cork and I had met that day, when I'd brought Polly to the country for some fresh air. The three stories made of brick, the many windows, the white fences. Even the chestnut horses and the sheep. "But I thought you said your uncle would buy *my* picture of his house!" I cried, only half serious.

Mr. Cork shrugged. "I'm afraid Mr. Guy got in ahead of you. It's quite the thing these days, to have Mr. Guy paint a landscape with your house in it. He's even got a waiting list, just as Mr. Stuart did when he set up shop to paint portraits in Washington City a few years since."

I'd never heard of Mr. Stuart, but I saw an opening to press my case. "That's what I want to try, doing a portrait. Even just a sketch."

"I've told you, Miss McKenzie, portraits aren't for beginners." Mr. Guy was seated before the table he was painting again. "I gave up the idea long ago, myself. Not that I couldn't execute them well, of course." I had to wonder about that. Maybe all the people in Mr. Guy's landscapes were tiny because he couldn't do faces.

"But you hold up a mirror to someone," he continued, "and they don't always like what they see. Then if you take out the wrinkles, or the fat at the chin, or what have you, they'll object that it doesn't look like *them*. Or the wife objects, or the husband — or the children. And the next thing you know, they've refused to pay you. No, landscapes are far safer. Or seascapes." He gestured to the table before him with a flick of his black hair as he stretched a hand to his snuff box. "The Finlay brothers have commissioned five of these card tables for their furniture concern, all to be done with scenes of the Basin."

"Has Mr. Guy told you about his ingenious invention for re-producing landscapes?" Mr. Cork asked me. "His painting tent?"

I shook my head. Just then Mr. Guy let out an enormous sneeze, no doubt the result of a large dose of snuff.

"When he undertakes to paint a scene from nature, or a house," Mr. Cork went on, "he sets up a tent that has a square opening in it — a window, if you will — the size of his intended picture."

"Then I take a piece of black gauze," Mr. Guy interrupted, having recovered from his sneeze. "And I stretch it over that window, on a frame. Then I take some chalk, and on the gauze I trace the outlines of what I can see through it: the shape of the land, the trees, the house, what you will. I take my canvas and press it to the gauze, and lo and behold, the chalk transfers itself and I have the sketch of my painting."

It did sound clever. "I wonder if you could do something like that with a portrait," I said, thinking aloud.

"Portraits, portraits, enough about portraits!" Mr. Guy said, in one of those explosions of his. He took his watch from the pocket of his waistcoat and glanced at it. "Now be off with you, we're done for today."

I began to put away the charcoal and the sketch I'd made, and Mr. Cork stood up from his armchair and stretched and yawned, as though *he'd* been the one slaving away, when it was *my* neck and back that ached, and my hand as well. Though I didn't mind, really — I'd much rather be sore from sitting and drawing than from hauling water back from the spring, or drag-ging in firewood.

Mr. Guy told me to wait a moment, then opened a chest and rummaged about, muttering where *is* the damned thing, I *know* it was here. "Ah," he said at last, and turned to face me. "This is for you."

He was holding a sort of case, about the size of a large sheet of paper, and made from dark red leather. Around the edges there were some curving designs done in gold.

"It's beautiful," I said. "But what would I need it for?"

"It's a portfolio!" he barked. Then, more gently: "It's to keep your sketches in. To protect them. No use making nice sketches and then having them get torn or soiled. Go on, you can take it home with you if you like."

"But." I extended a hand and felt the softness of the leather. "It must have cost a heap of money."

He thrust it towards me. "Just take it and be gone," he growled. "The both of you. I've work to do."

Once we were out on the street, Mr. Cork took the portfolio from me and admired it. "Don't let Mr. Guy scare you off," he said. "He's an odd little man, set in his opinions, but he'd give you his last penny." And then he told me a story about how his friend Mr. Harmer had been walking along Market Street with Mr. Guy when they met a boy carrying a canary in a cage. Mr. Guy decided he must have the canary, for some reason, but had no money with him. So he borrowed five dollars from Mr. Harmer and bought the bird and the cage.

"Not three minutes later," Mr. Cork went on as we made our way down High Street towards the Falls, "they encountered Mr. Malone, who complimented Mr. Guy on the bird he was carrying. And do you know, Mr. Guy immediately made a present of the canary and its cage to Mr. Malone. Insisted that he take them!" Mr. Cork laughed and shook his head. "Harmer never did see his five dollars again. But where shall we go for supper?"

Supper! So he was going to buy me a meal. I was happy to hear that, as my stomach had been rumbling for the last half hour. And I was convinced I had no reason to fear that he remembered me from the Legrands', for surely he would have mentioned it by now.

"I know a tavern on the other side of the Falls," Mr. Cork went on. "It's a bit ripe around here."

It's true there's an odor in Old Town that will put you right off your food. So we turned onto York Street and could see the bridge not far ahead of us. It was a lovely April evening, warm but with a gentle breeze. I could hardly believe my good fortune: drawing lessons, the portfolio, supper at a tavern. And walking along with Mr. Cork, just like we were friends.

But then he said something about how we had business to discuss, and I recalled our arrangement. I began to feel ill at ease, not knowing what he'd expect me to tell him about Mrs. A, and not having much to tell. We were at the bridge now, walking across it.

"My father worked on this bridge," I said. "A year ago, making repairs. That was before he started on the mud machine."

Mr. Cork raised his eyebrows. "Dredging mud from the Basin? Dirty work, that. I've seen those men, out there in the water. I thought they were all ..."

He stopped himself, and I knew why. "They *used* to be taken from the jail," I said, keeping my voice even and staring straight ahead. "But not when my father worked there."

I was quiet for a time after that, thinking of how my father would come home, covered in that foul grime and so tired he could hardly eat his supper. Most of the men didn't last more than a few weeks on the machine, but my father was there a good three months and would have stayed longer if the sickly season hadn't come on and brought the work to a halt. He got more than six dollars a week there, better than what the bridge work paid. It takes me a month to make six dollars. I thought of the story about Mr. Guy and the bird that cost five dollars, and wondered at the very idea of it.

We were at the tavern now, one called the Sow's Ear, and as soon as we opened the door the smell of roasting meat set my mouth to watering. I've only been in a tavern once or twice before, and I had a good look about. It was smoky and dark, and almost all the other people in the room were men, and there was a good deal of noise. Mr. Cork ordered some ale and a meat pie for us, and we found a seat at a table in the corner, by ourselves. As soon as the tavern keeper brought the ale I poured quite a bit of it down my throat.

Mr. Cork watched me, and then took a small swallow himself. "And how is your mistress these days, Margaret?"

I shrugged. "I told you, it doesn't fall to me to know much of what she does." I felt my heart beating and took some more ale. I thought if I didn't tell him something he might decide not to pay for any more lessons with Mr. Guy, or take me out for any more suppers. "But there are lots of people who come to the house. In the evening, mostly. Lots of foreigners, speaking different languages.

And there was one gentleman, he stayed in the house for a week or so, until he found a place to live. It seemed he had just come to town from somewhere. He didn't speak much English."

He nodded. "I told you, she adores all things European. Like that *Madame* Bonaparte, who she's on such intimate terms with."

It seemed to me that most of these foreigners were there more at the Doctor's invitation than at Mrs. A's. She sometimes complains about having so many people to the house, and says she doesn't have enough peace and quiet to do her work. But I decided not to mention that, as Mr. Cork seemed pleased to think it was all on her account.

"Can you recall anyone else in particular?" he asked. "Any names?"

The tavern keeper arrived with the meat pie, which smelled better than just about anything that had ever been set before me. I took some, quickly, but it was too hot and burned my mouth, and I had to spit it out.

"There's a Frenchman who comes round a lot," I said after I'd had a gulp of ale, staring at the pie and hoping it would cool. "They speak French together. Or at least I think it's French."

"There are a lot of Frenchmen in this town." Mr. Cork took a small forkful of pie, chewed, and swallowed, all the while looking straight at me. "Can you tell me anything else about him?"

I wondered why he should care so much about who was visiting the Doctor and Mrs. A. "I think he's called Mr. God-for-something."

Mr. Cork raised his eyebrows. "Godefroy? The drawing master?"

I shrugged. And then I shuddered, remembering who else had been there one afternoon, speaking French: Miss Legrand, visiting Mrs. A. I'd gone into the sitting room with the tea and nearly dropped the tray when I saw her. I went back to the kitchen and told Mrs. Morris I was feeling ill, which was true, and that I needed to take to my bed. Mrs. Morris grumbled at me, and the next day she kept exclaiming about how fast a recovery I'd made, and not in a friendly way.

"And what about the Observer?" he asked. "Do you know what she's planning for the next number?"

I rolled my eyes at him and swallowed some pie, at last. "Do you imagine she discusses such things with *me*?" I took another swill of ale. "But she's been out of sorts quite a bit. Or up and down, I should say. Laughing and excited one minute, raging about something the next. People who don't pay their bills, sometimes. Or people saying bad things about her, I suppose. I don't know, really. A few days ago I heard her complaining to the Doctor, very loud it was, and it was something about spectacles, of all things."

At this Mr. Cork smiled slowly, and I could see his lovely white teeth. I smiled back, relieved that he seemed so pleased, but puzzled as to why.

"Spectacles?" he said. He threw his head back and laughed, then leaned across the table, so close I could almost feel his breath on my face. "Do you recall that I told you some friends of mine were undertaking to start a new paper? Well, they've done it. And the name of it is Spectacles."

I was beginning to understand. "You've written things about *her*?"

"I have simply pointed out that a publication that ridicules and insults its readers isn't likely to last long. I suspected she was displeased, given what she wrote about me in today's number of the Observer. But one never knows how much of what one reads is simply for show. It's gratifying to hear that she was genuinely agitated. Perhaps she'll have second thoughts before printing more of her vicious slander. Or perhaps she'll realize that she simply lacks the proper temperament to edit a literary miscellany."

I was pleased that I'd managed to find something to tell him that he found useful, and turned my attention to the meat pie. I think I ate more of it than he did, but he didn't seem to mind. He was occupied in talking about how if Baltimore was to take its place among the leading cities of this country, it needed a decent weekly paper—like one called The Port Folio, just like the leather case Mr. Guy had given me, that he said was in Philadelphia.

"What's needed is a publication that holds up to the world the accomplishments of our citizens," he said, pounding his mug of ale on the table, "not one that exaggerates our defects and renders us even more of a laughing stock than we already are. Finished with that pie, are you?"

I was. Mr. Cork walked me as far as the corner of Hanover and Market, but said it would be best if he didn't come any closer to the Doctor's house. He gave me the portfolio, which he'd been carrying for me, and I asked him if I would see him at Mr. Guy's next Saturday, and he said perhaps, he didn't know. I felt my insides drop a bit. I wanted to see his hair glint in the sun again, and to hear him talking and jesting with Mr. Guy, and I wanted another meat pie.

"I might have something more to tell you about Mrs. A, next week," I said. "And perhaps you'd let me do your portrait, in charcoal. I don't care what Mr. Guy says, I'm sure I could do a good job. I've practiced lots, with my sister, and I've done some sketches of Polly. I can show you. They're good, honest they are."

He cocked his head at me and smiled, and there were those nice teeth again. "I don't know that Mr. Guy would approve."

"We could do it afterwards then. After supper." I smiled back at him, keeping my lips together to hide my teeth. "They don't mind how late I come back on Saturday evenings. Perhaps we could find some quiet place. It could be just the two of us. Mr. Guy needn't know anything about it."

Mr. Cork said nothing, but his face went a bit pink. I imagine mine did too, when I realized what I'd said, and how it might sound. But he hadn't said no.

"Saturday, then," I said, and went off up Hanover Street. It was all I could do to keep from skipping.

From the Observer, April 11, 1807:

BEATRICE IRONSIDE'S BUDGET.

A friend stepped in to pay me a visit this evening, just as I had taken up the pen to furnish my weekly budget. Our conversation turned upon the various passions that interest and occupy the human mind, and the good or evil that result from them.

Amidst the topics of discussion that occurred to us was the rage for gambling, which gains daily and dreadful ground in our city. Good heavens! How many desolated families, how many ruined reputations, how much prostrated virtue and blasted honor form the train of this hell-born passion! It beckons to woe, it leads the way to guilt and infamy.

You at least, my young readers, who are not yet enslaved by habit, remember that "the gods are just, and of our pleasant vices, *make instruments to scourge us."*

Chapter Nine: Eliza

W hat a lively and edifying evening party we had last night, with such engaging and intelligent conversation that none felt the need for gambling at whist or loo or any such trivial yet dangerous pursuits to help us while away the hours. It was Betsy who urged me to include in my recent budget a timely admonition against this variety of dissipation, especially as it regards our extremely susceptible younger citizens.

Nor, although it was a mixed company, did any of the ladies present (even including Bess Caton) endeavor to charm the gentlemen through coquettish wiles or affectation, but I am pleased to say that all contributed to the conversation in equal measure and all were heard with equal respect, regardless of their sex. Perhaps it would be presumption to say that I am worthy of a place amongst the great *salonnières* of Paris, but given the more modest bounty at my disposal in Baltimore, I believe that my harvest of artists and wits would have met with their approval. Indeed, I reaped an unexpected prize when Mr. Godefroy asked if he might bring his friend Mr. Latrobe, who had returned to town to supervise construction at the Cathedral.

We had several of our usual visitors — Mr. Godefroy of course, the Italian singing master Mr. Cecchi, the German violinist Mr. Nenninger — but feeling that our gatherings have been generally too heavily weighted towards the male sex, I had prevailed on Father to allow me to invite a few of my female friends. I confess I also hoped to restore my friendship with Bess, which, despite my explanation and apology, has never entirely recovered from the Tabitha Simple episode. And I was able to muster the presence of Henriette Legrand, so that although in the end the ladies were outnumbered by the gentlemen, it was less so than usual.

It was indeed a privilege to entertain Mr. Latrobe, whom I had never met — although we did, of course, correspond concerning the two essays on fine arts he wrote for the Observer before the press of other duties interfered. Given his residence in Washington City, where he has been much engaged in the construction of the Capitol building, he was able to enlighten us on many topics of the day, most particularly what is being said there regarding Vice-President Burr's designs on the Western territories, and the shocking prospect that he would soon be brought to trial on charges of treason.

But delighted as I was to include Mr. Latrobe in our little band, I confess that much of the interest of the evening, for me, was the opportunity to learn more of Mr. Godefroy's personal history, for though I have tried to extract it over these last few months, he has proven resistant to my attempts. Bess, with her encouraging smiles, induced him to reveal much more than I had heard before, and the presence of Mr. Latrobe, to whom he has apparently unburdened himself fully, was also invaluable in this regard. The tale was even more romantic than I had imagined, and has only served to increase my admiration for the gentleman.

As Bess had never made Mr. Godefroy's acquaintance before, some of the preliminaries he divulged to her were known to me: his having arrived in this country some two years since, first attempting unsuccessfully to find employment in Philadelphia, and then, on the recommendation of a friend, securing a position at St. Mary's.

"And what was it, sir, that induced you to leave your native land?" Bess inquired guilelessly.

At first Mr. Godefroy demurred, saying — as he has to me on more than one previous occasion — that it was but a long and dull story that would only ruin an otherwise pleasant evening. But Mr. Latrobe protested that on the contrary, it was a story the company would find highly interesting, and proceeded to tell it — with the inevitable result that Mr. Godefroy stepped in to correct one or two minor inaccuracies in his friend's narrative, and soon began to relate the tale himself.

At the dawn of the Revolution in France, Mr. Godefroy — who, being some fifteen years older than myself, was already then a young man—sympathized with those who called for an end to tyranny, although he was himself (as Mr. Latrobe declared) a member of the aristocracy, his father having died and passed to him the title of Count St. Maur. Mr. Godefroy cast his eyes down modestly at this revelation, and I was surprised that he had never mentioned it—although given the rabid democratic fervor of some in this part of the world, perhaps his reticence has been no more than circumspect. But the high position of his family, and the education that was no doubt afforded him as a result, do serve to explain the immense breadth of his knowledge, fresh evidence of which is constantly manifesting itself to me.

Taking up the tale, Mr. Godefroy attempted to pass over the tumultuous events of the Revolution and its aftermath, merely saying that his own principles—those of equality before the law balanced by public order—had never altered, despite the rapid changes in the circumstances surrounding him. But I could not resist pressing him for a fuller description of what he had witnessed, and he acknowledged that yes, he had seen blood run in the gutters of Paris, he had seen crowds carrying heads on pikes, and had generally witnessed scenes of depravity and savagery that he could not bring himself to inflict on so polite a company.

"It is *affreux* – terrible—what people will do when they join together in a ... what do you call it? A bob?"

"Ah, a *mob!*" I interjected. "Yes, we're quite familiar with mobs in this town, unfortunately. And if mobs can commit such outrages in a city as civilized as Paris, imagine what they might be capable of doing in these parts."

We were all silent for a moment, perhaps recalling scenes we had witnessed in the streets of our fair city: faces contorted in rage, drunken brawls spilling out of taverns. Once I saw a man staggering away from such an encounter clutching his eye, which appeared to have been gouged out by another combatant.

"And of course on every Election Day," Mr. Latrobe put in bitterly, "we're treated to the scene of our noble electorate thronging to the polls under the influence of the favors dispensed by their favorite candidate—their favorite candidate being whichever one has provided them with the greatest amount of intoxicating fluid!"

"Yes, our much vaunted democracy," I said, holding out my glass as Margaret made the rounds with a bottle of claret. "But never say a word against it in public, Mr. Latrobe, or they're liable to have your head on a pike."

Bess then gently brought the conversation back to Mr. Godefroy's personal history — for which I was most grateful — asking him if it was the tumult of the Revolution that had prompted him to flee. He replied no, that he had weathered those storms by remaining as inconspicuous as possible: serving in the army ("if not brilliantly," he said with a shrug, "then at least honorably"), pursuing instruction in drawing, then being trained and employed as a civil engineer. But he said, he could no longer keep his silence when a man arose who threatened to recreate the very tyranny that the Revolution had endeavored to end: Napoleon Bonaparte. I shuddered as he pronounced the name, and exchanged a glance with Father.

"I had the ... unwisdom," he said, coining a new but useful word, "to see that this abuse of liberty would bring forth the despotism." He smiled sadly. "And the greater unwisdom to say these thoughts freely."

For a few moments Mr. Godefroy was silent, as was his audience, breathlessly awaiting his next words.

"And what, pray tell, did the Emperor do to you?" cried Henriette at last.

"Ah, Mademoiselle, not nearly so much as he did to others," Mr. Godefroy replied.

"But tell them, Maxim," Mr. Latrobe interjected. "Tell them of your imprisonment, and your escape!"

Bowing to his friend's urging with apparent reluctance, Mr. Godefroy then recounted his arrest in Paris, succeeded by confinement to a prison in the Pyrenees. While there he received word that the Duchess of Orleans, who sympathized with his plight, had arranged for a boat to meet him in Barcelona, and he was able to slip away through the mountains — though being tracked like a savage beast, as he said, by hounds. But after crossing the Spanish border he was informed that the commander of the prison had been falsely accused of aiding him in his escape and was to be court-martialed. Unable to allow such an injustice to go forward, he sent a letter to Napoleon himself, stating the truth of the matter and offering to give himself up.

Such nobility of spirit, such courageous self-sacrifice could not help but produce murmurs of admiration from the company.

I myself felt a choking sensation in my throat and the pressure of tears at my eyes.

"And what was the Emperor's response?" I managed to say. "I could imagine him ordering you summarily to be shot, but the evidence before my eyes indicates that you were somehow able to avoid such a fate."

Mr. Godefroy gave me one of his melancholy smiles. "No, Bonaparte was able to appreciate such conduct. Or so it appeared, at least. I asked him to allow me to enter the army of Spain, or to go to the United States. I had his word that I could go to Spain, but instead I somehow found myself in prison once again, this time at the Chateau d'If — perhaps you know of it? — where it is impossible to escape. I was there for some months, and then I was ordered — *ordered* – to go to America." He drew himself up. "I would have chosen to come here freely, but no — he would not allow me such freedom, but ordered me, like a dog."

"And tell them, Maxim, how you passed your time at the Chateau d'If," Mr. Latrobe urged.

Mr. Godefroy twirled his wine glass, fixing his gaze on the tiny waves he was stirring in the ruby liquid. "The Chateau is ... not a pleasant place. A rocky island, you know, all alone in the sea, a full mile from Marseille. My hair, it was black when I went in, and like this when I came out." He raked a hand through his snowy mane. "To preserve my sanity, I turned to the one thing that has always sustained me: art. I had only some scraps of paper — the backs of letters and such — and the stump of a pen, and for ink only a solution I made from the soot of my stove-pipe. But in my mind I could see a heroic scene, the great battle between Charles of Sweden and Peter the Great at Pultowa."

He took a sip of his wine and shrugged. "I don't know why that is what came to me. But I saw Charles on his rearing horse, telling his soldiers they must fight even though they were ill, even though they were hungry, even though they were so few. And so I spent my endless solitary hours in drawing, on the little bits of paper, over a hundred of them. A horse's leg here, a man's arm there, all on the floor like the pieces of a puzzle. I say it was to preserve my sanity, but my jailers surely thought I had already lost it."

"And what became of it, this drawing?" Bess asked. I could see her dark eyes shining with moisture in the firelight, as no doubt my own were as well. "Did you leave it behind?"

"Indeed, no!" cried Mr. Latrobe. "It's right here in Baltimore."

At this we all gasped, and Mr. Latrobe explained that during his voyage across the Atlantic Mr. Godefroy had carefully glued together the various parts of his drawing, then colored them with sepia wash and India ink upon his arrival in Philadelphia. "It's magnificent," he added. "Full of life and action. Even if you don't know the circumstances of its creation, it's a wonder to behold."

"But I must ask you, please, my friends," Mr. Godefroy said urgently, leaning forward in his chair and looking around at our attentive faces, "not to discuss any of this with others. I don't like to talk about the past, for many reasons. But one is that there are those in this country with strong feelings concerning the French government, as you know. And I prefer not to be drawn into politics. I am done with that!"

"Oh, of course!" I cried. "We shall all be discreet, for your sake. But know that there is not one amongst us who does not sympathize with and applaud you. And I, for one, am determined to see your magnificent drawing—and to see it displayed for public admiration."

Again murmurs of agreement arose, and suggestions of a suitable venue for the drawing's display. Henriette proposed the Library Company, and Father, who is on good terms with several of its directors, promised that he would speak to them about the matter the very next day.

"You know, Mr. Godefroy," Father then said, "that you are not the only one in this room to have had your life threatened by that imperial scoundrel. My daughter also encountered his wrath."

Bess and Henriette were familiar with my overseas adventure, but the gentlemen had never heard the tale. I begged to defer the telling to another occasion, so as not to weary those who knew it—and to spare myself the reliving of it. But my friends began to recount it all: Betsy's determination to present herself before the Emperor and plead the case for the legitimacy of her marriage; my reluctant agreement to join the couple on their dangerous journey, as Betsy was expecting a child and desired a female friend to be present at the delivery; our slipping away in the dead of night, so as to evade the English ships on the alert for Jerome, the brother of their sworn enemy; our discovery, upon arriving at Lisbon, that Napoleon had forbidden Betsy to disembark at any port under his control; Jerome's departure, under guard, for an audience with the Emperor, and his promise to send for Betsy; and our difficult sea voyage thence to Amsterdam, where Betsy hoped to land and deliver her child—Napoleon's nephew—and be reunited with her husband.

"We had thought Amsterdam was sufficiently neutral that we would find refuge there," I put in, taking up the story at its most dramatic point. "But we discovered we were wrong. Not only had Napoleon issued orders forbidding us from landing, but the Dutch—who hadn't the faintest idea who we were, or what supposed danger we might present—would neither let us land or leave. And our stores of food, which we had taken on weeks before at Lisbon, were nearly exhausted. We were reduced to a few scraps of salt beef and some hard biscuit."

I paused to steady myself, and took a sip of wine. "We were growing desperate, and particularly concerned for Madame Bonaparte, in her condition. Some of the gentlemen—the doctor Jerome had left behind to attend her, a few seamen—decided to set off in a small boat, in order to secure some provisions. But as the boat was being lowered the captain cried out—the Dutch gunships that had been guarding us for days had aimed their cannons directly at the boat, and were preparing to fire. We could see the flames of the tapers they had lit."

Then I had to smile, which the company must have found odd, but in my mind I saw the image of Dr. Garnier, so anxious to escape the small boat that he fairly rolled from it onto the ship's deck, like a portly caterpillar in the path of a looming foot.

"I had no idea," Mr. Godefroy said with a seething quiet. "Of course I knew something of the humiliation Madame Bonaparte was subjected to—even at the Chateau d'If, one heard of these things. And I know all too well what the Emperor will do against one he sees as an enemy. But to threaten two harmless females! I had not thought him capable of that."

I assured Mr. Godefroy that once the Dutch admiral was made to understand the situation, he sent along a full supply of food and drink, including an assortment of wines and liquors, and we soon received permission to depart for another port. "Of course, the only port where we could be assured of a welcome, and that was nearby, was England, and so the choice was made for us. It was unfortunate, but unavoidable, that we should end by taking refuge in a country that was at war with the very government we were seeking to appease. And that the child should have been born there."

I paused for a moment, recalling Betsy's extravagant welcome when we disembarked, the throngs that greeted her, the newspapers that reported her every gesture and excursion and sang frequent paeans to her beauty—while occasionally noting that she was accompanied by "another American lady." Most women would have shrunk from such a glare, but Betsy turned to it like a flower opening to the sun. I have always wondered whether we stayed in London so many months because she was still hopeful of receiving word from Jerome, as she claimed, or whether she simply couldn't tear herself away from such adulation. And it was beguiling, indeed, to be courted by the great and the refined, to be invited into grand homes where masterpieces graced the walls and *bon mots* leavened the conversation. Had I not been so anxious concerning Polly and Father I doubt I should have been so eager to return to Baltimore myself.

And although, once I returned, I was greatly relieved to find them both alive and well, it seemed to me—as it did to Betsy— that, compared to what I'd known in London, my life in this place was unbearably colorless and small. I suppose that is what induced me to begin sending in contributions to the Companion, the need for something beyond the daily round of managing a house and caring for a child and discussing the weather or the price currents at evening parties. I wanted to introduce into my life—and into this place—something approaching what I'd experienced abroad.

"But enough of these sad tales!" I cried. "Mr. Latrobe, how goes the work on your Cathedral?"

"It goes very little at all, I fear," he said, pushing his spectacles on his forehead and rubbing his eyes wearily. "And when it does go, it goes so badly I wish it would stop. Did I tell you, Godefroy, that the builder read my plans upside down and told the Bishop they were absurd? He mistook the crypt vault for reversed foundation arches. Such incompetence! I refused to have anything to do with the project unless I was assured the man would be kept as far away as possible from the site." He placed his elbows on the table before him and used his hands to pull his cheeks down into a comical expression of mourning. "The trouble is, the builder's one of the Cathedral trustees!"

"And what of my little church, then?" Mr. Godefroy exclaimed. "The carpenter, he made the windows in the *chappelle basse* like the windows for a kitchen! If I'm not right there to stop them, they do anything they want with my plans. And Father Tessier, he's happy to do what the workmen want if it saves him a little money."

"At least they're allowing you to do it in the Gothic style," Mr. Latrobe retorted. "What would have been more fitting than a Gothic cathedral? But no, the Bishop and the trustees, in their wisdom, insisted on a classical design. Of course, there are far worse atrocities on view in the streets of Baltimore on a daily basis. No taste whatsoever here, as far as I can tell. Do you know, we went to the theater last night, Godefroy and I, and saw the most absurd spectacle — an actor subjecting himself to the most painful contortions in order to produce a few notes of song!"

"Ah, that would have been Mr. Webster," I sighed, as Mr. Cecchi nodded his head vigorously. "He seems to perform in nearly every theatrical production. You would scarcely believe the attitudes he sometimes strikes in the pursuit of his art!"

"My dear Mrs. Anderson," said Mr. Latrobe, "I would believe anything that can be said of the Vandalism of the Baltimoreans in the arts, provided it is exceedingly absurd and ridiculous."

"Yes, *Vandalism* indeed!" I laughed. "You do have a talent for a turn of phrase, Mr. Latrobe."

"But we are to be treated to some true art the week after next," Mr. Cecchi interjected, "at Mr. Nenninger's concert. Mr. Nenninger has invited a number of musicians, including some from the orchestra at the theater. And I will sing a few airs myself."

"Oh, excellent!" I clapped my hands with delight. Earlier in the evening Mr. Nenninger, who had brought his violin at my request, had played us a most delightful tune on the violin, which he said had been composed by Herr Mozart, and executed it admirably. "Some virtuoso talent on display here at last."

Mr. Nenninger, whose hearty looks belie the delicacy of his technique, folded his hands atop his rounded belly and nodded in acknowledgment of the compliment. "I hope it will bring enough money so that I can take not so many pupils, and perhaps not play so much for the dancing at the Assembly. Very dull, these lessons and these dances, very dull indeed. The dancers, they cannot keep the measure!"

Mr. Cecchi, who has an exquisite tenor voice but must give singing lessons to keep body and soul together, shook his head vigorously. "The young ladies, I tell them to sing E, but they can come no closer than C or D!"

"It's outrageous," said Mr. Latrobe heatedly, "that artists of your quality—and yours too, Godefroy—should be condemned to waste their gifts in instructing brats with no ear and playing cotillions for dancers who only want to chatter and flirt! There's no respect in this country for genius, for inspiration—no distinction made between the artist and the mechanic—no greater admiration for a man who can create a fine drawing than for the tradesman who creates the paper he draws it on."

"It's true!" I cried. "Do you know there's a man here, a Mr. Guy, who tries to pass himself off as an artist, when in fact his only training is as a tailor and dyer? He'll paint a landscape with a flattering depiction of your house one day, and then the next he'll take your measurements with his stay tape and conjure you a nice suit made of buckram! How are we to educate the public to respect the arts when we have those amongst us who persist in sowing such confusion?" I now feared that the conversation had once again taken too somber a turn. "But let us hope for the best for Mr. Nenninger's concert. Let's toast its success, shall we?"

I reached for my glass and found it empty, and then observed to my dismay that the others' glasses were in a similarly depleted condition. The four bottles of wine on the side table were drained as well. We hadn't the means to provide a full meal for so large a group, but I had persuaded Mrs. Morris to produce some tea cake before she departed for the evening, and the least I could do was to ensure an uninterrupted supply of the fruits of the vine. I was moving towards the door to call for Margaret when I nearly stumbled over her, standing quiet as a mouse in the shadow of a bookcase. I can't think what she was doing there, but I was pleased not to have to go to the trouble of finding her and immediately directed her to fetch us two more bottles from the cellar.

While we were awaiting her return, I announced that I would do my best to bring public attention to the concert through the pages of the Observer. I only regretted, directing an accusatory look in Mr. Latrobe's direction, that I could not depend on some writer of taste and discernment to contribute a regular essay on the fine arts.

"A thankless task, I fear, in this town," Mr. Latrobe responded. "And yet, for you, Mrs. Anderson, I would nevertheless undertake it had I the time to spare. But why not draw upon the excellent judgment and knowledge of Mr. Godefroy? He lives right here and has ample opportunity to observe how the arts are flourishing — or rather, languishing."

Mr. Godefroy gallantly said that nothing could please him more, but protested, as he had before, that his writing in English still suffered from many defects. "But, Madame, if *you* write the essays, I am more than happy to provide whatever aid and advice I can. I am sure you will do an excellent job of it. It is all very well to criticize the gambling, the affectations of the young ladies." He made a dismissive Gallic gesture and a small moue with his lips. "But is it not more important to encourage the arts? Especially here, where there is so little of them. It is like we are in some *Siberia* here, is it not?"

"Indeed it is! A Siberia of the arts. But ..." I hesitated. Of course, it had been my original intention to write about the fine arts myself — it was only that wretch Cork who convinced me I was inadequate to the task. True, I lack expertise. But with Mr. Godefroy to advise me, that seems a not insuperable obstacle. After all, one needn't be an artist oneself to discern merit or decry ineptitude. Writing regular essays on the fine arts, in addition to reviewing and editing submissions and producing Beatrice Ironside's Budget, will leave me little time for sleep. But one must make sacrifices in perilous times, I told myself, for the general good.

"I'll do it, then!" I cried. "But what of the rest of you? I'm in dire need of contributions! I can't be expected to produce sixteen pages of entertaining and edifying material each week without assistance."

"I'm already supplying you with my translation of *Adelaide*," protested Henriette, which was true, and I thanked her — although I cannot say that I entirely share her enthusiasm for the novel, which she is providing to me in installments. We've only published two chapters so far, though, and I haven't relinquished hope that the narrative will yet improve. And judging from the correspondence I've received, our readers are far more enthusiastic about *Adelaide* than I am.

"You can't point your finger at me," Father put in. "You've had four installments of my series on quarantine, and there's much more to come."

I agreed that he was absolved from any additional responsibility to fill the Observer's pages, keeping to myself any further thoughts. Mr. Patterson sent a note last week approving Father's argument that the quarantining of goods has no effect upon the progress of disease, since it's impossible for contagion to be spread through the air or by contact. But he expressed reservations about Father's assertion that epidemics are useful in limiting the growth of what would otherwise be a dangerously burgeoning population, fearing the unpopularity of such a view. And he betrayed some impatience with Father's lengthy disquisitions on the habits of various specimens of the insect world (last week's essay was devoted largely to the plant louse), demanding to know instead what Father *does* identify as the cause of disease. I replied that all would be explained in the near future, but I could not help but wonder whether Mr. Patterson will be so approving when — and if — Father reaches that point in the development of his theory.

"What about you, Bess?" I said. "Can I not tempt you to undertake an essay, or perhaps a bit of poetry?"

"Oh, I'm afraid I couldn't," she said, a look of horror clouding her face. "Mamma would never allow it. She doesn't approve of ladies attracting public attention."

"But she needn't know anything about it," I coaxed. "You could make up any name you please — you could write in the guise of a man! You can be anyone you like, in print."

Bess pursed her lips in a tight smile. "You're tempting me. I could see writing something about ... oh, perhaps taking to task a certain Baltimore lady who persists in giving herself *imperial* airs, when the empire to which she seeks to attach herself wants nothing to do with her."

My own smile froze. It would be impossible to publish something mocking Betsy, given our ties of friendship — and the matter of Mr. Patterson's loan, which we as yet have no hopes of repaying. Why Betsy and Bess have conceived such scorn for one another I can't fathom; of all the Catons, Betsy reserves her most ardent vitriol for Bess. It has been no small feat to maintain friendships with both of them. I desperately searched my brain for a diplomatic way to discourage Bess from such a plan.

"But no, I couldn't risk it," Bess continued regretfully. "Mamma would have my head."

I shook my own head in outward sympathy, while my insides proceeded to gratefully uncoil.

Mr. Cecchi and Mr. Nenninger offered to contribute essays in their native tongues, but I explained regretfully that I knew no one proficient enough in Italian and German to translate whatever they might produce.

Just then, Margaret arrived with the wine and announced loudly that these were our last two bottles—as though this were information to be shared with guests! I laughed and told her that was no matter, we would replenish the cellar tomorrow (although heaven knows if we can find the money to do so, especially after the expense of all the candles we burned this evening), and that she should please fill everyone's glass without further delay.

"What really needs translation, of course," Mr. Latrobe continued after our toast to the concert had at last been accomplished, "is Godefroy's memorial. Surely he's mentioned it to you, Mrs. Anderson?"

I replied that Mr. Godefroy had been reticent on a number of topics, and this memorial—whatever its subject—was among them. Mr. Latrobe then explained that Mr. Godefroy, drawing on the extensive knowledge of military fortifications he had acquired in France, had written an essay on the subject, intended to be presented to the gentlemen in Congress to assist them in planning for our country's defense in the event of an attack by a European power. Indeed, there are many who consider such an attack imminent, even if they cannot tell which power will be the first to pounce: France, where Napoleon's imperial ambitions know no bounds; or England, in such desperate need of warm bodies to counteract those ambitions that it scruples not to impress American seamen to aid in its exertions.

Alas, Mr. Latrobe continued, there has been little interest in the memorial, no doubt because of the violent prejudice of both parties against the land of Mr. Godefroy's birth—the Federalists having an antipathy towards all things French dating from the days of that country's Revolution, and the Republicans indiscriminately despising anything that does not originate on America's own peerless soil.

"Nevertheless," Mr. Godefroy said, "perhaps if it weren't in French—if I could find someone to translate it—I might have better success. I only want to assist the country that has welcomed so kindly and generously a poor refugee."

He directed a glance at Father and then myself, with unmistakable gratitude.

"Henriette," I cried, "couldn't you translate Mr. Godefroy's memorial, once you finish with *Adelaide?*"

Henriette has never given any indication of a keen intelligence, and her translation of *Adelaide* has at times evidenced a dearth of literary sensibility. But her French is fluent and no doubt adequate to the task at hand. Alas, Henriette protested that she knew nothing about military fortifications, and while she was sure the subject was a highly important one, she admitted she found it of little interest.

"What about you, Mrs. Anderson?" Mr. Latrobe said. "Your command of French is excellent, is it not? It would be a great service to the country if you were to undertake the translation. And a service to Mr. Godefroy as well."

At this Mr. Godefroy raised his dark eyes to me, their customary mournfulness supplanted by a hopeful gleam.

"I'm afraid I couldn't possibly manage it, unless I could somehow duplicate myself!" I replied. "I've just vowed to take on the role of critic of the fine arts, I'll remind you. And I haven't had an hour to give Polly her lessons these last two weeks. The poor child is becoming a little unschooled heathen."

"Of course, of course, it's too much to ask," Mr. Godefroy said quickly.

And I saw the light vanish from his eyes like a snuffed-out candle. My throat tightening, I thought of all the poor man had suffered, the terrible falling off from what must have been a promising youth. How could I deny him the chance to display his talents to the world, and to receive the recognition that was undoubtedly his due? So I began to ask him questions: how long was the memorial ("Not long at all!"), how difficult the French ("Very simple!"), until at length I found myself somehow agreeing to shoulder the task — although I warned the company that I might well expire from exhaustion as a result.

"I think not, Madame!" Mr. Godefroy said, rising from his chair in his enthusiasm. "I declare that you have more energy, and more wit, than any lady I have ever had the pleasure to encounter. You will have this done before breakfast, I think!"

He now strode to where I sat and gallantly kissed my hand. I felt my face grow warm, and I protested that he had vastly over-estimated my abilities—although I confess I succumbed to the temptation to tell the entire company of the poem that had recently arrived from someone styling himself "P," entitled "The Ironsidiad." With some reluctance, I divulged a few of the more memorable couplets ("Fair Beatrice slays the foes of wit and sense/Her words deliver us from dull pretense!"). To the cries that I must publish this worthy epic, I demurred, pleading modesty—although in truth I also entertain some doubts as to the quality of its composition. But, I hastened to add, in tomorrow's number of the Observer they would find an even more edifying epigram, which I was able to recite for them in its entirety:

> *Bickerstaff once declared, should his wit e'er offend,*
> *He would quit his position for no man,*
> *He adhered to his word — tho' 'tis true in the end*
> *He has fled from the wit of a woman.*

This declamation was greeted by a round of cheers and applause, and we lifted the few drops left in our glasses to toast the bright prospects that lay before us: the publication of the epigram, the translation of Mr. Godefroy's memorial, the success (once again) of Mr. Nenninger's concert, the continuations of *Adelaide* and Father's series on quarantine in the Observer—and the initiation of a regular column of much-needed criticism concerning the fine arts.

I bade farewell to our guests in the highest of spirits, and was so giddy that it was hours before I was able to find respite in the arms of Morpheus. It is only now, in the harsher light of day— and suffering from a grievous deficiency of sleep—that I am beginning to fully comprehend what Herculean labors I have promised to perform. There is nothing for it but to forge onward, and so, as a weary and battle-scarred soldier might yet again hoist arms in the service of a noble cause, I take up my sharpened pen.

From the Observer, May 23, 1807:

FINE ARTS.
MUSIC.

We have heard a delightful performer on the violin this week; it was Mr. J. Nenninger, *a German musician whom the commotions of Europe have led to the United States in pursuit of peace; peace! which has usually been the tutelary goddess and nurse of the genius of fine arts!*

But what will this Virtuoso *do here? We have neither large theatres; nor church choirs; nor subscription concerts; nor military music; nor national academies, where exiled talent might receive those honors which are the vital principles of genius, and find resource against* indigence *and* want!

Our dullness, our insensibility is Vandalism *indeed — yes, Vandalism, we cannot refrain from giving its true and merited epithet.*

What then, we repeat, will *this virtuoso do here? He will be viewed in the light and treated with the consideration thought due to a* mechanic! Ah! 19ᵗʰ *century, how great will you be in the history of our America if it is thus that the elegant arts which embellish life continue long to flourish!!!*

We hasten however to announce that Mr. Nenninger *will on Tuesday give a concert, and we hope the distinguished musicians of our city will combine their harmonious sounds to banish from our memories that we are here,* in the very Siberia of the arts.

Chapter Ten: Margaret

Yesterday was a merry day at Mr. Guy's studio, for not only did Mr. Cork show himself at last (he's not been there since he bought me that lovely supper), but he brought some friends along. One was a Mr. Patterson, who I take to be a brother of that Madame Bonaparte's—for her name used to be Patterson, and there's a marked resemblance between them, both small and dark, though the features they share look better on her. Another was Mr. Harmer, who is the editor of that paper Mr. Cork writes for, Spectacles. And the third was a Mr. Webster, an actor and singer at the theater, and no doubt the same Webster I heard Mrs. A and her friends discussing at her evening party last week.

It seemed that the gentlemen were all well acquainted with Mr. Guy, and at first I kept my distance as they came in and greeted one another, moving Mr. Guy's canvases and brushes and paint bladders from the chairs in the room in order to find a seat. It was like an invasion of puppies, them all talking at once and tossing Mr. Guy's snuff box about, which he objected to loudly. I nodded towards Mr. Cork and smiled, and he nodded back, but we said nothing.

It wasn't long before the conversation turned to Mrs. A's paper, and the number that appeared just yesterday. There was a letter in it about the Vice President, Mr. Burr, and his trial for treason, and Mr. Cork and the others thought the letter was far too kind to the scoundrel (for that was what they called him). They said that justice can never be done, as the letter-writer claimed it would be, when the trial judge is known to be a sworn enemy of President Jefferson, just like Mr. Burr himself. And there was also an article about art, which got them all complaining about how Mrs. A said people here were like Vandals, and that Baltimore was like Siberia. Siberia must be a very bad place, because the gentlemen seemed to find it quite an insult.

"As though that concert, by that German, was to be the only bright spot in a desert of dullness!" said Mr. Webster, whose speech has more than a trace of Ireland in it. He's a black-haired man with skin so pale I'd say it has some gray in it, which makes his hair and eyebrows appear that much darker, and he's tall with a large chest. "What of the theater, then? What of the two plays each evening during the season? Last week we alternated 'School for Scandal' and 'Othello,' along with the usual farces afterwards. Are Sheridan and Shakespeare to count for nothing? And what of our orchestra and its fine musicians? Are they no more than *Vandals*?"

"And for that matter," said Mr. Harmer, who seemed a bit older than the others and had on a fine pair of blue pantaloons, "what of *you*, Webster? One of the finest performers in this country, and she takes no notice of your gifts."

"What happened, then, with that concert?" Mr. Guy called over his shoulder. He was hard at work on a landscape, another of his country houses, but he must have been listening as I was. "I went to buy tickets, for Mrs. Guy and myself. But they told me at Bryden's that it wasn't to be put on that evening after all."

"Another outrage," said Mr. Patterson. "They'd scheduled it for the night before the benefit for Webster at the theater. Well, if the public were all going to the concert—and they'd sold a couple of hundred tickets—they wouldn't be likely to go out a second night to the theater, would they? And what would come of the benefit?"

"Fortunately," said Webster, "my friends interceded." Here he nodded towards Cork and Harmer. "The manager of the theater let it be known that any member of the orchestra who participated in the concert would no longer be welcome in his employ. And since Nenninger was relying on the services of the entire orchestra, there was an end to his plan right there."

Mr. Guy let out a small whistle. "Well played, well played. But is there to be no concert then?"

"Oh, it's only been postponed, to the eleventh of June," said Cork. "Even though it's after the end of the season—the mayor was prevailed on to give them a special dispensation. But we did get one oversight corrected. We pointed out to Nenninger that the public would be dismayed not to see Mr. Webster's name on the program. How could the man have planned a concert without an appearance by our theater's leading light? They were going to have that little Italian singing master instead."

Mr. Webster nodded at Cork, as if to say thank you, but then made a sour face. "But do you know the man had the audacity to expect me to perform for free? He made it out to be sheer greed that I should ask for a trifling compliment for my services, when it's always been customary for performers at these concerts to receive some little compensation."

"I imagine the *German* always planned on being compensated," said Patterson. "Him and the Italian. But then, Americans are only Vandals!"

"Speaking of Vandals," said Mr. Guy, pausing in his work to take an enormous pinch of snuff, "have you seen the drawing that's on display at the library? The one by that Frenchman? Battle of Something-or-other?"

My ears perked up at that, for I knew it must be Mr. Godefroy he was talking about. It seemed Mr. Guy had little admiration for the drawing. Too busy, he said it was, such a jumble of horses and bodies that one could scarcely tell who was coming or going, and the figures too stiff and out of proportion. He would find no buyers for it in this town, Mr. Guy said, for people here would have little interest in a mess of soldiers and horses in some battle they'd never heard of.

Mr. Guy paused to take some snuff, which caused one of his violent sneezes. I took advantage of the lull to say a word, for I could no longer restrain myself, even though the gentlemen had taken no notice of me.

"I heard Mr. Godefroy say he did that drawing in a prison, in France," I told them. "He said all he had to draw on were little bits of paper, and he had to make ink from the soot of his stove."

They all turned and stared at me, as though a piece of furniture had just spoken.

"Miss McKenzie is employed at Dr. Crawford's house," Mr. Cork explained. "No doubt she overheard this remark at some gathering there, when Mr. Godefroy was in attendance. Is that not right, Margaret?"

I nodded. "Aye, that's it. It was him and a bunch of others."

Mr. Guy snorted as he turned back to his canvas. "Bits of paper! That explains a lot. As for the soot, there's nothing so remarkable about that. I use wood soot myself to make black ink. Though coal cinders are better to make blue. I should say the man is lucky to have been hired as a drawing master, given his skills."

He came over to where I sat drawing the vase of flowers he'd told me to sketch, took the charcoal from my hand and added a few strokes. I suppose he'd reminded himself of what he was meant to be doing. "And the way that woman—Ironside, or whatever she calls herself—speaks of mechanics," he said as he turned away from me, "as though there was anything dishonorable about making an honest living!"

Mr. Cork and Mr. Harmer began telling Mr. Guy he had to write something for Spectacles about how Mrs. A had been wrong—that he should say artists are working people, just like mechanics, and that there's no reason to treat the one with any more consideration than the other. And Mr. Guy said yes, by Jesus, he would do it! Then Mr. Patterson started asking Mr. Guy about an exhibit *he* is to have, of his paintings, next month, along with another artist named Mr. Groombridge, and Mr. Cork said he would write all about it for Spectacles.

After a while Mr. Cork seemed to recall that I was sitting there. "Well then, Margaret! What else can you tell us of what transpires at the Crawford-Anderson manse? Any other morsels of conversation that were of interest?"

I put down my charcoal and turned to face them, and I swear I could hear my heart beating, and only hoped it wasn't so loud they heard it as well. I'd been wanting to tell him all about what I'd overheard that evening, as I'd lingered in the room for that very purpose—even though Miss Legrand was there, and I spent the whole time in mortal fear that she might recognize me. But I'd expected to tell Mr. Cork alone, not him and these strangers together. I swallowed.

"Well." My voice was soft, but I couldn't seem to make it any louder. "They talked some about democracy, and how they didn't like it."

"Is that so?" I could see I'd gotten Mr. Cork's attention, for he came and leaned against the table where I sat, and his friends followed, leaving only Mr. Guy at the other end of the room, still painting. But he was listening too, I could tell. "Tell us more."

So I told them about how they'd talked about France, and the mobs there, and how Mrs. A said the mobs here would be worse, and that they'd have your head on a pike. And how people only voted for the candidates who gave them liquor, which is probably sometimes true but not always.

"And anyway," I said, my voice louder now and my heart back to normal, "there they sat drinking glass after glass of wine — all we had in the cellar. And them complaining about honest working people taking a drop before going to the polls!"

The gentlemen all laughed and cheered at that, and Mr. Cork patted me on the shoulder and told me I'd done well to hear all that, and I thought my smile would near jump from my face. Then Mr. Guy said it was time for him to go home, and my lesson must end, and we would all have to betake ourselves elsewhere as this wasn't a public tavern. It seemed as though Mr. Cork was going to go off with the others and leave me on my own, and not buy me another supper. So I whispered to him that I had some further information to communicate, of a private nature, and I could tell only him alone. So he told the others they must go on without him, and Mr. Patterson glanced at me and then gave Mr. Cork a nod and a wink, which made him blush a bit.

The three gentlemen headed east then, towards the Point, and Mr. Cork and I made our way west, over the bridge, me carrying my portfolio with the gold trim and him with his hand at my elbow, and I was pleased to think that anyone might assume we were a couple, even husband and wife. But then he asked me what it was I had to tell him, and I felt a shiver, for I had no idea, and said it would have to wait until we were sitting down.

Instead I began to talk some more about what I'd heard at that party, and how Mrs. A had talked of Mr. Guy being both a tailor and an artist, and how ridiculous it was for someone to be both things. I hadn't been able to bring myself to say that in front of Mr. Guy himself, fearing the explosion it might spark. But Mr. Cork said right off he would have to tell Guy about *that*, for it would certainly light a fire under him and ensure that he'd write something about Mrs. A for Spectacles.

"And the things they were saying about democracy!" I went on. "When I think about how it was when my father went to vote, how he came back with such pride afterwards, and said we were blessed to live in a country where ordinary people had a say in their government, not like when he was a lad back in Ireland and the great people made all the decisions and devil take the hindmost."

"Didn't I tell you?" said Mr. Cork, pulling me back from a horse and chair that was throwing up mud in its wake, for we were at Market Street now and not far from the tavern. "She and her friends, they despise all that this country stands for."

"But he lost the vote anyway, my father did," I said as we crossed Market. "When he lost our farm. He said they wouldn't let him vote anymore because now he had no property, and that wasn't fair, for wasn't he the same man he'd been before?"

Mr. Cork then asked how my father had come to lose the farm. At that I exclaimed over a handsome chestnut horse that was tied to a post, thinking to change the subject. But he asked again, and I decided to tell him the truth: that mother had taken sick when Fanny was born, and then she died, and out of grief father had begun to drink more than was good for him, and we'd had to sell the chickens and then the cows, and at length we'd had no choice but to leave and come to the city in search of work. I didn't tell him all of it — not about my brother John, and the way he and father had argued so violently — for though I was liking him better and better, I didn't know Mr. Cork well enough for that.

And then he said something that riled me, which is that he wondered that my father hadn't acquired some property when we'd moved here, for surely an able-bodied man could find a good job in a city like Baltimore, where there was so much building and trading going on, unless he was lazy or stupid. And I told him no indeed — that my father had worked till he was near dead, day in and day out, and that no matter what he could barely scrape together the money to keep us in a room at Mrs. Brooks', let alone buy a house of his own. And that if now and then he drank a bit more than he should, who could blame him when all he had to look forward to was day after day of breaking his back with so little to show for it? And it wasn't *his* fault if they shut the mud machine down during the sickly season, and the winter, and there was no other work to be had.

"All right, all right, Margaret!" said Mr. Cork, making it sound as though it was all a jest. "I won't say another word against your father, I promise."

99

I wanted to explain that it wasn't only my father, that there were many in his situation — and worse, as well — but we had arrived at the tavern and he was holding open the door for me, and I could smell frying potatoes and onions from inside, and all I could think of just then was getting some of that into my stomach.

It was dark and smoky in the tavern, which suited us fine, as it wouldn't do to be seen together. After Mr. Cork had ordered us some ale and fish chowder, he leaned forward and rested his forearms on the table. "Well?" he said.

I felt a wave of fear sweep across me, but I took a breath and started to talk, for I knew I must say something, anything, now that I'd gotten him to bring me here. "It's that Frenchman," I said. "That Mr. Godefroy."

"You mean there's something between them? Between him and your mistress, something improper?"

I don't know why I'd chosen to say what I had, for I rather liked Mr. Godefroy, and what he'd said about how art and drawing had kept him from losing his mind in prison. I'm not in prison, not like he was, and yet I sometimes feel the same way — like the only thing that gets me through the washing and the dusting and the hauling of coal is the thought that come Saturday I can draw. But there was no turning back now. And the truth is, I do have a feeling about those two.

"I don't know that there's anything *between* them, as you say." I swallowed a gulp of ale, as it had arrived at the table. "And they talk French to each other most of the time, so I don't rightly know what they're saying. But the way she looks at him, you can tell she's fond of him. Very fond, I'd say. And on Friday he came by, to give her something he'd written, and I saw him kiss her hand and then press it to his chest, like this." I put my hand on my heart. "And they stood there for maybe a whole minute, just looking into each other's eyes." I did an imitation of what they'd looked like that afternoon, apparently so taken with each other that they couldn't be bothered to notice I'd come into the room to dust.

Mr. Cork leaned back and crossed his arms and considered. "A kiss on the hand, that's nothing by itself. A Frenchman will do that to any lady. But the rest of it ..." He frowned and cocked his head. "How often would you say he comes to the house?"

I told him once or twice a week, sometimes for supper or an evening party like the one I'd told him about, and sometimes during the day, when it's just Mrs. A at home. "And now she's translating what he wrote, something about the military." Then I remembered something else I'd heard at that party. "They say he's some sort of count, or duke or something."

Mr. Cork leaned back and made a snorting noise. "Oh, every Frenchman in town is a count or a duke, to hear *them* tell it. I wouldn't put much store in a tale like that. Besides, we've no need of titles in this country! Let him claim to be the ghost of Louis the damned Sixteenth, if he wants. It's only Mrs. Anderson and her fine friends who go weak in the knees over such things."

He was right, of course. I don't know why I'd allowed myself to think there was anything wonderful in Mr. Godefroy being a count, if that's what he was. The fish chowder came just then, and we were silent for a minute or two, eating. Lovely, it was, all creamy and studded with bits of potato and onion and salt pork.

"There's nothing much we can do now, but I'd say it's worth keeping your eye on those two," Mr. Cork said after a while. "She's a married woman, you know — no matter that her husband has vanished, she's still bound by her vows. And if she sets herself up, as she's done, as the town's guardian of culture and morality, the town has every right to know whether she practices what she preaches. Not that what she preaches is always so pure!"

He reached into his coat and pulled out some papers, and I could see it was today's number of the Observer. "Have you read this? No? Here, let me find the blasted thing ..." He was looking for something, turning the pages. "This series of Dr. Crawford's — ridiculous. This one's about caterpillars, and how extraordinary it is they turn into butterflies. Three pages of it ... But that's not what I wanted to show you."

"I don't know," I said, thinking of how kind the Doctor has been to me. "I should like to read about caterpillars and how they turn into butterflies."

"Well, perhaps you would," he said, laughing again, "if you picked up a book about insects, but the gentleman is meant to be writing about quarantines, not caterpillars. And do you know what he said about things like the yellow fever, a couple of weeks back? That they were a good thing, because otherwise there would be too many people in the world!"

"I don't think the Doctor would ever say a thing like that," I said in a soft voice.

101

"Ah, here it is." Mr. Cork had gone back to looking for whatever it was he wanted to show me. Then he put on a high voice, like a girl's. "'Adelaide,'" he read, "'or: a Lesson for Lovers.' What a vile piece of trash!"

I could feel my heart start to pound, because I recognized that name. It's the book Miss Legrand has been translating.

He held it out for me to read, but the very thought of Miss Legrand sent my head spinning, so I told him my eyes were hurting because of the smoke in the room, and could he read it to me.

He began to read, in that same high voice. "'We repeated the insidious piece, which spread its flame through our hearts, which felt new and strange palpitations.'" He looked over at me and explained that the piece was some music the young man had brought to the girl, for the two of them to sing together. Then he began to read again, not in the girlish voice, but not in his own voice either. It was deep and full of feeling, as though he was up on a stage in front of an audience.

"'I was standing behind Adelaide, my head leaning over her panting bosom. One of my boiling tears fell on her breast.'" Then he said in his real voice, "Hold on a bit, let me find ... ah, yes, here." He drew himself up again. "'Love, held in by a remains of timidity, broke his curb, forced every barrier that until then had opposed him; and I fell again at the feet of Adelaide ... I started up ... threw myself in her arms. Mechanically she folded them round me.'" He paused and said loudly, "*Adelaide's innocence was lost forever!*"

Then he stopped, although I very much wanted him to continue, for it seemed as though the story was just becoming interesting. "What does it say next?" I said, leaning across the table over the remains of my chowder.

"Just this." He showed the paper to me and I saw a series of dots. "At least she has the delicacy to do that much," he said. "Leaves it to her readers' imaginations to supply the little she left out. Corrupting the fancies of innocent young girls with this filth! And her talking about morals. The woman should be ashamed of herself."

I laughed a bit, I couldn't help it, for he was so wrought up about it, and I couldn't see the harm in what he'd read. The truth is, I was imagining me and him in one another's arms, like Adelaide and her young man, one of his hot tears falling on my panting breast. I put my hand out, as though to move the paper so I could see it better, but I did it so that my hand brushed against his, and then I let it rest there, on top of his palm. He stared at it for a moment, his face getting flushed, and then he drew his hand away like it had been burnt. I couldn't figure it: he appears so cool and sure of himself when we're only talking, telling me how pretty I am, but now that I'd touched him he was shrinking from me like a bashful child. I'd never had a fellow do that with me before, and I had to wonder if there was something amiss with him or if he just didn't fancy me.

"Anyway," he said, suddenly all briskness and business, "it's good that you're keeping your eyes and ears open. But it's nothing we can really use, so far. We need more details, something more specific."

"Oh, more details, easy for you to say!" I was put out now, my blood rising. "You're not the one who's risking your neck, waiting on Miss Legrand and trembling lest she point a finger at you."

I was sorry as soon as I heard myself say it, and cursed myself for being so heedless. But it was too late.

"Point a finger at you?" he said, his golden eyebrows narrowing. "Whatever do you mean?" I said nothing and looked down, but he seemed to be putting things together on his own. "Ah, so you did work at the Legrands. I thought so. And something happened there?"

I shook my head hard as I could. But the tears were starting to come, and I was having trouble catching my breath. What might he think if I didn't tell him? Something far worse than it really was, perhaps. Murder, even. I couldn't bear the idea of him thinking I'd done something like that, for he's the only person who's taken any interest in me in months. Even if he doesn't like me the same way I like him, it seems he wants to be my friend. I haven't had someone to call a friend in so long, not since Alice, back at Mrs. Brooks', and who knew if I'd see her ever again.

And then it all came out of me, like the freshets that burst from the hills after the spring rains. I told him how I'd had to find work last August, when the mud machine closed down, and Papa could find no other job, and what I was earning from slop work wasn't enough to pay for our room and keep us in bread and cheese. The Legrands took me on as a maid, but then three weeks later they decided to leave for the country, because the fever was beginning to cross the Falls to their part of town. I could see they were going to let me go, for they weren't taking all the servants with them. And I wouldn't have gone with them anyway, not with Papa and Fanny still in the city.

"I couldn't bring myself to tell my father and my sister I was to lose the job," I said, "not when they were counting on my wages. We'd been in the almshouse once, and the thought that we might find ourselves there again ..."

I stopped to wipe my nose on my sleeve, and next I knew he had taken out a clean white handkerchief, trimmed with lace it was, and given it to me. I blew my nose into it, just a bit, for it seemed a shame to dirty it.

"That last day before they left, I was told to polish the silver and then pack it up in its wooden case, so it could be put away until the family came back. It was me and another girl doing it, one of the Negroes. And I didn't like that, working alongside a slave as though I was no better than she was. And of course, *she* was going off to the country with Mr. Legrand. *She* wasn't going to have to stay behind and wonder where her family's next meal was coming from, and worry about catching the yellow fever. So she was humming and singing to herself, happy as a wren. And then the cook called her to do something in the kitchen, and I was glad to be left to myself."

I stopped and felt a rising in my throat, and the tears began to come again.

"Margaret." Mr. Cork's voice was quiet, and his eyes had a kind look to them. "If you took some of the Legrands' silver, I wouldn't blame you for it."

I could feel not just one tear but ten or twenty, rushing from my eyes and trickling down my cheeks. I'd been carrying this secret around like a pack on my back, that no one could see, but weighing me down nonetheless.

"It was just three spoons," I said, my voice choked. "They had so many. I thought perhaps they wouldn't even notice. I took them to one of those shops, the ones that will give you money for jewelry and pretty baubles. But the man there, he looked at the spoons very carefully, the backs of them and all, where there was some tiny writing. He looked at them through a glass that he put to his eye. And then he looked at me all suspicious and asked me where I'd gotten them from. And I didn't know what to say, I was so frightened. I thought the writing on the spoons must have had the name Legrand, or something that told him where they'd come from. So I ran from the shop and never went back." I put my face in my hands. "I never even got a penny for those damned spoons."

Mr. Cork was silent for a moment, waiting for me to stop crying I suppose. Then I felt his hand on my arm, very gentle like, as though he was petting a wounded bird. "I can see now why you were afraid, waiting on Miss Legrand. It was very brave of you to stay, on my account. I should never have asked you to do such a thing, if I'd known."

I looked at my arm, to make sure it was really his hand. "If she'd recognized me, she could have me thrown into jail with a snap of her fingers." I closed my eyes, thinking of the jail, the sounds you sometimes hear when you walk by it. "It's a good thing you rich people don't pay much mind to the servants, else I wouldn't have a prayer."

"*I* recognized you," he said. "I said I thought I'd seen you before, that first day at Mrs. Anderson's."

"So you did," I said, and for a moment we just looked at one another, smiling. And then I put my hand on his, where it rested on my arm, and this time he didn't take it away. I looked down at them, our hands one atop the other, and it sent such a warm, giddy feeling through me that I had to close my eyes.

Then he said there was something I should know. "I believe the Legrands did notice the missing spoons, when they got back to town."

I was suddenly thrown back into my fear. "Did that man from the shop tell them?"

Mr. Cork smiled and shook his head. "No, I don't think they would have heard from the man at the shop. Someone must have just counted and saw they were short. Anyway, I remember Henriette — Miss Legrand — saying that one of their Negroes had been caught stealing the silver."

"Effie? Did she say it was Effie?"

"She didn't say a name. But it was a girl."

I felt a chill creep over me. I could see Effie's broad, dark face, and her smile. I could hear her singing, the way she was doing that day, sitting next to me in the dining room. Her voice was lovely, clear and strong. "What happened to her? Did Miss Legrand say?"

"She said they'd had to sell her down South. She'd said it was too bad, because before that she'd been a good worker. But you just could never tell about these people—that's what she said. And you couldn't afford to take chances. The Legrands came here from Santo Domingo, you know. They had to leave when the rebellion broke out. I suppose you don't forget something like that, all the slaves running amok and threatening murder."

I said no, I suppose not, and then I was quiet, thinking of Effie. Maybe she was only a slave, but she didn't deserve to be punished for something I'd done. I felt that heaviness again, the pack on my back, but now it wasn't the fear that I'd be caught. It was knowing I was the cause of someone else's suffering.

Then the tavern keeper was there, with the bill, and Mr. Cork paid and we left the filmy dark of the tavern for the clear air outside, a velvet dusk with a few stars out. We walked west towards Hanover Street, and I was quiet, still thinking about Effie. When we reached Light Street Mr. Cork stopped and said he regretted having to send me the rest of the way on my own, but he didn't dare come closer. And he took my hand, to say goodbye.

"You mustn't blame yourself for what happened to the Negro girl," he said. "You couldn't have known."

I held onto his hand and thanked him, and asked him would he come again to Mr. Guy's next Saturday. He said he would try, and I told him that I hadn't forgotten about doing his portrait. And he said maybe next time. And then I did something that surprised us both, but I couldn't help it: I stood on my toes and gave him a peck on the cheek, just like that. And then I turned and ran off, without daring to look at him. But something told me he was pleased.

From the Observer, June 6, 1807:

For the Observer.

MR. NENNINGER'S CONCERT

We announce with pleasure that the opposition and delay to Mr. Nenninger's concert has had a happy effect in advancing his interests; and the little intrigues which retarded it have given occasion to some articles in the papers which have piqued the curiosity of some and the self-love of others. A great number of tickets have been disposed of, and we flatter ourselves that this excellent musician will receive in some measure the tribute due to his talents. The concert is fixed for the 11th of the month, when Mr. Nenninger, and a number of amateurs, will delight the ear with a variety of both vocal and instrumental music.

Chapter Eleven: Eliza

Yesterday evening was quite the event in our fair metropolis: a respectable crowd of two hundred or more, all dressed in their finest, treated to harmonious strains sublime enough for an imperial court! And Bryden's Assembly Room, one of our few fine structures, with its Doric pediment and balustrade at the roofline, glowed with elegance. There were moments when I scarcely believed myself in Baltimore. And then, alas, there were other moments when I was all too conscious of the fact.

It was, indeed, no easy feat merely to ensure that the concert would go forward as planned, what with the obstacles thrown up by Mr. Cork and his cabal at nearly the last minute. If they want to disprove my assertions about the dearth of taste in this city, it would seem the last thing they should do is raise a hue and cry against a concert because it doesn't include performers of their own choosing. A concert is not a democratic undertaking, with representation from all who desire it!

And to portray me as a traitor to my country, merely because I have pointed out that the good citizens of Baltimore are more likely to worship Mammon than the Muses—that is a low and ridiculous blow, indeed. But there are those who are ready to believe that any well-intentioned criticism, justified as it may be, is tantamount to calumny—or, perhaps, they are so fearful of being tarred with the brush of "treason" that they will concede to any demand, no matter how absurd.

Such, I fear, is the description that must attach to the esteemed Mr. Bryden. One might have thought the hysterical alarm raised by Spectacles, and the flurry of notices in the Gazette and one or two other papers rushing to endorse it, were edicts from on high, so quickly did Mr. B first cancel the concert, and then two days later announce that it would go on with an altered roster of musicians — Mr. Webster having been substituted for Mr. Cecchi, although the latter's voice is a far superior instrument.

But I race ahead. First I should record that I attended the concert wearing my best blue silk frock and a bonnet newly dyed for the occasion, fitted with a new white plume. Unfortunately our meager resources would not stretch to accommodate a new pair of slippers, but when I went to say goodbye to Polly, at supper in the kitchen, the dear girl told me I looked beautiful — more a tribute to her affection for her Mamma, surely, than testament to her judgment in these matters. (Margaret, for her part, smirked at the compliment, but I see no reason to set any store in *her* opinions on beauty and fashion.)

Mr. Godefroy soon arrived to accompany Father and myself to the assembly room. He too appeared to have taken special care with his toilette, and looked even more striking than usual. Alas, Father's black silk coat has gone shiny with age, and a large and apparently indelible stain of some sort adorns the right sleeve, but I flatter myself we made an impressive little band as we strolled up Market Street towards Calvert. The evening air was moist but pleasant, and as we approached the assembly room we found ourselves part of a small stream of ladies and gentlemen wearing similar attire and expressions of cheerful anticipation.

We arrived in plenty of time, for I was anxious to secure seats at the front, so that Mr. Nenninger might take encouragement from the presence of his friends. Right at the entrance, however, we encountered my Aunt O'Donnell — a surprise indeed. But the fountain of the arts must be open to all who sincerely wish to drink of its restorative waters, and as one must never despair of the conversion of Philistines, I greeted her with as much warmth as I could muster.

"A word, Eliza, if you don't mind, I must have a word," she commanded, tapping my forearm with her folded fan.

I gave an inward sigh and implored Mr. Godefroy and Father to go ahead and find seats, and then turned meekly to my aunt — who, as she holds the title to our modest abode, in which Father has only a life estate, has us somewhat in her thrall. If I am ever to inherit the roof over my head, I must endure her lectures and her company from time to time.

"Is it true what I hear, that you have something to do with this paper ... what's it called? The Spectator?" She waved the hand holding her fan and pursed her rouged lips. "You and this Mrs. Iron ... Ironwill? You are one and the same?"

I looked about to see if there was any danger of being overheard. "Iron*side*," I whispered. "I would prefer that it not be generally known, but yes, that is my *nom de plume*."

I was pleased to think our fame had spread sufficiently that someone so outside the fashionable current as Mrs. O'Donnell had heard of the Observer, even if she had unintentionally flattered me by confusing it with the far more eminent periodical once so ably edited by Messrs. Addison and Steele.

"Ah, so Mrs. Caton's information was correct. And yet you mentioned nothing of it to me, your own aunt."

So Bess hadn't preserved my secret. But in truth, it's hardly a secret anymore. Several times a week now I am approached, and often congratulated, by friends and acquaintances, and on occasion the near stranger, on some article or bon mot in a recent number. And once in a while I find myself the target of cold stares and pointed snubs from those who have taken umbrage at our satirical jibes or are disappointed at not seeing their immortal words enshrined in our pages, but such things are to be expected when one is in the public eye. Still, I could see no reason why I should have informed Mrs. O'Donnell of a fact that did not concern her and which I have not generally advertised. But of course I had to apologize to her for my "omission," nonetheless.

"Well, Eliza, I must say I am saddened, deeply saddened." She raised her nearly invisible eyebrows in an expression of aggrieved concern, and shook her head so that the flesh under her chin trembled slightly. "I am only relieved that your uncle did not live to see you come to this."

I steadied myself. Fool that I am, I should have anticipated a dressing-down rather than an encomium! Mrs. O'Donnell has never missed an opportunity to trumpet her general displeasure with my person and character.

"I'm afraid I fail to take your meaning," I said, bristling, although a voice inside my head warned that I should hold my tongue. "There are many who believe that the Observer is performing a public service in its efforts to raise the cultural tone of our city."

"Raising the tone! Is that what you call publishing that … that … offal about some hussy named Adeline? You consider *that* to be a tale that will have an improving effect upon your readers?"

I felt a warm flush rise to my face. Indeed, the last two installments of Adelaide have been rather more lurid than I had expected, and there have been a few complaints. Three weeks ago, when I read what was to be the next chapter, I hesitated to the point that I chose not to publish it. But I was soon inundated with the most piteous demands for the story's continuation, and one must be conscious of the wishes of one's readers. If there are those who pick up the paper to read of Adelaide and her heaving bosom, but then find their interest piqued by an essay on architecture, or a report on the recent calamities in Europe, is not any harm more than balanced by the resulting benefit? Our youth, and especially our young ladies, know so little of art, and history, and geography, and what transpires in the world beyond card games and fashion. If one must lure them with a bit of sugar in order to slip them some true nourishment, then I am more than willing to bait the trap.

Mrs. O'Donnell went on for some minutes more about how it was embarrassing enough that I had chosen to make a public spectacle of myself with this paper, which was no fit occupation for a female, but that for me, as a *lady* (a word she invested with such sarcasm that it sounded very like an insult) to infect the impressionable minds of others of my sex with such lewdness … well, it was really too much to bear, and she was ashamed to show her face in public, as everyone knew of her connection to me. I had little choice but to stand there in the appropriate attitude of contrition, with downcast eye, until fortunately we were joined by Mr. and Mrs. Howard, who had apparently arranged to accompany Mrs. O'Donnell to the concert.

"Ah yes, do please go in, I'll be there in a moment," Mrs. O'Donnell told them, suddenly shedding the harpy demeanor she had directed at me and supplanting it with a serene smile. As soon as they'd gone inside she turned back to me, her momentary transformation entirely reversed. "If I were you, I would disassociate myself from this unbecoming enterprise entirely. But at the very least, if you wish to have a chance of staying in my good graces —

which, I may remind you, would be very much to your benefit —
then you will cease publishing this disgusting story of Adeline immediately, and issue an apology to your readers." She flipped open
her fan and drew herself up. "If, that is, you have any."

I was nearly trembling with rage as I watched Mrs. O'Donnell's
ample posterior ascend slowly up the steps and disappear, at last,
through the arched doorway. I closed my eyes and prayed silently for strength and composure. My first impulse was to defy my
aunt's edict, merely because she had issued it. But after a moment
or two of reflection I considered that although *Adelaide* is no worse
than many novels one might find at Cole and Bonsal's bookshop,
I would most likely not have agreed to publish it had I read the
entirety of it beforehand. I have no objection to descriptions of irresistible passion if they are anchored to literary quality and true
morality, but alas, that has not proven to be the case with this
tale. Yes, I could dispense with further installments of Adelaide's
amorous adventures without compromising my principles.

I had just resolved to inform Henriette Legrand that her
translation services, faltering as they were, would no longer be
required, when I saw another sight that tested my equanimity:
none other than James Cork, striding up East Street in the company of that tailor-cum-painter Mr. Guy — the author of the article
in last week's number of Spectacles that attempted to ridicule me
for stating the simple truth about the lack of appreciation for the
arts in this city, and vehemently protesting that there was no dishonor in being a mechanic — as though I'd ever said there was. It
wasn't difficult to identify him as the author, for he actually had
the audacity to sign the piece with his own name!

I hied myself up the assembly room steps as though I had
failed to spot the pair on the horizon and made my way towards
the front, where I could see the back of Mr. Godefroy's head rising from the crowd — for he is well above average height, which
adds to his innate air of dignity and command.

"And what members of the insect family will we be treated to
next week, Doctor Crawford?" I heard Mr. O'Neill saying to Father as I inched past the others in our row on the way to my chair
next to Mr. Godefroy.

I winced. I have pleaded with Father to have done with his
near encyclopedic account of the members of the insect kingdom and their habits, and at last arrive at what is meant to be the

subject of his disquisition, namely the practice of quarantine. I believe Mr. Patterson has given up on ever finding anything useful in Father's lucubrations, for we have lately heard nothing from him, either directly or through Betsy. Fortunately, now that we have increased our list of subscribers — some of whom have been honorable enough to pay for their subscriptions — I have reason to hope that we won't be forced to return to Mr. Patterson with the proverbial hat in hand, which I am quite sure would be returned to us empty in any event. I only pray that the subscribers added since we began publishing *Adelaide* do not desert us when they find less sensational fare in its stead.

"Ah," I heard Father say, apparently oblivious to the mockery in Mr. O'Neill's manner, "the next installment will first discuss the corn weevil, and the unfortunate depredations which that tiny creature wreaks on the granaries of farmers — and the ingenious method employed by some in combating the scourge, namely the introduction of ants who feast on the weevils. Next I will turn to the Capricorn beetle, and the way in which the female of the species deposits her eggs beneath the bark of wood that has been felled but not stripped, using a flat tube appended to her body that she may retract at will." Father held up his hands and used them to outline the shape of the structure, albeit many times larger than it presumably appears on the beetle. "The larva, a sort of worm, then emerges, and — "

"Oh Doctor, please!" Mr. O'Neill cried, as his eldest son, a lad of about fifteen who was seated next to him, struggled to stifle his mirth. "Tell me no more, as I want to savor the freshness of the information when I read it in the paper."

Father nodded and smiled uncertainly, and my heart ached to think he might, if he reflected a bit, understand that Mr. O'Neill's remonstrance was something less than sincere.

"Mr. O'Neill," I quickly interjected, "did you not enjoy the letter from Richmond that appeared in the Observer concerning the trial of Colonel Burr?"

As soon as the words were out of my mouth, I reflected that perhaps some other subject would have been safer. There are those in this city who violently defend the former Vice-President, and maintain that he never intended to foment rebellion in the Western territories, and others who just as violently insist that the charges of treason are well justified.

"Indeed, very judiciously written," I was relieved to hear Mr. O'Neill remark. "Whatever one thinks of the man—and I'm inclined to believe he's a thorough scoundrel—one must agree that … how did the author put it? That it's better to let a thousand guilty men go free than to let one innocent suffer? I certainly hope your man in Richmond will be sending you further dispatches, Mrs. *Ironside*."

I smiled, almost ready to forgive Mr. O'Neill his recent mockery of Father. "Have you made the acquaintance of Mr. Godefroy?" I asked, nodding towards him. "Mr. Godefroy is the author of a highly interesting work concerning fortifications, and the methods best calculated to defend our country from foreign attack."

"Indeed?" Mr. O'Neill widened his eyes. "And I thought you were a drawing master."

Mr. Godefroy bobbed his head in acknowledgment of the fact, and smiled at Bobby O'Neill, who I now recalled as being a student at St. Mary's. "Yes, it is true. And architect. But in France I was educated as engineer. Engineer military?"

"Mr. Godefroy is a gentleman of many talents," I put in, lest Mr. O'Neill assume that his continuing difficulty with English reflected any lack of intelligence.

"Well, sir, I hope you don't believe we're about to be attacked!" Mr. O'Neill said, reaching for Bobby's hand as though afraid the boy might decide to enlist then and there.

"Ah, let us hope no," Mr. Godefroy said, just as a rustle went through the audience indicating that someone had stepped onto the stage. "But we must always prepare, yes?"

Mr. Bryden was repeatedly calling "Ladies and Gentlemen" to a group that appeared determined to put the lie to that honorable appellation. It was evident that the audience included many who viewed the occasion more as an opportunity to chatter with their neighbors than to attend to and honor the efforts of the performers, and eventually Mr. Bryden had to make his peace with a hum of voices that no remonstrance or pleading could silence.

The first piece was described on the program as "A Grand Military Overture," played by the "Full Orchestra," but it was rendered with such listlessness, and performed on instruments so lacking in volume, that any soldiers hearing it would likely have been induced to shed their weaponry and collapse into languorous repose. Whistles and cheers nonetheless greeted this feeble attempt, apparently because the rowdier elements were looking for any excuse to exercise their lungs with abandon.

After a decent concerto rendered on the flute, the unfortunate Mr. Webster took the stage to sing "Oh, Climb the Rock With Me My Love," accompanying it with such grimaces and contortions that it seemed he was attempting to scale an actual boulder, and slipping dangerously backwards. I'll admit the sounds he produced were pleasant, especially if one closed one's eyes, but I observed a good deal of tittering at the spectacle. If Mr. Cork has any concern for his friend's reputation, he will ensure that the gentleman learns something about how to conduct himself in public before he attempts such a performance again.

At last Mr. Nenninger took the stage, and immediately the tone of the evening was lifted — or would have been, had certain members of the audience been able to refrain from whispering, coughing, cracking nuts, and generally attending to their own business rather than maintaining the respectful silence this genius deserved. The way his fingers flew over the frets, quick as a flock of hummingbirds, was a marvel to behold, and his expression of dignified but passionate absorption invited a similar attitude on the part of his more sensitive listeners.

At the end of the program, Mr. Nenninger and his violin once again appeared and worked their magic, producing a concerto that brought me to tears with its sublimity. The audience, to its credit, gave him an enthusiastic round of applause, albeit punctuated by a few undignified cheers and whistles, and I could not restrain myself from shouting, "Bravo!"

I had hoped to avoid an encounter with Mr. Cork, but as we made our way out of the hall we found ourselves nearly face to face with him and Mr. Guy, and I had no choice but to acknowledge them.

"I trust," Mr. Cork said after bowing to me stiffly, "that you find the attendance here this evening gratifying?" He waved an arm towards the exiting crowd. "As you can see, Baltimore is hardly Siberia, whether one is speaking of the arts or of the weather." At that, he took out a handkerchief and mopped at his brow, for the hall had been warm. This display of wit was evidently too much for Mr. Guy, who began to shake with laughter.

"Alas, one concert does not a season make," I told Mr. Cork with as much politeness as I could muster. "If we were treated

115

to performances such as this each week, or even each month, instead of once in perhaps a year, I should begin to take heart. And it should have been far easier than it was to induce people to purchase tickets sufficient to fill the hall. In any event, as you may have noticed, many of those in the audience were strangers to this town."

"Why, you'll never be satisfied, will you?" This was Mr. Guy, to whom I don't believe I'd ever spoken before—and given the rudeness of his first utterance to me, I think I should prefer to avoid the experience in the future. "I suppose you'd also say that if there were any *mechanics* in the crowd, they shouldn't count as well?"

"I am certainly delighted whenever such individuals seek a means of improving themselves," I managed to say, keeping my voice as steady as possible. "And I'm happy, Mr. Guy, to observe that you, for instance, have been able to take leave of your labors in stay tape and buckram for a few hours and nourish your spirit with an excursion into the finer things of life."

He and Mr. Cork exchanged a dark look, and Mr. Cork tried to speak, but Mr. Guy stopped him with a hand on his arm and stepped forward, his small black eyes shining with what I presume was fury. "I'm not ashamed to say that I know a thing or two about stay tape, and that I can construct as fine a suit of clothing as ever you'd wish. But I haven't depended on tailoring for my income in quite some time. Perhaps you've seen the frescoes on the walls at the Fountain Inn? Or the paintings hanging in some of the finest houses in Baltimore, for that matter? If you don't believe I'm an artist, I invite you to come by Mr. Cole's store next week and see my work for yourself."

"Indeed, I intend to," I said, not mentioning that my primary interest would be in the paintings of Mr. Groombridge, an artist of undeniable merit. "The Observer, as you know, takes a keen interest in the state of the arts in this town, and we feel it our duty to provide the public with discerning criticism of all such exhibitions, if we can."

"And I take it that you, Mrs. Anderson, will act as the discerning critic?" Mr. Cork inquired, his voice laden with sarcasm. "If, as you argue, mechanics are incapable of producing art, then how is a woman equipped to judge artistic merit? For surely the ranks of great artists, and great critics, are at least as devoid of females as they are of mechanics."

I felt a flood of hot rage sweep through me. So here we were at last, I thought, arriving at the truth: he despises me not because of my views on art, or my satirical stabs at the follies of our fellow citizens—for did we not found the Observer in order to add such weaponry to our arsenal? No, it is because I am a *woman*, and a woman who has presumed to criticize him—not to mention a woman whose paper's circulation undoubtedly exceeds that of *his* wretched excuse for a periodical. No doubt many of the few who pick up Spectacles do so merely in order to laugh at his weekly jibes against the Observer and myself.

"If women have not been able to place themselves in the first ranks of artists—and philosophers, and writers, and mathematicians," I told him, as calmly as I could manage, "it is only because they have been denied the necessary education and encouragement. By *men*. It is no reflection on their native abilities."

"No, indeed," Mr. Guy interjected, "no more than it is a reflection on the native abilities of mechanics, who have been subjected to similar deprivations!"

I was in the process of composing a retort to this remark when Father inserted himself into the conversation. "My dear sirs," he said, with a bow, "I'm afraid I must prevail upon you to excuse my daughter from further intercourse this evening, as my ancient bones are succumbing to fatigue, and we must now begin to set our course homeward."

I suspect Father's interruption was prompted as much by his solicitude for my reputation as by weariness on his part, for as we made our way back up Market Street I was treated to a gentle discourse on the dangers of unleashing my tongue without first pausing to consider the wisdom of my words. I murmured some dutiful promises, but in truth I regret nothing of what I said, nor would I retract it had I the chance.

Indeed, I only regret that I was deprived of the opportunity to explain to Mr. Guy that women are often blessed with the leisure necessary to improve their minds and hone their artistic or logical abilities—and then deprived of the opportunity to put those minds and skills to good use—nay, told that it is damaging to their health and deleterious to the welfare of society for them to do so! Whereas if one is trained as a tailor—or a carpenter, or a tanner, or whatever the trade may be—and if one devotes the greater part of one's waking hours to tasks that call for no mental or spiritual exercise, and indeed exclude it, how can one suddenly leap from that mundane realm to the lofty heights of true art?

Poor Mr. Godefroy was, I think, entirely confused by the exchange between Messrs. Cork and Guy and myself, for he understood no more than a few words of it. And so, once Father had retired for the evening, I gave him a thorough account of what had transpired, in French, and translated some of Mr. Cork's hysterical fulminations in Spectacles, and I was highly gratified to hear Mr. Godefroy's expressions of sympathy and encouragement. Indeed, our conversation continued late into the evening, over some wine and bread and cold meat that I had Margaret bring us (for some reason she lingered in the room until I told her, rather sharply, that she might go). I should have gone to bed like Father, but I was in such a state of agitation that I couldn't have slept without first unburdening myself. And I can think of no one I would rather unburden myself to than Mr. Godefroy.

In truth, I don't know what I should have done, these last few weeks, without Mr. Godefroy to confide in. I don't know that I have ever met another man whose mind is so open to what a woman may accomplish, if allowed to spread her wings. I told Mr. Godefroy of the unfortunate necessity of discontinuing *Adelaide*, and he suggested that I consider publishing another novel that has been popular in France, touching on similar themes but far better handled, with more delicacy and a firmer moral sense. I recognized the title, *Claire d'Albe*, but told him I hadn't had the opportunity to read the work, and indeed had heard that it was of questionable morality. But Mr. Godefroy urged me to judge for myself, and promised to provide me with a copy — for me to translate, he insists! For he says the translation I have completed so far of his essay on fortifications has been most impressive, and he believes I could easily do a better job with a novel than Henriette Legrand.

In that, I think, he may be right, though I only laughed and told him he was far too kind. But the small glow of ambition that he kindled burned within me for hours after he took his leave, indeed grew into quite the conflagration, keeping me awake with excitement nearly till dawn. Could I, I kept asking myself, and ask even now? *Could* I? There was, after all, a time when I never imagined I could edit a weekly literary miscellany.

What might my life have been like, I wonder, had I encountered Mr. Godefroy, or someone like him (if there be anyone else like him) before I met that scoundrel Henry Anderson? What if I had linked my being and my fortunes to someone who encouraged my yearnings rather than ridiculing them? Indeed, who not only encouraged me, but who urged me on to ambitions that I myself would never have had the confidence to imagine?

But no, I mustn't allow myself such fantasies, tempting as they are. I have a husband, at least in name, and I must remain resigned to the fact that I am chained to him forever. I will treasure Mr. Godefroy as a friend, a true friend, and nothing more. But I shall at least allow myself to look forward to Saturday afternoon, when he has promised to escort me to the exhibition of paintings at Cole and Bonsal's. It's Margaret's afternoon and evening off, time I usually spend instructing Polly in her letters, or trying to. But as Mr. Godefroy cannot manage to accompany me at any other time this week, I shall have to postpone our lesson and ask Mrs. Morris to mind her for a while. And with a guide as knowledgeable and discerning as Mr. Godefroy, I feel confident that I will prove to Messrs. Cork and Guy—and anyone else—that a woman is as capable of judging artistic merit as any man. Of if not *any* man, then at least as capable as they are.

From the Observer, June 13, 1807:

FINE ARTS.

In speaking of Mr. Nenninger's musical talents, we accused our country of vandalism with regard to the elegant arts. Yes, of vandalism, and we repeat the accusation. The number of tickets disposed of prove nothing against our previous observations. One concert, favored by the whim of the day, cannot entitle us to pretend to be connoisseurs *and* patrons of the arts.

We will add that we were not a little amused with the indignation which fired some artists in stay tape and buckram at the incongruity we committed in exclaiming against the vandalism of classing an eminent musician amongst MECHANICS.

We regret to announce to these levelers, who would place in the same rank the poet with the manufacturer of the paper on which he writes the productions of his genius, that in Parnassus this equality, which can only reign in taverns on electioneering days, does not exist – the Muses are rather saucy, and do not admit workmen to their levees.

***

TO READERS AND CORRESPONDENTS.

We received the story of Adelaide from a friend, for whose trouble in having gone through the lengthy translation we cannot be too grateful: but we must nevertheless observe that had we seen it altogether, we must at once have declined its publication. To go on with it is impossible. It is too glowing, too impure, to be presented by a female to the chaste eye of female modesty.

We have proceeded with it even further than propriety would justify already, for, whilst some extracts we have made from the most valuable works are passed by, this love-tale excites the liveliest interest, and when its publication has been suspended for a week, the office door has not stood still a moment for the constant, the continual enquiries that were made to know when it would be continued, and to urge its speedy publication. But the gratification of such readers must yield to our sense of right. Mistress Beatrice cannot consent that through her means, manners or morals should receive the slightest attaint.

Chapter Twelve: Margaret

This afternoon, instead of the usual Saturday drawing lesson, Mr. Guy proposed that we take an educational excursion, as he put it, to see the exhibition of his paintings at Mr. Cole's store. For, to my delight, he said that I may soon be ready to begin using oils, and he thought I would benefit from a careful observation of his technique.

It seemed to me I could just as easily have made the careful observation when the paintings were leaning against the walls of Mr. Guy's room, and covered with cloth to protect them — and he has once or twice unveiled some of them and pointed out this or that, the angle of a fence or the way a shadow fell on the grass. I suspect that mostly he wanted me to see his paintings in all their glory, nicely framed and hung on a wall for the public to admire. I don't begrudge him that little vanity, for I've grown fond of the man, and of his paintings as well.

I was pleased to see Mr. Cork already at Mr. Guy's studio when I arrived, but then dismayed when Mr. Guy told Mr. Cork that no doubt he'd prefer not to accompany us, as Mr. Cork had already seen the exhibit, and written about it favorably in his paper. But fortunately Mr. Cork said no, he should very much like to see the exhibit again. What with this exhibit and the concert last week, he said, Baltimore was having quite a flowering of culture, as he put it, and that remark of course led to another round of them both talking about how mistaken Mrs. A was in saying we all lived in Siberia.

It was near a twenty-minute walk to the bookstore, and we were rather damp from the heat when we arrived, but in excellent

spirits. I was pleased to be out walking alongside these two gentlemen—for I do consider Mr. Guy a gentleman now, for all his
roughness, as he knows a lot about a great many things—and
them treating me almost as an equal. From time to time Mr. Cork
put his hand to my elbow and guided me around the leavings of a
dog or a pig, just as if I were his lady friend and in need of protec-
tion from such things.

But as we walked down Market Street towards the bookstore,
and grew nearer to Mrs. A's house, I began to feel anxious about
someone seeing us together, and told him so. He shrugged and
said he and Mr. Guy would go in first and make sure none of
Mrs. A's friends were in the shop, and then signal that it was safe
for me to enter. And perhaps, he said, it would be best if I kept
my distance, so that we didn't appear to all be together. Mr. Guy
didn't much like that, as he had wanted to use the opportunity to
instruct me, but he agreed. Mr. Cork said he would linger near
the door as much as possible, to act as lookout.

When we got to Cole's they went in and I waited across
the way, in front of Russell's silver shop. I stood there for what
seemed like ten minutes, trying to interest myself in the plates
and teapots in the window, and to look as if I had some business
that kept me there, standing in the street. At last Mr. Guy came
out and waved me to come in, and I ran across.

I tried to walk in as though it were nothing out of the ordinary. I've passed by the store many times but never stopped in,
for I have had neither the time to look at the books and other fine
things on display there, nor the money to buy them. A man at the
door, who I suppose was Mr. Cole or Mr. Bonsal, said good day
to me, but in a surprised voice, maybe even suspicious, as though
he could tell I was only a serving girl and had no business there.
I straightened my bonnet and smoothed my frock, which was the
patched green one that Mrs. A gave me when I first arrived, and
tried to look as presentable as possible.

The light inside was dim, at least as compared to the sunny
day outside, but once my eyes got accustomed to it I saw there
were perhaps fifteen people there, including myself and Mr. Cork
and Mr. Guy. It was a large room, and the center of it was taken up
with tables full of books, more books than I had ever seen before
in one place—more books, even, than are in the Doctor's house,
and near every room is full of them there—and the paintings

hung along the walls. People were standing about in little groups of two or three, peering at the paintings and sometimes talking in low voices, as though they were at church.

Mr. Cork was studying a painting by the door, or pretending to, and appeared to take no notice of me. Mr. Guy was farther back, conversing with another gentleman, older than himself and taller too, with a small chin and a large nose that held a pair of spectacles. Mr. Guy was being very polite and calling the man "sir," which he doesn't often do. When I heard the man talk, I could hear he had an English accent, but not quite like Mr. Guy's. It sounded more like the way an English gentleman would talk — one with money, I mean. And yet his boots were down at the heel and marked with gray streaks where he'd scuffed them.

Now that I had taken some stock of my surroundings, I turned my attention to the paintings. Mr. Guy's paintings I recognized at once, like old friends, although they did look more handsome up there on the walls rather than stacked willy-nilly on the floor. There was the Jones Falls, with Pennington's mill next to it, and two men in the foreground loading barrels, just the way we'd seen it not half an hour before on our walk here — indeed, I realized, it was the view from the very bridge Papa helped to build. And there was another view from the same bridge, but this time looking downstream instead of up, with a coach and horses walking along the river on the left, and on the right the fine white house with the two chimneys that I have often admired. It made the bridge more important somehow, seeing the view framed on the wall like that, and I even felt a bit important because of my connection to it, and to Mr. Guy. I was wishing Papa could see it, and Fanny too.

There were two views of Baltimore, done from hills outside the city, and the painting of Mr. Cork's uncle's house, with the white fence and the sheep, and the few small figures that Mr. Guy always puts in, for "scale," he says. It was lovely to see places that were so familiar but looked like better versions of themselves, with skies that were pink and blue and softened with swirling clouds, and the branches of trees feathery against them. It was like seeing a lady who has taken extra care with her dressing, before going out, her hair just so, and perhaps a bit of rouge at her cheek or a new plume in her bonnet, so that you know it is her and yet you marvel at the change. I thought of how Mrs. A looked, that evening she went to the concert, when Polly exclaimed over how beautiful she was. She'll never be a true beauty, not like Mrs. Bonaparte, but she was changed, her cheeks all pink and creamy like one of Mr. Guy's skies. I don't think it was paint, not with Mrs. A. More likely it was the thought that Mr. Godefroy was coming to collect her, for I've noticed she looks like that, younger and prettier, when he's about. I had to smile then, thinking of Mrs. A going all giddy over Mr. Godefroy, and how I should tell Mr. Cork about it when we were alone.

Then I looked at the paintings by Mr. Groombridge, which were further towards the back of the store. I recognized nothing in them, for they didn't appear to be of Baltimore at all, but more like something you might imagine when someone tells you a tale. There were tall mountains, and rivers that snaked off into the distance, and sometimes what looked like a castle or a ruin on a cliff. And the skies were done differently from Mr. Guy's, much calmer like, with similar colors but not so mixed together, and his clouds were tame where Mr. Guy's were wild.

I was just looking at one of Mr. Groombridge's paintings that was a night scene, with a full moon and a ruin up on a crag, very eerie it was, when I felt a tap at my elbow and heard Mr. Cork's voice whisper, "She's *here*. With her Frenchman." I whipped about and saw them just coming in the door, and prayed that their eyes would take at least as much time as mine had to adjust to the light, so they wouldn't see me.

I took a breath and swallowed. "What should I do?" I whispered.

"There." He cocked his head towards where Mr. Guy and the other gentleman were standing near the back of the store. "Behind that curtain."

There was a dark green velvet cloth hanging behind the two of them, and I made my way there as quickly and quietly as I could and slipped behind it, saying nothing to Mr. Guy and hoping the man he was talking to wouldn't think it was anything worth remarking on. I didn't know if people were supposed to go behind the curtain, or what I might find there, but I had no choice and could only hope Mr. Cole or Mr. Bonsal wouldn't discover me. All that was there was a tiny room with a lot of wooden boxes, the kind you see being unloaded from ships, and I used one for a seat.

I could hear quite well from behind the curtain, and at first what I heard was Mr. Guy and the other gentleman, who turned out to be Mr. Groombridge, the other artist. They were talking about Mr. Gilmor, who I have heard Mr. Guy speak of before. He's a very rich man who has a lot of art, and he let Mr. Guy copy some of his paintings when Mr. Guy first came here, which Mr. Guy said was one of the best ways to improve as an artist, copying the work of others, if they're good. And Mr. Guy said Mr. Gilmor has some of the best. I don't remember the names of the artists, but a number of them sounded Italian.

"You say he's given you three commissions?" Mr. Groombridge was saying, sounding like he was trying not to be sad. "I haven't been able to interest him in a single one of my paintings, although heaven knows I've tried."

"Perhaps I could have a word with him," Mr. Guy replied. "That painting over there, with the moon, that's a fine one. I think it would look quite well on his library wall, next to my view of his country seat."

"Very kind of you, sir." There was a little breeze that sent the curtain my way, which must have come from Mr. Groombridge bowing. "I would be most grateful."

Then I heard Mrs. A's voice, which is hard to mistake, for she speaks loudly and her voice goes up and down, very dramatic like. "Why, I see one of the artists is here, in the flesh!" she said, only she pronounced it "ar-TEESTS," for some reason.

"Both of them, Mrs. Anderson," Mr. Guy said. "May I present Mr. William Groombridge?"

Mrs. A then introduced Mr. Godefroy, and said, "So we have three ar-TEESTS in the room at once, quite a blinding conclave of talent!" She went on to tell the others about that drawing of a battle that Mr. Godefroy did, and they both said they had seen it at the library.

"A very impressive work indeed, sir," Mr. Groombridge said. And the curtain moved again, which must have been Mr. Godefroy bowing. I noticed Mr. Guy said nothing, which was just as well.

"And we," said Mrs. A, "are quite taken with *your* work, Mr. Groombridge. The effects of light, the brushwork, the composition—all are most original, and most enchanting! One can tell you have been well trained."

I noticed she didn't say anything about Mr. Guy's pictures. Now they were talking about where Mr. Groombridge had studied painting, and how he had exhibited at something called the Royal Academy in London before he came to this country.

"And to think that your paintings here are to be disposed of by lottery," Mrs. A exclaimed, "as if they were prizes at a country fair!"

"I beg to differ." This was Mr. Guy. "I see no dishonor in a lottery. And lotteries have served me well. Some years ago I had a large exhibit at the Fountain Inn, of fourteen sizeable canvases, and the lottery for them yielded me no less than fifteen hundred dollars."

"Really!" said Mr. Groombridge, and this time you could hear the sadness in his voice more clearly. I tried to imagine a sum as large as fifteen hundred dollars, but it was beyond me.

"Well," said Mrs. A, sounding like she'd just tasted something sour, "I'm glad to hear you collected such a large amount, but I'm not sure a lottery is a fitting method of selling Mr. *Groombridge*'s works of art."

"And why might that be, Mrs. Anderson?" This was Mr. Cork, who must have come up and joined them, and his tone was that polite one rich people use when they're angry. "Why might it be a fitting means of disposing of Mr. Guy's art but not Mr. Groombridge's? Or Mr. Godefroy's, for that matter. I don't believe you found any takers for your battle drawing, did you, sir?"

"Alas, no," Mr. Godefroy said.

"That proves nothing," Mrs. A said, "except that those with the funds to buy true art in this city lack the education and taste to recognize it when they see it. As for when a lottery is appropriate, there may be some ... *productions* that are pretty and pleasing, and for which some people may be induced to enter a game of chance. But a connoisseur whose spirit is stirred by a work of genius will certainly do the artist the honor of a specific and suitable offer for that work."

"Ah," said Mr. Cork, still using that false polite tone, "so you consider Mr. Guy's paintings to be mere 'productions,' and not art?"

There was a pause, and I could imagine Mrs. A taking in that little breath she does when she's riled, and chewing her lip. "I mean no insult to Mr. Guy, of course, and it is quite clear he has a good deal of native talent. But." She paused again. Her voice was high and cold. "When one uses a piece of gauze and some chalk to take the measure of a landscape, as though one were measuring it for a new suit of clothes, it strikes me that there is more of the mechanic at work than the artist. As when one merely copies the techniques of other artists who have gone before, rather than striking out in new and original directions. And then, of course, there is the choice of subject matter."

"You don't care for landscapes, then?" It was Mr. Guy now, and he didn't sound at all pleased. I could only pray he kept his temper in check. "Mr. Groombridge and I both do landscapes, so why should you object to my subject matter and not to his?"

"Ah, but it isn't merely a matter of landscapes or not," Mrs. A. said. "Mr. Groombridge, you see, has used his imagination to conjure up stirring scenes of nature, the kind that have the power to transport the soul and ennoble the heart. Merely painting what one sees around one … well, even if it is an excellent copy, one wonders if it can be called art."

"Oh, *does* one?" said Mr. Guy, with a snarl in his voice.

"May I suggest that there is room in the house of art for both varieties?" This was Mr. Groombridge, sounding anxious. "It can be as difficult to render what you see before you as to depict the products of your imagination, and the results may be equally pleasing."

"A generous sentiment, sir," said Mrs. A. "But surely the rooms in the house of art, like the rooms in any house, are not all of the same quality. One would never place the kitchen, for example, on the same level as the sitting room or the dining room, where guests are ushered in and welcomed. And may I suggest that the most ennobling subjects for art—its grandest parlors, if you will—are drawn from history and mythology and literature."

"So you would have us ignore our surroundings and comb the pages of books to find our subjects?" Mr. Guy shot at her.

"Mr. Guy, I would have *you* do nothing more than you are doing at present—your paintings, as I said before, are quite pretty. And not everyone has the genius necessary to ascend to the highest peaks of artistic endeavor."

Then I heard Mr. Godefroy say something about it being time for them to go. I imagine he wasn't able to understand every word of the conversation, but no doubt he could tell that it was heading in a dangerous direction. There were some hurried goodbyes, and some quick footsteps—a heavier tread, which I took to be Mr. Godefroy's, and Mrs. A's lighter one. And then, after I heard the door open and close, the bell on it jangling, I found the courage to come out from behind the curtain, relieved that I hadn't been discovered.

Mr. Guy, as I had expected, was near shaking with rage, and his fists were clenched. "How dare the woman!" he was saying, as he paced back and forth in the narrow space between the tables of books, and "She knows nothing, nothing!" He went on about how she'd accused him of copying techniques from other artists, as though it were stealing, when it was no more than what artists have done from time immemorial.

"Never mind all that, sir," Mr. Cork said, with a gesture as though he were swatting a fly. "We'll get back at her in the paper. I can refute all she says, point by point."

"Aye, you do that," said Mr. Guy, "and I shall refute her as well. Not just by words, but by deeds."

This sounded like a threat, although I couldn't fathom what he meant by it, and I feared it would only arouse his anger further if I asked. Mr. Groombridge was looking highly uncomfortable, and when he saw an acquaintance at the door to the shop, he took the opportunity to excuse himself.

There was a brief silence, and Mr. Guy said it was growing late, and he must take himself home. I had hoped that, now that the danger had passed, he'd perhaps do as he'd said and use the paintings on the wall to instruct me, but I could see he was far too agitated now for that sort of thing. And then, after he left and it was just me and Mr. Cork, I thought we might go to the tavern and have some supper. But Mr. Cork said no, not this evening, he must write about what Mrs. A had said while he still had it all fresh in his mind, and that we must do without our supper tonight.

So I had no choice but to go back to the Doctor's and see what scraps Mrs. Morris could spare for me. It was much poorer fare than what the Sow's Ear can offer up, and I took it up to my room and ate by myself, not wanting Mrs. Morris's company—or even Polly's, which, dearly as I love the child, is a poor substitute for Mr. Cork's. And so I sit here now, feeling rather sorry for myself, and knowing that but for Mrs. A I might have had a far more amusing evening.

From the Observer, June 20, 1807:

FINE ARTS.

Mr. Nenninger's concert took place on Thursday the 11ᵗʰ, and was rendered delightful by the united exertions of the most distinguished talents in the musical art. It was impossible not to admire the graceful ease of Mr. Nenninger's execution, and the perfection of his taste.

It would be difficult for us to pronounce on Mr. Webster's voice and method of singing; we have here too few points of comparison to enable us competently to judge of his merit. It is, however, impossible that without a considerable degree of natural talent and some science, he could do what he does. Nevertheless it really is to be desired that he would not distort his features with the horrible grimaces he makes whilst singing, and that in his trills he would not assume the appearance of gargling his throat with his notes, nor make his transitions so sudden and unequal. We have observed him on the stage as well as in the present instance, and in viewing the contortions of his body, and the contraction of his muscles (when he would astonish the natives by the wonders of his skill), our imagination has always presented us the agreeable idea of a man laboring under the operation of a strong emetic.

Music, painting and poetry are sister arts, and have therefore one common cause. In speaking of the first, we are under the necessity of saying a few words of the second.

For us who have never been able to devote ourselves to acquiring the knowledge necessary to judge of painting, we content ourselves with recurring to the decision of such persons as have an acknowledged right of pronouncing on these points.

They will say then that the genius of Mr. Guy is a wild plant; that nature had intended him for a landscape painter, as is evident by the pretty frescoes he has painted at the Fountain Inn; but they will also say that he has not studied, that from want of encouragement reduced to the necessity of making coats and pantaloons, he has not had it in his power to cultivate his talent, nor has he made a single striking step in the art. If Mr. Guy's genius is a diamond, it is one without polish.

Real connoisseurs will say that as for Mr. Groombridge, he views nature with an artist's eye; that he is familiar with good schools; that he has a great deal of facility; and that to produce paintings really fine, he needs only to meet with persons sufficiently generous and discerning to indemnify him for the time and expense the necessary studies would cost him.

If the paintings which are placed in lottery at Mr. Cole's are admirable, it is then very true that this is the Siberia of the arts, where the authors of such fine pieces can derive no profit from their talents, and where they are suffered to vegetate unemployed, or are compelled to make small-clothes, to procure themselves the means of existence.

Chapter Thirteen: Eliza

This afternoon I received a communication from Her Highness Madame Bonaparte (alas, still not in possession of a proper title—or should I say, a concocted title—from the *soi-disant* Emperor, who doles them out as freely as he invents new principalities to accompany them) and obediently hied myself to an immediate audience at South Street. For the Pattersons will soon depart *en famille* for one of their country places, leaving the hot, dusty, insalubrious streets of Baltimore to the likes of me—and the wretched patients of Father's Dispensary—until such time as cooler temperatures and healthier air render the place habitable for more refined beings.

In fact, envious as I am, I was pleased to receive the summons to Betsy's presence, and threw aside my plans for the afternoon with alacrity—even though I had intended to spend the time giving instruction to Polly. I hadn't seen Betsy in weeks, her preference now being to spend as much time as possible in Washington City, and I knew this might be my last opportunity for many weeks more. Infuriating as she can be, there is a bond between us that I cherish—and of course it is to my advantage to enlist her continuing support for the cause of the Observer.

My only hesitation arose from the prospect of encountering Mr. Patterson, for although our subscriber list has now reached beyond five hundred, we are not yet in a position to repay him his money. The expenses associated with a publication of this sort—the printing costs and the postage, which I often must pay for submissions whose authors have seen fit to send them unstamped, and which are sometimes useful only as fodder for the fire—are higher than I had anticipated, as are the number of sub-scribers evading their pecuniary obligations. But as Mr. Patterson generally keeps to his counting house during the day, and would be particularly likely to do so on the eve of his departure from town, I thought it safe to venture into the lion's den.

Betsy received me with her usual cool elegance, and Mrs. Patterson with her usual enveloping warmth—and with little Bo af-fixed as usual to her hip—in the hall. But Betsy and I soon retired to the garden and settled on the bench under the plane tree that so faithfully sheltered us throughout our girlhoods, when we would read to one another of a long afternoon. I felt a shiver of bittersweet recollection as I lowered myself onto its hard, though somehow welcoming, stone surface, and wondered if Betsy was experiencing similar sensations, remembering younger and hap-pier days. If she was, she betrayed no sign of it.

"How tiresome it is, all this packing and boxing," she sighed as she leaned back and gazed up at the brilliant sky through the tree's branches. "I only just returned from Washington City last week, and now we must leave again for Springfield!"

I murmured some words of sympathy, trying not to betray how much I yearned to go somewhere, anywhere, to see some-thing other than the same muddy streets and blandly similar houses. Even Washington City, which Betsy paints as no better than a few half-finished structures scattered across a wilderness, for me gleams on the horizon like some mythical kingdom, re-splendent with glittering foreign dignitaries who somehow mus-ter up the necessities for nightly entertainments. And Springfield would at least offer rolling green hills and fresh country air. Nor did it seem that Betsy herself was overly engaged in the tedious work of packing and boxing. No doubt some servant, or perhaps two or three, was up in her bedroom at that moment surrounded by silks and muslins and chemises destined for departure.

"Any word from the French minister?" I inquired, to be po-lite. I was fairly sure the answer would be no, for otherwise I should have heard something of it.

Betsy sighed, crossed her arms, and looked away. "Only one excuse after another." She switched her tone to one of mockery, and her accent to something approximating that of a Frenchman. " 'You must understand that the Emperor, 'ee eez extremely oc-cupied—we are at war, you know—and he cannot attend to this leetle matter of a title and a pension for you on a moment's notice, *Mademoiselle Patterson!*'" She closed her eyes and took a breath. "He persists in addressing me by that insulting appellation. And of course the Emperor is not too 'occupied' to attempt to find another wife for his married brother!"

I had heard the rumors, of course—there was one about Napoleon trying to forge an alliance with the Queen of Etruria, one of his made-up "kingdoms." But the Queen, to her credit, was reported to have said she would give up her crown rather than marry Jerome Bonaparte (it was not reported whether this objection was based on the deficiencies of his character or his legitimate marriage to Betsy, but either would of course suffice).

"If only the Emperor had allowed you into his presence," I mused, "if he'd given you a few moments to show him who you really are, your true self! Things might have transpired so differently."

"My true self!" She turned her head away and raised a hand to her throat. "I am nothing, no one. Not anymore. When I think of what was almost mine." Her voiced had a choked quality to it, and when she faced me I saw tears spilling from her eyes. "I put on a brave face, act a public role, but the truth is I feel myself sinking into a black abyss, lower and lower each day. It's all I can do to force myself from my bed in the morning."

"Dearest girl!" I clasped her to my bosom, all my little resentments and annoyances forgotten. "You mustn't let the gloomy Monster take possession of so fine a mind as yours." I drew away from her, but held her by the shoulders. "Don't you think I've had experience of such despair myself? But you must call forth every latent spark of energy, exert your faculties. I know what it is to feel that all hope is lost, that life holds no charm. But there is a style of metaphysical reading that I delight in at such times, and oh Betsy, I know it would exactly suit you. You must get Smith's *Moral Sentiments*—and Kames' *History of Man*—oh, and Paley's *Moral Philosophy*, of course. I can send some of them round, Father won't mind, and you can take them to Springfield. Oh, and Baron Helvetius on man and the mind—"

"Eliza, please!" She pulled herself from my grasp and stood, then put a hand to her brow as though her head was aching. "I'm not *you*. I couldn't possibly read such things in my present state. I can scarcely manage to read the paper these days." She took a few steps away from the tree, her back to me and her arms crossed, and stood there for perhaps a minute or more in silence. I thought perhaps I had been dismissed. Wounded, I stood and prepared to take my leave, when suddenly she turned back to me, and I saw that she was entirely composed again, her brave public face firmly in place.

"Ah, but I did read the article in the Observer on the art exhibit on Cole and Bonsal's," she said with a cool smile. "Most interesting. It was you that wrote it, was it not?"

I felt like a rider whose horse now gallops wildly, now slows to a dignified trot, thrown off balance and uncertain whether to stay the course or dismount. But the Observer was the one topic I could not run from, no matter how tumultuous the course, so I forced myself to match the calm lightness of Betsy's tone, as though we'd just been exchanging pleasantries.

I nodded and dipped my head modestly. "I'm no expert in the arts, of course, but I had help from Mr. Godefroy. Not in the writing, but in distinguishing between true talent and mere competence. I knew what I preferred, as between the two artists, but until Mr. Godefroy took me under his wing I did not understand *why*."

"Ah, so you are still enamored of your Mr. Godefroy, then?" There seemed to be a mocking edge to her voice.

"I find his company to be pleasurable and stimulating, and I am honored to call him my friend." I heard the chill in my tone but was powerless to infuse it with much warmth. "We only discuss art, and philosophy, and literature—he's given me the most extraordinary French novel to read, *Claire d'Albe*. There are few in this town to equal his breadth of knowledge and delicacy of taste, especially as *you* are now so frequently absent from it. I must have *someone* I can talk to!"

"Oh, I know," she said with feeling. "Why do you think I spend so much time in Washington City? The French, the English—I tell you, they truly appreciate me. Not like the small-minded dullards who populate this place. But ..." She raised her eyebrows and lowered her chin. "Just be on your guard you aren't talked *about*."

"Why?" Alarm began to creep over me, causing my breath to catch. "Have you heard something?"

"Oh, this town! You know what they're like." She lifted a small white hand in a dismissive wave and resumed her seat on the bench. "Always ready to gossip, especially if one has fallen afoul of them in some way. I should pay it no mind."

I swooped to her side, placed a hand on her arm, and clutched it. "Pay *what* no mind?"

"Really, it was nothing." She patted my hand and then moved her arm so as to displace it. "But if you must know, it was that Cork fellow. He was at the Catons' the other day for tea — somehow they suffered me to cross their threshold and pollute their domain. I should much rather not have gone, but Mother insisted. At any rate, Mr. Cork was spouting some nonsense about you and Mr. Godefroy and how it didn't become you, as a married lady, to engage in so intimate a friendship with a gentleman."

"Cork! I knew it." I stood up and began pacing. "I swear to you, Betsy, nothing improper or dishonorable has passed between me and Mr. Godefroy, nothing. You know I've renounced all interest in men but that of a friendly nature. But James Cork is determined to destroy me, simply because I am a woman — a woman who has had the audacity to defy him and expose him for the fool he is, rather than fall at his feet like all the simpering little misses of this place. I should have known he would resort to slander!"

"Oh, he hasn't gone that far. Not yet, anyway." Betsy shook her head.

"But what am I to do? He and that paper of his won't leave me alone for a moment. Every week brings fresh denunciations! Am I to bear it in silence? And now he's brought others into the enterprise. There's some awful little rag that just appeared last week, called Moonshine — I can't imagine it will last more than a month or two, given their feeble attempts at what I suppose is meant to be wit, but they were happy to launch a sally or two at me, or try to. And then Tuesday — " I had meant to tell her of this, and could not believe I had forgotten it until this moment. "Did you see the Federal Gazette? The letter signed 'An American'?"

She shook her head no, and I asked her if there might be a copy inside the house. Within a few moments we were in Mr. Patterson's library, with a copy of the offending missive in my trembling hand. My eye raced through the author's tedious verbiage — his paean to America, blessed with peace and prosperity while Europe is convulsed in war, et cetera, et cetera, and then his eventual admission that if there is one field in which we must

yield pre-eminence, it is that of the arts. At last I found the passage that had nearly caused me to choke on my tea two days ago.

"'Do not misunderstand me, sir,'" I read. "'I am not about to
join in the ungracious attempt to stigmatize my dear Columbia as
hostile to the arts. I will not call her sons Vandals, nor denounce
the territory as a cold Siberia, where the best plants sicken and
die.'" I paused, glancing up to satisfy myself that she was listening. "'No, I value the intelligence of her citizens at a higher rate,
and I esteem her climate and her soil as of a kinder nature.'" I
looked up again. "There, you see? How can I not answer when
such ridiculous claims are leveled against me!"

Betsy shrugged. "If you ignore these people, they'll go away.
Why bring further attention to the fellow? If you hadn't just read
that letter to me, I should never have known about it."

"But ..." It crossed my mind to say that responding to it
might well bring the Observer new subscribers, as we have seen
an increase every time there is a riposte to a barb such as this. But
I thought better of it. "His arguments make no sense! He agrees
with me on every point, and then tries to disassociate himself
from my position. And I never claimed that this country suf-
fers from any deficiency of ..." I glanced at the paper, still in my
hand. "*Soil*, or climate! The man has no sense of metaphor. And to
call himself 'An American,' as though my criticism of this country — which is no different in substance from his — somehow renders me unfit for citizenship. No, this, *this*" — I rapped the paper
against Mr. Patterson's heavy dark wood desk — "simply cannot
be ignored."

Betsy rolled her eyes and sank onto Mr. Patterson's leather
armchair. "Well then, answer him if you must. But don't be surprised if you're accused of being ungracious, or worse, if you go
on in this vein. There are bound to be some who will label you an
outright traitor."

"But Betsy." I perched on the arm of her chair. "Is it not true
patriotism to try to *correct* our nation's flaws when we perceive
them? Is it not in fact disloyalty to coat the painful truth with such
fawning praise that readers will think they're being lauded when
in fact they're being faulted?"

"Very noble of you, indeed, to try to correct flaws that I fear
are not susceptible of correction. But perhaps the author of the
letter was only trying to be diplomatic." With an indulgent smile,

she patted my arm as though I were a small child. "That is a characteristic no one will ever fault *you* for, my dear."

I rose to my feet and backed away a few steps. "Diplomacy, you call it? Cowardice, is what *I* say!" I might have added that she, of all people, was not one to lecture me on diplomacy, but I had enough self-possession to hold my tongue.

"Now, now, I meant no insult. But why not publish more essays in a humorous vein? People like that sort of thing, you know, and it's less likely to rile them. I don't mean things like that Tabitha Simple letter," she added quickly when she saw me begin to open my mouth to respond. "Something milder. You know the type: a letter about 'an old maid of my acquaintance,' with a fondness for cats and a head full of superstitions. You see that everywhere."

"Yes, you do, and it's one reason I would prefer not to publish such pabulum." I crossed my arms and looked out at the garden through the open window. Some nagging voice within told me that Betsy might have a point. "I did receive something in that vein just yesterday. Now that I think of it, it *was* about an old maid—his Aunt Prissy, the author called her—with a fondness for cats!"

"There you are. That sounds perfect."

I was about to tell her of my unfortunate experience with *Adelaide*, when we heard raised voices in the front hall.

"That's Father," Betsy said, her brows raised in surprise. "What is he doing home at this hour?"

The door to the library opened and Mr. Patterson strode in. He stopped when he saw Betsy, and then pivoted his fierce head until he was staring at me. "Why, it's Mrs. Anderson. Taking time away from your editorial labors? Has your worthy father at last finished cataloguing every inhabitant of the insect kingdom?"

I tried to smile winningly. "Nearly. Next week's installment is devoted to the Ichneumon fly, but he does understand that readers are growing impatient, and he's promised that in another week or two—"

"Yes, well, never mind that now." He turned to Betsy, and I was relieved that he apparently had no intention of pursuing the subject further, or of demanding the repayment of his loan. "Young lady, you should be in your room overseeing the boxing of your clothes. We leave for Springfield at dawn tomorrow."

"Tomorrow?" Betsy was clearly displeased. "But I thought we were not to go until Saturday. And I'm engaged for dinner at the Browns tomorrow!"

"Well, you'll need to send your regrets. No point in lingering in town when there's talk of war."

We both were silent for a moment, thinking we must have misheard. "War?" Betsy said at last. "Who is talking of war?"

Mr. Patterson moved to his desk and began gathering up papers. "One of our ships just came in from Norfolk. The captain said that two days ago the British fired on an American frigate — the *Chesapeake* — that had just left port there, on its way to the Barbary Coast. It was the usual thing, the British claiming a right to search the ship because there were deserters from the British Navy on board. Or so they said. The captain of the *Chesapeake* refused to allow the search, and rightly so, and the British began firing." He picked up a sheaf of papers and tapped them on the edge of the desk to neaten the edges, then tucked them under his arm. "It ended badly, I'm afraid. The captain I spoke to wasn't sure of the exact numbers, but he thought at least two American seamen were killed, maybe more, and at least a dozen wounded. And four were seized by the British as deserters. I'm surprised they didn't take more, as they're none too scrupulous these days."

"And you think the President will declare war?" Betsy's tone was steady, but I wondered if in fact her heart was racing as much as mine was. I thought of poor little Bobby O'Neill at the concert two weeks ago, and his father's fear that war might snatch his son.

"I think if he has any spine he will." Mr. Patterson now stood at the door, poised to make preparations for his flight to the countryside. "Not that I welcome it. It's been bad enough for business, trying to send our ships across the sea with the French and British at each other's throats. If we're in it as well ..." He shook his head. "And our navy is no match for the British — apparently the *Chesapeake* fired only one shot before surrendering. Still, I don't see that it can be avoided. The news is spreading along the docks, and there's not a soul but what's clamoring to defend the nation's honor."

He turned again to me, and lowered his abundant eyebrows, looking for all the world like a prophet of doom from Scripture. "I should be careful of what I put in that paper, if I were you, Mrs.

Anderson. There'll be little kindness for those who show naught but scorn for the nation at a time like this." He extended a long, bony finger, and uttered his next remark in a near whisper so ominous that the result was more threatening than a shout. "You'd best change your tune, or you're liable to find yourself shackled and hauled up for treason like Colonel Burr."

And with that he opened the wood-paneled library door and vanished. For a moment I was quite overcome, as though the hand of the Lord had suddenly reached down and pointed a celestial digit at me. I suppose it didn't help that Betsy had uttered the word "traitor" only minutes before.

"I see your father agrees with you that it would be best to confine the paper to essays concerning old maids and their cats," I mumbled.

"Oh come, Eliza, I'm sure no one will put you in irons for your comments on the fine arts," Betsy said briskly. "But it wouldn't hurt to throw a bone to the patriots lusting for British blood. Something about our having the best system of government ever devised by man, the most fertile soil on earth, the most prosperous commerce ... you know the sort of thing. There's no requirement that you believe it."

"Oh, I do know the sort of thing—it's exactly what that *American* was spouting in the Gazette!" I swallowed and tried to soften my voice, which I could hear was sounding a trifle strident. "I won't give up the mission I undertook. The Observer will not flinch, war or no war!"

Betsy shrugged and began to move towards the door. "Suit yourself. For my part, I shouldn't care if the British did reclaim us and put an end to this miserable experiment in mob rule." She turned back to me, her hand on the doorknob. "But I'm afraid I really must see to the packing now. And send my regrets to the Browns." She shook her head and briefly directed her gaze to the ceiling. "Dawn tomorrow!"

A thought had just struck me. "But there *is* something I can do, something that will prove I'm a loyal American and won't require that I compromise my principles. Did I tell you of Mr. Godefroy's memorial? On fortifications? The one I've undertaken to translate? He's tried to interest several members of Congress in his proposals, but to no avail, so he's now resolved to publish it in pamphlet form."

"Mr. Godefroy again?" She placed her hands on her hips and shook her head.

"This has nothing to do with the friendship between us. It's a stroke of luck! I can publish excerpts from the memorial in the Observer, and once people see what he recommends … It's all so sensible, so clearly laid out. It's sure to cause a sensation, especially with the prospect of war hanging over us. I tell you, the Observer will be praised for its service to the public!"

"Well, I should publish it as soon as possible, then." Her hand was on the doorknob again.

We said some hasty farewells, and she remarked vaguely that I really should come out to Springfield for a while if I could manage it. But I hesitated to press her for an actual invitation, and I suppose I'll be condemned to remain here, where my existence is now threatened not only by the usual scourge of yellow fever but also by a British invasion—for Baltimore, with its busy harbor, is almost sure to be a military target.

True to my word, as soon as I returned home I threw myself into Mr. Godefroy's manuscript, so absorbed in the work of translation that I was surprised to hear Mrs. Morris ringing the bell for supper. I suppose I shall have to lay aside for a while the translation of *Claire d'Albe*. And I had intended to write a series of essays addressed to mothers, on the topic of raising and educating daughters, a subject as to which I flatter myself I have some expertise!

But perhaps I can find the time to work on all of these simultaneously, and still manage my editorial duties. I feel a strange and deep energy coursing through me, almost as though I could work straight through the night without tiring. It is now nearly eleven, and I feel no hint of fatigue. Indeed, I have put aside Mr. Godefroy's memorial in order to turn my attention to composing my response to "An American."

I intend to wield my words without fear, undaunted by the clumsy missiles hurled by ignorant foes. Oh, I shall be diplomatic—I'll show Betsy that I can engage in those little charades if I need to. But I shall be firm, and there'll be no mistaking my meaning.

From the Observer, June 27, 1807:

BEATRICE IRONSIDE'S BUDGET.

A letter which appeared in the Federal Gazette of Tuesday last evidenced that the author is no less formed for the love of the arts than he appears to be attached to his country, and it is with pleasure that Mrs. Beatrice takes up the gauntlet thrown by such an adversary.

I faithfully transcribe this passage:

"The paintings of Mr. GROOMBRIDGE, in vain were they exhibited, while the sensibility of this gentleman was wounded by neglect, and his works valued only for their frames."

Permit me, sir, to ask if it was by such arguments you expected to make those repent of their sincerity whom you accuse of having stigmatized our young nation? Ha! It is impossible but that fundamentally you must agree with me on all I have advanced upon this point.

I will take the liberty of saying that it is wrong to assume names or titles which preclude freedom of opinion. In adopting the signature of AN AMERICAN, does this writer mean that all those who do not take Philadelphia for London, New-York for Paris, Washington for Rome, and Baltimore for Athens, are unpatriotic citizens, and stigmatizers of Columbia!

From the Federal Gazette, June 27, 1807:

It is much to be lamented that professed information should at any time be converted into instruments by which to convey the foul effects of party spleen and mischievous and false aspersions.

I was led into this strain of thinking on reading a communication in the Observer of Saturday last under the head of "Fine Arts," in which the author has drawn an odious and insulting comparison between America and every other part of the civilized world, by calling this country the Siberia of the arts; and, with all the egotism of a self-conceited pedant, soundly asserts that Americans, as respects their knowledge of the arts, are in few instances more enlightened than the savages of that uncultivated desert.

C.

Chapter Fourteen: Margaret

A most remarkable day, today was, and one I warrant I won't soon forget. I had thought only to take Polly out for some fresh air and exercise, for the child has been looking pale lately, and has nearly given up eating entirely. She only wants cakes and sweet things, and Mrs. A and Mrs. Morris agree she can have none of that unless she eats the other things first. I suppose they have the better of the argument, but I can remember when I myself was small and there was still money to be had for sweets. And I thought perhaps if I tired Polly out with a walk and stirred up her appetite, she might be willing to eat whatever was placed in front of her.

We had gone but a little ways out of town on the Reister's Town road, our pace slow because Polly's short legs cover little ground, when she began to complain and ask to turn back.

"But look up there!" I said, pointing to a group of tents I had just spied, arranged in what looked to be a circle, perhaps a quarter of a mile down the road in an open field. "Don't you want to see what that might be?"

I wanted to see myself, as judging from the number of carriages and wagons there were a multitude of people there, and even at this distance I could hear what sounded like singing. Polly squinted at the curious light brown structures, squatting in the distance like some overgrown stand of mushrooms, and considered.

"Is it a market, do you think?" she said, turning her round brown eyes up to me, full of hope. "Do they have cakes there?"

"Perhaps they do," I said, though I had my doubts. And even if they did, I had no money for cakes. "Let's go find out."

I felt a little guilty, luring the poor girl on with false hopes of cake, but I reflected that it was for her own good, and that Dr. Crawford, who is a great believer in exercise, would surely approve. Perhaps it was my guilt that moved me to pick her up, when she began complaining again that she was tired, and carry her the last hundred yards or so. I was tired myself, and small as she is I struggled a bit under her weight. And yet it was sweet to hold her so close, and feel the puffs of her warm breath on the side of my neck where she nestled her head like a bird come to roost. I used to be reminded of Fanny, when I held Polly like that, and I would feel a stab of joy and grief. But Polly is her own little person, and the truth is I've come to love her for herself, and not because she puts me in mind of my sister.

As we got closer, I began to hear loud voices, mixed with odder sounds like shouts and moans. I began to think perhaps we shouldn't have come so close, for it appeared to be one of those camp meetings I've heard of, that the Baptists and the Methodists sometimes have. But there was a large, jolly-looking woman at the entrance to the tent who saw me stop and hesitate, and she called out, "Come, sister, come and hear the good news!"

At that Polly lifted her head and scrambled down from my arms, her spirit suddenly returning to her, and ran a little ways towards the woman. She must have thought the good news had something to do with the rumblings of her stomach, for before I could stop her, I heard her ask if there was cake inside.

"Cake there is, my girl!" said the woman, bending over to pat the soft brown curls atop Polly's head. "We shall have a love feast soon. Nourishment for the spirit and for the body."

Polly was not to be put off now. "You were right," she told me, taking my hand and pulling me forward. "There *is* cake."

I thought it could do no harm to look about the place for a minute or two, and the prospect of some food before we started back home was cheering. Although I wasn't sure I liked the sound of the words "love feast."

Polly pulled me to where the woman was directing us, through a passageway between two of the tents, and we came into a large open circular space covered in patchy grass. At one end of this circle was a raised wooden platform, hammered roughly together. There were a few other people strolling about—curious visitors like us, I supposed—and occasionally peeking into the tents, from which those odd sounds could be heard. Polly broke from me and ran towards the tent on our left, perhaps hoping she would find the promised cake.

I hurried to catch up with her and arrived just as she had drawn back the curtain covering the entrance. We both stared at the strange scene before us: a circle of perhaps twenty young men and women, all kneeling on the straw that had been strewn to make a sort of floor, their arms and heads supported by piles of more straw. And in the center a tall, thin young man dressed all in black, his arms stiff at his sides, speaking so rapidly I could scarce make out his words, except to know it was something about Jesus. But the people kneeling in the circle seemed to understand him, for they were shouting out "Jesus" and "Glory be to the Lord!" as if in response. And then I saw that a number of these people had tears running down their cheeks, and some were sobbing outright. One young woman, her hair falling loose down her back, had her features entirely distorted by what appeared to be agony, and the young man next to her had his arm about her neck to comfort her. But she began to shake with agitation, and he along with her, and the next I knew the two of them had fallen forward with groans and a kind of low howling and were writhing about on the straw, apparently overcome by whatever it was the grim young man in the center was saying.

I glanced at Polly, who was taking in the scene with an open mouth and wide eyes. "Let's come away now," I whispered to her. "I don't think they have any cake here."

She offered no resistance, but when I suggested that we begin our journey homeward she shook her head fiercely and insisted there must be cake somewhere, for the lady had said so. And just then we heard a horn blow, and people began coming out of all the tents and gathering in the open circle in front of the raised platform.

"*Now* there will be cake," Polly said firmly, and began to march toward the platform along with the others who were streaming from the tents.

I thought of snatching her up and carrying her away, but I suspected she would protest loudly, and I didn't want to do anything that might attract attention, so I meekly followed along, quite as though I were the child and she the adult. The best I could do was to prevent her from stationing herself right at the base of the platform and coax her instead into a position off to the side, where I took her up in my arms so that she might see what was to transpire. There was a multitude gathered in the circle now, perhaps two or three hundred, mostly young people and mostly women, all dressed in simple clothing. At the far end was a cluster of perhaps twenty or thirty Negroes, which surprised me, as generally they have their own churches. But here they were greeting and being greeted by the others just as though they were white, even exchanging embraces and kisses with some of the people near them.

It had been a long time, years perhaps, since I'd been in a church—although rightly this wasn't a church at all, for even aside from it being out of doors, it looked and felt nothing like the churches Papa would sometimes take us to down at the Point, when his conscience would nag at him, or the one we went to with Mother every Sunday back in Bel Air. There we all had to be quiet, and dress in our best, and keep our hands in our laps and our eyes downcast or fixed on the preacher while he read us verses from the Bible. Here I began to wonder if there would be a preacher at all.

But soon a tall, thin man dressed in black appeared on the platform, older than the one in the tent but with a similar burning look in his eye, and a mane of black hair flowing down about his shoulders and a scraggly black beard that partly hid his long face. Out from the midst of all this dark hair there jutted a beaky nose, which, along with the dark hair and clothes and his hunched shoulders, gave him the appearance of a large and unnaturally narrow crow. Even at a distance, I could see that his clothes were far from new, with mud stains and tears in the fabric.

"Brothers and sisters!" he called to the people in a high, whining voice, "we are here gathered to cast out sin from our lives, and to commit ourselves to the love and care of our Lord Jesus Christ!"

There were shouts of "Amen!" and "Jesus, Jesus!" and "Glory!" Then, to my surprise, the preacher began to talk, not about Jesus, but about America. It was no accident, he said, that this land, which had lain undiscovered for thousands of years, had been revealed to us now. And it was no accident that it was here that the common people had at last been given a say in their destinies. No, he said, it was all part of God's plan. We were at the dawn of a new golden age, an age of democracy.

"We don't need the gentlemen, or the nobility, to tell us what to do, not in this country!" he cried, as the crowd made approving noises. He paced the stage with stiff strides, as though, like a crow, he had no knees. "Do they not put the common people on a level with animals, do they not think us peasants, and expect us to bow and cringe and scrape? Oh yes, we see it and we feel it daily."

"We do, yes indeed!" said a voice from the place where the Negroes sat, and several others called, "Amen!"

"But we know we're every bit as good as they are, in the eyes of the Lord and under the law of this land." One of the preacher's arms, which had dangled at his side, jerked up above his head, a finger pointed at the sky, like he was a puppet and someone had pulled on his string. "It's high time for us not only to think, but also to act, for ourselves, to see with our own eyes, and to take all our measures directly from the Divine standard!"

I had never heard such words from the mouth of a preacher, and they went straight to my heart. They put me in mind of the kinds of things Papa used to say, and that I'd always felt in my bones were true. I thought of Mrs. A, and the way she orders me about and puts on airs, when in truth she's no better than I am. Why, she can't even be bothered to raise her own child, like any natural mother would, leaving it to me instead—and I daresay I do a better job than she could, anyway. Just then Polly tugged at my bonnet strings and said something about cake, but I gave her a kiss and hushed her, for I wanted to hear what the preacher would say next.

"And we'll not submit to the yoke of monarchy, we'll not let the cursed English enslave us again. No, we'll fight for our freedom, and our sacred rights, even unto death, for the Lord demands no less of us!"

The crowd cheered at this, and I reckoned he was talking about that ship, the one the English fired on, and that everyone says will bring on a war. Last Saturday when I arrived for my drawing lesson, Mr. Guy told me he was occupied in making a painting of that ship, the *Chesapeake* they call it, and that I must go away, or else I could stay and watch him paint. I chose to stay, mostly in hopes that Mr. Cork would come, which he did, soon after I arrived. Mr. Guy apologized but said it was important that he finish the painting, for it's to be exhibited at a tavern in town on the Fourth of July. He said it was to show Mrs. A and the rest of them that he could paint something more than houses, but Mr. Cork said he doubted Mrs. A would come see the painting, when she and her crowd most likely believed we should just surrender without a fight and put ourselves again under England's thumb.

Mr. Guy waved his brush about and said it would be an outrage if she didn't come, after she'd taunted him about not painting historical works, even if it's houses and landscapes most people want to buy. In fact, he said his paintings at Mr. Cole's store had brought in quite a tidy sum, while poor Mr. Groombridge hadn't found any takers for his, and that when he had the time he would write a public statement answering Mrs. A and put it in the Gazette. Then I told them about the scene that morning, when Mrs. A read a letter in the Gazette that attacked her, as she said, for claiming we all lived in Siberia. Mr. Cork was particularly interested when I said she thought *he* might have written the letter, as it was signed "C." He laughed and said no, it wasn't him, though he was happy to let Mrs. A think it was, but that it was cheering to know that others had taken up the cause.

I had hoped Mr. Cork would take me to supper again, but he said no, not this week, he hadn't the time. Sometimes I think we may never speak alone again, or even that he might stop coming to Mr. Guy's at all, and it gives me such pain I feel the tears coming on. It seems like everyone else I've ever cared about has been taken from me, one way or another. Except for Polly, of course, who was growing heavier in my arms by the minute.

"Right now," the preacher was saying, "*now* is the time for anxious sinners to wrestle with the Lord. Do not be afeard, for I — I, who was a sinner, and now know the joy and peace of salvation — I am here to help you. Come forward, come to the pen, and be saved, and know the love of Jesus!"

At the mention of the word "pen," the crowd fell back from the platform several feet, leaving an open space in front of it, into which the preacher now jumped, his long arms flailing. He stood there for several minutes, his eyes closed and his arms outstretched as though to receive the sinners. And then in his whiny voice he began to sing a hymn that was all about sinners coming to Jesus to be saved, and many in the crowd joined in, and I began to think how comforting it would be to be part of such a crowd. For their voices were clear and their faces were lifted upwards, and many of them were holding one another's hands, or had their arms about each other's shoulders, as though they were a family.

Then people began coming forward, mostly young women—perhaps my age, some even younger. Some of them were groaning, and some uttering a howl, and some were in such distress that they had to be helped forward by others. As one of the young women turned in my direction I saw to my astonishment that I recognized her features, distorted as they were by her transports. It was Alice, who lived across the hall from me and Papa and Fanny at Mrs. Brooks', down at the Point. Papa used to tell me to keep my distance from her, as he didn't approve of how she earned her bread, but she was kind to me, and made me laugh. I gasped and gave out a small cry when I saw her, but I don't think she noticed me, for her dark eyes were glassy and blank, like she was in the grip of a fever. And yet she was still pretty as ever, with her heart-shaped face and a small mouth that put me in mind of a kitten's.

"Let us pray!" said the preacher, and the girls dropped to their knees. But soon that position was not enough for them, and they began to sprawl on the ground and writhe around like snakes, their limbs jerking this way and that and tangling with one another. And the sounds that came from them were truly terrifying to behold, all manner of sobs and shrieks and groans, and even what sounded like a dog barking. Some of the girls were deathly pale, but one, screaming "Take me, Jesus" over and over, was so red in the face that I feared she would burst.

I had nearly forgotten Polly in my arms, but now I heard a little sob, and a small frightened voice saying that she wanted to go home.

"In a bit, my girl, in a bit," I whispered. I put her down on the ground, both to spare my arms and to shield her view, and she buried her face in my skirts.

The preacher was going from one penitent to the next, now bending down and whispering what appeared to be encouragement, now listening to some tale of woe and sin. He would put his face very close to them, and they would sometimes wrap their arms about him in a way I had never seen strangers do before, and he would even kiss their cheeks. When he got to Alice, she began to cry out.

"Woe, woe to the backsliders!" I heard her shout between her sobs. "When I was fifteen, my mother died, and I backslided. Oh, hear me, Jesus! Take me home to her, for I am weary. Oh, Jesus, let me sit beside her on the sunny bank of salvation, let me sit with my own dear mother. Shall I, Jesus, shall I? Oh, take me home, take me home."

I was amazed, for she had never spoken to me of her mother dying, and here she was announcing it to a crowd of strangers. I thought it odd indeed, but at the same time I felt tears rising for her. Or perhaps not just for her. Had I not lost a mother too? Didn't I want to see her again, and sit with her on a sunny bank? Suddenly I was seized with the desire to make my own way forward to the pen, and to hear that black-clad preacher's whisper assuring me that Jesus would bring me back to my mother — and my father, and Fanny. I could see us all — my brother John, too — in bright sunshine amidst fresh and plentiful grass, a family again. I could feel the gentle touch of my mother's hand on my cheek. I had at that moment entirely forgotten about Polly, and I began to move towards the platform, almost as though my feet were thinking for me. But then I felt a sharp tug on my skirts, and Polly's voice wailing, "Margaret, where are you going?" And I stopped and shook my head and came back to myself.

"Nowhere, sweet girl, I'm right here," I whispered to her, kneeling by her and taking her into my arms. She was shaking with sobs. I knew we must leave, though I longed to speak with Alice, and I gathered her up in my arms and found an opening in the tent through which we made our escape.

The walk back home was long and slow, and I had to carry Polly much of the way, and listen to her complaints when it occurred to her at last that she had never gotten her cake. But after we had dragged ourselves up the steps at Hanover Street and made our way inside, and washed off the dust and mud, I was quite pleased to see her devour a chicken leg for her dinner and ask for more potatoes, and to overhear Mrs. A exclaim so approvingly at her appetite. I suppose she has quite forgotten about all we saw today, for children flit so easily from one thing to another.

As for me, it's not so easy to put it all from my mind. What I saw and heard today, and the vision I had of us all on the sunny bank, they are all still with me and will not let me rest. And Alice — I see her pretty pale face, streaked with tears, the black-clad preacher leaning over her. I hear her voice, sounding like my own, asking Jesus to bring her to her mother, to her home.

From the Observer, July 4, 1807:

BEATRICE IRONSIDE'S BUDGET.

The analysis I made in my last budget of a letter signed An American *might serve as an ample reply to the virulent attack of C, who has honored me with his notice. But the stormy indignation of this exasperated hero is so pleasant, I cannot resist giving it a moment's attention.*

This personage appears to agree that we should have literary works whose object is to ameliorate the present state of taste, but he chooses that they should flatter and cherish the errors of our day! Such a mode of amelioration is gentle, it is true, but can it be efficacious? This, I believe, no one will attempt to assert. It is ridicule *alone that corrects mankind. Banish criticism, satire, and raillery, there will be no longer any salt in society; no longer will absurdities or follies be reformed.*

Alas! poor Beatrice; bitterly are you assailed by the sapient *clamors and blazing philippics of these modern Demosthenes! Must I bend the knee to all that surround me? Must I admire our incontestable excellence and sublimity in every way? Well then, I will chant my recantation.*

Yes, Baltimore is greater than Athens and the federal City than Rome. *Our edifices, our baths, our public gardens are delightful. In fact we are more than ever was, we surpass all that is, we are now greater than we* ever shall be. *Is this enough? Or shall I praise the* yellow fever *too, for this is also a production of the Country.*

TO READERS AND CORRESPONDENTS.

Some time ago, several judicious persons expressed to us a desire that a military memorial *which they had seen should be translated and given to the consideration of the government, as they deemed it of great importance to the country. Its author is a* military stranger *whom the course of events has cast upon America.*

It is our purpose to translate it with the utmost expedition, and until it is completed, we will give in the Observer such parts of it as can be extracted.

Its object is to consider the best mode of defense for the United States. *Our enlightened fellow citizens will decide on the logical and political part of this memorial, which at this juncture is of such importance to every true American. We confine ourselves to observing that it is impossible to write on such a subject with more elegance, precision, and simplicity.*

The work undoubtedly merits the attention of the government; and under this impression, it is in translating it with the utmost speed we shall best prove our regard to the country, and reply to the base calumnies which have been insinuated against us.

Chapter Fifteen: Eliza

I have made a discovery today of a most unsettling nature, one that has caused me seriously to question certain domestic arrangements that have suited my convenience, but which I now fear have subjected my dear child to the utmost danger.

Yesterday evening, in celebration of Independence Day, Father and I took Polly to the fireworks display that had been advertised in the papers, even though it required the expense of hiring a carriage to take us up the Reister's Town turnpike road to Chatsworth—and, once there, the admission price of one dollar for each of us. I was loath to attend, myself, as the crowds and the noise at such spectacles are rarely to my liking, and indeed I had a faint moment of hope when some dark-hued clouds appeared on the horizon just as the sun was setting. But shortly thereafter three rockets could be seen and heard to the north, signaling that the fireworks would go on as planned.

Polly was beside herself with excitement, as she had never seen a fireworks display before, and was imagining something far more spectacular than she would likely witness. The child was barely able to ingest a morsel of food at supper, and I was forced to threaten her with confinement at home if she didn't consume at least a few bites of what was placed before her. No doubt her beloved Margaret had been fanning the flames of her anticipation, for I overheard her telling Polly that while she had never seen fireworks herself, she had been given to understand that they were one of the great wonders of the world, and that some even said there was magic behind them. I was forced to interrupt and set matters straight by revealing that it was chemistry that was responsible for the fire and colors, and that indeed there was no such thing as magic. In light of what I was to discover later that evening, it makes perfect sense that the wench has been beguiling my child with such devilish superstitions!

Polly even begged me to bring Margaret with us to Chatsworth, as we had an extra place in the carriage, but I thought it just as well that I should have my daughter to myself for an hour or two. In any event, we had promised the place to Mr. Godefroy, and the prospect of his company presented itself to me as compensation for the ordeal.

Aside from Polly's fervid desire to witness what she persisted in calling "magic," I felt it wise to put in an appearance at this public display of patriotic sentiment. The announcement in today's Observer that we shall soon be publishing excerpts from Mr. Godefroy's memorial should be enough to satisfy those who discern treachery in the Observer's clear-eyed criticism, but one cannot be too careful in time of war, or near war. So, not only did I subject myself to the noise and fumes of gunpowder, I even affixed a red, white, and blue rosette to the brim of my bonnet, a sign to all that I too am an "An American." And although I have resolved to ignore the base insinuations apparently circulating concerning my friendship with Mr. Godefroy, it occurred to me as well that our appearance together at so wholesome an occasion, in the company of my father and my child, might serve to dispel any unseemly suspicions.

And so we made our halting way up a road jammed with carriages and wagons, some filled with rowdy passengers who had concluded that their patriotism was best displayed by exhibiting the effects of the national fondness for strong drink. Polly was nearly weeping with distress, convinced that we were to miss the display, but Mr. Godefroy gently calmed her, explaining that Monsieur Rosainville — an acquaintance of his, it seems — had assured him he wouldn't begin until all those attending had taken their places. Whether or not this assertion was true I cannot say, but it had the desired effect on Polly, who slipped her small hand into Mr. Godefroy's as though he were her oracle and protector.

"Madame," Mr. Godefroy said to me, once Polly's cries had quieted, "I must thank you, but you did me too great an honor today in the pages of the Observer, with your description of my little memorial. It brought the blood to my face as I read it."

"I spoke only the truth," I told him, feeling some blood rush to my own face. "The words came from my heart." Believing it would be prudent to channel the conversation in some less personal direction, I asked him whether he had found time to peruse the volume of Lord Kames on criticism that he had borrowed from us last week.

"Ah yes!" he said. "I found the section on the emotions caused by fiction most intriguing."

"Indeed! That was the very section I wanted to discuss with you. How extraordinary."

And then we were off, our words colliding into one another's, tumbling out like water from an overflowing well: What did he think of Kames' argument that fiction, because of its vividness, was better able to stir our sympathies than history? Did I agree with Kames' assertion that the emotions aroused by painting could never equal those aroused by fiction? Was that not at least partly contradicted by his later assertion that a truly masterful painting could, like well-wrought poetry, employ bold fictions while still engaging the viewer?

Mr. Godefroy was just beginning to explain that he believed Rousseau, in his second preface to *La Nouvelle Héloise*, had taken a rather different view of the utility of fiction when, alas, the driver turned in at the entrance to Chatsworth, and we became occupied in the process of readying ourselves to disembark. How I relish these conversations with Mr. Godefroy, how I yearn for them to continue and ever regret their termination! But indeed, it seems that we are engaged in one long conversation that is only punctuated by our temporary separations. Even when we are apart, I feel that we are speaking yet, as I ruminate over what he said at our last meeting and compose a response to be delivered at our next.

What a pleasure it is to have found someone whose mind runs in the same course as my own, whose mind indeed seems to be a part of my own, and who never seems to tire of the very subjects I find endlessly fascinating! It has been so long since someone listened to my ideas, and responded to them, as Mr. Godefroy does. Betsy did once, and Father still does occasionally when he has the leisure. Every now and then I feel that I might have a conversation of this sort with Bess Caton. But I don't believe I have ever encountered anyone else — any man other than Father, certainly—with whom I have felt so free to express myself, so unafraid to be mocked as a pedant or berated as a bluestocking. I soon learned not to try to speak with Henry Anderson in such a vein, as there was no surer way to propel him from the room, if not from the house.

"Look, Mamma!" Polly cried after we had purchased our tickets, and a dirt path had at last brought us in sight of a wooden amphitheater specially constructed for tonight's festivities. She was anxious to run ahead to secure us all seats, and Mr. Godefroy kindly offered to accompany her while I stayed back with Father, whose gait can scarcely match the trot of an eager six-year-old.

"An excellent gentleman," Father said when Mr. Godefroy was out of earshot, gesturing towards him with his walking stick.

"Polly seems quite fond of him," I said briskly.

"Ah yes." Father's tone bore a trace of amusement. "Polly."

I had intended to have at least Polly, if not Polly and Father, between myself and Mr. Godefroy, but somehow when we arrived at the row where Polly had chosen us seats, I found myself adjacent to Mr. Godefroy rather than safely at a distance. But as it would have brought even more attention to the situation to attempt to carry out a change in seating, I resigned myself to our proximity.

The spectacle below us was indeed grand, with wooden towers and wheels and platforms, all stoically prepared to sacrifice their brief existence in a burst of pyrotechnics for our entertainment. And off to one side, at what I presume had been determined a safe distance from the coming conflagration, sat a small string orchestra, preparing to fiddle while all around them burned. I noticed with some dismay that the ubiquitous Mr. Webster was once again set to entertain us, albeit unintentionally, with his grimaces and gyrations.

"Is that not your friend Mr. Guy?" Mr. Godefroy said in French, pointing his chin down and to his left.

"Indeed it is," I replied in the same language, recognizing the tailor's black hair and wide-legged, battle-ready stance. He was still down on the lawn—which in truth was more dirt than grass—next to a tall woman that I took to be his wife, and they were conversing animatedly with another couple. I hoped to avoid an encounter, as I expected he would only harangue me about whether I intended to praise his latest *oeuvre*, a rendition of the *Chesapeake* skirmish, in the Observer. "But I don't believe he considers himself my friend."

I felt a tug at my sleeve, followed by Polly's demand that the fireworks start *now*. I explained that it was not within my power to cause them to begin, and told her that she must sit quietly and wait. Her face formed a pout and she crossed her arms.

"But I *have* been waiting!" she complained in a high voice that scraped against my nerves like a nail dragged across a splintery board. "How much longer will it *be?*"

I was mortified that Mr. Godefroy, and who knew how many others seated near us, should witness such unpleasant behavior from my child. "If you cannot wait quietly," I whispered, desperate to calm her, "we shall leave right now."

At this Polly's eyebrows shot up and the corners of her mouth fell, and then the dreaded tears began to flow down her cheeks. What on earth had I said to cause this outburst, I wondered? I tried to hush her, but my efforts only seemed to cause additional tearful freshets and louder wails. Father, too, attempted to soothe her, to no avail.

"Ah, the poor child must be tired!" said Mr. Godefroy, which I thought most generous of him—although it was, in fact, past her usual bedtime. He issued an invitation to Polly to come rest on his lap, and to my surprise she eagerly climbed upon his knees and nestled against his chest, her sobs reduced to quiet whimpers.

A moment later the orchestra took up "Yankee Doodle Dandy," with vocal accompaniment by a relatively subdued Mr. Webster, whose only obvious symptoms of distress were redness in the face, bulging of the eyes, and visibly taut vocal cords at the neck. Then a short man with a protruding belly stepped onto the stage and announced—in a French accent that identified him as Monsieur Rosainville himself—the order of events: a running changing sun, and then a large vertical wheel, followed by the battle of Don Quixote against the windmill, the whole spectacle eventually culminating in a reenactment of the bombardment of Tripoli by the American fleet, at the mention of which a cheer arose from the bellicose crowd. There were the usual promises that nothing resembling this display had ever been witnessed in Baltimore, and the audience must prepare to be astonished, et cetera, et cetera.

Polly, her fatigue and impatience having vanished with no other trace than a slight redness about the eyes and dampness on the
cheek, sat bolt upright throughout this speech, her mouth open.

As the orchestra did its best to conjure a mood of excitement—
despite its small size, inadequate instruments, and poor coordina-
tion—one of those small rockets called a "pigeon" streaked across
the sky from our right and landed on one of the wooden structures, a sun's face painted on the top of a pole. A ring of shoot-
ing fire immediately began to blaze in a circle around the sun's
face, changing colors from yellow to red to blue, accompanied by
rhythmic loud bangs that more or less kept time with the music.

Polly began to bounce up and down on poor Mr. Godefroy's
knees, clapping her hands with delight, her transformation from
hellion to cherub nearly complete. Mr. Godefroy and I exchanged
fond smiles, almost as though we were both the child's proud
parents.

Once the sun's blaze had run its course, there was a brief musical interlude while the next display was readied, a process that
fortunately absorbed Polly's attention and distracted her from
the delay.

"May I ask, Madame Anderson," said Mr. Godefroy in French,
"whether you have yet read that novel I gave you, and what you
think of it?"

"Oh, *Claire d'Albe*! Alas, I've had time only to peruse the first
fifty pages or so, but I'm finding it very much to my liking. The
author's use of language, her powers of description, are most impressive. And the character of Claire—so virtuous in her respect
for her husband, and her affection for her children! And yet, underneath it, her sadness, her sense that something is lacking in
her life. I find the situation intriguing."

"And have you met Frédéric yet?"

"Ah yes, the husband's young cousin. A passionate soul, certainly, but I'm not entirely sure I like him. His expressions are so
blunt, so impolite. An odd sort. I think Claire is very good to put
up with his fits of impudence."

Mr. Godefroy nodded his head and pursed his lips. "Yes, he's
all that you say, but he is more as well. He is impolite because he
has no use for the conventions of society. What is more important
to him are his emotions. The truth, I suppose you might say." He
smiled. "But I will let you discover the story for yourself."

"And so I shall, as soon as I possibly can—if I can tear myself away from your excellent memorial!"

Mr. Godefroy made a modest dismissive gesture just as a loud boom signaled the beginning of the next display. Polly emitted a shrill squeal and buried her face in Mr. Godefroy's coat, her hands pressed to her ears.

"Hush, Polly," I told her. "And you must open your eyes, or you'll miss the fireworks."

"It's too loud!" she said into Mr. Godefroy's chest. He, dear man, only smiled and shrugged tolerantly.

As I watched the sky rockets soaring and sending off blue sparks, and then the vertical wheel spinning in its fiery glory, all while Polly's eyes were clenched tightly shut, I couldn't help but feel some annoyance. We had, after all, undertaken this excursion at her insistence.

Monsieur Rosainville then took the stage to announce a brief intermission during which, he promised, even more spectacular entertainments were to be prepared for us. The orchestra took up a jolly rendition of "The President's March," and people began to rise from their seats to stretch their legs and go off in search of refreshment. Polly, understanding that it was now safe to emerge from the sanctuary of Mr. Godefroy's jacket, blinked and looked around, then pointed to the stall that had appeared on the grass below us, where cakes and ginger beer were being sold. She announced that she wanted some cake, and then began babbling something I couldn't make sense of, about how she hadn't gotten any cake "last time." But before I could remind her that she had refused to finish her supper, and was therefore ineligible for this sort of treat, I heard Mr. Godefroy assuring her that he would be delighted to procure some cake for her.

I tried to protest, but he wouldn't hear of it, and the end of it was that he and I went off in search of Polly's cake, while she remained behind with Father. As we reached the bottom of the steps, I heard my name being called—or rather, I heard myself being addressed as "Mrs. Ironside," an appellation to which I am almost becoming accustomed. I turned to find a portly, redheaded gentleman I vaguely recognized from church, a Mr. Harris if I recalled correctly.

"Well, well," he boomed, "you certainly gave that Mr. 'C' quite a drubbing in your paper today! Who do you think he is?"

I smiled in acknowledgment of what I took to be a tribute. "I couldn't tell you, sir, although I have given the matter some thought. Not Cato, certainly, as *this* 'C' would proscribe all criticism. And not Cupid, either, as he has so little gallantry!"

I didn't add that there was one "C" I suspected, by the far more mundane name of Cork.

We had progressed now to the back of the line that had formed at the ginger beer and cakes stall, with Mr. Harris continuing his loud commentary on today's installment of my Budget.

"Might as well praise the yellow fever!" he laughed. "I liked that one. You're quite right, we surely have our defects in this country, and those who won't admit it are either dishonest or blind."

A lady and gentleman standing in front of us exchanged a concerned look, and the gentleman turned to face us. "I beg your pardon, sir," he said with an exaggerated bow, "but those are rather ill-fitting sentiments to express on the anniversary of our independence, and at a time when our sacred liberty is under threat."

Mr. Harris crossed his arms and jutted out his chin. "And does not that sacred liberty include the right to express one's sentiments, whether others believe them ill-fitting or not? Is that not what our heroes fought and died for?" He turned to me and shook his head. "You're quite right, Mrs. Ironside, there's no use trying to reason with these people."

I noticed that others in our vicinity had grown quiet and were stealing surreptitious glances at us.

"As it would not become me to engage in argument with a lady," the man said icily to Mr. Harris, "I will continue to address myself to you, sir. But the views expressed in the paper that *she* is associated with—" Here he shot a cutting look in my direction. "They are not the views of a patriot, and anyone endorsing such calumnies should be ashamed of himself!"

Mr. Harris took a deep breath and drew himself up, much like a large cobra preparing an attack.

"Please, gentlemen!" I cried in alarm, not knowing what might happen next. But then I stopped, uncertain what more to say. "I beg you ... I beg you to remember there are ladies present."

They continued to stare murderously at one another for another second or two, and then Mr. Harris, his eyes narrowed to slits, turned to me and bowed. "If you'll excuse me, Mrs. Anderson," he said. "I find I've quite lost my appetite."

With that he turned and strode back toward his seat, leaving Mr. Godefroy and myself facing the irate Defender of Our Nation's Honor, still trembling with anger.

After a moment's awkward silence, Mr. Godefroy quietly suggested to me, in French, that we needn't both stay there to obtain Polly's cake, and that perhaps I would be more at my ease back at my seat. Although I was reluctant to leave him alone to face the wrath I had somehow managed to engender, I was relieved by this suggestion and accepted gratefully.

"But where are the tents?" Polly asked, incomprehensibly, after I had returned and explained that her cake would be arriving in a few moments.

"Tents? I haven't the slightest idea what you're talking about."

"Last time," she said, looking around at the clearing where the amphitheater had been erected, "there were tents."

I told her we had never been here before, and that she must be confusing the place with something else, although I couldn't imagine what. And then Mr. Godefroy arrived with her cake, which she greeted with cries of delight. I was delighted, as well, to see that he had returned apparently unscathed.

"Thank you for rescuing me," I whispered to him as Monsieur Rosainville mounted the stage to announce that the second half of the program was about to begin. "Did that man cause you any further trouble?"

"Oh, he and his wife said a few more foolish things." He waved a dismissive hand. "But I pretended not to understand them."

Ah, the prerogative of the foreigner, I thought, as more wooden structures were wheeled and dragged into place below — including a figure on horseback that I presumed was meant to be Don Quixote, and a windmill at which he would no doubt soon be tilting. I took Polly on my lap now, both to save Mr. Godefroy's coat and trousers from the cake crumbs she was liberally spewing, and also to impart to her the rudiments of the story of the great Spanish knight. I was pleased that this next conflagration at least afforded me the opportunity to acquaint my child with one of the foremost works of Western literature.

I had only just introduced the character of Sancho Panza when sparks and rockets began to boom and fly, illuminating both Don

Quixote and his windmill and silencing my narrative. Although Polly immediately put her hands over her ears (despite the fact that one hand still held the remnants of her cake), she mustered the courage to keep her eyes open throughout the display. Indeed her eyes were quite wide, and I could see tiny reflections of the bursts of fire in her pupils. Perhaps, I thought as I watched her rapt expression, it hadn't been such a mistake to come to this spectacle tonight. There are times when I look at Polly and am so overcome with affection that tears rise to my eyes and I am seized with an urge to embrace her. This was one such time. Not wanting to distract her from the fireworks, however, I contented myself with brushing the cake crumbs from her hair.

The charred remains of Don Quixote were taken away, and the orchestra launched into military marches as preparations were made for the grand finale depicting the bombardment of Tripoli. Wooden ships and battlements were brought into place.

"This will be the best of all!" I told Polly as she wriggled to and fro on my knees.

A moment later a loud boom signaled the opening salvo, and then came the squeals of several rockets simultaneously ascending skyward. More booms and flashes followed, and showers of many-colored sparks fell to the ground. The volume and multitude of explosions surpassed anything that had been on the program until now. Cheers arose from the crowd, and a few fevered cries of "Death to the British!"

The British, of course, had nothing to do with our bombardment of Tripoli, and I shuddered when I recalled that during that attempt to stanch the depredations of the Barbary pirates three years ago, an American warship packed with explosives prematurely erupted in fireworks similar to the ones now being displayed for our amusement, killing all aboard. Would the crowd be cheering thus, I wondered, if real British rockets were bursting over Baltimore's harbor, threatening our homes and our lives? It was one thing to take a stand against Tripoli, and quite another to take on the world's pre-eminent military power. In either case, I could derive no pleasure from a display that mimicked all too realistically the horrors unleashed by war.

I now glanced at Polly, expecting to see that same expression of wonder that had gladdened my heart a few moments before, but instead her face was a mask of terror. As more booms and squeals and sparks surrounded us, seeming to come ever closer, she opened her mouth and released a scream so loud that it managed to penetrate the din. Next I knew she was sobbing hysterically, catching at my dress, and saying she wanted to go home.

"But it's only fireworks, Polly!" I cried. "There's nothing to be afraid of."

"No, no, no!" she yelled, shaking her head and pounding at me with her fists. "I want to go! I hate this place."

She went on in that vein for another minute or two, again saying something about "last time," and that she never wanted to come here again. I looked at Father and Mr. Godefroy, and we all signaled our agreement that we should make a hasty departure, even though the spectacle was not yet over. We had, despite the competition from the bombardment of Tripoli, managed to attract a good deal of attention, and I suspected our neighbors would not be disappointed to see us depart.

Mr. Godefroy valiantly carried the still sobbing Polly down the path leading away from the amphitheater, through the murky darkness, and after some long minutes we managed to find our carriage and driver in the midst of a jumble of nearly identical vehicles, whereupon we bundled ourselves inside.

"Whatever did you mean," I said to Polly when she had calmed down a bit, although her breath was still coming in little catches, "about 'last time'? I told you, we were never there before."

"No, not with you." She sniffed, and Mr. Godefroy offered her his handkerchief, as he had done several times before. "I was there with Margaret."

"With Margaret? Whatever for?"

"There were tents." She rubbed an eye. "And they said there was cake, but I didn't get any."

I looked at Father and Mr. Godefroy, then leaned closer and took Polly's hand. "Who said there was cake?" I kept my voice quiet and even, so as not to alarm her. "Who was there?"

"I don't know. A lot of people." She yawned. "First they were in the tents, and they were crying and rolling on the ground and hugging each other. And then they all came out, and there was a man who was talking about Jesus, and then some girls were lying on the ground and they were crying and yelling and making noises. One of them kept saying she wanted someone to take her home. And I told Margaret I wanted to go home too, because I was scared."

"Of course you were, you poor dear!" I put my arm about her and drew her to me, then turned to Father.

"It must have been one of those camp meetings," I whispered to him in a tone I struggled to keep calm. "She took the child to a camp meeting! Without telling me, without asking me. It's one thing to tell the girl that fireworks are magic, and nonsense like that, but to expose her to the Lord knows what ... I cannot, cannot allow it!"

"Now, now," Father said quietly, although I could see concern in his expression. "We mustn't judge before we know all the facts. There may be some innocent explanation. Please, Eliza, let me talk to the girl."

I closed my eyes and took a breath while Polly leaned over and put her head in my lap, exhausted. I stroked her hair, and within moments her breathing had become deep and regular, and I knew she was asleep. I turned to Mr. Godefroy, thinking that I would make some apology for Polly's behavior, but as soon as I opened my mouth he put a finger to his lips, and I could see from his eyes that no explanation was necessary.

Indeed, the only explanation that appears to be necessary is one from Margaret, for I can see no excuse for what she did. Yes, Polly seems to love the girl, but children have been known to love things that aren't good for them—cakes and sweets, for instance. I have forced myself to overlook Margaret's deficiencies, her general surliness and her constant sketching when she should be attending to her duties. But there is a limit. Exposing my child to scenes that terrify her, and to outlandish ideas that may infect and pollute her mind—that I cannot, and will not, overlook. I promised Father that he could speak to Margaret first, but I must satisfy myself that nothing like this will ever happen again. And it seems to me that the only way to ensure that is to give the girl her notice.

From the American and Commercial Daily Advertiser (Baltimore), July 8, 1807:

A grand Historical PAINTING by GUY, representing the late atrocious attack of the Leopard on the Chesapeake, and which was exhibited on the 4ᵗʰ of July at Wharfe's tavern, will remain there during this day for the gratification of those who may be inclined to view it.

From Spectacles (Baltimore), July 18, 1807:

The author of the communication relative to the "Observer" is informed that I will not fill my sheet with remarks upon so stale and so dry a subject. The vindication of GUY was admitted to serve a man of genius, and to expose a most uncharitable but impotent attempt to injure him. That object having been effected, there is nothing in the "Observer" sufficiently interesting to attract my further attention.

Chapter Sixteen: Maragaret

As I had some unexpected liberty yesterday afternoon — Mrs. A having decided to try to teach Polly her letters again, and Mrs. Morris for once not having any need of me — I decided to do something I've wanted to do ever since Polly and I found ourselves at that camp meeting, weeks ago now: I went off to see if I could find my old friend Alice. I didn't know if she still lived in that same room at Mrs. Brooks', down at the Point, but as I knew no other place where she might be, I thought I might as well try there.

I've had reason to regret happening upon that camp meeting, as it nearly cost me my job. The Doctor was kind enough about it, understanding that it had been an accident, me and Polly going there, and that I meant nothing by it, and that aside from a bit of a fright the girl had suffered no harm. But Mrs. A was furious, scolding me as though I'd let Polly wander into the path of a runaway horse, or pushed her into the harbor to see if she would sink. I protested that I would never do anything to put Polly in danger, and indeed there had been no danger at the camp meeting — that the people there were all good Christians, whether or not they prayed in the way Mrs. A happened to approve of. But she would have none of it. I believe Mrs. A would have sent me packing if it hadn't been for the Doctor. And I was so angry myself that I had half a mind to quit, right then and there, even though I had no place to go and no prospect of finding another position in service. The only thing that stopped me was the thought of leaving Polly.

And so we've managed to go on, Mrs. A and I, though there's no love lost between us. But then, there never was. The main thing that's changed is that Mrs. A is spending a bit more time with Polly, I suppose because she fears I'm a bad influence, and who knows where I might take the child next. Indeed, I'm forbidden from taking her from the house without first securing Mrs. A's permission. It's clear that Polly prefers to spend her time with me, playing and going out for walks and drawing, rather than being drilled on her letters and numbers by Mrs. A. But I do have more time to myself now, although Mrs. Morris is generally apt to fill it with chores like polishing the silver or ironing the table cloths.

But as I said, yesterday afternoon she could find nothing she needed me to do, and so I set off down Market Street towards the bridge across the Falls to Old Town, and then on down York Street to Fells Point. It was a lovely warm summer's day, and I could see one of those volunteer regiments that are everywhere these days, practicing their drills on the green by the bridge. The young men looked so fine, wearing their regimental colors and sporting feathers in their caps and silver swords at their hips—at least, those who could afford such things. There were some that not only had no uniforms to wear but also lacked weapons, and had to pretend they were loading muskets and bringing them to their shoulders to aim and fire.

Mr. Cork wrote something for Spectacles mocking the volunteers, or some of them, for looking so ragged and having no weapons, but when he read it to me at the tavern last Saturday, I told him just what I thought, which is that it was cruel and unfair. I said the young men were brave to be risking their lives to defend us all, and it wasn't their fault if they couldn't afford uniforms and guns, and that gentlemen like him who *could* afford such things would do better to join up themselves rather than make fun of those who did. It all just came out without my thinking, and afterwards I was worried I'd offended him, for he just frowned and said nothing for a moment. But then he nodded and said perhaps I was right, and he hadn't seen it that way before. He looked me right in the eye and smiled and told me that he'd never really known anyone like me, and it seemed he meant it in a good way, so I smiled back and told him I'd never really known anyone like him, either. We sat there just smiling at one another for what seemed like a good minute, and my heart started beating fast, and I entirely lost my appetite, which almost never happens with me. When it came time to part, and we were in the street, I hoped he might kiss me. He didn't, but he told me I should call him James. I must remember that: James. It seems odd, after thinking of him as Mr. Cork for so long, but I expect I'll get used to it.

If I see him again, that is. That very morning, there was a notice in Spectacles saying they would publish nothing more about the Observer. Mrs. A had been in quite a dudgeon about it at breakfast, railing on at the poor Doctor for nigh on fifteen minutes, for it seems a friend of hers had wanted them to publish something he'd written taking her side. For two weeks ago there was something in Spectacles accusing her of knowing nothing about art, which riled her no end, and then last week there was something in another paper, Moonshine, mocking her for fawning over Europeans and despising Americans — something I happen to know Mr. Cork wrote, though he didn't call himself "Bickerstaff." But if Spectacles won't publish more about Mrs. A, and if Moonshine does the same, I don't know that Mr. Cork will want to continue our arrangement — him paying for my lessons with Mr. Guy, and our suppers together.

I asked Mr. Cork, I mean James, if it what the notice said was true, but he only shrugged. He said Mr. Harmer had decided that what Mrs. A wanted more than anything else was attention, and that perhaps the best way to silence her was simply to ignore her, as you might a whining child. I could see how they might be right about that, but I didn't say that of course. Instead I said again that I thought there was something afoot between her and that Mr. Godefroy, for he always seems to be coming round the house these days. And he said, well, I should keep an eye out, but that it had to be more than a mere kiss on the hand to make it worth him writing about it.

I was thinking about all this as I walked along, and so absorbed in my thoughts I suddenly realized I had gone right past Apple Alley and had to retrace my steps. When I reached it again, I turned left and walked the two blocks past Dulany and then Smith Street, doing my best to keep my skirts from the muck and animal leavings that littered the narrow space between the houses on either side.

My stomach began to turn from the smell, and I thought I might cast up my accounts right there in the alley, though I don't recall feeling so sickened by the place when I lived there. I suppose I've gone soft, living for nigh on a year now in a part of town that generally doesn't carry so strong an odor. But as I drew closer to Mrs. Brooks' door with its peeling blue paint, I felt myself begin to tremble and sweat. I don't know if it was the smell, or the prospect of seeing Alice again, or the memories that suddenly hit me like a blow to the head: my father and Fanny moaning in their last hours, in that upstairs room at the back, their skin and the whites of their eyes all yellow, and the blood coming from places it wasn't supposed to, and me not having the power to stop any of it. Whatever it was, I had to lean against the wall for a minute and catch my breath.

I was about to turn around and go back, no longer remembering why I had thought it so important to see Alice, but just then the blue door opened and I found myself face to face with Mrs. Brooks herself, carrying a jordan full of someone's piss, which I suppose she meant to throw out in the alley.

"Well, my soul, if it isn't Maggie McKenzie!" she greeted me, setting down her burden and wiping her hands on her apron, which was torn and stained. Next I knew she had thrown her thick arms about me and was clapping me on the back. "Where have you been keeping yourself, child?"

I told her I was in service to a family in town, and she clapped me again and said, "Oh, a mopsqueezer, are you? Well, that's very grand now, you've come up in the world! But then, you did that before too, didn't you, for those French?"

I managed to tell her yes, though I was still feeling unsteady, and the memory of the Legrands didn't help. Mrs. Brooks must have seen something in my face, for she bustled me inside, her piss pot forgotten by the door, and bade me sit in a chair in the kitchen, which was very warm but at least smelled of boiled potatoes, and that was better than what the air smelled of outside. She took out a pitcher and poured some beer into a mug and handed it to me, saying I must be tired from my long walk. Evidently she thought I'd come to see her, not Alice, and as she was being so kind I hadn't the heart to tell her different.

"I suppose you've come to settle up with me at last," she said after I'd taken a sip or two of beer, her plump reddened hands folded on the rough wood table in front of us. Ah, I thought, that's why she's being so kind. I had entirely forgotten that I still owed her rent, and that it must have been at least three dollars.

I told her I had but fifty cents with me but that she was welcome to have it, and that I would bring the rest as soon as I could. Her mouth turned down a bit at that, and she said something about how I must be making good wages, and I should be sure to pay my debts before spending them on ribbons and fripperies. But when I brought the fifty cents from my basket, she took it right up and slipped it into the pocket she had at her waist, and smiled and said she expected she would see me again soon.

It was then that I asked if Alice still lived there. Mrs. Brooks sighed and cast her eyes to the ceiling and said, yes, the poor romp was still about, and might well be in her room upstairs, as she'd come in very late last night. I was surprised to hear that, and even more surprised to hear Mrs. Brooks call her a romp, after what Alice had said at the camp meeting.

Walking up the familiar slanted, creaking stairs, I had the fleeting thought that Papa and Fanny would be at the top to greet me, healthy and alive and waiting to see what I'd brought for dinner. When I got to Alice's door, I did my best to keep my eyes away from the door across the hall that used to be ours.

"I told you, leave me be!" was Alice's response to my knock, in a voice that sounded more animal than human. "I want no more of your gum, you old dog!"

But then I said my name, and the door flew open. When she saw me she cried out and threw her arms about me, and I was glad I hadn't turned back. But after she released me and I got a good look at her, I saw that her left eye was swollen and purplish. I said nothing, just sat myself on the one chair in the room and put my basket on the little table next to it, and Alice took the bed. I told her I had seen her at the camp meeting last month.

"Oh, *that*," she said, as though it had been years ago. She leaned back on her elbows on the bed and crossed one thin bare leg over the other. The bedclothes were rumpled and she was wearing nothing more than her shift, which only reached her knees. "That preacher said the Lord would provide if I kept to the straight path, but apparently he forgot to tell the Lord about the arrangement."

I couldn't help but laugh. I was sad she hadn't kept to the straight and narrow, but also relieved to find she was still the same Alice. "You're out on the streets again, then?"

"I was working Oakum Bay last night." She pointed to the rope strands on the table that sailors give to girls to untangle and sell to the papermakers. She drew herself up a little straighter, as though gathering some pride. "I don't always get just the oakum, of course. Most of them give me money outright. And look what I bought, two days ago."

She sprang up from the bed and took a pink muslin frock from a peg by the door and held it up against herself, turning this way and that to show it off.

"Very nice," I said, and it was, nicer than anything I could afford. I tried to smile, but then I looked down at my hands in my lap, remembering what she'd said at the camp meeting. "You said your mother died, when you were fifteen. And that you backslided. You said you wanted Jesus to take you home, to a sunny bank where you could sit with her."

I'd thought of those words so many times since I'd heard her say them, it was like they were written inside my head. I'd imagined talking to Alice about her mother, and telling her about mine.

Alice put the frock back on its peg. "I told you, I tried," she said, her back to me as she leaned her hand against the wall and bowed her head, "but there was no way. I tried slop work, but I'm no good with a needle. And then I tried buying some cherries at the market and selling them down by the harbor, but at the end of a long day I had only a few pennies to show for it." She turned to me and crossed her arms, and the corners of her lips curled upwards. "The sailors were more interested in my notch than my cherries, truth to tell, and willing to pay more for it."

I felt my face grow warm, for I've gotten out of the habit of hearing people speak so plainly of their private parts. "Is that how you got the black eye?" I asked. "From one of your sailors?"

Alice's smile vanished. "Not this time. It was a damned old dog of a night watchman, who said he'd haul me off to jail if I didn't service him. Took his filthy Thomas out right there in the street and shook it at me!"

"And you said no?"

"I called him a fathead and told him I had to work for my living, and charge all comers for my favors." She touched the skin around her eye, testing it. "I reckon I shouldn't have called him a fathead. Anyway, I got away before he did too much damage."

She smiled. "His head wasn't the only part of him that was fat, lucky for me, and I could run a deal faster than he could.

"But tell me," she said, floating down onto the bed once more, her white chemise blowing out around her like the sail of a ship, "tell me where you've been, and what you're doing. You're in service still? With that nice old doctor who came here, that day?"

I nodded, and silently thanked her for the way she'd said "that day," as though the memory was still sharp for her as well, even though it was my kin that had been taken.

"Must be pleasant," Alice said. "Getting all your meals, and a bed, and money on top of that. And not having to bend over for all and sundry."

I shrugged. "The money's not bad, but you wouldn't like it. You don't have to bend over, exactly, but you have to do some bowing, and biting of your tongue, and smiling and saying 'Yes, ma'am' when you feel like telling them to go to the devil." I couldn't imagine Alice taking in silence the kind of huffing I'd gotten from Mrs. A after the camp meeting. "But you'll never guess," I said, wanting to brighten the conversation, "I'm taking drawing lessons!"

Her mouth flew open and her eyes grew wide. "You never are!" she cried. "I remember now, you used to draw sometimes, you and Fanny." She shifted her weight to the edge of the bed and leaned forward and touched my arm. "Oh, Maggie, could you draw me? I've always wanted a drawing of myself."

Mr. Guy has only just started to teach me how to draw faces, and he's been so distracted during our last couple of lessons he's hardly taught me anything at all—for he's lately developed a potion of some sort that he swears is a cure for the toothache, and every few minutes there's a knock at the door from someone in desperate need of it. But Alice looked so excited and earnest I didn't have the heart to say no. And I'd brought some charcoal and paper in my basket, as I always do when I go out, just in case I see something I want to sketch. "I don't know that it would be any good."

"Of course it would—I remember you drew a chair once, and I almost thought I could sit in it, it was that lifelike! And I'm sure it will be quite the best drawing anyone has ever done of *me*," she said with her saucy smile, which I was sure meant that no one had ever undertaken to draw her before.

I had her sit on the bed near the window, although it was so grimy that the light coming through wasn't much, and she picked up a comb from the table and ran it through her hair, which was loose about her shoulders. I asked her to turn her head to one side so that I wouldn't have to draw her nose straight on, which is the hardest. I also thought it best not to have the damaged eye in the drawing. But Alice said no, she wanted her whole face in the drawing, not just one side of it. I suppose she'd forgotten about the eye.

I started with those light little strokes, the ones like feathers, that Mr. Guy has told me to use, and the upside-down egg shape he says I must use for faces, then the faint lines where the mouth and nose and eyes would go. I started with the mouth, and it was a pleasure, as I'd always found myself staring at Alice's mouth — the middle of her upper lip like two tiny mountains, and the way the corners sloped down but didn't make her look like she was frowning — and now I could do it without seeming rude. It was lovely to see that mouth taking shape on my paper, where nothing had been just a moment before — like magic, I always think when I see it happen.

When it came time to sketch in the eyes, I decided there was no need to draw the bruise around the left one, for it would be gone in a week, and why should the only drawing that Alice had of herself include a reminder of such unpleasantness? So I drew both of the eyes the way they usually look, dark and cat-like, slanting slightly upwards, with almost no crease at the lids.

I had to keep telling her to sit still, for she kept yawning and shifting about and scratching places on her body, saying she couldn't help it, she had bites from the bedbugs. But she did her best. You could see she was pleased about the whole thing, saying she felt like quite the grand lady.

"How much do they cost you, these drawing lessons?" she asked while I was trying to do her nose, starting with a dark little flying bird shape for the nostrils, as Mr. Guy has told me to, and then shading the rest in. It wasn't coming well, and I had to fish in my basket for the gum to rub some of it out.

"I don't rightly know what they cost," I said absently. "It's not me that pays for them."

"That Doctor pays for the lessons, then, on top of your wages?"

"No, not him. Another gentleman."

She sat up and cocked her head, and I had to ask her to move it back into the position I was drawing. "And what gentleman might *that* be?" she asked. "And what's that blush coming to your cheeks?"

I put a hand to my face. "He's a friend, that's all."

She cocked an eyebrow. "And what does this *friend* expect in return?"

"It's not like that, and can you stay still please? But sometimes he wants to know things about my boss — the Doctor's daughter. So I tell him things I happen to see and hear, and he pays for the lessons."

"And the drawing lessons are a kind of payment, then, for what you tell him?"

The nose wasn't coming, so I moved on to the hair. "It started like that. But now I'd do it even if he wasn't paying for the lessons. She's a sorry hussy, she is, and James has good reasons for wanting to know things about her."

"Ah, *James*, is it?" Her mouth was smiling now, which wasn't how I'd intended to draw it, and I had to ask her to stop talking and keep her lips together. But she couldn't do it for long. "And just how friendly are you with this gentleman?"

I put down the paper and charcoal. Why not tell her, I thought, for I've wanted to tell someone, and there was no one else to tell. I had thought I'd come here to talk to Alice about my mother, but now it seemed that what had led me here was James.

"The truth is ..." I took a breath and swallowed. "I'm very fond of him. I've never felt like this about anyone before. I don't know, I suppose I love him." My voice was so low I wasn't sure she'd heard me.

"Do you now?" Alice crossed her arms and shook her head at me, suddenly serious. "Careful, Maggie. It's all very well to take your amusement where you can find it, but never give your heart to a gentleman. You'll only get it back in pieces. And you'll end up with a swelling in your belly as well, like as not."

"It's not like that between James and me!"

"Hasn't he tried to wap you yet?"

I shook my head. "He hasn't even kissed me."

"No? Well, then, it's clear that all he's interested in is the spying you're doing for him. Sounds to me like your mistress is the one he's sweet on."

I felt like throwing my charcoal at her, I was that riled. How could she know what was between James and me? To say that he was sweet on Mrs. A! And yet I'd asked myself a million times why James has scarcely even touched me, when the men I knew down here at the Point used to try to put their hands up my skirts when given half a chance, even one of Papa's old messmates did that once. It seemed James liked me well enough. Did he not think I was pretty enough for him?

"If you want this drawing finished," I said to Alice, "you'd best get back to how you were."

"All right, all right then. No need to get your back up, I was only giving you my honest opinion. Is this how I was?"

I started sketching again, and I found myself drawing Alice's left eye just the way it really looked, though I didn't have the colors I needed to do the job right. But I put in the puffiness, and started shading around it. Why not show her as she truly was, I thought? Hold a mirror up to her and blast away her imaginings of herself as a fine lady, simply because I was sketching her face, and force her to see that she was nothing more than a two-bit whore who'd had a bad night? The strokes I was making on the paper were thicker now, and darker.

Then I heard myself saying something that surprised me, for I don't know where it came from. "The truth is, James treats me the way he would treat a lady. Gentlemen don't go about wapping ladies they're fond of, that's not how they do things." I thought of that Adelaide story, and how shocked James was about the hot tears falling on her breast. "The truth is, he wants to marry me."

Alice leaned forward, her eyes wide—or at least the good one—and her mouth open. "*Marry* you? He's asked you, then?"

"Not in so many words. But we have an understanding." Quickly, I started rolling the paper I'd been sketching on and putting it back in the basket and told Alice I needed to go.

"Is it finished?" she said, reaching for the drawing. "Can I see it?"

I snatched it away and told her no, it needed more work, and that I'd bring it back when it was done.

"Ooh, make it soon, then!" She came and put her arms about me, and drew me to her, though I stood stock still. "It's so good of you, Maggie, to come and see me. I've missed you, you know. And I never thought anyone would ever do my portrait!" She stood back and looked at me, smiling. "To think that our old Maggie is taking drawing lessons, and is to be married to a gentleman. I can hardly believe it."

I wondered if she meant it, or if she was saying she *didn't* believe it. "My mother took drawing lessons, you know," I said, "when she was a girl. Her family had the money for it, then. And anyway, we've got no titles in this country, and no aristocrats. Anyone can rise if they want to, it doesn't matter what you were born to. That's what I believe, and James too."

"Does he! Well, that's very modern of him, very modern indeed." She crossed her arms and cocked her head. "But if I were you, just to be sure, I'd give him a taste of my wares. Not the whole store, mind you, just enough to make him want more. Let him feel one of your boobies, or even put a finger or two in your notch. If he's a normal man and not a Miss Molly, that should put the seal on it for you."

"Oh, it's sealed, don't you trouble yourself about that," I told her. "And he's no Molly."

She shrugged. "Suit yourself. Only don't forget about the portrait! Promise you'll bring it back?"

"Next week. I promise." Although the truth was, I only wanted to get away from her and what she was saying about James, and away from Apple Alley and all its smells and memories.

"All right, then, I'll be counting the days." She put her arms about me again, and I stood stiff, but she didn't seem to notice. "And if you should ever find yourself in trouble—you know, because of that gentleman of yours—you come down and see your old friend Alice. Because I know a thing or two about solving problems like that." She leaned closer and lowered her voice, though there was no chance of us being overheard. "But mind you, come as soon as you suspect something, as the longer you wait the more trouble you'll have fixing it."

I bristled even more and told her I was sure I wouldn't be having any such problems, and quickly took my leave. I told myself I shouldn't blame her for thinking James would get me with child and leave me, for that's surely the way it's been for *her*. But I couldn't help it, I was furious, and I fear I muttered to myself like a madwoman all the way back to Hanover Street.

When I got to my room, I took the drawing of Alice from my basket and almost threw it into the fire. But at the last moment I stopped and looked at it closely. The fact is, it has the makings of a good likeness — there's something about the eyes and mouth that's both sad and hopeful at the same time. I began to think that if I took out the bruises I'd begun to put in and got the nose right, Mr. Guy would see it as proof that I'm ready to do portraits and not just sketch the flowers and bowls of fruit that he sets me to week after week. So I drew back from the fire and instead slipped the drawing into the leather portfolio he gave me, which I bring to his studio every Saturday.

It's true I promised it to Alice, and if she saw herself the way she really looks perhaps it would be enough to make her change her ways. But then again, it might only rile her. And anyway, the portrait is likely to be of more use to me than it ever could be to her.

From the Observer, July 25th, 1807:

BEATRICE IRONSIDE'S BUDGET.

A COALITION really terrible *has burst forth against Mistress Be-atrice. The parts have been distributed, the attacks combined, to harass her as if from every side.*

A mischievous genius expected to derive a double advantage from this stratagem: that of multiplying in appearance *the clamors against the Observer, and by concealing himself, of escaping the contempt which such ridiculous attacks could not fail to excite in all judicious minds.*

But notwithstanding his various metamorphoses, I recognize in the fury of his onset, in the coarseness of his language, in the affectation and folly of his images; in short, in the deformity of his various shapes, the pitiful buffoon who had already declared that he would annihilate the Observer with the fillip of his finger.

It may be judged if the Observer can possibly escape his indignation when this paper has the misfortune of being edited by a WOMAN, *and by a* woman *so impious as not to recognize his literary supremacy, and when those who contribute to the Observer have the audacity to write without a* permit from this pretended *viceroy of Apollo!*

When the Observer had occasion to speak of the fine arts, it said what no one amongst us in possession of their senses could contest. Did it not speak of Messrs. Guy and Groombridge in terms which would have flattered men of great reputation in Europe?

But our detractors, so jealous of national glory, have not hesitated at turning our MILITIA into ridicule *in one of their late numbers; when the zeal of these volunteers is so praise worthy; when it is so neces-sary to offer them every species of encouragement; when it is so just to testify our gratitude to them. This has sufficiently proved to every* true American *that the motive of Spectacles, and of the whole set, was no other than to injure the Observer.*

It is not without the extremest repugnance *I have descended to reply to such adversaries, but I thought it proper to make known to these wretched enemies that WOMAN as she is, Mistress Beatrice does not fear their logic, and their rhetoric highly amuses her.*

Chapter Seventeen: Eliza

Ah, it is very Arcadia here, the air fresh and the breezes mild, the cows lowing and the birds chirping, the dogs and horses frolicking like the proverbial lions and lambs! All that is missing are some picturesque shepherds and shepherdesses to make the summer idyll complete. I suppose the local rustics will have to do in their stead, although with their grimy faces and muddy boots they bear faint resemblance to the Silvius and Phoebe of time-honored lore.

What a pleasant surprise it was to receive Betsy's note, some two weeks ago, inviting us all to spend a month at Springfield! I had nearly abandoned hope, but I suppose even the bucolic charms of these surroundings begin to pall without stimulating companionship, which Betsy can hardly find in the bosom of her family. And it was gratifying to see that despite her elevation in the world, she still values the company of an old friend. I can't imagine that Mr. Patterson encouraged the overture, given my persistence in editing the Observer and the matter of our still-outstanding debt. But no doubt his benevolent consort took the opposite position on the matter, for Mrs. Patterson, dear soul, has ever been my champion.

As I expected, Father refused to abandon the Dispensary on the very cusp of the sickly season, but he insisted that Polly and I should accept the invitation. We are no longer expecting an imminent British invasion—the drumbeats of war having given way to the stately minuet of diplomacy—but the seasonal specter of disease looms as large as always, or perhaps larger. There have been alarming reports of influenza outbreaks everywhere along the coast from New York to Savannah, and Father fears it is just a matter of time before the scourge strikes Baltimore. I was loath to leave him at such a time, but I could see that he was right: it would be far preferable for Polly to spend a few weeks in a healthy situation, as she recently suffered a brief but acute bout of fever that gave us quite a scare. The child appears to have a naturally weak constitution, and I fear that she is destined for a lifetime of ill health, especially if she persists in her habit of preferring cakes and sweets to real nourishment.

And truth be told, I have not been in a healthy state myself, although my affliction has been more mental than physical. Much as I have enjoyed my modicum of fame in our city—the nods and smiles that greet me when I am out in the world, and the various encomiums I receive in the post, which modesty largely forbids me from publishing—I confess to having been oppressed by the virulent attacks against me and the Observer by that self-appointed censor, that self-important imbecile, that self-satisfied ignoramus who formerly went by the name of Bickerstaff and now adopts any number of fanciful appellations in a multitude of scurrilous periodicals, but whom I will ever recognize as none other than the despicable James Cork. All this continuing nonsense about my supposed lack of patriotism and my appalling ignorance!

I confess I was for several weeks so agitated by his onslaught that my sleep was much disturbed and my appetite little better than Polly's. I suspect Father was at least as worried about my own well-being as about hers when he urged us to flee to the countryside.

I was fatigued as well from the endless round of editorial duties that I have had to perform, week after unrelenting week, even whilst translating Mr. Godefroy's memorial—which, as the work progressed, I began to realize was somewhat less lucid in its composition than I had originally thought. I do not complain of this, as I have taken great pleasure in our *tête-a-têtes*, puzzling over *le mot juste* in English for this or that French term. Moreover, I have had the satisfaction of performing a vital service for the public in disseminating parts of the memorial, which will resound further when the entire work is published by Mr. Hill in the fall.

Gratifying as the undertaking was, it took its toll, and I yearned to recuperate amidst the pastoral splendors of Springfield.

At first I couldn't fathom how I might contrive to leave the city without suspending the publication of the Observer, which would no doubt cause consternation among our subscribers, some of whom have paid their bills and rightly expect a new number to arrive at their doorsteps every Saturday. But Father pointed out that I had at least two more installments of Mr. Godefroy's memorial already translated, as well as the continuation of his own essay on quarantine and perhaps a dozen other submissions lying about that I have not yet found room for in the paper—because I felt they were not of the highest quality, it's true. But, as Father urged, a slight lowering of my editorial standards could be justified under the circumstances.

At length my exhaustion served to convince me that he was right. And as Mr. Patterson was sure to have a regular courier carrying letters from Springfield to Baltimore and back, I could avail myself of that service to send each number's articles to the printer before the end of the week. If I brought Margaret along to look after Polly, as Father urged, I realized I might have the rest and refreshment my mind and body so sorely craved.

Perhaps most pressing of all, I yearned for some undisturbed peace in which to finish my translation of the remarkable novel brought to my attention by Mr. Godefroy, *Claire d'Albe*. I've found that he was correct, that the accusations of immorality leveled against it were quite mistaken. Now that I have read it through, I am acutely sensible of the urgency of bringing the tale in all its beauty and poignancy to a broader audience. Surely once Americans are able to read the novel for themselves, they will see it for what it is—at one and the same time a sympathetic account of the uncontrollable passion between Claire and Frédéric, and a warning against the perils of succumbing to such illicit desires.

I have spoken of the novel so often to Betsy since I arrived here a few days ago that she prevailed upon me to relinquish it long enough for her to read it herself—without the knowledge of her parents, of course. I have been eager to hear Betsy's thoughts on the book, and to have someone with whom I could discuss my own—someone other than Mr. Godefroy, that is, for I confess that some of my thoughts are rather too delicate for me to deliver to that particular repository.

And so I was pleased that this morning after breakfast, Betsy and I found ourselves alone on the piazza at the side of the house—a sprawling brick edifice graced by columns of the Tuscan order—not far from where Polly was playing on the grass with Betsy's little brothers Henry and Octavius. Margaret was keeping watch over their game, as I had instructed, to guard against Polly's overtiring herself or the boys becoming too rough with her, as has sometimes been their wont. I took a chair with its back to the frolicking cherubs, the better to concentrate my attention on Betsy's commentary on *Claire d'Albe*. Yesterday evening she told me she had nearly reached the end, and I saw that she had brought the volume with her, presumably with the intention of returning it to me.

But alas, I had only just opened my mouth to ask if she had finished the book, when who should heave into view but Mr. Patterson, holding a bundle of recently delivered correspondence. There was a letter for Betsy from her brother Charles, who is still in Baltimore attending to Mr. Patterson's business interests, and a most welcome missive for me from Father. As I was eagerly perusing its contents, finding to my relief that he was well, I became aware that Mr. Patterson was still present, leaning against one of the piazza's columns and blocking the path of the sun. I looked up and saw that he was scanning, with a frown, the most recent number of the Observer.

"What's this your father's saying here, then?" he barked at me. "That all disease is caused by *insects*?"

I had rather hoped that Mr. Patterson had forgotten about the matter of quarantine and Father's views on the subject. "Well, yes. That's why he devoted so much time to describing the behavior of various insect species, and the ways in which they cause disease in animals. But as to quarantine—"

"But that's animals! Does he means to say that we, *we* who have been created in God's image, are no different from ..." He gestured towards the fields nearby. "From sheep, and cattle?"

"Oh dear no, of course not!" I shot a quick glance at Betsy, but she was absorbed in Charles's letter. It seemed I could expect no reinforcements from her in this skirmish. "If you recall, several numbers ago when he discussed that very point, my father said quite clearly that man's immortal soul distinguishes him from animals. But our mortal aspect, our bodies—those are subject to the same laws of nature as the bodies of all other living beings. And that's why quarantine—"

184

"And just how does he think that these insects cause ..." He glanced down at the Observer, open in his hand. "Yellow fever, and cholera? And without our being aware of its happening?"

"Well, you see ..." Hadn't he read the explanations Father had provided in his many installments? Why should it fall to me to explain to him the disgusting details Father had laid out? "They might be very small, these insects, so as to be invisible to us. Or perhaps they're not, but unbeknownst to us they may lay tiny eggs on our skin, or ... near some openings into our bodies. And then ..." I paused, trying to find words that would allow me to express Father's ideas without sounding indecent; this information would have been much easier to convey in writing. "The eggs enter our bodies, and perhaps even our bones. And the insects that emerge cause disease. If you recall what Father wrote about the ichneumon fly, and horses—"

"I don't need to hear about horses. Why, I've seen worms taken from my children that were over a foot long. And I never saw the worms go in, so they must have hatched inside."

"Exactly!" I felt a surge of relief; perhaps Mr. Patterson could actually be led to embrace Father's theory. "It's very much the same idea. And so, you see, we don't contract our fevers from other people, or from goods that have arrived from other cities or countries—we get them from these insects, whose movements we cannot control, try as we might. And that's why quarantine is so senseless and useless!"

Mr. Patterson uttered a brief "hmmph" that could have signified agreement or skepticism, tossed the Observer on a small table that stood nearby, and crossed his arms.

"A very strange argument, very strange indeed," he said after a moment. "I suppose he could be right, but I don't think he'll find many who'll agree. People don't like to be told there's nothing they can do to prevent illness. And from what I've read, he's arguing we shouldn't even try, that if we didn't die from these plagues we'd all suffer worse deaths from war and starvation! *That* sort of thing won't win him many followers, I can assure you. And it's not going to bring down that damned lazaretto, where right now I've got two shiploads of cotton rotting because they've come from Charleston and are thought to carry the influenza!"

I tried to explain that Father did say that things could be done to prevent disease—that the victims should be moved to a healthy situation, where the disease-causing insects were not prevalent, rather than confined under quarantine. But Mr. Patterson took his leave abruptly, saying he had pressing correspondence to attend to. I bit my lip and played with the neck of my frock as I watched him go, wondering if he might soon be demanding the repayment of his loan. We had been in a position — just barely — to repay the money, but then I had to pay Mr. Hill for the printing of Mr. Godefroy's memorial, and soon I'll need to finance the printing of my translation of *Claire d'Albe* (Mr. Hill having given us a cheap rate if we employed him as the printer for both volumes). I have no doubt we'll recoup that money, and more, once the books are published and copies begin to sell, but it may take months for that to happen.

"That's not *fair!*" I suddenly heard Polly cry from behind me, in a tone I knew to be a prelude to tears. I quickly turned to find Henry and Octavius tossing a ball between them, high out of Polly's reach — she was jumping and extending her arms in vain attempts to catch it, her thin little face screwed up in desperation. I stood, intending to scold the boys for excluding her from their game, but before I could utter a word Margaret stepped up and snatched the ball in mid-air.

"No one plays unless all can play!" she said sharply, tucking the ball under her arm. There was a moment's silence, all three children frozen, apparently waiting for Henry — the elder of the two boys — to make his decision. "Oh, all right then," he muttered at last, whereupon Margaret tossed the ball to Polly and the game resumed.

"She seems to know how to manage the little brats," Betsy said as I resumed my seat, "even if her manners could use some improving."

"Her manners aren't the only thing that could use improving," I replied, although I had to admit to myself that Margaret has a decent way with children. In fact, that consideration induced me to bring her along to Springfield rather than entrust Polly to the care of Patience, who tends to the many Patterson offspring while also fulfilling various household tasks, and hardly lives up to her name — I knew Polly would be running to me every five minutes with some complaint or request unless Margaret was with us.

But taking the child to a camp meeting, where she might encounter the Lord only knows what sort of fanaticism and wildness!

One more incident like that, I've told Father, and Margaret will be out the door, no matter what excuses he puts forward in her defense. And it's not merely the atrocious judgment she displayed in bringing the girl to so unsuitable a place. Polly is in some ways an odd child, fearful and awkward with other children and often lost in her daydreams, and I suspect that Margaret's encouragement of her fanciful drawing and storytelling is only making her odder. I shudder to think what she may suffer at the hands of other girls once she goes to school—for I know, from my days of teaching them (or trying to) what cruelties young girls can inflict on one another.

But I now put thoughts of Polly from my mind and took a breath, preparatory to asking Betsy, at last, for her opinion of *Claire d'Albe*. Before I could speak she took the opportunity to inform me, in some detail, of all that Charles had conveyed to her in his letter.

Apparently there are reports in the papers that Bonaparte has created a new kingdom, Westphalia, and intends to install as its King no other than his brother Jerome. Betsy tried to feign indifference as she communicated this intelligence to me, but I knew what she must be feeling: had things transpired differently, she might now be planning her coronation as Queen of Westphalia rather than sitting on this piazza in the wilds of Maryland, surrounded by the shouts of bickering children.

"Oh Betsy, you mustn't think about what might have been," I told her. "You would have had no security in any event—that man, the Emperor, is no more than a despot who will change his intentions on the slightest whim. Surely you wouldn't want your fate to be placed in his hands?"

"My fate *is* in his hands," she retorted. "And I've told you, Eliza, I don't want to hear anything against him!"

We sat for a moment in uncomfortable silence, me thinking her deluded, and her no doubt thinking me equally so. I cannot fathom her admiration for a tyrant who has ruined her prospects of happiness—and nearly had us both killed for doing nothing more than attempting to procure food when we were in danger of starvation. I wondered whether she had seen any of the essays in the Observer on the political situation in Europe—excellent articles, all taking a very dim view of the supposed hero of the French. I rather hoped she hadn't.

"Charles also has news of your friend Mr. Cork," Betsy said at last, in what I took to be an attempt to heal the breach that had suddenly opened between us. "He's gone to Ballston Spa for a few weeks, and apparently has his eye on some Philadelphia heiress who's sojourning there." She looked down at the paper in her hand, densely covered with small writing, and squinted. "A Miss Scattergood. Odd name. A Quaker, it appears, from quite a wealthy family. Which is not something one could say of the Corks, although of course they have their pretensions."

"Well, perhaps this Miss Scattergood can manage to scatter some good as well as some money in Mr. Cork's direction—heaven knows he hasn't much of that to draw on, either. And perhaps he'll remove himself to Philadelphia and leave me in peace."

"Oh, he may leave you in peace in any event." She squinted at the letter again. "Charles says that Cork's friend Mr. Harmer is planning to sell that paper."

"Spectacles? Sell it? To whom?"

She consulted the letter. "Someone named Barnes. Apparently the editor of the Gazette, Mr. Hewes, is lending him the money."

"Hewes! One would think he'd keep his distance from something as disreputable as Spectacles. I can only hope you're right in surmising that this new owner will refuse to publish Cork's effusions, but I don't think that would be enough to put an end to him. He seems to have no difficulty finding other editors willing to aid him in spewing his venom. But if he were to marry and leave town ..." I threw back my head and filled my lungs with sweet-scented air, imagining a world without Cork/Bickerstaff. "Now *that* would be something to celebrate indeed!"

"Would it? Are you sure you don't enjoy these battles of words you engage in?" She began to fan herself with Charles's letter, as the day was growing warm. "Isn't it something of a pose, all this indignation of yours?"

I was pleased to hear that she had been reading my little sallies, as I'm never sure how much attention she pays to the Observer. But I hesitated before answering her question.

"I do find it amusing to compose my attacks—and even more amusing to read *their* pitiful attempts to injure me." This was far from the entire truth, of course. But if I unburdened myself to Betsy about my distress, I was sure she would only scorn such weakness.

"It's just becoming rather tiresome," I went on, keeping my tone light. "I know he's only jealous of our success, and he can't bear the idea that a woman—a mere woman!—is besting him at his own game. I'd much rather use the space in the Observer for more important matters, but I simply can't let his outrageous accusations pass without defending myself."

"But does the public actually want to read about more important matters? I'd wager that this jousting with Spectacles and the like has brought you some new subscribers."

I drew myself up in my chair. "Yes, perhaps—I think we've got seven hundred now. But who's to say why they subscribe? Perhaps some want to read my retorts to Bickerstaff or one of these other fools. But I'm sure there are at least as many others who want to read the poetry, or the essays on politics or moral philosophy."

"Or your worthy father's disquisitions on the insect kingdom," Betsy said with a smirk.

"I don't see why not. *Your* father's been reading them." Although not with particular care, I almost added, but I decided to allow the remark to pass without further comment. "Does Charles have any further details on Mr. Cork's courtship of this Philadelphia heiress?"

Betsy shrugged. "You can ask him yourself—he'll be here the end of next week. They're great friends, you know."

I did know. Charles has never been my favorite of Betsy's brothers. And I imagine I'm no favorite of his, not after I rejected that essay he submitted under the guise of "Cloanthus."

But enough of this talk of Cork and Spectacles, I thought. Hadn't I come here to rid myself of such unpleasant thoughts? At last I turned to the topic that had been burning in my mind— *Claire d'Albe.*

"Oh yes, it's well done, I suppose, if you like that sort of thing," was all the response I received to my eager inquiry. I asked Betsy what "sort of thing" she meant.

"Oh, tales of young love thwarted. Agonies of yearning. Irresistible passion. Like that other novel you were printing, the one that caused you all that trouble."

"*Adelaide*? Oh no, *Claire d'Albe* is nothing like *Adelaide*!" It was true that the bare facts that Betsy had outlined might have described either novel, but the bare facts tell far from the entire story.

"The lovers in *Adelaide* are shallow creatures, merely lusting after one another's physical charms. Whereas Claire and Frédéric—"

"Are entranced by the beauty of one another's souls. Yes, yes, I know. But if they'd been able to solemnize their union, I have no doubt they would have soon tired of one another's souls, just as husbands and wives tire of one another's physical charms. Perhaps sooner."

"How *can* you be such a cynic!" I rose from my chair and began pacing the length of the piazza. "Just because *your* marriage proved less than entirely successful—"

"Oh, and *yours* was of course a complete triumph! Did you learn nothing?"

"I learned that I married the wrong person! If I had met someone who could have brought me true happiness ..." I strode to where Betsy was sitting and picked the book out of her lap. "Did you read the scene where Frédéric risks his life to save Claire's husband from the bull? And then together he and Claire tend to the wounds of the old peasant who's been gored?"

I resumed my place in the chair across from her and began madly searching through the book's pages, but Betsy only waved a hand. "Yes, I read it. It was well executed, but it has nothing to do with my point. If Claire hadn't already been married—or if she hadn't died at the end—she and Frédéric would have eventually grown indifferent to one another, bull or no bull. Or perhaps they would even have come to secretly loathe each other, like ..." She leaned forward and lowered her voice. "Like my parents. *Your* father may cherish the memory of your mother, but that's easy to do when a wife dies young." She sat back and crossed her arms briskly, as though about to deliver a definitive pronouncement. "Disillusionment is simply the way of the world, and if you can't see that, it's only because your own brain has been addled by some romantic passion."

I felt my face grow suddenly hot, and I clutched the book to my breast. "I haven't the slightest idea what you're talking about."

"You know very well that I'm talking about that Frenchman. Godefroy."

"Betsy!" I looked behind me, to make sure no one had overheard her. "I've *told* you, I've renounced all that. I'm a married woman."

"As is Claire," she said drily. "And *her* husband has a far greater claim on her loyalty than yours does. He's a good man, an excellent provider. Whereas yours, like mine, is a bounder and a rogue. I imagine you must have asked yourself why Henry Anderson should have the power to deny you happiness, simply because he bears the title 'husband.'"

I was speechless for a moment, my mouth open. How Betsy had penetrated into my most secret thoughts was a mystery to me. And I saw before me the image of Mr. Godefroy's face, its strong features and immeasurably kind eyes, eyes that hold that deep sadness I long to assuage. It's a face that comes unbidden into my imagination every night — keeping me awake as much as the abominations produced by Mr. Cork's pen, and throwing me into a state of agitated confusion.

"Perhaps I have, on occasion." I tried to keep my tone calm, but I was suddenly seized by a desire to confess all that I have been feeling and thinking these past few months, things I haven't dared breathe to a soul. I leaned closer and placed a hand on her bare arm. "Do you recall that passage in *Claire d'Albe*, the one about two hearts being moved by a single passion, communicating with one another without speaking? I tell you, that's how it is between us. He'll voice things that I have thought but never said, as though not only our hearts but our minds are one. I think he feels it too, though he's never quite said as much. But there's a bond between us. And I crave his company as a starving man craves food or drink."

Suddenly a scream erupted behind me, followed by a wail — a scream and a wail I recognized as belonging to my child. I rose and turned to see that Polly had tripped and fallen, on a tree root or a stone, perhaps, but just as possibly on a foot extended by a mischievous Patterson boy. My impulse was to run to her, but before I could Margaret had the girl in her arms, and her sobs were already beginning to subside. I could see no blood. No doubt she was more tired than injured, I thought.

"Margaret," I called, "take her inside, she needs rest!"

The insolent wench began stomping away from me even as I spoke, calling back over her shoulder that she'd already decided to do that — quite as though it were her decision and not mine.

I turned back to Betsy, trembling — but whether that was the result of the topic under discussion, or the anxiety occasioned by

Polly's cries, or the irritation caused by Margaret's rudeness, or the combination of the three, I couldn't say.

Betsy seemed almost unaware of the contretemps. She appeared to have been considering my blurted confession throughout my exchange with Margaret, and now, with an expression of alarm, continued the conversation as though it had been uninterrupted. "But are you saying that you are prepared to follow Claire's example? To follow where your passion leads you?"

It seemed that my words had managed to penetrate, at least temporarily, the fortress she had erected against the possibility of genuine emotion. But I hesitated before I answered, unsure of how my words would be received.

"Sometimes, reading this book, the thought has entered my head," I ventured. Betsy leaned forward, her mouth open. Before she could speak, I quickly added, "But of course, no, I could never! It didn't work out very well for Claire, did it? And I must think not only of my own reputation and honor, but that of my child. And Father's, of course."

Betsy sat back. "I'm very relieved to hear it." She directed her gaze towards the green hills in the distance, and began to flutter the red fan that had been dangling from her wrist. "I suppose we're both the victims of our own mistakes. I should tell you I've been considering a divorce. Not immediately, of course, but if the Emperor should prove entirely impervious to my efforts to obtain a pension and a title ..."

A divorce. What I would give to be unyoked from Henry Anderson! "You would divorce Jerome? Have you investigated the possibility?"

"Only preliminarily. It requires a private bill in the legislature. Massively expensive, and it could take years to get it through. One needs to know the right people, and so on." She shot a glance at me. "For someone in your situation I'm afraid it would be impossible."

"Of course." I closed my eyes and tried to shake the thought from my head.

"And even if it were possible, it would only make sense if you were planning to marry a gentleman of some wealth, or at least a decent income. I grant you that Mr. Godefroy would be a vast improvement over that vulgar husband of yours, but he looks scarcely able to provide for himself, let alone for a family. No, the only thing for you to do, if you want to put an end to these vile rumors, is to cut off all contact with him."

"But ..." I gasped as though she'd kicked me in the shin. "I couldn't do that, couldn't possibly. I told you, seeing him—conversing with him—is the only bit of happiness available to me these days." I could feel a small flame of indignation kindling within me, building to a mighty conflagration. "I've done nothing wrong, and I refuse to be cowed by Cork and his friends, and their baseless, insolent insinuations. If I choose to conduct a perfectly honorable friendship with Mr. Godefroy, I have every right to do so!"

"Suit yourself, then. I warn you, though: it may be an honorable friendship, but it could also be a dangerous one." She rose from her chair and moved to the edge of the piazza to survey the view. "I think I shall take a ride in the carriage before it grows any warmer. Join me?"

I declined, telling her I needed to proceed with my translation, now that she'd returned the novel to me. But the truth was I was stung by her brusque dismissal of all I had confessed to her. There was a time when my situation would have evoked more sympathy from her, I felt sure, for had she herself not defied her father and even the Emperor Napoleon to be in the company of the man she had loved? Could she not remember that yearning in herself, and respect it in me? Had her disappointment deadened her soul to such feelings?

Or, in fact, had she never yearned for anything more than the title and wealth she thought marriage to Jerome would bring her? There were times, during our Atlantic crossing, when Jerome would try to soothe her anxiety by saying never mind, *chérie*, if my brother refuses to recognize our marriage we will simply return to America and live our lives somewhere, quietly but happily. And I would see a flicker in her eyes, like the glint of a blade in the firelight, and I knew what it meant: oh no, the quiet life will never do for me.

But for myself, I would ask for nothing more. If I could obtain the refuge for my soul that would come with marriage to Mr. Godefroy, I should be content even in the humblest and most obscure of situations.

I spent the remainder of the morning attempting to finish my translation, for I have only one chapter remaining before I can send the manuscript to the printer. But my mind was elsewhere, turning the conversation over and over: What, exactly, were the "vile rumors" she alluded to about myself and Mr. Godefroy? And then again, why should I trouble myself with such nonsense? Alas, in the course of several hours I was able to finish no more than a page of the novel.

But with Betsy's last remarks resounding in my ears, I did at least come upon a suitable title for my translation. I shall call it *Dangerous Friendship; or, the Letters of Clara d'Albe.*

From the Baltimore American and Commercial Daily Advertiser, August 11, 1807:

An infallible cure for the Tooth Ache.

I know that various opinions exist concerning my advertising the price of curing the tooth ache — some suppose I am joking with the public, others say if I have really discovered a cure for that tormenting malady, I ought at least for the sake of humanity to make it public, and support the fact by all necessary and convincing evidence. I have taken their advice, and therefore declare that I have given my newly discovered Essence of Sulphur, *to near one hundred different persons who were afflicted with the pain arising from hollow or decayed teeth, and I do not know of one instance where it has failed in producing a cure, nor do I believe it ever will, if used according to my directions. I have swallowed it often and will at any time drink it, to remove the scruples of the timorous.*

If ever the above mentioned essence should fail in producing the desired effect, and the tooth or teeth for which it was taken to cure should at any future period be extracted, all money received by me for such cure shall be returned, and double the sum if required.

FRANCIS GUY.
Baltimore County, August 10, 1807.

Sworn before me the subscriber a justice of the peace for the county aforesaid

JOHN ASQUITH.

From the Baltimore American and Commercial Daily Advertiser, August 24, 1807:

SPECTACLES!

Having purchased the "Spectacles," the present editor hopes to conduct it in such a manner as to ensure the approbation and encouragement of his fellow citizens. Several literary friends having generously proffered their support, the columns of the "Spectacles" will be rendered useful, interesting and amusing. It will be neatly printed, regularly and early distributed, and no pains will be spared to give the most complete satisfaction to its patrons. It will again appear on Saturday next.

SAMUEL BARNES.

Chapter Eighteen: Margaret

I had thought, when Mrs. A told me we were coming out to the country for a month, that there was no luckier girl anywhere than me. And indeed I've felt that way for the past three weeks, most of the time. Polly has been out of sorts now and then, but still, we've had our fun, taking walks in the fields and petting the lambs and feeding the baby goats, sometimes finding a spot to do some sketching. Mrs. A has allowed us more time together than she did in the city, and it's all put me in mind of my own childhood and the days when my mother was alive, and we still had the farm. Truly, I haven't been so much at peace and so content in years. Until last week, that is, when I was watching Polly play with the Patterson boys and I happened to hear Mrs. A talking to Mrs. Bonaparte, while they were sitting out on that thing they call the piazza, and my whole world seemed to turn upside down.

The last time I saw James before we came out here, I still had my conversation with Alice in my head, and my own words too, about how he wanted to marry me. I suppose because I was thinking of all that, I was determined to make something happen, to figure out once and for all if James liked me that way, maybe even loved me. So when he appeared at Mr. Guy's the Saturday before we left town, I told him I had something important to communicate to him that I could only tell him in private.

We walked out together and I drew him down a quiet alley, and that's where I told him I'd seen Mr. Godefroy kissing Mrs. A, and not just on the hand. It wasn't true, of course, but I reckoned it would give me the opportunity I needed. Like this, I said, and I put my lips on his and pressed. He went all stiff at first, but after a moment he began to press back, even opened his mouth a bit, and it was as lovely as I'd known it would be, kissing him, like sinking into a satin cushion. His lips were that soft, and his kiss so gentle. He said nothing afterwards, I suppose from surprise, but I could tell he'd liked it, and wouldn't have minded doing some more.

So when Mrs. A announced a few days later that we were to leave town, I was distressed that it would mean not seeing James for a whole month—and me not even having the chance to tell him I was leaving, though I went round to Mr. Guy's to let him know. But I felt that we had an understanding now, James and me—that what I'd told Alice about him loving me, and us getting married, wasn't far from the mark, that it was only a question of time. I began to imagine all sorts of rosy things for my future: a fine home with lots of rooms, and nice new frocks for me to wear, and my own servants to haul water and fetch the firewood. And best of all, money to buy pastels and paints, and endless hours when I could use them.

So when I heard Mrs. B say the name Cork that day, and then the two of them talking about his planning to marry some rich lady from Philadelphia, it was quite a shock. It was all I could do to keep myself from bursting into tears, right there in front of Polly and the boys. I kept listening to what they were saying as best I could, and got quite the earful—Mrs. A talking about how she was in love with the Frenchman, as I'd suspected all along, and Mrs. B saying why should it make a difference that she already had a husband. But they said nothing more about James, except something about Spectacles being sold. Which he also hadn't told me, although you'd think he would have mentioned it. What else had he been keeping from me, I wondered? Had I been entirely mistaken, and did he only want me for what I could tell him about Mrs. A? Had that kiss meant everything to me, but nothing to him?

Then, when that nasty little Henry Patterson tripped Polly and she began to cry, I didn't know whether I was glad to have to take her inside or sorry—for I was torn between wanting to know more concerning this Philadelphia lady and wanting to run away and allow the tears to come.

But before I went inside I also heard Mrs. B say that her brother was coming to the country, and later I wondered if that could be the Mr. Patterson who had come to the studio with James once or twice. I hoped it would be, because then I could ask him outright about James and the rich lady. But then again, I had to hope it wouldn't be, for wouldn't it be dangerous to have someone in this house who knew about me and James, and that I'd been telling him about Mrs. A's doings?

So when Mr. Patterson got here, a few days ago, and I saw it was indeed James' friend, I was both pleased and scared. It seemed he recognized me, although thank the Lord he was smart enough not to make it plain to anyone else. It was just a nod, a little flicker in his eyes. That made me feel a bit better, that he was keeping our secret, and I began to try to think of a way to catch him alone. But he always seemed to be in the company of at least one of his brothers, or his father. Sometimes, though, when I passed near him, I saw or felt his eyes on me, and I thought maybe he was watching for a chance as well, that he had something to tell me.

Then this evening, after supper, after I'd made sure Polly was in bed and sound asleep, I decided I would walk outside for a bit. The day had been hot and close, but now the air was cooling and the stars were just coming out against a clear sky of a beautiful gray-violet color, and a large moon was hanging low. I was on the far side of one of the barns, feeling the slight breeze against my skin, my neck craned upwards, when I heard a noise behind me. I turned and saw it was Charles Patterson. I greeted him with a smile, and he smiled back, though he looked uncertain.

"It *is* you, isn't it?" he said. "Molly? Mary?"

"Margaret," I answered.

"Of course. Margaret. Margaret the little spy."

I felt my face grow warm, for it reminded me how easy it would be for him to say something to Mrs. A, who was in the house not a hundred yards away from us. Maybe the only reason he hadn't said anything to her yet was that he hadn't been sure it was me.

"A pleasure to see you again, sir." I thought it best to be as polite as I could be. "I hope Mr. Cork was well when you left him."

"When I left him? He left me, is more the case. I haven't seen him in nearly a month. The lucky dog went up to Ballston Spa."

"Really?" I pretended surprise. So he must have left for this Ballston place at near the same time I came out here, I thought, though he hadn't told me he was going. Mr. Patterson and I were walking along together now, away from the house. The sky was darkening, and I thought perhaps I should turn back, but I needed to know more. "And why did he go there?"

"The usual reasons. To take the waters, play at billiards and backgammon, dance at the balls."

"Ah, of course," I said, as though he was reminding me of what I'd already known. "I suppose he must be enjoying himself. Perhaps he's written to you?"

He looked at me sideways, a corner of his mouth pulling up a bit. "He has, as a matter of fact. He's having quite a gay time. A crowd of beauties there this year, he says, and the balls go on till all hours." He paused. "You're not jealous, are you?"

"Me? Of course not!" It was all I could do to sound unconcerned. "Only, it sounds lovely, that's all. I'd like to be there myself, going to balls and such."

"Then that makes two of us. Nothing much to do here, is there?" He stopped walking, so I did too. Then he turned to me and asked me if I knew how to dance. I almost lied and said of course, but I thought he might ask me to prove it. So I told him the truth. And then he smiled and bowed, very gentlemanly, and said it would be his pleasure to teach me.

"What, here?" I said. "In the middle of a field? With no music?"

And he said he could provide the music and began to hum a tune. I thought of James taking his amusement with all those beauties and thought I might as well make merry too, as best I could. So I laughed and said all right, then, and Mr. Patterson began showing me steps, this way and that, and I tried to keep up, but I kept treading on his feet. And then we were both laughing and had to stop. But then he grew quiet and I saw him looking at me the way the men down at the Point used to do sometimes. He put his hand under my chin and drew my face towards his. I closed my eyes and let him kiss me. And it felt good. Not as good as when James kissed me, but who knew if I'd ever see James again. And Mr. Patterson wasn't bad looking, not bad at all really, and he was being so nice.

He stopped kissing me for a moment and looked about. It was dark now, but we were out in the open, so he took me by the hand and led me to a stand of trees about twenty feet away. When we got there he leaned me up against a tree and started in on kissing me again. Then after another minute or two he started to pull down the front of my frock and kiss my breasts. I was torn, I was, for I knew I should insist that he stop, but at the same time I was afraid that if I did he would go to Mrs. A, and that would be the end of me.

Then he began to unbutton his britches, and I could see what he was planning. "No, please, sir," I said, though weakly. "I must go back now."

"Oh come now, Margaret," Mr. Patterson said, his hand moving up under my skirts, "I can give you a better wapping than Cork has ever done, you'll see. And you'd best forget him, anyway, for he's as good as married now."

I don't know what riled me more, that it was true about James marrying that rich lady, or that he'd told Mr. Patterson we'd done the deed when we never had.

So I let him go on. And the truth was, I didn't entirely want him to stop. He began to rub me under my skirts, and it felt as though all my insides were melting, in the most lovely way, like a plate of butter left too close to the fire—the way I'd felt when James read me that story about the hot tears falling on that girl's breast. True, it was James I'd been wanting. But it was also *this* I'd been wanting, and if James hadn't given it to me, and now never would, I thought I might as well get it from Charles Patterson. Although it's not quite the truth to say "I thought," for I wasn't thinking at all by this time, I was only feeling. And then the melting began to feel like an explosion, fire and magic. Like those fireworks I had been able to just catch sight of on the Reister's Town road on the Fourth of July, but happening inside me.

Next I knew we were both down on the grass, between the trees, and he was pushing himself into me. That part hurt, as I'd been told it would the first time. And it was only then that I truly understood what I'd done, or what I'd let him do, but by then it was too late. And how could I have said no to him, anyway, with him having my fate in his hands?

When he was finished, he picked himself up and dusted off the dirt and the leaves on his britches. He leaned down to where I sat on the grass, arranging my frock and feeling stunned by it all, and kissed me on the cheek and told me I was quite the game pullet. "Come now," he said, extending a hand. "Time to go back."

And we walked along in silence, except for him whistling, until we reached the outbuildings. Then he told me to go on ahead, for perhaps it was best if we weren't seen coming back together, and I nodded. I started to go, but then I turned back.

"You won't tell Mrs. Anderson, will you?" I asked him, for I had to know. "About me spying for Mr. Cork? Or your sister, neither, because they're friends."

"Of course not." He glanced up at the second floor of the house, where a candle was burning in Mrs. A's room, and the look on his face was dark. "Anything you can do to bring her down a peg or two is fine with me."

I almost said: and don't tell Mr. Cork about what we did tonight. But then I thought, no, let him talk, if that's what he wants to do. Let James know what he could have had, and maybe he'll be sorry.

From the Observer, September 19, 1807:

For the Observer.

CLARA D'ALBE.

The public has been presented this week with a novel translated from the French by a lady of Baltimore, entitled, "Dangerous Friendship, or the Letters of Clara d'Albe." *Of novel reading to the extent which it is generally pursued, we totally and entirely disapprove. But since it is in vain to aim at changing general taste, and the most miserable trash will be read with untiring avidity, it is at least some advantage that works of this kind should have correctness of sentiment and beauty of style to recommend them.*

The volume before us excels in both; its language is at once simple, flowing, and elegant, its sentiments correct, and its moral good: *since those of its characters who yield to the dominion of passion become the victims of the aberrations from virtue into which it leads them.*

We doubt not that many a tear will dim the bright eye of beauty in sympathy for Clara's fate. The translator has, we think, done justice to her original, and although translation is but a secondary department in literature, yet it is no very easy task to transfuse the impassioned style of French love and sentiment into English, and whilst tempering it down to suit our colder language, not to lessen the grace and vivacity of the original. As it is a new thing amongst us for a lady to engage in literary pursuits, we should be happy to see her encouraged to more useful and important undertakings.

From the Baltimore American and Commercial Daily Advertiser, September 23, 1807:

FOR THE AMERICAN.

CLARA D'ALBE.

The French, in the happy talent of telling a story with liveliness & ease, are universally allowed to excel every other nation. And the translator of Clara d'Albe is not among the least of those who have been successful in copying the ease and graces of the French composition. I am proud to find in my native city a lady who to a thorough conception of the force and delicacy of her own language joins such brilliant powers of mind: and I have only to regret that such estimable talents should be employed in the servile task of translation.

But the period so anxiously awaited by the friends of true taste and learning approaches with tardy and hesitating steps — that period when a generous and enlightened public will reject the spurious and tinseled productions that are thrown to us by surrounding nations and explore and cultivate that native mine of genius which has hitherto been suffered to molder and decay.

PETRONIUS.

Chapter Nineteen: Eliza

M r. Godefroy has just left me, and I am still trembling to think what has transpired — or almost transpired.

I have been in a state of distressing confusion since our return from the country two weeks ago, now anxious concerning the gossip my innocent friendship with the gentleman has apparently engendered, now determined not to allow such nonsense to determine the course of my behavior. And Betsy's question that day — why should I allow Henry Anderson, my husband in name only, to deny me happiness? — has haunted me with ever-deepening intensity. Although for her it was but a momentary thought, soon dismissed, for me it's as though she had taken a needle to the faint pattern of yearning that was sketched on my consciousness and embroidered upon it in bold and vibrant colors. I've even found myself thinking of Mr. Godefroy by his Christian name, Maximilian, murmuring it to myself at times as though I were a love-struck schoolgirl.

And so, when I discovered the gentleman himself in the sitting room an hour ago (Margaret having uncharacteristically answered the knock at the front door before I could respond), my heart beat faster and my skin began to flush — these particular organs having betrayed me in this way on each occasion when I have encountered him since my return from Springfield. Apparently unaware of the effect his presence was working upon me, he gave me his customary tender, melancholy smile.

"I have come to offer you my congratulations, Madame Translator," he said in French, with a gracious bow. "Your *Clara D'Albe* has met with great success! As I knew it would."

I felt myself blush deeper still, and hoped he might attribute my color to modesty alone. Despite my agitation, or perhaps because of it, I found myself asking Mr. Godefroy if he might have the time for some tea and cake. Why yes, I heard him say, that would be most kind. And so I told Margaret, who was still standing in the doorway, to bring us some.

"You must be pleased, Madame, with the review in Saturday's number of the Observer," he said when he had taken Father's chair and I had placed myself on the settee across from it.

"Oh, I scarcely think I can count the Observer as an objective source of praise," I said, my eyes flitting about the room. "There may be some in this town who don't know that the 'lady of Baltimore' who translated *Claire d'Albe* and Mistress Ironside of the Observer are one and the same, but the many who do will discount the compliments accordingly. I only published it because Mr. Tyson, the author, insisted that I would be a fool not to bring as much attention to the book as I could. And as he has been one of my most reliable contributors, I felt I should oblige him."

In truth, it was I who had approached Mr. Tyson about the possibility of writing something for the Observer concerning *Dangerous Friendship*, but once I raised the idea he greeted it with such enthusiasm that I'm sure he would have suggested it himself had I not done so first. And at the time, I hadn't been confident that any other publication would take notice of the book—not even Spectacles, which certainly would have found in it something to condemn, but which has so far failed to appear in print under its new ownership. Perhaps Mr. Hewes and Mr. Barnes have concluded the paper is beyond salvation.

"But what about this review in the American?" Mr. Godefroy continued, reaching for the copy of today's number of the paper, which sat on the side table next to him, open to the article in question. "This 'Petronius' has taken note of your ..." He scrutinized the paper for a moment, and read the phrase he was looking for in English. "'Brilliant powers of mind.' Surely it must be gratifying to hear such praise from one with whom you have no connection. Whoever he is, he has stated my thoughts exactly."

In fact, the essay had been presented to me in advance of publication by Mr. Arnold, like Mr. Tyson one of my frequent contributors, and contained no surprises. But I thrilled to the words nonetheless, because of Mr. Godefroy's endorsement of them.

Perhaps some women revel in a compliment to their eyes or their complexion, but the rare occasion when a gentleman praises my intellect—that is when *I* blush and flutter.

"You're too kind," I managed to murmur. "But of course, as usual, there are those who disagree."

I then told Mr. Godefroy that although Mr. Pechin had been pleased to publish Petronius's review in the American, Mr. Hewes at the Gazette had first rejected it. Such was the level of his outrage that he had even refused good money to publish an advertisement for the book, and sent me a note sputtering that his paper would never be associated with so grossly indecent a tale, as he called it.

Mr. Godefroy shook his head and drew his eyebrows together. "Ah, this country. I don't know that I will ever understand it. To think that Mr. Hewes would label such a beautiful story indecent! Was he serious, do you think?"

"Oh, I expect so," I said. "Unless it's just that he's still irritated at the public drubbing I inflicted on his correspondent some time ago, the one who styled himself 'C.' But no, difficult as it may be to credit, I rather think he meant it."

We smiled at one another, and I was conscious of that invisible coil that connects us, felt its tug as sharply as though we were ships roped together in the harbor, tossed separately by the waves but ever united. My stomach leapt like some small restless animal within me, and we were silent a moment.

"Of course, I don't see why Mr. Arnold—I mean, Petronius— felt it necessary to characterize translation as a 'servile task,'" I said, as lightly as I could manage. I rose and moved to the bookshelves, where I began to run my fingers along the spines of the volumes. "You and I both know it's far more than that."

"It's true, translation is an art, and you have a gift for it," he said, and even though I was no longer facing him I could feel his eyes upon me. "There are few in this world who are conversant in two languages and also have the talent of finding the correct correspondences between them. But perhaps this Petronius is right, that you are capable of even more—of writing something original."

"Oh, but I write original things every week!"

"Yes, but I'm not speaking of articles for the papers. I mean something more permanent, more artistic. As Petronius says, perhaps instead of translating European novels, you might help to establish a native literature in this country."

I paused, startled. "Did he say that?"

"Well, not in those words, but I think that's what he means to suggest."

He came to where I stood and handed me the paper, and I reread the review's last paragraph, with its remark about cultivating a native mine of genius. I had taken it, at first glance, as merely one more patriotic denunciation of all things European, but now I saw that it could be read to support Mr. Godefroy's interpretation.

"Me, write a novel?" I laughed and flung the paper onto the settee.

"Why not? If you want to move people, to affect their moral sense and their sympathies, fiction is a far stronger tool than essays. Is that not what Lord Kames says? That it's fiction that arouses our passions and strengthens the bonds of sympathy between us?"

"Well, yes, he does make that argument." I picked at a particularly frayed book cover and tried not to dwell on the mention of passion. "But what on earth would I write a novel about?"

Margaret had come in, at last, with the tea tray, which she set down on the table between us. I resumed my place on the settee as she began to pour.

Mr. Godefroy shrugged. "I suppose it would be in the form of letters, like most novels. And I suppose that the main characters would be lovers. Is that not generally the case?"

I blushed again at the mention of the word lovers. But my mind had already begun to race with possibilities. "I suppose it could run along the lines of *Claire d'Albe*, only it would take place in the United States. Perhaps even in Baltimore."

"Yes, an American version of *Claire d'Albe*."

"But there would be certain differences. Claire and Frédéric are drawn to one another because they perceive each other's virtues. You know—Frédéric sees Claire tending to the sick, Claire sees Frédéric risk his life to save others from the bull. And that's all well and good." I was speaking faster now, swept up in the rush of my thoughts. "But *my* characters would also be drawn to one another because they admire each other's intellects. It would be a 'marriage of true minds,' as the Bard says."

I had to render that last phrase in English, given its source, and I wondered if Mr. Godefroy would grasp the reference.

"But there would be some 'impediment,' would there not, to this 'marriage of true minds'?" he asked, using the English words. He smiled, and I realized he knew the sonnet as well as I did. "I am no novelist, of course, but it seems to me you cannot have a plot unless there is an impediment."

We laughed, and I told him he was quite right. I was beginning to feel more at my ease with him, almost as I have in the past. Then I noticed that Margaret was still lingering in the room, although she had finished pouring, and I had to tell her she was dismissed. She shuffled slowly to the door, as though reluctant to go. Such an odd girl, she is.

"An impediment," I mused aloud, returning to the game. "Yes, of course, we must have one of those. They would be a little older than Claire and Frédéric, these two—I think that would make them more interesting, don't you? As their minds would have had more time to develop?"

He nodded encouragingly. "Yes, but not too old. They would still retain some of those physical charms that stir the heart."

"And at least one of them would be married. Let's say it's her. There's your impediment." My tea forgotten, I found myself standing again and began to walk about the room, as I often do when my mind is racing. "But he's not an honorable man, like Monsieur d'Albe. That made it too difficult for Claire. What if the woman had discovered, after marrying, that her husband was not a decent person at all? Perhaps he can't bear the idea that she, a mere woman, is more intelligent and well read than he is. And whenever she proves that she knows more than he does, which she can't help doing, he mocks and berates her."

As I said this, of course, the image of Henry Anderson rose to my mind: I could see that dark bewilderment about his eyes when I had sketched an argument he couldn't follow, or made some allusion he failed to recognize, a bewilderment that was quickly replaced by some dismissive insult about educated women and their supposed vanity, his desperate weapon against me in a battle he knew he could never truly win.

"Her husband, in fact, has abandoned her—her and their young child," I went on. "And she wasn't sorry to see him go. In fact, she decides that she wants nothing more to do with men, at least not in any romantic manner. And how could she, in any event, as she's still married to the scoundrel?"

"But then," Mr. Godefroy interjected quietly, "she meets someone. A man who appreciates her intellect."

I stopped my pacing, startled. In the fever of creation, I had nearly forgotten he was in the room. But now I turned to him and saw that he was looking at me in a way he never had before—or at least, that I had never noticed before. There was an earnestness, an intensity in his gaze.

"Yes." I swallowed, trying to steady myself against a wave of panicky emotion that I felt might knock me to the ground. I knew I should put an end to this tale-spinning, but I felt compelled to continue. "She realizes that she can speak her mind with him, that she can be the woman she truly is and not the one that people may expect, and that it doesn't lessen his regard for her. It seems only to increase it."

I took a breath before willing myself to go on. "But it's not only that he admires her. She also sees the beauty of *his* intellect. She sees that he's acquired great knowledge—not only from books and study, but from all that he has experienced. He has more than knowledge, he has wisdom. And all of that has opened new possibilities for her, new ways of looking at the world. She realizes that never before has she met anyone whose mind was so much in harmony with her own, and she fears she never will again."

We were silent for a moment, frozen in place, our eyes locked. The clock's ticking had never seemed so loud.

"But there is, of course, the impediment," Mr. Godefroy said at last.

"Yes, the husband. And so these two people, the man and the woman, must decide what to do—whether to continue as friends, despite the baseless, vicious gossip of those around them." I swallowed. "Or to renounce their innocent pleasure in one another's company for the sake of their honor and their families."

"Are those their only choices?" Mr. Godefroy took a few steps towards where I had come to rest, by the bookshelves again. "For isn't their marriage, the marriage of their minds, far truer than the supposed marriage between the woman and her scoundrel of a husband?"

I closed my eyes for a moment, then opened them to find him just inches away, still intently gazing at me. "Yes, but don't they already have that, through their friendship? The marriage of their minds? Is it so necessary for them to have … the rest of it?" My voice sounded small and far away.

"Isn't it?" And then Mr. Godefroy took my hands in his, and he was so near I could feel the warmth of his breath as he exhaled. "Isn't it only human nature to want more?"

Paralyzed, I watched as he took both my hands in his and brought them to his lips, holding them there, his eyes closed. The touch of his soft, warm flesh against mine sent such waves through me that I was nearly overcome. He had kissed my hand on previous occasions, of course, but never like this. This kiss roused in me feelings I had never experienced before, not even in the marriage bed with Henry.

I thought of Claire and Frédéric, and particularly that scene in the garden towards the end, at Claire's father's grave, when Frédéric comes upon her and she succumbs to him. Yes, she suc-cumbs — and those who rail against the novel would no doubt prefer a sublimely virtuous heroine who manages to resist. But that is what makes the novel so beautiful and true, I thought: the characters are not flawless paragons, but living, breathing people. And then Mr. Godefroy lifted his head, with its tousled mane, from where it was bent over my hands, and brought it close to mine. Closer and closer he came, until our lips were nearly touch-ing, and he placed a hand gently on my cheek. My mind was numb, frozen; I was no more than a pounding heart encased in a trembling body.

What might have happened next I cannot say and shudder to contemplate. But just then the door opened — with no heralding knock — and Margaret walked in. We jumped apart instantly, Mr. Godefroy's leg knocking into the settee and sending the newspa-per crashing to the floor as though it too were startled.

"I thought you might want me to take away the tea things," Margaret said after a moment, her eyes wide and her face flushed.

"Yes, fine, take them away," I said, in a voice louder than I'd intended. The impertinence of the girl, entering the room unan-nounced! I would take her to task about that later, I thought — but then considered that to do so might only cast the scene in a more lurid light than it deserved. For whatever was in our hearts, we had done nothing improper.

"Well, I mustn't keep you from your labors," Mr. Godefroy said in the awkward silence that followed Margaret's departure. I had removed myself to the window, while he remained at the bookcase.

I gestured towards the library across the hall, where piles of submissions were awaiting my attention. "Yes, alas, like Sisyphus, I find my work is unceasing. Each week brings a fresh stone to push up the hill." I heard myself emit a brittle laugh.

"But you have far more to show for it. A new number every Saturday!"

"Which perhaps only serves to wrap the fish bought at the market on Monday."

We both laughed at that, perhaps more than the pleasantry warranted.

"I doubt that," Mr. Godefroy said, but then his expression turned serious once more. "But consider what I said, won't you, about writing something more permanent? And if you should write that novel …" He paused for a moment, seeming uncertain whether to go on. "Somehow let them have a true marriage, one that involves more than the mind. Nature intended—God intends—that such powerful feelings should have a physical expression." He paused again. "I noticed, in your translation … that scene in the garden, by Claire's father's grave, when Frédéric finds her …"

I felt myself color, and my heart again began to beat hard and fast. That scene again.

"You left out certain phrases. About Claire's feelings, how she at last tastes that delight that love alone can bring, that rapture, that bliss. How her soul unites with her lover's."

"Yes," I managed to reply. I had struggled to translate the scene without verging on indecency. Although, I reflected, I wasn't entirely sure I had grasped its full meaning until just now. "I thought those phrases would prove too much for certain sensibilities in this town. Only imagine what Mr. Hewes would have said if I'd left them in!" I laughed again. "And in truth I thought that part wasn't necessary to the story."

He came to where I stood, and once again took my hand and pressed it to his lips. And again I burned and melted, both at once.

He raised his head to look into my eyes. "But, my dear Madame, I think that part will be necessary to *your* story," he said.

And with that he was gone, leaving me in a state that was entirely inadequate to the undertaking of my editorial duties, or indeed of anything else—and all too conscious of the fact that I have somehow allowed this friendship to enter territory even more dangerous than that it occupied before.

Chapter Twenty: Margaret

All has changed in the last few weeks, since we came back from the country. I hadn't wanted to leave Springfield, thinking that James was set on marrying someone else, and that I might never see him again. Coming back to the dull round of sweeping and dusting, after being free to roam the green fields and cool woods, seemed the prospect of hell itself, even if I would still have Polly to play with and care for. All my dreams — of marrying James, and being a lady who could spend her days drawing and painting, and having my own children someday as well — they were all crumbled to dust.

I nearly didn't go to Mr. Guy's studio that first Saturday after we returned, for I hadn't any idea whether James was still paying for the lessons, and I didn't want to hear Mr. Guy send me away. But I did go, in the end, and it's a lucky thing, for all was as it had been before. Mr. Guy was strutting about, taking his snuff and working at his landscapes, while at the same time tending to a moaning wretch who'd come in search of the toothache cure. And there, in a chair by the corner with his feet up on a window-sill, was James.

I just stared at him, but he greeted me with a wide smile, his lovely white teeth shining, and it was all I could do to stay upright. Mr. Guy instructed me to sketch a statue he has in his studio of a man called Hercules — practically naked it is, for that seems to be how people went about in olden times. Mr. Guy said it would be useful to me if I wanted to draw people, knowing where the muscles are under the clothes, but the truth is I've never seen a man with as many muscles as that statue (although I haven't seen any men wearing as little clothing as that, so perhaps I don't rightly know).

I had a terrible time keeping my mind on it, for all I could think of was James sitting there. He and Mr. Guy were talking about Vice-President Burr's trial in Richmond, and how the jury had found him not guilty of treason, and what an outrage it was, and it was only because the judge is a sworn enemy of President Jefferson and had kept certain evidence from the jury, and on and on. And every few minutes their conversation was interrupted by someone else at the door with the toothache, so even if I hadn't been so riled up about James I would have been distracted.

After a while Mr. Guy said I must leave off my lesson early, as he had an appointment, which was certainly agreeable to me. I looked over at James as I was packing up my things, and I could see him looking at me, and he seemed to be waiting. Fortunately none of his friends were there, and to my delight he suggested that we repair to the Sow's Ear for supper, with no need of a hint from me.

I was wary at first, expecting him to tell me the lessons and our meetings must come to an end. But instead as we walked along he touched me under the chin and tucked my hair inside my cap and even took my hand, just like we were a courting couple. It gave me hope, but it also threw me into some confusion. After a while I could bear it no more, and once we got to the tavern I simply asked him whether it was true he was going to marry a rich lady who lived in Philadelphia.

He raised one of his golden eyebrows and asked me where I'd heard that, and I told him I'd overheard Mrs. Bonaparte saying as much, and he told me not to place my trust in idle gossip of the kind she retailed. So it's not true, I said, my heart beating faster? He shrugged and said it was true enough that his father would *like* him to marry this Miss Scattergood, or someone with a purse as full as hers, but that he was his own person, and he had no intention of doing so, and he'd only pretended to pay court to her to please his father.

I thought it was impossible for me to be any happier than I was at that moment. But then he said more, which was that this Miss Scattergood was a bony, awkward lady with a long sharp nose, and that if he were to marry he would only marry someone as pretty as me. I could do nothing but look at him, my mouth wide, until he laughed and said if I didn't close it one of the flies buzzing about the Sow's Ear would soon take up residence inside it.

I found I could eat no more than a few morsels, which was very unlike me, and after a while James asked if I'd go to a room upstairs with him, where we could talk in private. He flushed red when he said that, but he had a determined look about him. I wondered what he might need to say to me in private, and whether it might have something to do with marriage, for he'd just said he wanted to marry someone like me. I couldn't account for the change in him, his being so forthright and bold, except that he must have realized he missed me while we were apart, just as I'd missed him. So I said yes, I would go upstairs with him.

He took me up to a small room that had nothing in it but a bed, so we sat ourselves on that, side by side. I waited for him to say something, nearly shaking I was. I think he might have been shaking a bit too. I was staring at the bare wall across from us, which had a crack running across it, and then at the floor, which had some streaks of red mud that whoever was there before must have brought in on his boots. At last, just to say something, I began to tell James what I'd heard Mrs. Bonaparte saying to Mrs. A in the country, about how she knew Mrs. A must be in love with Mr. Godefroy, and why should she let her husband stand in the way of her happiness. I thought he'd be interested to hear that, but he only grunted a bit, so I asked him didn't he want to write something about that for Spectacles. He just shrugged and said that Spectacles might have come to an end, that the new owner hadn't put out a number since before he'd left town.

I began to wonder what we were doing in the room, since he hadn't said anything about marriage, and he didn't seem to want to talk about Mrs. A. And then next I knew he had his arms about me and was kissing me, and at first I was so surprised I felt as though my head had been pushed under water and I couldn't breathe, but then a minute later it was lovely, it was everything I'd been dreaming of. True, he'd said nothing about marrying me yet, but I didn't want him to stop. I recalled what Alice had advised me, weeks ago, about giving him a taste of my wares but not the whole store. And there was a moment, when he was lifting my skirts, when I tried to say no, we mustn't. But he didn't seem to hear me, and then things happened rather fast, and it was too late. I suppose it was wrong, but it was far nicer than it had been with Mr. Patterson, so I can't say I'm sorry it happened. It surely proved he's no Miss Molly, and that he likes me just the way I thought he did. I felt a bit uneasy that we hadn't talked of marriage, but then again, I told myself, James is an honorable gentleman, and surely that's what he has in mind.

The next Saturday James was at Mr. Guy's again, and again we went to the Sow's Ear and the room upstairs afterwards, just as though it had been arranged between us. I felt all tingly as we left Mr. Guy's, just thinking of what was to come, but at the same time I knew I must say something. So I asked him did he love me, and he said of course he did, and I told him I loved him too. I felt better for a bit, after that, but when we got into the room upstairs and he began kissing me, which he did immediately this time, I pushed him away and asked did he intend to marry me, for I was a respectable girl. And he said of course, he'd told me he loved me, hadn't he? And that put my mind at ease, and we went to bed and it was even lovelier than the time before.

But then last Saturday, though James was at Mr. Guy's as usual, I saw he'd brought his friend Mr. Webster with him. When the lesson was over, I began to pack up my portfolio, hoping that James would make ready to leave as well, but he and Mr. Webster and Mr. Guy were engaged in conversation, and James seemed to be paying me no mind. So I took him aside and whispered that I had something most particular to tell him, which was true, and that it must be done in *private*, if he took my meaning. He sighed and looked away and said that he was sorry, but he'd promised he'd take supper with Mr. Webster. He seemed rather cool, which worried me. So I told him it was quite a grave matter I had to discuss with him, and it would be very much to his advantage to break his plans with Mr. Webster and come along with me.

At last he said he would, though I couldn't fathom why he was so reluctant. I asked him was something wrong, had I said or done something to displease him, and he said no, but what was it that was so important? I'd meant only to tell him about what I'd seen a few days before when Mr. Godefroy was visiting, and I came into the room and the two of them jumped apart. I started with that, of course. But then he said, is that all?

"No, of course not," I told him, as it seemed not to be enough. We were at supper now, at the Sow's Ear, and I lowered my voice and leaned closer. "Her frock, it was all undone. And her bosom, it was quite bare. All hanging out, she was."

His eyes widened at that, with all their different colors. I almost forgot what I was saying, looking at his eyes. "Anything else?"

I swallowed and put down my fork. "Well, *him*. The Frenchman." I wasn't sure what I was going to say until I heard myself say it. "His britches, they were unbuttoned. And her hand was there, inside. She took it out as soon as she saw me, of course, but I saw where it had been."

"Good Lord." James sat back, his mouth open slightly. "Well, this changes everything. This is far more than just talk, or even a kiss. And combined with that obscene novel she's just published!"

"You mean *Clara Something*?"

He looked at me suspiciously. "You've read it?"

"No, I've just heard them talking. Something about lovers, is all I know. And the lady is married to someone else."

"That's it. That's all you need to know. It fits, doesn't it?" He took a drink of his ale.

I was beginning to feel uneasy, wondering what I'd just done. I couldn't come out and tell him I'd made it all up, but I felt I should say something. "But she didn't *write* the novel. She translated it, from a French book."

"Oh, yes, but who's to know what she might have added? A few embellishments from her own experience? And why did she choose to translate that particular novel in the first place?" He leaned back in his chair and crossed his arms and smiled. "I'll need to have a word with Mr. Barnes about this. And Mr. Hewes. I believe this is reason enough for another number of Spectacles to appear at last. It's a filthy tale, that book, and it's all the filthier when one knows where it's come from." Then he brought his face close to mine and put his hand to my cheek, and I felt myself begin to tingle.

"Shall we see if there's a room for us upstairs?" James said. "I'm of a mind to celebrate."

"Celebrate what?" I asked, thinking that it might be something to do with us. But James said it was the reappearance of Spectacles he was thinking of.

There was a room, and it was sweet to be together again, after I'd thought he might be done with me. I did feel bad that I'd told him things about Mrs. A and Mr. G that weren't exactly true, but I wouldn't be surprised if something like that goes on between them while I'm not looking. You could just about smell it in that room, their hunger for one another.

I asked James again would he marry me, and he said of course, someday. And I said when would that be, and he said as soon as he could manage it, but he didn't think his father would ever consent, so he'd need to make some money first, to give us something to live on. And then he fell off to sleep.

He looked so lovely lying there in the bed, his chest bare and his golden eyelashes curled down on his cheeks, that I had to draw him. So, very quietly, I took out my charcoal and the few pastels Mr. Guy had given me, and I did my best to catch him on paper: the soft curve of his cheek, and the roundness of his lower lip, his slightly hooked nose and his high forehead. I had to do his chest as well, and I thought of the Hercules statue. James's chest hasn't nearly so many muscles, but in truth I think it's far nicer. I didn't know that he would want me drawing him, so I was careful to put the paper back in my portfolio before he awoke. I was only sorry his eyes had been closed, for I do think they're his best feature.

Once I got home I took the drawing from my portfolio and tucked it carefully under my mattress. I certainly won't show it to Mr. Guy—or to anyone else, not even James, at least not yet. But I do think it's one of my best. Every night I take it out and give it a kiss, and then I blow out the candle and wait for sleep to come, thinking of what lies ahead: the two of us together as man and wife, and me not having to haul and dust and launder all the time. And then I'll paint him, and his golden hair and golden eyebrows, the smooth pink of his lips and the white of his teeth, and of course the green and gold and brown of his eyes.

From the American and Commercial Daily Advertiser, October 10, 1807 (printed as well in the Observer of the same date):

For the American.

CLARA D'ALBE.

Do the critics who thunder the fulminations of their ignorance against this tale know what the word novel *means? Do they know that it is a heightened representation of nature, and that though the coloring should be strong, the characters must have their origin in real life?*

But let us not be deceived — it is not the improper tendency of the work that arms these chaste *spirits against it. Such is the delirium of passion, such the supernatural influence of ENVY, that the* Spectacles *that had long ago been cut to pieces by criticism, viper-like, rejoined its scattered members on Saturday last and resuscitated to new purposes of malice.*

Clara d'Albe *can in no way lend a color to the poisoned philippics which these* Spectacles *have directed against it, and by the infamous and* palpable *falsehood they assert concerning its origin, they only evidence their gross ignorance of style and language to be equal to their impotent and contemptible malice. Can anyone who has the least discrimination in the English tongue fail to perceive in a moment that every page stamps it a translation!* Clara d'Albe *has been announced a considerable time, and it is easy to know that the lady who translated it was no other than the* female *against whom this champion has waged a gross and indecent war!!!*

The conscientious *Editor of the Federal Gazette too, remembering the retort courteous given to his correspondent C in the Observer some time ago, or rather perhaps, because he had no interest in the sales of the work, inveighs against it as being vile and contaminating. When this oracle of uprightness is* moved *to teach morality to the youth of* Columbia, *he will doubtless begin by teaching them that they must never* sell *their honor and their consciences, like Esau, for a mess of pottage!!!*

E.A.

☞ *The original from which* Clara d'Albe *was translated, printed in Paris, may be seen at Mr. Hill's Book-store by anyone who may be curious to see attested the degree of reliance to be placed on the veracity of the Spectacles.*

From the Observer, October 10, 1807:

For the Observer.

THEATRICAL.

"Paul and Virginia" was the farce, in which Mr. Webster was the hero of the piece. We have before had occasion to speak of this actor, and we regret very sincerely that his last night's performance has not changed our opinion of him. For ridiculous affectation, vanity, and impertinence he verily stands without a rival.

If Mr. W. would modestly content himself with using his musical powers in a natural way, he might soon become an agreeable singer, and on this score a favorite with the public — but when with his hideous grimaces he treats us to the wretched caricature of an ape, while every look and motion announces the plenitude of his vanity and conceit, it is impossible to look at him with common patience, or to listen to him without disgust, and were he on the London stage, he would most indubitably be hissed off with the contempt he merits.

From the Federal Gazette and Baltimore Daily Advertiser, October 10, 1807:

This day is published & for sale
BY GEORGE HILL

Military Reflections
On four modes of defense for the United States, with a

Plan of Defense.
Adapted to their circumstances and the existing state of things.

*By Maxim ***_____*
Ex-Officer of the État major.
Translated by Eliza Anderson.

Price 25 cents.

Chapter Twenty~one: Eliza

E very day, it seems, bring fresh insults, until it is almost more than I can bear. I had expected this to be the week when I would bask in the reflection of Mr. Godefroy's well deserved glory, as encomiums were heaped upon the service he has rendered to our nation in his newly published memorial. I also hoped that a further modicum of praise might be coming to me in my own right for my translation of *Claire d'Albe*, and that my name might be invoked favorably in the more discerning quarters of town. Instead, thanks to James Cork and his crew of malicious demons, I have been hurled to the hounds of gossip, and the appearance of my name on the title page of Mr. Godefroy's slim volume has only served to sharpen their lust for my blood — and, I fear, for his.

I had thought Spectacles to be dead and safely buried, for to my delight the publication had not appeared in at least six weeks. I credited Mr. Barnes with having realized that the best he could do with the wretched thing was to put it out of its misery, like a rabid dog. Perhaps, I thought, he had purchased it with the very intention of ridding the community of its addled and incessant barking, its frothing about the mouth, its baring of its jagged yellow teeth, and for that he would have my undying gratitude, along with that of the thinking portion of this city's populace.

But no, it seems that Barnes and the rest of them were only lying in wait for an opportunity to prove just how craven and unprincipled they truly are. What better reason for Spectacles' ghoulish resurrection than to spread vile and outlandish lies about the origin of a novel translated by the very person who had formerly given the periodical its *raison d'être*? I can only imagine the cackling joy with which they concocted a tale sufficient to drag my reputation through mud so foul that one would think even they might have hesitated to tread upon it.

But after my initial horror I was struck by the ridiculousness of the whole affair. Who would lend any credit to the accusation that I had drawn the details of *Claire d'Albe* — the novel I had *translated* — from the supposedly sordid events of my own life? Who could possibly believe that my chaste acquaintance with Mr. Godefroy was the inspiration for the moral transgression portrayed in the book? Of course, to preserve the veneer of propriety the anonymous author of the article in Spectacles (clearly none other than James Cork) refrained from alluding to me by name. Oh no, its editors are far too delicate for such open accusations! Instead they contented themselves with sly phrases whose meaning no one could mistake, such as: "The author has been able to render immorality in such vivid colors because she has been *the Observer* of such wicked scenes herself — nay, not merely *the Observer*, but indeed the participant!"

I also was sure I now knew precisely why Mr. Hewes had refused to publish anything regarding *Claire d'Albe* in the Gazette, and why he had fulminated against it so in the note he sent me: behind the smokescreen of moralistic outrage, it was clear, was hidden a base and mercenary motive arising from his financial association with Mr. Barnes and, by extension, with Cork. Had he not lent Barnes the money to purchase Spectacles? And would he therefore not do all he could to further the interests of Spectacles, and to destroy mine? I see now that it's a cabal, no doubt orchestrated by Cork, and that the Gazette and Moonshine and the Lord knows how many other papers are all conspiring against me. Perhaps only the American can still be counted on as a voice in my favor — although of course Mr. Pechin will publish nearly anything he thinks will cause consternation at the Gazette.

Bolstered by the many notes that immediately arrived from friends expressing outrage at the filth that had appeared in Spectacles, or dismissing it with the derision it deserved, I gleefully composed my response, confident that Spectacles had gone so far that its doom was now sealed. So invigorating was this exercise that I immediately went on to pen a review of a performance by the unfortunate Mr. Webster that I had suffered through at the theater the evening before.

Determined to reach the greatest number of people I could, I resolved to publish my response to Spectacles' accusations not only in the Observer but also in the American. I immediately sent it off to Mr. Pechin and was gratified to receive word a few hours later that he would be pleased to publish my letter in Saturday's number. It was only later that I mentioned all this to Father — who has been noble and gracious throughout this ordeal, never once complaining that I have embroiled him in scandal — and I saw him blanch. When I asked him why, he was reluctant to tell me, as the deed was already done, but at last he opined that perhaps a letter in the American would only serve to bring the whole affair to the attention of those who might otherwise never have heard of it.

Alas, his words proved all too prophetic. For this afternoon my Aunt O'Donnell came to take tea, at Father's invitation (would that he had consulted me before extending it!). No sooner had we relieved the good lady of her wrap than she began to hurl queries and insults at me: What was this she had read about an immoral novel I had undertaken to translate? How could I have put myself in a position to be attacked in such a way by Spectacles — a publication she hadn't previously heard of, but with which she had supplied herself immediately upon reading my letter in the American? What brazen and indecent behavior, exactly, had I been indulging in? She should have known what this would lead to, when I undertook to call myself an editor — that I would lose the gentlewoman in me, and descend to vulgarity. That *Adelaide* episode had been bad enough, but this! How did I expect her to hold up her head in society, given our unfortunate connection? Had I made it my purpose in life to embarrass and humiliate her? And — for good measure — she added that she had come upon yesterday's number of the Observer and had been highly offended by my vicious and unfair remarks concerning a favorite of hers, Mr. Webster of the theater.

Naturally, I was seething inside, but I flatter myself that with heroic effort I managed to draw a veil of politeness over my feelings, explaining patiently that there was absolutely no truth to what Spectacles had printed, and that its lies were motivated only by rancor and envy (I thought it best to let her misplaced admiration for Mr. Webster go unchallenged). Father did his best to bolster me in this effort, but I fear we fell somewhat short of success.

Mrs. O'Donnell swept off after only a sip of tea and a nibble of cake, declaring that even if Spectacles had exaggerated the situation, I must have done something improper to attract their notice in the first place, and if I wanted to live out my days in any degree of respectability I must immediately take steps to mend my ways. She didn't need to spell out the consequences of my refusal, as we were all acutely conscious of the fact that title to our house will revert to her upon Father's demise.

"Perhaps, Eliza my dear," said Father quietly after her departure, after we'd spent a moment in stunned silence, "you should be more careful."

"But what am I to do?" I cried, pacing the carpet. "Abandon the Observer, now, when to do so would be seen as an admission of defeat? Would you have me give Cork that satisfaction?"

"No, no, of course not," Father began.

"Or cut off all contact with Mr. Godefroy, when I have done nothing in the least dishonorable?" I was conscious, of course, that I had indeed approached the brink of dishonor, that day when we were interrupted by Margaret—but the fact was, I had turned back. "Must I keep him at a distance," I continued, "simply because some fools who are jealous of my success take it upon themselves to create a scandal out of thin air, when his friendship is to me the one ray of joy in an otherwise bleak existence?"

After a moment I noticed that Father hadn't responded, and I stopped my pacing to look at him. The poor man, he looked quite defeated and deflated. I immediately ran to where he sat in his chair, knelt by his side, and took his hand in mine, overcome by remorse.

"Oh, Father," I said, "you know I didn't mean that! Of course you are a great source of joy to me, you and Polly both. No one could ask for a kinder, a more generous parent, and one who has nurtured not only my body but also my soul, and my mind. It's just that … I only meant …" I was at a loss for words that would convey my meaning and at the same time appear neither too critical of Father nor too inappropriately admiring of Mr. Godefroy.

He patted my hand. "It's all right, my dear. I understand, I assure you. I couldn't ask you to do either of those things, not unless you wanted them yourself. It's unfortunate about Mrs. O'Donnell. And all the rest of it. But." He rose to his feet, struggling a bit, and I gripped his arm to steady him. "We shall manage, we shall manage. We've weathered storms before, and we'll find a way through this one as well, somehow. And now if you'll excuse me, I think I'll take some rest before supper."

And with that he hobbled slowly from the room, looking as though he had somehow aged ten years since Mrs. O'Donnell's arrival. Would that the witch had never darkened our door, and caused my dear father such distress! Surely there are many parents who would have taken her side against me, and denounced my behavior as shocking and intolerable. But if I have been unlucky in many things in life, I can never question the good fortune that sent me a father who truly comprehends what stuff I am made of, and is made of even stronger stuff himself.

From the Federal Gazette and Baltimore Daily Advertiser, October 12, 1807:

MISTRESS "E.A."

The Editor of the Federal Gazette can never be forced into a newspaper controversy with any person: When the malicious assailant is a WOMAN, he can wage no possible war except that of defense.

Several weeks since, an essay signed "Petronius" was offered for the Gazette. The essay was intended to sell a novel translated by Mrs. "E.A." which we thought unfit for female perusal. We refused to publish the essay: This, and only this, is what has armed against us the fierce FURY who edits the "Observer."

We never have published in this paper one line, or word, against the infamous tale entitled "Clara d'Albe." It was because we were too conscientious to praise it, that we have been piously attacked.

Our defense is this—No "lady" of any tolerable delicacy can read "Clara d'Albe" without being filled with disgust at the horrible scene described in the garden. A once lovely woman, reduced to a mere skeleton, is offering up orisons at the tomb of her father; a barbarian rushes upon her—seizes the trembling dying Clara, and .... shame! shame! .... Let the "lady" of delicate taste and refined feeling who has offered it to the females of Baltimore tell the rest. We cannot defile these columns by publishing a chapter, for censuring which we have incurred the high displeasure of the phenomenon in Hanover Street.

To the Public.

The paltry attack against me in Saturday's "Observer" should have been treated with silent contempt had it not plainly appeared to me as the effect of my non-compliance with a requisition previously made. On the 2d of October I received a letter, the purport of which, as near as I can recollect, was as follows:

"In the course of the theatrical season many attempts will be made to injure you by means of newspaper criticisms. I feel for you, as you have many enemies, particularly in the Theatre. *A weekly publication (printed at No. 4, Charles street) may assist you. It is not the Editor's intention to criticize the performers: but should an attack be made, it can be answered in your favor.* The subscription is five dollars a year; *the paper is circulated all over the continent," &c &c*

BEATRICE IRONSIDE.

Could I have anticipated so infamous an attack, I would not have to regret having mislaid this letter. It was impossible to foresee that an accomplished lady, and a Translator *too, could have behaved thus: but for the satisfaction of any person who doubts my word, I will make* affidavit.

Beatrice *is not sorry I did not subscribe; for no doubt she has made more by her scurrilous stuff than the five dollars she applied for — as all my enemies (with whom she seems to be well acquainted), if not already, will soon become subscribers to the "Observer."*

I never have, nor will I, BUY PRAISE; *nor do the* feeble attempts *to injure me trouble me in the least. So long as the audience assembled to witness my performance bestow on me their approbation, I shall laugh at* BEATRICE *and her accomplices.*

W.H. WEBSTER.

From the Federal Gazette and Baltimore Daily Advertiser, October 15, 1807:

Mr. Webster

It appears by a publication in the Federal Gazette of the 13th inst. signed W.H. Webster that some remarks on the gentleman's manner of singing and acting have given him deep offense. If Mr. Webster has suffered from unjust criticism, he will necessarily rise above it; if, on the other hand, judges and men of taste have formed the same opinion as Mistress Beatrice, her advice to him is that he should endeavor to improve by it, instead of wasting his time in abusing a lady.

Beatrice declares, in the most solemn and unequivocal terms she declares, *that no person,* Friend or Enemy, *has she ever yet solicited, personally or* by letter *to become a subscriber. The public will therefore judge of her surprise to find it asserted by Mr. Webster that he had received a letter from her, dated the 2d of October, in which he says she proposed* to prostrate to his use the pages of the Observer for five dollars. *Mr. Webster regrets that he has* lost *the letter which contains this proposal, and suggests if there are those who doubt its veracity that he will "make* affidavit."

The world will judge how far an affidavit *could establish its authenticity.*

Chapter Twenty-two: Margaret

A ll is changed, all is lost, all my pretty dreams vanished like the smoke from last night's fire. I see now that Alice was right, that James never meant any of it. He's no more than a scoundrel, and I a stupid fool.

Today at Mr. Guy's, James was there, and Mr. Webster and Charles Patterson too—and I was far from pleased to see those two, especially Mr. Patterson, for I hadn't seen him since that night in the country and the memory of it made me uneasy, especially with James sitting right there. Also, I feared James would go off with the two of them afterwards instead of having his supper with me, and it had been two weeks since I'd seen him alone. I wanted to ask him more about us getting married, and how long it would take him to get the money we'd need, for I thought it would do me good to have some plan in my head, some date I could look forward to.

But there I was, off in my corner with my drawing paper and the few pastels Mr. Guy has let me use, and the gentlemen were at the other end of the room, Mr. Guy occupied with a woman who'd come in holding her mouth and groaning. The others were talking about what Mrs. A had said about Mr. Webster, and what Mr. Webster should do. I haven't read all the papers they were talking about, but I've certainly heard Mrs. A going on about a letter Mr. Webster says she wrote, and which she says she didn't. James was saying there was no point in Mr. Webster swearing he'd received the letter—that those inclined to believe Mr. Webster would simply accept his word, and those inclined against him would scarcely be convinced by his swearing to it. And Mr.

Patterson was saying Mr. Webster could simply say he'd *found* the letter, perhaps under a pile of papers. From the way they were talking, I was pretty well convinced there'd never been any such letter, but of course I didn't say so.

"Oh, never mind the letter," James said, sounding weary of it all.

"But the letter was your idea in the first place!" Mr. Webster spluttered.

"Yes, but it's time to let the matter rest. Her ship will soon sink, and you'll be part of the reason for it—that's all that's important. She can't go on much longer. Not with all that's being said and whispered about her. She's proven she's no lady, swinging her fists at all and sundry, and abandoning all decency with that Frenchman. And did you see the article about his memorial in the American?"

"The one calling Napoleon a Corsican adventurer?" said Mr. Patterson. "And saying that the French had degenerated into a nation of plunderers and assassins? I'm surprised the American was willing to publish it, even if Pechin did add a note condemning the insults to France."

"That's the one," said James. "So you see, her lover has been exposed as a sworn enemy of Napoleon and all things French— no doubt because he was foiled in his plotting against the man, and still wants his revenge. And her father has become a laughingstock, what with his insistence that man is no better than the animals, and that all of us dying from disease is a benefit devoutly to be wished. Not to mention his veritable obsession with the insect kingdom."

Mr. Guy turned from the festering open mouth into which he had been peering. "Did you see he recommended crushed ladybird as a remedy for toothache? What nonsense!"

"The fact is," James continued, "she's proven the dangers of allowing a woman to assume a position of responsibility. They can't help it, it's their natural vanity that leads them astray. They acquire a smattering of learning, and they grow so puffed up with pride they become convinced they know more than anyone else. That, combined with their inability to restrain their emotions ... well, this is a perfect example of what can happen." He sighed. "I blame myself, at least in part. Not that I ever intended that she become editor of the blasted paper, though. That was all her idea! Anyway, I say let her be, and she'll be hoist by her own petard."

"But here now, Cork," Mr. Webster whined, "she's made me look a fool. There must be something I can do!"

I was growing tired of listening to all this, and agitated as well—for I still felt bad about what I'd told James Mrs. A and Mr. G were doing that day in the sitting room, and also I was sorry to hear people are laughing at the Doctor, whatever he may have said to bring it on himself.

Mr. Guy had set me to sketching a bowl of apples again—the same bowl I'd sketched the week before, and judging from the flies buzzing round the wrinkled fruit, the same apples as well. He's been distracted lately—for in addition to the usual landscapes, he's agreed to paint seascapes on three card tables for Findlay's furniture shop, and also two tavern signs, not to mention all the toothache patients coming round for his cure—and he seems to have forgotten that he said he would help me learn to draw faces. So I got up my courage and interrupted the conversation to tell Mr. Guy that I'd been drawing some portraits on my own, and that I'd brought them with me in that portfolio he gave me, and would he please be so good as to look at them and tell me what he thought.

He said he supposed he would have to, though of course he didn't approve of my embarking on such attempts without supervision, and after sending the patient off with a vial of his potion he strutted to where I sat, his feet sticking slightly outwards like a duck's, the other gentlemen trailing after him. I hadn't intended for them all to come, but I didn't mind, for I was proud of my work.

I brought out my sketches, which were mostly of Polly, but I had a few others as well: one of Mrs. Morris that she'd allowed me to do while she was making a stew one day and was in unusually good spirits, and one I'd done from memory of the Doctor. And the one of Alice, which I'd never shown him, though I thought it had come out well in the end, and I was glad I'd decided to take out the bruises around the eye. But the portrait I liked best, of course—the one of James asleep in bed—was safely back home, under my mattress.

Mr. Guy nodded and squinted at the drawings, and I was holding my breath, waiting for him to tell me what he thought.

"Not bad," he said at last, "not bad at all. Some of the proportions aren't quite right—you see that eyebrow there, how it's off by at least an eighth of an inch? But you've got a real talent for drawing faces, my girl, that you do. If you work hard enough at it, someday you may become a true portraitist."

I began to breathe again, and to smile as well, and I felt a warmth spread all through me. I was so pleased that I scarcely noticed Mr. Patterson taking James by the elbow and drawing him away, and them talking in another corner of the room. And then it was time for my lesson to end, but the gentlemen— including James—made no move to leave, so I took my time collecting my things, hoping that James would come over and invite me to supper, or at least make some excuse for why he couldn't. But he said nothing, and I couldn't catch his eye, try as I might.

So at last I mustered my courage and walked right over to him and said, "Mr. Cork, might I have a word with you in private? Outside?" Just like a fine lady, I said it, though my heart was pounding. I suppose Mr. Guy's praise had gone to my head.

James sighed and looked like he was about to say no, but then he made an apology to his friends and said he would return shortly. He didn't even put on his hat. We went down the stairs and out to the street, me frantically searching my brain for what I would say to him.

"What is it?" he barked when we were outside. "Has your mistress been up to more mischief with her Frenchman?"

A chill wind was blowing, and I bundled my cloak about my neck. "No, it's not that." I'd done enough damage there and was determined to say no more on the subject, even if it were true.

"Well, then, what do you want with me? My friends are waiting."

I couldn't account for the change in his manner. It seemed I was the last person in the world he wanted to speak with, that I was nothing more than a nuisance. What had happened to all the affection he'd shown me, and the sweet words he'd whispered? I tried to think what I might have done or said that had turned him against me but could think of nothing.

"I thought we might have supper this evening, you and me. Like we usually do. And then, you know, we could be together." I put a hand on his sleeve but he brushed it away.

"I promised Webster and Patterson I'd dine with them." He was looking off into the distance, and his manner was so cold he might have been talking to some clerk in a shop.

"James!" I said, my voice beginning to tremble. I could feel the tears coming on. "I don't understand. Tell me what's wrong, what's happened."

He looked at me at last, his eyes boring into me. "What's *happened*? What's happened is I've realized who and what you truly are. You could at least have been honest with me."

"But I have been!" I began to panic, thinking of the lies I'd told him about Mrs. A. Had he somehow learned the truth? "And anyway, what about you and your Mr. Webster? You know she didn't write any such letter to him, and yet you went and told him to say she did, just to make her look bad. I don't see that that's anything worse than what I've done."

James looked at me as though I'd begun to speak a language he didn't understand. "I don't know what you're talking about. What you've done is entirely different."

I still thought he meant what I'd told him about Mrs. A. Somewhere inside me I knew what I'd made up about her was worse than the letter, but I wanted to convince him that we were the same. "At least I didn't invent something out of whole cloth! All right, perhaps the front of her frock wasn't open, and his trousers weren't unbuttoned. But I know there was something going on between them, I could feel it in the air."

Now James looked truly puzzled, drawing his head back and screwing up his face. "You're saying you invented those things? You lied to me about what you saw?" He closed his eyes for a moment and bit his lip, as though trying to keep himself from losing his temper. "I should have expected as much, I suppose. I should have known you had a filthy mind, given what you've come from."

Now it was my turn to draw back. "What I've come from? Whatever are you talking about?"

He glanced behind him at the door to Mr. Guy's studio, as though he longed to be back in its warmth, or longed to be anywhere other than standing in the street talking to me. "That drawing you took out today, the one of that girl—the whore. She's a common bunter, works the docks. And you told me you were a respectable girl, that you came from a good family, even if a poor one. But if that were true, how would you have known a girl like that, let alone drawn her portrait?"

I stood for a moment with my mouth hanging open, so stunned I forgot I was shivering with cold. "Alice? But she's a friend! Or she was. From when I lived down at the Point. And yes, it's true she gets her living that way, but that doesn't mean she's an evil person—it's the only way she can keep body and soul together, that's all."

He drew his fingers through his golden hair and turned away, and it looked as though he was about to go back inside.

"But what ho, then!" I cried. "If *you're* so virtuous, how is it that you recognized Alice's portrait? How do you come to know a girl like that yourself?"

"I don't." He hesitated a moment and drew his jacket tighter, but his face was still turned from me, in the direction of the door. "It was Patterson. He told me who she was."

I froze for a moment, wondering what else Mr. Patterson might have told him. But I couldn't let him go, not knowing if I would ever see him again. "Just because I know a girl who gets her living that way, that makes you think I've done it too? After all I've told you, all we've said to one another?"

"I know there's something you *haven't* told me." He turned around, and his eyes were narrow and cold. "Something else Patterson did tell me."

So he knew. I swallowed. There was no point in denying it. "When did he tell you?"

"Right after he came back from Springfield, and I came back from Ballston. At first I was furious at you, allowing him such liberties. But then I gave the matter some thought, and I realized that must be what girls like you expected, what you wanted. I realized I'd been a fool. Why should Patterson be the only one to take his pleasure with you? Why shouldn't I have some amusement as well?"

I leaned against the brick wall of the building, to steady myself. "So that's all I've been to you? Some amusement? Because that's not all you've been to me. Yes, I wanted you to kiss me, to hold me. But only because I loved you. And I thought you loved me."

A man and a woman walked towards us, laughing together. James waited until they'd gone past, his arms crossed in front of his chest and his head downcast, then when they were out of earshot he turned back to me. "Perhaps I did love you, for a time. I don't know anymore." He moved closer, putting an arm on the wall above my head, and lowered his voice to a harsh whisper. "When Patterson told me what the two of you had done, laughing about it, I didn't know what to think. There were times when I thought he must have made it up, just to irritate me. But now ..." The muscles in his face tightened like a line pulled taut by a fish. He took his arm from the wall and stood straight before me. "I see now that it was true. And perhaps worse is true as well."

"But I only went with him because I thought you were going to marry that Philadelphia lady! I was vexed with you." The tears were spilling from my eyes, and I wiped my cheek with the back of one of my freezing hands. "Not to mention that he could have easily had me booted from my position and tossed out on the street if I'd refused him, with all he knew about me and you. *And* he seemed to think you'd already had me, and where would he have gotten that idea from, if not from you?"

"I never told him that. He drew that conclusion on his own, because that's the type of fellow *he* is, and I suppose he couldn't imagine anyone else behaving differently."

"But you never corrected him, did you? You never told him I was something more to you than a cheap moll who was good for a wapping now and then." I swallowed hard and tried to keep my voice steady. "Why didn't you tell him you loved me, and that we were to be married?"

James moved so that his back was towards me, his arms crossed and his shoulders hunched.

"He's the only man I've ever been with, aside from you," I said, sobbing now despite my best efforts. "Why is it so important? I don't love him. I don't even like him!"

He turned and stared at me. "And you think that makes it all right?" He shook his head and narrowed his eyes at me. "I should have known better than to think I could ever ..." Now he looked up at the brick wall above my head and seemed almost to be talking to himself. "That you could be my *wife*? That my family would ever welcome you? A woman who counts prostitutes among her friends? No, it could never have been. We're just too different, you and I."

My tears stopped, and I felt a fierce anger begin to take their place. I had thought he had liked me being different, and telling him things he'd never have heard from his fine lady friends. Now I could see it had all been talk and play-acting for him.

"And do you think I would *want* to be the wife of someone who was ashamed of me, who wouldn't want his friends or his parents to know me?" I felt more tears rising, but these were tears of anger. I swallowed them down. "Oh, we're different all right, you and me. I would never have led someone on the way you did, telling them I loved them when all along I thought they were no better than the dirt beneath my feet. Yes, *we*'re different, but you're just the same as *she* is, thinking you're better than others just because you have money and know which fork to use at dinner. At least Mrs. A is honest about it, and comes out and says she doesn't believe in democracy and equality and all those things you pretend to love!"

He glared at me, and when he spoke again his voice was quiet and cold. "How dare you? When it's clear all you wanted from me was what my money could buy you—first the drawing lessons and the suppers at the Sow's Ear, but then when that wasn't enough you wanted more."

I stood there, stunned, feeling warm tears running down my frozen cheeks. I wanted to tell him it wasn't true. But I couldn't speak, maybe because part of it was true, in a way—I didn't know. I could only look at him, wondering how I ever could have loved someone like him, someone so cruel and hateful, wondering whether I'd been lying all along, not just to him but to myself.

"Go home now, Margaret," he said in a dull voice, moving away again. "Your teeth are chattering."

And then he opened the door to Mr. Guy's studio and disappeared, taking all my fond hopes with him.

From the Baltimore American and Commercial Daily Advertiser, October 20, 1807:

To the Editor of the American.

SIR,

Whatever may be the nature of my private opinions, every reader of the Military Reflections *I have just submitted to the attention of your countrymen will perceive I have not suffered them to appear in any way in the treatise. I believed that I owed this tribute to the country where I had found liberty and peace, and this has been the only motive which induced me to take up my pen. I have repeated to the Americans that which I would have said to my own countrymen:* Be on your guard. *And France more than Spain or England was not the object of this general advice.*

Accept the assurance of consideration with which I have the honor to be, Sir,

Your humble & obedient servant,

MAXIMILIAN.

Chapter Twenty-three: Eliza

I have been called onto the carpet by Her Highness the Duchess of South Street, and it seems I have no choice but to obey. Or to state the case more precisely, I now understand what I must do, and it is perhaps a matter of coincidence that it corresponds to Betsy's wishes.

The summons arrived early this afternoon, and I dutifully hied myself to the Patterson manse within the hour. I suspected the reason, although no explanation was offered: no doubt Betsy, having recently returned from the country, had become aware of the unfortunate controversies in which I have been embroiled, including most recently the accusations against Mr. Godefroy's memorial. What nonsense—the volume is hardly biased against the French government or the French people, although Mr. Gode-froy surely has every right to rail against the former. It was only the writer of the review in the American who expressed, rather crudely, an antipathy towards the French, and in such a way that unsophisticated readers might mistakenly attribute such views to Mr. Godefroy himself. The likelihood of such a mistake was then compounded when Mr. Pechin, whose adoration of the French has apparently remained undimmed despite the outrages committed by their Emperor, railed against the article he had just published in his own paper in the most intemperate terms.

Thus, when I arrived and was ushered into the sitting room, I was not surprised to see Betsy wearing a stern expression and holding the offending number of the American in her hand.

"It's all nonsense of course," I told her even before she'd had an opportunity to speak. "Nothing to do with what's actually in

Mr. Godefroy's memorial, I assure you. Here, I brought you a copy so you can see for yourself."

I proffered the slim volume, even though we can scarcely afford to give them away, what with the printer's bill looming over us. But she made no move to take it.

"It's not a question of what's actually in the memorial. I cannot have my name associated with someone who is perceived to have disparaged the French nation and more particularly its Emperor. Calling him, what?" She scanned the paper for a moment. "A Corsican adventurer? Really!"

I knew better than to venture that the statement had some truth to it. And I presumed it would make no difference that Mr. Godefroy himself had said no such thing — and had even published a letter in the American defending his absolute neutrality. Nor did I point out that with Jerome now married off to a German princess, the chances that the Emperor will do anything for Betsy are faint at best. But she persists in nursing hopes that he'll confer some title on her, or at least on little Bo — who, if legitimized, would immediately achieve an enviable position in the line of succession, Napoleon having no heir and little chance of producing one with the aging Empress.

"But Betsy." I strove for a soothing tone. "How is your name associated with any of this? You have no connection with Mr. Godefroy."

"No, but I have a connection with *you*, one that is well known to the French authorities, since you were with me at Lisbon and Amsterdam, and then at London you were listed as one of the official witnesses to Bo's birth."

Yes, I thought, along with a small host of others, with the document even authenticated by the King of England's own notary, as though such trappings would ensure royal status for the child.

"And not only does your name appear as the translator of this memorial," Betsy continued, "*your* connection with Mr. Godefroy is well known. One might even say notorious."

"Betsy!" I stood from the silk-upholstered chair I had taken. "How many times must I defend myself to you against that villain Cork? Surely you don't believe —"

"Whether I believe it or not isn't important. I've told you, it's what people perceive that matters. And I'm quite confident there are French agents in this city reporting back to the French government on every word they read in Spectacles, or the American, or the Gazette, without any scruples as to its truth. And the whole *Clara d'Albe* affair doesn't help matters, I can assure you."

"Oh, Betsy, really! You read the novel, you know what nonsense this all is. And you're asking me to do what, cease publication of the Observer?"

"That would certainly be the wisest course, but it's not entirely necessary. Indeed, some good has come from the undertaking, and you may be capable of effecting more, if you handle matters correctly."

I was about to express my relief, but she held up a hand to stop me and continued. "But what I do need from you immediately is an assurance that you will sever all connection with Mr. Godefroy. Really, I don't understand why you haven't done it already. This has gone on long enough."

Once again, as at Springfield that day, she betrayed no understanding of what a wrenching loss such a renunciation would be to me. And to demand it of me, as though it were her right!

"I'm afraid I cannot give you such an assurance," I said, standing and reaching for my bonnet, which was lying on a side table. I no longer cared about sparing her feelings, or humoring her delusions of impending grandeur. "I'm sorry if my friendship with the gentleman ruins your chances of a title, but it can't be helped. I suppose you're condemned to spend the rest of your life as a commoner in Baltimore, like the rest of us."

She placed a hand on my arm, to halt my preparations for departure. "Eliza, please, it's not only for my sake, or even that of my poor little Bo, that I ask this of you." Her voice had softened now, and when I looked up I saw that her features were suffused with concern. "What of your father, whose life has been darkened once already by the disgrace brought upon him by his offspring? Really, Eliza, can you bring yourself to inflict such pain upon him yet again?"

Now her arrow had hit its mark, and I felt myself flinch. I had almost managed to convince myself that the scandal caused by Thomas's behavior had been forgotten, that Father and I were the only ones in the town who remembered. But here in Betsy's words was confirmation that the story lived on.

It's been six years since we last had direct word from Thomas, five years since the news of his fate reached us. There are times when I almost forget that I ever had a brother, although as a child I worshipped him, wanting no greater reward in life than his company and his approval. Father should have known better than to expend a small fortune—one that we could ill afford—to send him to England to study medicine, for Thomas never showed much inclination for science or study of any kind. But it was Father's fond hope that a child of his should take up his own noble profession and perhaps continue his research and develop his theories. And as I was a female that mantle fell to Thomas, whether it fit him well or not.

We had begun to suspect, when his letters came less and less frequently, that, alone and far from the benevolent influence of his family, Thomas had abandoned his studies and given himself over to a life of idleness and indulgence. But still, when the news came from Father's friend Mr. McCalmont that Thomas had been arrested and thrown into Newgate, it was nearly beyond our comprehension. He had always been mischievous—the sort of boy over whom a parent must keep close watch—but neither of us could have anticipated the depths to which he had sunk.

For it was not merely debtors' prison to which Thomas had been sent—although no doubt he would have been an eligible candidate for that barbaric institution as well. Mr. McCalmont had chosen his words with delicacy, but it was nevertheless clear that Thomas had committed unspeakable crimes against nature, that he had fallen in with a circle of debauched aristocrats who themselves escaped censure or punishment while ruining the lives and reputations of the young men whom they employed for their amusement.

How such news—of events that transpired an ocean away, and which was communicated to us in strictest confidence—should have spread so quickly through Baltimore is a mystery to me. But then again, the hunger for gossip and scandal in this place is so fierce, so rapacious, I shouldn't have been surprised. So small is the world here, so narrow the minds, that a few words in a letter from a business connection in London, or some whispered hints by a traveler freshly returned from Europe, are sufficient to light a merry fire that races from house to house, consuming one dinner party after another. I can recall several occasions during that time when Father and I made our entrance and perceived the assembled guests immediately fall into a guilty silence, broken only when some brave soul led the retreat to a safer subject, the weather or the price of coffee.

Through it all, Father would brook no discussion of the matter, even when I tried to reassure him that Thomas must have been led astray by evil companions, that he would never have committed so monstrous a sin had he not been lured into it by deception or forced by financial necessity. At last he cut me off with the chilling words that in his mind he no longer had a son. We have not spoken of Thomas since.

But I shook these distressing memories off, reminding myself of Father's words to me after that unfortunate visit from my Aunt O'Donnell. "No, Betsy, you're wrong. Father has paid no attention to all this nonsense. He would never ask me to end my friendship with Mr. Godefroy because of it. He told me so himself."

"Oh, did he?" Betsy pursed her lips and looked down at the carpet for a moment, as though unsure whether to continue. "Eliza, I hadn't wanted to tell you this," she said, looking up, "as it was told to me in confidence. But you leave me no choice."

A chill went through me, and I lowered myself once more onto the chair across from her.

"Your father met with mine a few days ago—something to do with the repayment of that loan, I believe."

"What? He never mentioned—"

She shook her head. "It isn't the loan I want to talk about. During the course of the conversation, your father confessed to mine that he had been much distressed of late, because of all the gossip concerning you, and the scandal. It appears that it has brought back to him the entire affair surrounding your brother, in the most vivid colors."

My mouth had fallen open, but I managed to speak. "But no, Betsy, surely you—you and your father—are mistaken. Father has never given me the slightest reason to believe that any of this has distressed him."

She cocked her head and gave me a sad and sympathetic smile. "But of course he wouldn't, would he? He's far too selfless, and too concerned for your happiness, to ask you to make any sacrifice on his account. And yet he's suffering, and no doubt doing his best to hide it from you. He told Papa that his sleep has been quite disturbed, and that his appetite has fallen off. All on account of your connection with Mr. Godefroy, and all that it has brought in its wake."

I drew my hands to my face and rubbed my forehead, trying to make sense of what Betsy was saying. It was true that Father hadn't been looking well these past few weeks. I recalled how he had difficulty rising from his chair after Aunt O'Donnell's visit, and the way he had shuffled weakly from the room. And how he'd admonished me to be "more careful." Had that been his gentle way of asking me to refrain from any further contact with Mr. Godefroy? It would be like him, very like him, to keep his anguish from me, and to refrain from making demands that would restrain my freedom.

I was seized with the deepest pangs of guilt and shame, thinking of how selfish I had been, so absorbed in pursuing my own happiness that I had been oblivious to his misery. Is this how I repaid his years of tender care and solicitude on my behalf?

I rose from my chair, swallowing hard in an effort to compose myself. "Betsy, I must thank you for telling me this. I should have realized …"

Betsy stood and embraced me, the first time she had shown me such affection in months. "I'm so sorry, my dear. I know how difficult this will be for you. But I also know you will do what you must, for the sake of your father." She stood back and looked at me levelly. "But promise me you won't tell him that I've told you this. He specifically instructed my father that you mustn't know how this affair has been affecting him!"

I gave Betsy my solemn oath that I would say nothing to Father, and set out towards home with leaden foot and aching heart, knowing that once I arrived I must put pen to paper and find the words to tell Mr. Godefroy that we must never meet again.

Chapter Twenty-four: Margaret

My monthly visitor is now more than three weeks late, and I've had a peculiar queasy feeling in my stomach of the mornings. I'm no midwife, but I've heard enough to know that chances are I'm with child, just as Alice said would happen. I suppose I should have been more careful. And I suppose a part of me thought that if it did happen, that would make James want to marry me, quick like, to give the child his name and make everything right in the eyes of God and the law. I've seen marriages come about like that more than once, down at the Point, when a fellow gets a respectable woman in the family way.

But of course, by the time I realized my circumstances, I didn't want to be married to James any more, and I was certain he didn't want to be married to me, if he ever had. I don't want to get rid of the child, Lord knows. It's a sin, of course, and besides that, I'd love nothing better than to have a little one of my own—a little girl, perhaps, like Polly, or Fanny. It would be someone to love, and someone who would love me back, someone at my side to help me get through life. But what would Mrs. A say, or even the Doctor, if they knew of my condition? I'd be out on my ear in a flash, that's certain, with no job and no place to rest my head. And how could I take care of a child if I couldn't even take care of myself?

So I resolved to go down to the Point and ask Alice how I might get out of this situation, as she'd as good as told me she knew a way to fix these things. I had an idea she might have found herself in similar difficulties once or twice, although she always said she knew ways to prevent the babes from coming (and now I wished I'd asked her what they were). All week I'd been having moments of terror, thinking of what lay ahead, but I'd always calm myself with the thought that come Saturday I'd find Alice and she would put it all to rights. And I decided to bring her portrait to her at last, for I felt guilty about keeping it, and for having such angry thoughts about her when it turns out she was the one who was seeing things clearly. Besides, I wanted to rid myself of the drawing, as it was part of what had caused the trouble between James and me.

But when I got to Mrs. Brooks' today I found that Alice had disappeared, and Mrs. Brooks had no idea what had become of her.

"Could be jail," she said, hacking away at a soup bone in the kitchen, "could be worse, knowing the kinds of things that wench got up to. Or maybe she just didn't want to pay the rent she owed me. All I know is, I haven't seen the hussy these last four days. Left all her fine clothes and things, and if she doesn't come back in the next day or two, I've a mind to sell it all and rent the room to someone else."

I'd almost stopped listening, for though I was afraid for Alice, I was equally afraid for myself. At the same time the smell from the greasy soup boiling on Mrs. Brooks' fire was having its effect on my stomach. Suddenly I felt my insides give a heave, and I had to run out to the street to cast up my accounts right outside the door. When I finished, Mrs. Brooks was standing there, her arms crossed and her lips pursed.

"Sorry," I said, drawing an arm across my mouth. "I'll clean it up if you can give me a bucket and a rag."

She did, and even filled the bucket with water for me, which was kind. I set about the task, and I thought she'd go back to her foul scum of a soup, but instead she stopped to watch.

"Sprained your ankle, then, have you?" she said after a minute.

No, I told her, my ankle was fine.

"No, I mean—you've got yourself a white swelling, don't you?"

Now I understood. I nodded, keeping my eyes on the mess I was collecting in the rag and trying to keep my skirts out of it.

"What are you going to do about it, then? You're not planning to have it?"

I stopped and shook my head. "I don't want to," I began. But I couldn't finish.

She was silent a minute. And then: "I know someone who could help you with that."

I dropped the rag into the bucket and looked up.

"But it'll cost you," she said. "At least ten dollars, maybe more."

"I haven't got near that much," I said, wiping my hands on my skirts. I've been saving my pennies for paper and charcoals, and even perhaps some pastels, for now that I can't go to Mr. Guy's I need to buy supplies if I want to continue drawing. I'd been thinking I could use that money for whatever Alice told me I must do, but it's no more than four dollars.

"Well, you'd best find it somewhere, and soon," Mrs. Brooks said. "Another month or two and it'll cost you a good deal more. Wait too long, and you'll find yourself a mother, like it or not." She sighed and picked up the bucket with my mess in it. "You go along now, I'll take care of this. And I'll not ask you for the money you still owe for that room, not this time. You get yourself taken care of, my girl, and then we can settle up. Come back when you've got the money, and I'll tell you where to go."

I thanked her, for she was kind in her way, but I stumbled back towards Hanover Street, scarcely able to think straight. Six dollars, all I make in a month. If I spend nothing in the coming month, only eat what they give me and buy no new ribbons for my bonnet or anything else, perhaps I can do it. No, I *will* do it. I must.

From the Observer, October 31, 1807:

ANATHEMA AGAINST NOVELS, THEATERS, & ACTORS, BY A RIGID MORALIST.

Have we not under our eyes an example of the infamy of novels in a recent production, terrible, odious, execrable, abominable, and infamous, which will forever destroy the innocence of our morals!! Yes, generation of vipers, you have before you this rock *of offense. Oh! had you profited by the assistance of some excellent SPECTACLES, you would have distinctly read a sign of malediction in these dreadful words: CLARA D'ALBE! Then if you had not been insensible to all compunction, you would have seized the bookseller, the printer, the printer's devils, the translator, the corrector, the paper-merchant, and the letter-founder; and you would have cut these impure pagans into pieces, joining in one bonfire with them the oil, the blacking, the ink, and even the pens which had served to convey such a stumbling block of abomination into the world.*

But I arrest my pen — for I feel that human weakness would tempt me to utter propositions contrary to that liberty of opinion which characterizes our nation, and to that spirit of toleration from which I can never deviate.

Chapter Twenty-five: Eliza

Today began on a note that was bittersweet—testament to the inestimable bonds of true friendship, and the generosity that we humans are capable of extending to one another at our best. And it ended, alas, with a shocking reminder of what depths some of us, at least, are willing to sink to, repaying trust and benevolence with cruel betrayal.

But first, to the morning, which I much prefer to revisit. I was delighted to find at my door none other than Bess Caton, even though I was in the midst of a lesson with Polly—and she was making good progress, for a change, for I had decided to make up a little story for her to read, and to my surprise the indifference she usually displays at deciphering the letters of a psalm or prayer turned to eagerness. But I broke off the lesson with little regret, for Bess had only just returned from one of her family's extended sojourns in Annapolis, and it had been weeks since I'd seen her.

There she was, her small red mouth smiling warmly as ever, her dark eyes beaming at me from beneath a turban of the latest style. "Oh, all these books," she sighed, as she always does when she enters Father's library. "Would that I had them all at my fingertips as you do!"

"Would you like to borrow one?" I said, thinking that perhaps that was the reason for her visit. I can scarcely credit that she would prefer my frayed, dusty hovel to the elegant Caton manse, but her expressions of yearning always have the ring of sincerity to them. "There's a new edition of the Edinburgh Review that might interest you, I just picked it up from Bradford's. I know it's here somewhere …"

"No, no, not today. But indeed it's a book that has brought me here. Yours!"

"Mine? You mean *Clara d'Albe*?" Although she gave every indication of being pleased, I couldn't help experiencing a small degree of trepidation as I awaited her response.

"*Clara d'Albe* indeed. What a marvelous tale, and so well told. And well translated, I might add." She gave a little sideways roll of her eyes. "I know I should have read it in French, but I'm far too lazy!"

"You, lazy? Never! But I'm pleased to have made it easier for you to sample the story, and even more pleased that you enjoyed it. Not everyone approves, you know."

"Oh, indeed, I do!" She settled herself into Father's chair, removed her turban, and patted her dark hair into place. "That letter in Saturday's number of the Observer, the one from the 'Rigid Moralist' — I might have thought the author was Mamma, only she wouldn't have written it in jest! I had to hide the book in the bottom of my clothes press and read it when no one was about. What a lot of fuss over nothing. I've lent it to Marianne, but I've sworn her to secrecy."

Our conversation continued at a sprightly pace, ranging over a variety of current topics: the news of Vice-President Burr's acquittal on treason charges, and the rumor that he would soon be stopping in our very own city at the house of his attorney, Mr. Martin; the dimming prospects of war with England, now that its government had officially repudiated the action of the *Leopard* in firing on the *Chesapeake*; and the rumors that Mr. Jefferson would bow to the clamor of those who demanded revenge through the use of some commercial measure of retaliation, perhaps even barring trade between the United States and England.

"Which would only inflict grievous damage on our economy," Bess remarked with her usual authority, "while scarcely affecting the vast commerce carried on by Great Britain."

I murmured that I was sure she was right, although in truth I've scarcely followed the controversy of late, being too caught up in my own concerns, and not much one for political debate even in the best of times. But there was one piece of news, of a far more domestic nature, that I had been eager to ask her about.

"What's this I've heard about a suitor?" I ventured. "A Mr. Greenfield of New York, is it not, whose eye you caught at

Ballston last summer? It's said he's quite presentable, and comes of a good family."

"Oh …" She gave her head a small dismissive shake. "He's presentable enough, I suppose, but not particularly alluring. Just another respectable merchant, whose main topics of conversation are the price of grain and the weather. Mamma is quite taken with him, but then she's not the one who would need to make conversation with him day in and day out."

"Ah well, you're right to be cautious. Once you're in a marriage, it's exceedingly difficult to get out of it." I gave her a rueful smile, which she returned in kind, as Margaret came in with the tea and cakes I'd asked her for. "But they say Miss Burton is engaged to be married to Mr. Haskins, and Mr. Littlefield to a Miss Briggs of New York."

"Yes, a veritable epidemic of matrimony breaking out! And did you hear that Mr. Cork is to be married to that lady from Philadelphia? A Miss Scattergood?"

I was just beginning to say that I had heard a rumor to that effect, although it was no concern of mine what that scoundrel did, when Margaret hurriedly set down the tray and ran from the room without pouring the tea. What rudeness, I thought, to abandon her duties like that, but rather than call the urchin back I poured it out myself.

"What about you, then?" Bess said after a pause, stirring sugar into her cup.

"Me?" I felt myself color, wondering what she might believe of Cork's lies concerning what had transpired between Mr. Godefroy and myself, despite the kind note she'd sent me shortly after the tale appeared in Spectacles. "Whatever do you mean? You know I'm already married, to my eternal chagrin."

"Of course." We were both silent for a moment, and then she added, "But one may still have feelings."

I stiffened. "I've done nothing dishonorable."

"Oh, I never for a moment thought you had! Anyone who knows you as I do couldn't possibly have believed those ridiculous insinuations. But …" She took a sip of her tea, then took a breath, and put the cup and saucer down on the side table. "I saw Mr. Godefroy recently, at the Legrands'. Such a charming, intelligent gentleman. And he speaks of you with the utmost respect and admiration."

"Does he?" My voice sounded high and cracked, almost not my own. I reached for my tea, hoping that I could mask some of the emotion that was beginning to engulf me by swallowing it. "I haven't seen him of late, myself."

I had written him a note as soon as I'd returned from Betsy's that day, some two weeks ago now, fearing that if I delayed my resolve would desert me.

"I hope you haven't let this ridiculous gossip distress you," Bess said gently. "It would be unfortunate if you felt you could no longer associate with the gentleman because of what a few un-principled fools choose to say. I've seen how the two of you take such innocent pleasure in one another's company."

"Oh, we do. Or rather, we did." I forced a smile and swal-lowed hard. "You wouldn't understand, Bess. It's not that I my-self care what the town says." I paused, fearing that any explana-tion might lead to a discussion of the scandal caused by Thom-as, a subject for which I hadn't the strength. "But I have other reasons. And really, I'm perfectly content. I have my books." I waved towards the bookshelves, then stood and approached them, my back to Bess, fearing that my face would betray my feelings. "The consolations of philosophy, as Boethius says. And of course, I have masses of work to do for the Observer, as usual. Now, where is that Edinburgh Review? It's here somewhere, and there's an essay I know you would ..."

My voice broke at that moment, despite my efforts, and the tears overcame me. I leaned against the books and tried to steady myself, but it seemed that all the emotion I'd been holding in check these last two weeks was now washing over me, a mighty Niagara against which I stood powerless. I'd been telling myself that I needed nothing more than my books, my work—just as I'd told Bess. But it was no use.

For once, the metaphysical reading that in the past has so often lifted me from my melancholy had failed to distract me, and I found myself staring at the same page of Smith or Kames for many minutes on end, unable to attend. As for producing the Observer each week, I scarcely know how I have managed it. Indeed, were there only my own interests to consider, I might well have brought the experiment to a close and refunded sub-scription payments to those few subscribers who have made them. But I know Father is intent on completing his series on quarantine, no matter the public reception, and there seems to be no end to it in sight.

"Oh, Eliza!" Bess was at my side, her arm about my shoulders, her mouth by my ear. "It isn't fair, that you should be bound to a man who is a husband in name only."

I turned to her and took the handkerchief that she'd extended. "And Mr. Godefroy has told me," I managed to say through my tears, as I dabbed at my eyes and nose, "that if I were free he would be honored to call me his …" I almost couldn't pronounce the word. "His wife."

He'd said this and a great many more things in the note he sent in response to my own, two weeks ago, a note that I've read over many times since, although I know that for the sake of my sanity I should have consigned it to the fire. Indeed, I've involuntarily memorized his words: "My dear Madame, I will of course respect your wishes and shall not trouble you again. But know that I will be waiting, should your disposition change. I have waited forty-five years to discover a woman like you, one with whom I would gladly share my humble life and modest fortunes, if she would have me, and I will continue to wait for you as long as necessary, forever if need be. For there is no one else in the world for me."

"Have you thought," Bess said cautiously, "of a divorce?"

I shook my head, remembering Betsy's words that day in Springfield — raising and then immediately dashing the possibility. "How could I? I have no money, nor any connections in the Assembly. I could never manage to obtain a private bill."

"Oh, that wouldn't be so difficult. I'm sure my grandfather could arrange it, under the circumstances. He's still a hero of the Revolution, you know. The Assembly will do anything he asks. And he'll do anything I ask."

I drew back from Bess's embrace, and for a moment I felt my heart jump in my chest. But no, I scolded myself. Even if I were to divorce Henry Anderson and marry Mr. Godefroy, the gossips would feast like vultures on my supposed lack of virtue — indeed, no doubt they would take our marriage as confirmation that in our passion we had thrown honor aside and only later sanctified our union in the eyes of God and the law. Not that such nonsense would matter to me, of course, but I now knew that for Father it would be too much to bear.

"No, Bess," I said, clenching her handkerchief into a tiny ball in my fist. "It's an extremely kind offer, but I'm afraid I must decline."

Bess and I were silent a moment, and I felt she wanted to inquire further, but her good manners prevailed. She only smiled and nodded before gathering her turban and gloves, and I fetched her cloak. As we stood at the front door, I thanked her again.

"You'll let me know if you ever change your mind, won't you?" she said, as though I'd declined an invitation to tea. But then, just as she went out, she paused on the front step and turned to me. "You know, Eliza," she said, her voice quietly earnest and her eyes boring into mine, "I certainly won't marry that Mr. Greenfield. I swear I shall never marry anyone unless I feel about him as you feel about Mr. Godefroy!"

I watched her sweep gracefully down the steps and alight into her carriage, and I felt my eyes brim once again, overcome with gratitude that I had such a friend. Perhaps I shall never have the husband I yearn for, I thought, but at least I know there is someone in the world who understands what is in my heart, and who would do whatever she can to accomplish my happiness. And that is something, I thought, something indeed.

I thought as well, though, of Mr. Godefroy — poor man, filled to the brim with so many sorrows, and now suffering for my sake as well. If I cannot continue our friendship, as we both so earnestly desire, perhaps I can at least protest the injustice of his situation, that of a prodigiously gifted artist forced to give lessons to keep himself out of the almshouse, and even then receiving but little custom from the natives of this place, for I recall his telling me that the preponderance of his pupils are from the French families who have settled here for one reason or another. Yes, I thought, I shall write something for the next number of the Observer lamenting his unfortunate situation, but couched in such general terms that no one could impute to it any impropriety.

And so I returned to my desk newly invigorated, donning the mantle of energetic indignation that the public has come to associate with Mistress Beatrice, and nearly forgetting my own limp melancholy in the process. Indeed, I spent the greater part of the afternoon absorbed in writing my essay on the fine arts and then editing the numerous submissions that were awaiting my attention.

Towards dusk I felt a tug at the back of my dress and a small voice crying "Mamma, Mamma!" When I inquired what crisis demanded my urgent attention, I was informed it was a lost doll, not to be found in her room or the kitchen. Polly was convinced she must have left the doll in Margaret's room but wouldn't venture there alone. My first impulse was to tell the child she must wait for Margaret to return from her errand—it seems she had gone out at Mrs. Morris's behest to procure a loaf of bread for supper. But then I recalled how I'd broken off our lesson earlier and never resumed it, and how diligently Polly had applied herself to reading the little story I'd concocted, about a girl who befriends a talking horse—a trifling tale, but one that seemed to catch her fancy. So I took her hand and together we climbed the stairs to the attic.

I hadn't had occasion to enter Margaret's room since we allowed her to move there from her pallet in the storeroom, a month after she arrived, and I was pleasantly surprised at its clean and orderly state. It seemed unlikely that Polly's doll might have found its way here, but Polly insisted that Margaret sometimes brought her here to play, and the doll might have slipped behind the clothes chest or the bed. We spent a few minutes looking in vain, and then, intent on demonstrating the hopelessness of the search, I lifted the edge of Margaret's mattress. "I suppose you think Liddy might have crawled under here?" I said.

To my surprise, I found, not the doll, but a sheet of paper, with a drawing of some kind on it. Pulling it out, I saw to my horror that it was the nude torso of a man, reclining in bed in a posture that spoke unmistakably of carnal desire and lewd abandon. And when my eyes settled on the face, I recognized it as none other than the smooth, deceptively cherubic visage of James Cork. Whoever had drawn this, it was clear, was on intimate terms with him. And there was only one person who could have drawn it. I let out a gasp—I couldn't help myself—and Polly immediately came clamoring, wanting to know what I'd found.

"Never you mind!" I'm afraid I snapped at her, clutching the obscene drawing to my chest to shield it from her view. "It's nothing that concerns you."

With that I took her arm and drew her from the room, promising that I would buy her a new doll, a better doll—anything to distract her from her curiosity about the drawing. As we made our way down the three flights of stairs, with Polly continuing loudly to lament Liddy's disappearance, it was all I could do to steady myself. One step, and then the next, I told myself, intent on not ending up as a heap of broken bones at the bottom.

Once I had delivered Polly safely back to Mrs. Morris in the kitchen, where I presumed she would find something else with which to amuse herself, I hurriedly retreated to the library and closed the door tight, my back pressed against it whilst I gathered my roiling thoughts. Difficult as it was for me to credit, there seemed to be only one possible conclusion: Cork had taken Margaret as his mistress.

I felt a shudder rack me and I closed my eyes. To think that I had entrusted the care of my precious daughter to a girl who clearly had no morals, no principles! Only an hour before I had been engaged in editing an essay concerning the dangers of camp meetings, and how in many instances they have sent young girls like Margaret careening from spiritual frenzy to physical abandon. What other dangers had she exposed Polly's soul to? Might she even have brought the child along to her assignations with that scoundrel Cork?

And why Cork, of all people? Suddenly a thought rushed into my befogged mind that caused my legs to weaken beneath me. I stumbled to the nearest chair and sank into it like a stone cast from a high window. *She's been spying on me.* It was clear now, Cork must have been relying on her for information about all that I did, all that I said, in what I had supposed was the privacy of my own home. It seemed absurd, that he would go to such lengths to pry into my affairs, and yet if I could believe it of anyone, it would be him. And hadn't Margaret seemed to linger, now that I thought back on it, whenever Mr. Godefroy had come to visit? Hadn't I more than once had to tell her she should quit the room, as her services were no longer required? And what of all the times I'd barely noticed her presence, as she dusted or swept, her ear cocked to all that transpired? I trembled to think of the day she had walked into the room when Mr. Godefroy and I had almost … I shrank from finishing the thought, even within the confines of my own mind. Who knew what she had carried back to Cork? And what might she have invented, spurred on by the lewdness of her own behavior?

She might return at any moment with the bread; I had to gather my wits, lay my plans. She would not remain a moment longer in my employ, of that I was sure. The only question was the best way to deliver the news, so as to cause the minimum amount of fuss—and of grief to poor Polly, whose distress at the disappearance of her beloved Margaret would no doubt be severe. The artfulness of the wench, cannily seducing my child into so staunch an attachment that I would be hard pressed ever to send her packing! Well, Polly's adoration of Margaret might have given me pause when it came to lesser offenses. But this—about this there could be no hesitation, no debate.

It must be done swiftly, before Polly had an opportunity to see her again. And before Father returned from the Dispensary for dinner. For although I was certain that ultimately, when acquainted with all the facts, Father would be in agreement with my determination—how could he think otherwise?—I had no stomach at the moment for discussion or delay.

I took up my watch at the front window, and within a few minutes Margaret came into view, the basket with the loaf hanging from her arm, a few strands of her coppery hair escaping from the muslin cap atop her head. I threw my shawl about my shoulders and stepped outside the front door, closing it behind me.

Margaret slowed her pace when she saw me, her face displaying confusion at what must have been the sternness of my expression. I beckoned her closer, then motioned her to meet me at the side of the house, where we were less likely to attract the attention of passers-by. Without speaking, I showed her the offending drawing, which I had been holding behind my back. She gasped and tried to snatch it from me, but I managed to whisk it away; I would need it for evidence, when it came time to explain matters to Father.

"Give that back!" she sputtered. "What right have you to go through my things?"

"What right have *I*?" It was all I could do to keep from raising my voice, but I reminded myself that we were in the public street. "What right have *you* to spy on me, and tell tales about what goes on in this house to one whose only object in life is to injure and malign me? How dare you hold yourself out as fit to care for my child? How do I know what filth you've exposed her to?"

"That's not fair, it's not true." The tears had started to gather at the rims of her blue eyes now, and her face was the very picture of distress. None of it moved me in the slightest. "All right, I've done you wrong, I've made mistakes, I'll admit that," she whimpered. "And I'm sorry for it. But with Polly, you've nothing to concern yourself about. I'd do anything for that girl, I swear it!"

"Well, you'll be doing nothing for her from now on."

She set the basket with the bread down on the ground and brought her hands to her face. Her head shook slowly from side to side. "No, please, don't take her from me, don't throw me out, I beg you," she said in a muffled voice. Then she drew her hands away and revealed a reddened, tear-stained visage. "It's all over now between me and Mr. Cork. I hate the very sound of his name, I do! I don't know why I kept that drawing, I should have burnt it."

"It would have been better for you if you had. But there's nothing you can say that will change the situation now, and I have no desire to prolong this interview." I picked up the bread basket. "You'll leave now. You can come back tonight, after nine, when Polly's sure to be asleep, to collect your things. I'll have them ready for you."

"But … I must at least say goodbye to her! And where am I to go?"

"Where you go isn't my concern." I felt myself waver for a moment, she looked so pitiful. But then I reminded myself of that drawing, the filth that Cork has written about me, the stories she must have been telling him. "All I know is that you're not to enter this house again. And don't ever attempt to speak to my daughter."

At last she turned, her head bowed and shoulders hunched, and began to shuffle slowly down Hanover Street, in the direction of the harbor, drawing her arm across her face to stanch the tears. I watched her until she turned left onto Pratt Street and was out of sight. Suddenly I was aware of my heart beating faster than usual, and I realized my brow and armpits were damp despite the chill wind assaulting me, a wind I had been oblivious to until that moment.

It was all I could do to drag myself back up the front steps, and as soon as I entered the front hall I burst into sobs, which I tried to stifle lest Polly hear me. Crying just like Margaret, I thought. And yet, surely not like her. I hoped that her tears sprang not just from her distress at losing her position, but also from shame over what she'd done. Whereas I had nothing to be ashamed of — except that I had foolishly placed my trust in someone who had proven so base, so unworthy. And so capable of destroying my one chance at happiness.

From the Observer, November 7, 1807:

Encouragement given to the FINE ARTS —

Their Rapid Progress Amongst Us.

With the exception of some tavern signs, Mr. Guy has been afforded no other opportunity of exercising his talents in perspective but in continuing the soul-inspiring avocation of making pantaloons.

Mr. Groombridge obtains no more employment than before, notwithstanding his distinguished talent for Landscape painting, which might be so well employed in decorating the Mansions and Villas of our Patricians and Grandees.

And in a celebrated University within our city, where there are 130 Students, a Professor of Drawing has but 15 pupils, and of this number five only are American.

It would not be difficult to demonstrate how completely such apathy must delay the period when taste will have reached perfection among us; how much it deprives us of the enjoyment of some of the most useful and elegant pleasures of life; and how injurious it is to the glory of a people who might aspire at holding a distinguished rank amongst the most polished nations.

B.I.

Chapter Twenty-six: Margaret

Here I am, then, back at the Point, back at Apple Alley, back in my old room at Mrs. Brooks', or nearly—just across the hall, in fact, in what used to be Alice's room. I sit here surrounded by all she left behind, the pretty frocks and bonnets, and even her hairbrush. It's almost as though I've slipped into her life, as easily as I might slip into the green slippers she left under the bed. Almost.

I could think of nowhere else to go, after Mrs. A tossed me out. I was hoping to find Alice returned here, and to beg to share her bed for a few days, at least when she wasn't sharing it with someone else. But Mrs. Brooks told me Alice hadn't come back, though she'd kept the room vacant .

"I'm the victim of my own soft heart, I am," she said, all mournful like. "When I think of the money I've lost, that room sitting empty all this time. I just can't bring myself to believe she's gone for good, though it's been over two weeks now. But what brings *you* here, then? Have you managed to scrape together the ten dollars we talked about?"

I told her no, I hadn't, and that I'd lost my job to boot. She clucked a bit and said dear, dear, what's to become of you. It was then that I asked if I might stay in the room, at least until Alice reappeared, as no one was using it anyway. I said I was sure Alice wouldn't mind. Mrs. Brooks considered a moment and sighed, and said she really shouldn't, and what about the rent I owed her, anyway? I began to tell her I'd pay her back, and for Alice's room too, once I managed to save the ten dollars and take care of my situation, and that I'd help her cook and clean or whatever she wanted me to do, if only she'd let me stay.

She crossed her arms over her bosom, which was more like resting them on a large pillow, and pursed her lips and said that was all very well, but how did I expect to earn the ten dollars, now that I'd lost my position?

"I don't suppose you could get a reference, under the circumstances," she said. I supposed she thought the circumstances were that my boss had discovered I was pregnant. I wish that was all it had been.

I told her no, but that I was willing to go back to slop work, and sew night and day if need be, and that I'd do any other work I could find. "I'll get that ten dollars, and more," I said, with as much confidence as I could muster. "You'll see." And I prayed she would believe me, even though I wasn't sure I believed myself, for I had no place else to turn except the almshouse, and I'd almost rather enter the gates of Hell than go back there.

She eyed me as though I was trying to pass bronze off as gold, but at last she said, "Lord love me, I know I shouldn't, but He gave me too soft a heart, He did."

I was so relieved and happy I scarcely heard what else she said, something about giving me a week or two and then seeing how much I'd saved. And something about how there was a line of work that would bring me more money than slop work, and quicker too, and no doubt the Lord would forgive me for it, under the circumstances. But as I said, I didn't pay it much mind at the time.

Early the next morning I set off for the slop shops to see what kind of piecework I could get, though I didn't relish the thought of bending over a needle and thread for hours on end, straining my eyes just to make six or eight cents for a shirt or a pair of trousers. I went to Mr. Barry's and then Mr. Clark's, hoping they'd remember me and recall that I'd been a good worker in the past. They remembered me all right, but there was little work to be had: a couple of pairs of trousers from the one, and four shirts from the other. All together, what I'd get paid for them would add up to less than a dollar. They both told me to come back for more when I was done, though they couldn't promise anything, what with the season ending soon.

Then I remembered what Mrs. Brooks had said the evening before, about a faster way to get the ten dollars. Could I do what

Alice had done, I asked myself? Fix myself up with the fancy frocks and hats in her room, gathering dust? Even dressed the way I was, I'd had men approach me on occasion, men who'd mistaken me for someone who sold her favors. It wouldn't mean I'd be a whore, exactly, I told myself. I'd just do it until I had the money to pay the doctor, or whoever it was Mrs. Brooks knew. It might not take more than a couple of weeks. I'd known other women who'd turned to working Oakum Bay during the winter, when the slop work dried up. If Papa hadn't been around to put food on the table — and to forbid me from ever thinking of selling my body — perhaps I'd already have done it myself by now. Now no one cared whether I sold myself or not.

Still, the thought of it made me shiver. It was one thing to go with James, or even Charles Patterson, for they were both young and handsome. But to spread my legs for anyone who thrust a few coins in my face, no matter how they looked or smelled, no matter how drunk or filthy they were, that was another matter. I remembered Alice's complaints, and all the times she'd appeared with a black eye or a swollen lip. And then I thought of James, and how I was no more guilty than he was, but he was going on about his business, without a care in the world. And I was facing either Oakum Bay or else the almshouse and another mouth to feed. I was just making my way back to the Point with my load, my head filled with these distressing thoughts, when I heard raised voices and the sounds of drums and a fife.

I was on Water Street, heading east to the bridge that would take me over the Falls, and the noise seemed to be coming from the north. It wasn't on my way, but I was curious — and, I confess, in no hurry to begin the sewing that awaited me, especially when it would bring me so little profit. So I decided to turn left and take the bridge that went off Market Street, thinking I might come across whatever the fuss was on my way. I headed up Gay Street, and when I got to Market I could see a crowd coming over the bridge from the Point — young men mostly, a few with masks covering their faces. They were carrying aloft four stuffed figures, with crudely drawn faces.

There were a number of others watching as well, and we pressed ourselves up against the buildings as the mob began to fill the street. I clutched the material for the shirts and trousers close, so that no mud or horse dung would get splattered on it.

To my dismay I found myself next to a gentleman who was puffing on a cigar. I worried that the ash might fall on the fabric, and I was choking from the smell, but we were all pushed together so tight there was nowhere for me to move to.

"That'll be Vice-President Burr, I guess," the man said to his companion, a smaller gentleman with spectacles on his nose, as the front part of the mob started to go past us. I craned my neck to see if I could catch a glimpse of Burr, for James was always denouncing him as the traitor who had schemed to steal the country away from the President.

"Which one?" said his friend.

"Must be the smallest one — the one with the stuffing coming out from the head."

They both laughed at that, and I realized they were only talking about the stuffed figures. Then they said who the other figures were supposed to be, but the only name I recognized was Luther Martin — James didn't like him either, because he was Burr's lawyer.

"Well, I suppose it's better for these bucks to be burning effigies than tarring and feathering the gentlemen themselves," said the man with the cigar. "They say there were windows broken at Martin's house last night, when Burr and the others were at supper."

The one with spectacles started saying something about a tumult breaking out if the figures were burned, and wondering where the constables were, but I stopped listening because just then in the crowd that was marching by, beating drums and blowing on fifes and yelling huzzahs to Jefferson and death to Burr, I saw James Cork.

Perhaps at another time I would have let him pass. But I'd just been thinking of him, cursing his name. I managed to break free of the tight line of people watching, dodge the feet of the marchers, and grab his arm.

"What do you think you're doing?" he said in a hoarse whisper. "I've nothing to say to you!"

"Oh, but I have something to say to you, and if you know what's good for you, you'll listen!"

He glanced around for a moment before ducking out from the crowd with me still holding onto his arm, for I was damned if he'd escape me. We turned off from Market onto a small side street that was deserted, for everyone's attention was trained on the mob.

"What do you want?" His voice was raised over the din, even though the mob was half a block away. "I need to catch up with them before they reach Gallows Hill. They'll be expecting me."

I told him I'd let him go on his way if he'd just give me twenty dollars. I figured that if I asked for twenty he might give me the ten I needed. But of course he wanted to know what it was for. When I told him, he grew pale for a moment. Then he glanced at my stomach, and he said it didn't look as though I was with child. I told him I wished I wasn't, but I was as sure of it as I was of my own name.

"And how am I to know it's mine, then?" he sneered. "And not Charles Patterson's? Or someone else's?"

I slapped him then, I couldn't help it. If I'd had a knife I might have killed him. He started to walk away but I pulled him back. "I know it's not Mr. Patterson's," I hissed, "and I told you, I haven't been with anyone else." Then I recalled what I'd heard a couple of years since, when a girl I knew named Mercy had been in my situation and said the father was Mr. Bellows, who owned the tavern at the corner. "I'll go to the almshouse and swear it's yours," I told him, "and they'll believe me, you know they will, especially if I name you when the pains are upon me. Then they'll go after you to pay my expenses, you and your father. And if you don't pay they'll take you to court, and the whole town will know of it. How will your lovely Miss Scattergood like *that*, I wonder?"

This seemed to have its effect. He stopped trying to get away and turned to face me. "You wouldn't," he said, his voice low. "You wouldn't dare."

"Oh, wouldn't I? And why shouldn't she know what kind of villain she's agreed to marry? I imagine it would make her reconsider."

"If you so much as whisper my name to anyone, I'll—"

"You'll *what*? What could you possibly do to make me any more miserable than I already am?"

Something passed over his face, some thought keen as a beam of sun, and he narrowed his eyes at me. "I'll tell the Legrands the truth about who stole their silver."

I froze, and my throat seemed to close in on itself. "But you said you understood!" I croaked. I remembered how he'd comforted me, and said it wasn't my fault that I'd taken the spoons. It was hard to believe that that kind soul, whose words had given me such comfort, was the same hard-faced man that was standing before me. "You wouldn't, you couldn't do that to me. They'd send me to jail for that."

There was a flicker in his eye, and I thought he might soften, but it passed. "I'll do it if I have to," he said, without a trace of pity in his voice. "So you'd best keep your mouth shut."

I closed my eyes and let go of his arm, and when I opened them again he was gone, lost in the rowdy band still marching up Market Street. Bad off as I am, jail would be far worse, from what I've heard. There were those who said the almshouse was like Bryden's Hotel compared to what they'd known in jail.

It's been six days since then, and every day I've plied my needle for hours on end, pricking myself and trying not to bleed onto the fabric, spending pennies I can't afford on candles so that I can continue working at night. There's no sign of Alice, and every day I find myself gazing at her red and pink frocks and her feathered hats, wondering if I should put them on and try my luck in Oakum Bay, before my belly begins to swell too much.

Today I brought my finished trousers and shirts to Mr. Barry and Mr. Clark and collected fifty cents from the one and thirty from the other. But when I asked for more slop work to do, neither one of them had any to give me. If I'm to get ten dollars, quick, I can think of only one way to do it, no matter how much the thought of it frightens and disgusts me.

Baltimore Federal Gazette and Daily Advertiser, November 17, 1807:

To the patrons of the Observer and the Public:

What do you think the Observer means by playing shuttle-cock with my poor name at every full and change of the moon? She will have Baltimore to be the Siberia of the Arts, say or do what you will — and to prove this favorite point, in her last number, amongst other learned arguments, observe the following: "With the exception of some tavern signs, Mr. Guy has been afforded no other opportunity of exercising his talents in perspective but in continuing the soul-inspiring avocation of making pantaloons."

Had the above not come from the pen of a lady, I should have bluntly stamped the lie upon it without further ceremony; but I must, for the sake of decency, content myself with proving it altogether and entirely false. Last spring I disposed of paintings in Baltimore to the amount of fifteen hundred dollars, and in the course of the last summer, I refused orders in landscape painting that would have occupied me above six months. I have now as many landscapes and sea-pieces bespoke as will employ me all the winter; here then is a picture of the Observer's veracity.

Mr. Groombridge, she likewise informs you, has no encouragement in his art. How true or false that may be, I cannot say. But if it is a fact, I am sorry for it; his abilities merit a better fate. If he is really neglected by the public, he may ascribe it to the friendship of the Observer; and never had man more reason than he has, to exclaim with Philip of Macedon — "O! ye Gods, what have I done that this person should speak well of me."

For my own part I freely confess that the Observer has rendered me essential service; and whilst my unsuspecting rival was gratefully bowing to the flattering encomiums of his friendly female Critic, I was reaping all the advantage of her scurrilous and witless opposition. The Connoisseurs of Baltimore will not be dictated to by insolence and abuse.

FRANCIS GUY.

From the Observer, November 21, 1807:

To Readers and Correspondents.

We have been in no small degree astonished at Mr. Guy's curious publication of Tuesday last, but shall only observe that Mr. Guy has given us pleasure by informing us that the sole and EVIDENT object of every line we have written with regard to him, that of drawing attention to his merits and obtaining for him the consideration and patronage he deserves, has been so fully answered.

* * *

In the masterly essay by An Impartial Observer, which we publish today, much matter of reflection is presented to every thinking mind. There is no truth more incontrovertible than that the horrible pictures of Hell's torments upon which some of the Clergy so much delight to dwell are injurious to the cause they would serve. At their camp meetings, the most horrible outrages are committed. Women are seen sprawling on the floors in ecstasies and postures offensive to common decency – and with their passions thus in fermentation, their nerves unstrung, and reason nearly driven from its seat, woeful are the consequences that result to many and many a luckless girl. Whoever has had much intercourse with the class of females who hire out for their maintenance must know many instances in confirmation of this fact.

Chapter Twenty-seven: Eliza

Polly has been gravely ill these last five days and given us a terrible scare, but thank the Lord, the worst appears to be over. And it is possible that we owe her recovery in part to a most unlikely source. At least, that is what Father thinks. For my part, I am in a state of confusion—although it is a happy confusion, as more than anything else I am thankful that my daughter, the dearest creature in the world to me, has been spared.

A week ago, she began to complain of a sore throat, and then a fever came on her. As she's often given to such complaints, at first we thought nothing of it—or at least, we were no more concerned than usual. But then she took a turn for the worse, and the fever grew higher. Father tried not to show his alarm, but I could sense that his veneer of calm was intended for my benefit and that underneath he was gripped by the same fear that had me in its clutches. As I have before when the child has been seriously ill, I silently berated myself for my failings as a mother—my impatience with her, my shortness, my yearning to be otherwise occupied when she begs for my company. And as always, I vowed that if the Lord would only allow her to recover her health, I should do better, and do it cheerfully.

At times, nearly from the moment she first fell ill, she began to ask for Margaret again. Polly had often posed questions to me about her shortly after the girl's departure—to all of which I answered that she had left quite suddenly, and I had no idea where she'd gone—but after a while she seemed to have grown accustomed to her absence and rarely spoke of her. Such is the benefit of childhood, that the urgent concerns of today are consigned to

oblivion on the morrow! Or so I had thought until this illness be-
fell her. But yesterday, nearly all day it was, "Where do you think
Margaret is?" and "Do you think she'll come back?" and "Why
did she leave?" over and over again. It pained me that in the
throes of illness my child cried out for a vulgar, duplicitous hussy
rather than for her own mother, but I made up answers as best I
could, telling her Margaret had returned to her people, wherever
they were, and that I was sure she missed Polly as much as Polly
missed her, for I was desperate to soothe the child's distress.

Then yesterday evening, after a particularly terrifying seizure
came upon her, Father insisted that we withdraw from her bedroom, where I had stationed myself for the previous twenty-four
hours, not even leaving to change my clothes. He said it was urgent, that we must talk. He sat beside me on the settee in the sitting room, took my hand in his, and looked at me with such grief
and pity that I almost stopped my ears. For I knew what he was
about to say: that I must prepare myself for the end, that there
was no more he could do for the child, that she would most likely
soon be in a better place.

He said all this, gently, as the tears streamed from my eyes;
but he said more as well. He said we must find Margaret and
bring her here, that it wasn't right to deny Polly something she so
desperately wanted — that this might be, indeed, her last request.
Could we let her go to her eternal rest believing that Margaret
had abandoned her? And what of Margaret? Was it right, was it
just, to deny her one last meeting with the child, if we had it in
our power to arrange it?

I protested of course, reminding him of Margaret's perfidy,
her lies about me, and the dangers to which she might have exposed Polly. But Father said we had no evidence that she had
endangered Polly, other than her unwise decision to bring her to
the camp meeting.

"As for the misery she inflicted upon you," Father said, "I
won't try to excuse it, of course. But we have a duty to try to understand — a duty to Margaret and to our Lord, who would have us
be merciful in all things, as He is. She's very young, remember, and
no doubt Mr. Cork took advantage of her, as young men are wont
to do. I feel certain that the sins she committed are more to be laid
at his doorstep than at hers. For as you know, young girls are apt
to do foolish things when their affections have been captivated."

He paused, meaningfully, and I took him to be alluding to my own situation, years ago, when as a headstrong nineteen-year-old I insisted on a marriage that he had warned me against, to no avail. I wavered. Yes, Margaret was young — and not only had she perhaps fallen victim to Cork's wiles, but her passions may as well have been unduly stirred by whatever wild rantings she heard at those camp meetings. But no, I thought: much as I wanted to be merciful and generous, like Father, I could not bring myself to allow Margaret back into my home, into my precious child's life, which now seemed to be ebbing so fast. Not after all she had done to me. I couldn't speak, but found myself shaking my head.

"All right, then," Father said, withdrawing a folded paper from the inside of his jacket. "I only ask you to look at this. I found it in Polly's hand this morning. She'd fallen asleep, holding it."

It was a sketch of Polly's head — Polly as she used to look, before the illness had sunken her cheeks and turned her eyes glassy. Polly smiling and happy, gazing directly at me, her lips slightly parted as though she were about to pose one of her many questions, her eyes seeming to sparkle. It was my daughter returned to vivid life.

"This is Margaret's handiwork," Father said as I contemplated the drawing through my tears. "And if Polly is taken from us, this bit of paper will be among our most precious possessions." He paused. "If you look at it closely, you'll see that it could only have been drawn by someone who loves the child, perhaps as dearly as you and I do."

It was true. Somehow every line, every smudge of the charcoal spoke of affection. I closed my eyes and swallowed hard before I spoke. "But how could we find her? She might be anywhere."

Father laid a hand on my arm and gently squeezed it. "Leave that to me," he said. "I shall go to the almshouse first thing tomorrow morning. That's the place to start, at least."

It was, in fact, the place to end as well. Father left at seven this morning and returned shortly before eight with Margaret, having hired a carriage to make the journey swifter — for Polly had endured a difficult night, and it seemed she might have little time left. I was in the chair next to her bed, where I'd spent the night again, and I had dozed off. Then, over the sound of Polly's rough breathing, I heard Father and Margaret enter, heard them

272

lower their voices so as not to disturb Polly — or, presumably, me. I chose not to open my eyes, hoping to put off the encounter with Margaret as long as possible.

There was a silence that lasted a few moments, and then I heard Margaret whisper to Father, "Is it true what I once heard, that you think it's a good thing people die from disease?"

I was taken aback at the impudence of the girl, though I moved not a muscle. But Father seemed unperturbed. He paused for a few seconds before responding, but then I heard him say softly, "It's never a good thing when someone dies. But we must consider the alternatives: death by war, death by starvation. If people didn't die of disease, prematurely in some instances, there wouldn't be enough food to sustain us all. It's all part of the Lord's plan, and the best we can do is to prepare our minds for our loss, and ease the suffering of the dying."

Another pause, and then another whisper: "But if His plan requires that some people die, why should He take innocent children, and not the old? Or the wicked?"

It was more or less exactly the question I had posed to myself, several times over the last few days. I knew what Father's answer would be, and I knew that I would find it unsatisfying, as always.

"It's not for us to know these things, Margaret," Father replied, as I'd expected. "But I can tell you that much of what my fellow physicians do, in attempting to cure their patients, has little effect, and some of it only makes them worse."

I opened my eyes at last, fearing that any further pretense of sleep would draw suspicion, and saw before me Margaret in a rough linen apron bearing the initials "BP," stitched in red — for Baltimore Poorhouse, I surmised. She seemed to have gained some weight since I had last seen her, which surprised me. Perhaps, I thought, the diet in the almshouse is heartier than one would expect. I could see, as well, that her eyes were reddened and there were traces of moisture on her cheeks.

She ducked her head and murmured, "Good morning, ma'am. I thank you for your kindness in allowing me to come see Polly, only I'm sorry for the circumstances." Another tear escaped, and she wiped it away with the back of a hand — a chapped and red hand, I noticed.

"Eliza," Father said, "go rest now, in your bed. I'm afraid I'm needed at the Dispensary for a few hours, but Margaret can sit with Polly. I've prevailed on Mr. Parker at the almshouse to allow her to stay until this afternoon. She'll wake you if there's any change—won't you, Margaret? And she'll have Mrs. Morris send word to me as well."

The only alternative was to remain in the room with Margaret, a situation I didn't relish. And my exhaustion was such that it overcame my reluctance to leave my child. And so, after instructing Margaret to hold a wet compress against Polly's forehead every few minutes, I allowed Father to take my elbow and escort me to my bedroom.

I suppose I slept as soon as my head met the pillow. When next I opened my eyes I realized that the sun was already high in the sky, and I sat up with a start. I had only meant to rest for thirty minutes, perhaps less. Margaret must have been alone with Polly for hours. I rushed to Polly's room as soon as I was able to stand upright without wobbling. But when I reached the door I was surprised to hear voices—two voices, one of them Polly's. She sounded clearer and stronger than she had in days. I paused for a moment, wondering what might be transpiring between them.

"But why did you go away?" Polly was saying. I held my breath, afraid of what Margaret might answer.

"I told you, my brother was taken ill. I had to go, very sudden like. I was sorry I didn't have the chance to say goodbye. Now take some more of this soup, there's a good girl."

Soup? Polly hadn't taken food in two days. It was all we could do to get her to drink a few drops of water.

"You never told me you had a brother." Polly sounded suspicious.

"Well, I do. He lives on our old farm, in Harford County. We hadn't spoken in a long time. Now, one more spoonful. That's it."

"I missed you," Polly said in a small, reproachful voice.

"I know, I'm sorry. But you've had your mother to take care of you, and Mrs. Morris."

"But I wanted *you*."

I'd known this of course. Still, it cut me like a knife to hear Polly say it.

I heard a small clatter that must have been Margaret setting the soup bowl and spoon on the table next to the bed. "But your mother can teach you all sorts of things that I can't, things you need to know to grow up to be a lady. She's a very clever woman, your mother. And she loves you very, very much."

I drew a breath in; I hadn't expected such words from Margaret.

"But she doesn't let me draw as much as I want to," Polly said, "and she doesn't play with me like you do. And she gets cross with me."

Again, a knife to the heart. Never again, I vowed: only let her recover, and I will be the very model of a patient mother. I will let the child draw to her heart's content.

"Well, mothers will do that, but only because they know what's best for you," Margaret said. "A mother is a very precious thing, Polly. My own mother—she died years ago, and not a day goes by that I don't think of her and wish she was here."

I thought of my own mother, taken from us when I was only two: a hand brushing a lock of hair from my eyes, a gentle kiss on my forehead. Or did I only think I remembered those things?

"My mother makes up stories for me to read," Polly said, and it sounded as though her voice now contained a note of pride. "There's one about a talking horse. It's a very good story. Do you want me to read it to you?"

"Not now, my sweet, you must rest. But another time, perhaps." Margaret was silent a moment, perhaps thinking there might never be another time, that we might not allow her to see Polly again. Then she said, "Making up stories! You see, I told you your mother was clever."

I came from behind the door at last, and exclaimed over Polly for a few moments: her color had begun to come back, and her eyes no longer had the false brightness that fever brings.

"I didn't like to wake you, Ma'am," Margaret said, standing as I entered, "but when she awoke it seemed the fever had broken. She said she was hungry, so I went down to Mrs. Morris for some soup. I hope you don't mind."

I told her no, I didn't mind, and tried to keep the tears from falling as I bent over Polly to feel her forehead and discovered that it was no longer burning to the touch. Just then I heard the front door open, and the sound of Father's footsteps. Soon he was with us, as delighted as I was by the improvement in Polly's condition. We all said a rather hurried goodbye to Margaret, as Father had kept the carriage waiting to take her back to the almshouse.

He said nothing more about the whole matter until this evening when we were by the fire in the sitting room, Polly sleeping comfortably upstairs, I struggling to stay awake over a submission for the Observer—for Polly's illness has caused me to fall woefully behind in my editorial duties.

"I can't say for certain," Father began, "that the girl's presence *caused* Polly's improvement, of course. No scientific evidence of that, certainly."

"None," I agreed, although I had been thinking similar thoughts. "I imagine it was entirely coincidental."

"Perhaps not entirely. Perhaps a shock to the mind—pleasant, as in this case, or painful—may have an effect on the physical constitution, for better or for worse. Modern medicine knows too little of the causes and cures of disease for us to be entirely certain of anything."

"But I thought you were rather certain of your theory of disease."

"In its broad outlines, yes. Insects, too tiny for us to see, have something to do with it, of that I'm sure. But there are many details that are not within my power, as yet, to grasp." He sighed. "But I fear, Eliza, that I won't be able to elaborate my theory to the public as fully as I would have liked."

"And why is that?" Perhaps, I thought, he had concluded that readers were not sufficiently attentive to his message—and that the few who did attend were far from convinced. That, at least, has been the tenor of most of the correspondence we have received on the subject, although I've tried to shield Father from it. But there are indications that he knows: he has on occasion made reference in his articles to those who would heap obloquy upon him, and a month or two since he promised to "trouble" our readers with only very short essays in the future, fearful of wearying them. In fact, though, his submissions have remained of the usual length.

Father sighed and reached for his pipe and pouch of tobacco. "I had intended to discuss this with you, but then Polly took ill." He began filling the pipe, tamping it down, lighting it with a straw held to the fire; I waited. He took a puff of the pipe and looked up. "I'm sorry Eliza, I know how much the Observer means to you. But the printer, the carriers—we grow deeper in debt to them every week. And there seems to be little prospect that our many delinquent subscribers will remit what they owe us. I've allowed it to go on this long, for you and for those subscribers who paid their six months in advance as they promised. But the last number of the year must be the end of it, or we'll be ruined."

"Oh, Father!" A flood of relief washed over me; nerves in my body I hadn't been aware of suddenly went slack. "That's quite the best news I've had in a long time—aside from Polly getting better, of course."

I hadn't realized until that moment how eager I was to be rid of it all: the constant deadlines, the stacks of unread submissions reproaching me from the corners of my desk, the printers' bills, the dunning letters to subscribers. And of course, the insults and imprecations hurled at me from all sides—if it isn't Mr. Guy abusing me for my well-meaning attempts to bring him to the public's attention, it's the local guardians of morality, predicting my eternal damnation for pointing out the obvious fact that our religious institutions are not what they should be. And in the most recent issue of Spectacles, Mr. Cork—having assumed his transparent guise as Benjamin Bickerstaff—in the midst of one of his tirades against me included several sentences in Greek, with no translation, and then had the audacity to comment that it was unfortunate that Mistress Ironside would not have the wit to decipher them!

"But I thought," Father began, his brow drawn in puzzlement, "I thought the paper was what you wanted, what sustained you. I had no idea—"

"No, neither did I, really." I found myself laughing, and I felt giddy, almost as though I'd had too much claret. I suppose it was the exhaustion. But I was quite sure that my relief was real. "I had such high hopes for it at the beginning—I thought it would raise the level of discourse in this town, that it would lead people to talk about higher things—the fine arts, and literature, and our obligation to support them—instead of the usual foolish gossip. But somehow it seems to have had the opposite effect."

Father nodded slowly. "Perhaps if you had simply ignored some of what was thrown at you. Or had been less ... vociferous in expressing some of your criticism—"

I stood up, tired as I was, and began to pace. "I couldn't have. It's simply not in my nature to ignore things, or to stifle myself for the sake of flattering people, you know that. There was no point in doing it if I couldn't tell people the truth as I saw it! Besides, it was what people wanted. You know our circulation went up every time I had one of those ugly skirmishes with Cork, or Guy, or Webster, or Hewes ... All those *men*. They simply can't stand to be bested by a woman!"

I stopped and turned to face him. "But I've proven a woman can do it, and do it well. Our circulation speaks to that, even if most of them don't pay their bills. And I simply don't want to do it anymore—why should I?" I paused as a thought entered my head. "Perhaps," I said slowly, "I'll find something else to do."

Father looked at me quizzically, but I couldn't bring myself to reveal the idea that had been lying dormant in my mind all these months, buried like myself under piles of submissions and deadlines: the novel that Mr. Godefroy had urged me to write. Now I could feel that sleeping fancy stretching its cramped limbs and blinking its eyes against the crack of light let in by the prospect of the Observer's demise. But I wasn't ready to let the idea out into the open yet, not even to parade it before Father's benevolent gaze.

"The only regret I have," I said, so as to put Father off the scent, "is that James Cork will no doubt congratulate himself for driving me out of business."

"Ah, Cork!" Father shook his head sadly. "I suppose you could see for yourself the predicament in which he has left that unfortunate girl."

"Whatever do you mean?" I asked, although as soon as the words had left my mouth I suddenly understood: Margaret was pregnant, and Cork was the father.

"She refuses to give his name to the authorities," Father continued, "although of course they're anxious to find someone to shoulder her expenses. And I couldn't convince her. She was most adamant, but she wouldn't say why. Perhaps she fears such an accusation would jeopardize his impending marriage to that heiress. Not that he deserves such consideration, of course, but the girl has a good heart. I know that may sound strange to you, after what she's done, but I'm convinced it's true."

I began pacing again, and running my hand through my hair. *A good heart*, I almost began to protest? But then I recalled what I had heard Margaret saying to Polly earlier, singing my praises, telling the child I loved her. Why she would do such a thing I couldn't fathom — perhaps her conscience was troubling her, as well it should. In any event, it hardly made up for the damage she had done me. And as for Cork ...

"That hypocrite," I fumed, "taking me to task for my supposed moral depravity, when *he* ..." I stopped. "I know what I'll do. *She* may not want to name him, but I'll put it all in the next number of the Observer, for the world to read about! Then he'll see what it feels like. Only in his case it will all be true."

"Eliza!" Father's voice was sharp. "Surely you wouldn't stoop to his level, attacking him personally in that way. And it's not your place to reveal this secret if Margaret chooses not to. It's her decision."

"I don't see why I should allow her a veto over what I choose to publish. What do I owe *her*?" I crossed my arms and turned away. If there were one last task I could accomplish with the Observer, one thing that would make it all worthwhile, it would be this.

"It's possible that we owe her at least some credit for Polly's recovery. But be that as it may, the most important object in this situation is not to stir further scandal, but to ensure that Cork lives up to his responsibilities towards the child." Father's voice, though tired, was firm. "I've decided to go see him, try and talk some sense into him. At least give me the chance to do that. And if that should fail ... well, we'll see. But I don't think it will come to that. He must have some sense of decency."

"I've seen no evidence of that."

"Still, I must try."

Father was quiet for a minute, puffing at his pipe. In the silence I felt the energy that had somehow been sustaining me through this conversation vanish from my body; I could no longer resist the urge to go upstairs and fling myself into bed and the blessed oblivion of sleep.

"One moment more, Eliza," Father called as I stood at the threshold, about to take my leave. "I don't like to pry into your personal affairs, but I must ask you: why it is that we no longer see Mr. Godefroy? If it's merely because of that vile story put out by Cork, I must say it seems that you've given him entirely too much power over your life."

I stood stock still, barely able to take a breath, then turned to face Father, my mouth agape. Once I had recovered the faculty of speech, I poured all of it out, although without alluding to anything Betsy had divulged to me: how I had recalled the scandal surrounding Thomas — whose name I now spoke aloud to him for the first time in years — and how I knew Father had suffered so as a result of it; how I had vowed not to bring upon him any further shame and distress.

"It's very considerate of you, my dear," Father said when I'd finished, "but I'm afraid your concern has been entirely misplaced. Your situation is quite different from your brother's. It wasn't the gossip that distressed me in his case — it was what he had done. In your case, I'm quite certain you're blameless. So why on earth should I care what some ignorant fools might be saying about you?"

"But ..." My mind was spinning. Was Betsy's tale no more than a web of lies, cleverly spun to entrap me into serving her own purposes? I could draw no other conclusion. And in fact, I didn't doubt that she was capable of such perfidy, for I know no one who is more zealous, or less scrupulous, in looking after her interests.

But I didn't want to trouble Father with so unpleasant a tale. And I remembered something he'd said that had inclined me to believe what Betsy had spun. "But what of Mrs. O'Donnell? Remember? You told me, that day, I must be more careful!"

"Did I? Well, it's true — she's an ignorant fool who unfortunately happens to have the power to turn you out of this house someday. But still, if your future happiness is bound up with Mr. Godefroy, as I suspect it is, we cannot let Mrs. O'Donnell or anyone else interfere. We'll find some way. And if you were to marry the gentleman, I imagine that even Mrs. O'Donnell would forget the gossip in time."

I swallowed. My heart was beating in my ears. "Marry?"

Father looked pained. "Perhaps I have presumed too much. Perhaps your feelings for the gentleman are not of that sort. Believe me, my dear, my only concern is for your happiness. You must do what you want, no more and no less. But go to bed now. You're looking quite pale."

And so I stumbled upstairs, in a daze of fatigue and confusion. Father said I must do what I want, but what *did* I want? I had thought I knew, and that I was only held back by my vow to spare Father further scandal. Now that the premise of that vow had proved mistaken, and I was free to follow my own desires, I found myself hesitating—indeed, terrified of what might lie ahead. Perhaps I secretly relished the idea of a tragic love, eternally condemned to the realm of the hypothetical—or of a friendship such as Mr. Godefroy and I had before, enlivened by an undercurrent of physical attraction but resolutely chaste. If I were to allow Mr. Godefroy back into my life now, all would be changed: he has declared his wish to make me his wife, and Bess Caton has made it clear that it's in her power to secure me a divorce from Henry Anderson. Even Father appears ready to give his blessing.

All the stars have aligned in the order I so desperately desired. Why, then, do I feel an impulse to shrink from the future they would spell? Am I—and not Father—the one who fears the whispers that will pursue me if I revive and indeed extend my connection with Mr. Godefroy? Or am I afraid that he will betray my trust as Henry Anderson did? Betsy's words that day at Springfield, mocking me for believing that romantic love could survive the marriage covenant, echoed in my thoughts. I had bristled at her cynicism then, but now I wondered if perhaps she had spoken the truth.

I willed myself to think of Polly, and her apparently miraculous delivery from the jaws of death, in order to still my mind and introduce some measure of calm to my thoughts. But thoughts of Polly led once more to thoughts of Mr. Godefroy. Did I not owe it to my daughter to supply the absent place of a father with a substitute whom she clearly adored? But then again, I thought: what if I am mistaken as to his character? Would it not be worse to have *two* fathers abandon her rather than just one?

I was too tired, too weak, to answer. I resolved to banish these questions from my mind and plunge into sleep, hopeful that in the morning all would somehow be clear.

From the Observer, December 19, 1807:

For the Observer.

BEATRICE IRONSIDE'S BUDGET.

It may be remembered that a certain Mr. BICKERSTAFF furnished us at first with some of his lucubrations, which he presented with the avowed and manifest intention of erecting himself into the Aristarchus of the City. Hardly had he supplied us with four numbers, after his fashion, *when the whim suddenly seized him to set his* veto *upon the Observer, and in quality of Grand Inquisitor of Baltimore, to mark his prohibition of every idea which should not have originated in his own most sapient brain.*

From this moment War was declared against the Observer, and every means, however underhand or contemptible, *were resorted to in the hope of destroying it. It was a* Woman *who was its Editor: this was all that was necessary to render its enemies BRAVE, and this was enough to embolden the most* pusillanimous Wight *to assume the garb of the Lion. It was a Woman who dared to speak the immutable language of reason and common sense. Could a scholar so profound as to know the whole Greek Alphabet by heart allow that a Woman should* know her own language? *Could he endure that she should venture to think and judge for herself, and what is much more sacrilegious, that she should presume to enter those lists of which he deemed* himself *in the whole Western Hemisphere the only able and redoubtable champion!!!*

On opening the Observer it will be found to contain reflections and opinions which we venture to predict will be one day more fairly appreciated, upon the various topics which properly came within its cognizance. On no occasion have we failed in doing justice to the talents of those who have come within our notice. Assuredly it is not Mistress Beatrice who is censurable if, in the intoxication of vanity, some persons have translated into sarcasms those expressions of approbation which originated purely in the design of obtaining for them the attention due to their merits. That Mistress Beatrice never pretended to speak of the genius of Mr. Guy, for instance, as of that of a Ruysdael, a Wilson, or a Claude Lorraine, is certainly most true – but she rendered the fullest and most ample justice to the degree of talent which he really does possess, as well as to those of every other artist of whom she has had occasion to speak.

And never have we sullied our pages with defaming and personal attacks, which others have for their pastime so liberally bestowed upon us.

But there is a measure in all things – Mistress Ironside is resolved to abandon a task as laborious as she finds it thankless and painful, & which she undertook only in the hope of being useful.

Before, however, she takes a final adieu, she must remind a vast *proportion of her Subscribers of the Claims which justice demands of them and urge their* ready discharge. *Of the* few *who have* freely *rendered* that which was due, *and cheered her on her toilsome way with the cordial smile of approbation, her memory is a true and faithful* Register – *whilst she consigns to the contempt they merit those pitiful Beings who have sought in mean subterfuge to evade compliance with their small and* just engagements.

B.I.

Chapter Twenty-eight: Margaret

I never was more surprised than I was this morning, when I looked up from my breakfast of bread and milk to see Mrs. A at the far end of the almshouse hall. I was almost as surprised as I'd been to see Dr. C there a week ago, when he came to bring me to Polly's bedside — though he's been here once since, to tell me that Polly was definitely on the mend, and he said he'd come by regularly to see how I was getting on. So if it had been Dr. C standing there, I would only have smiled and risen from the table to greet him. When I saw it was Mrs. A, though, such was the shock that I froze at my place.

Because I was rooted to the spot, my mouth hanging open, it was left to Mrs. A to pick her way towards me through the length of the room. I could see her doing her best to pretend she didn't notice the stench and the noise (one of the lunatics was banging a spoon and screaming "No! No!" and a lot of worse things, as he usually does at mealtimes), and at one point she only narrowly escaped the clutches of Mad Martha, who has a habit of reaching out for peoples' clothes and hanging on for dear life. I could only pray that none of the men called out anything rude as she walked by, but it seems that the sight of a fine lady in our midst was enough to keep even them quiet. Not that Mrs. A is all that fine, with her frocks often stained or patched in places, but compared to the rest of us she seemed a very princess.

"Good morning, Margaret," she said to me, her voice chilly. She looked decidedly uncomfortable. "I'd like a few words with you. But not here." She darted a glance at my tablemates, all of them sitting with their bread in mid-air, staring at her. Only

Susannah, across the table from me, was moving, and she was scratching herself vigorously as usual. "Come with me, would you? We can talk in Mr. Parker's office."

I couldn't imagine what Mrs. A wanted to talk to me about, but whatever it was I hoped it might make me late for work. Untangling old rope all day and picking out the oakum in the cold is the kind of work that makes me long for the time when I was only hauling firewood or stitching shirts in near darkness, and my hands have gone all rough and raw. I wondered, though, what Mr. Parker would say about my not going to the oakum shed on time, and taking his office from him. But when we got there he was all smiles and "why yes, of course, Mrs. Anderson, take as long as you need." I suppose he and Mrs. A know one another through the Doctor, who I gather often comes here on medical business (they say he sometimes does experiments on the residents, though I don't know whether to believe it).

As soon as Mr. Parker was out of the room, Mrs. A asked me to sit in the chair in front of his desk. She took off her bonnet and cloak, like she was prepared to stay a while, and then she took Mr. Parker's chair from behind the desk and brought it round next to mine, so that we were sitting facing one another. She had a shawl about her shoulders, and she drew it close against the cold. For even in Mr. Parker's office there isn't much of a fire.

"I trust Polly is well?" I asked, because a chill had entered my mind at the thought that she might have come to impart the news I had most dreaded to hear.

"Polly? Oh yes, nearly her old self again, thank the Lord. I've come to talk to you about something else entirely." She pressed her lips together and seemed uncertain what to say next. I waited. "Margaret," she said at last, "I must ask you a question. And it's very important that you tell me the truth."

I could only stare at her, barely breathing, afraid of what might come next.

"Did you ever steal anything from the Legrands?"

"No!" I said immediately, knowing that any hesitation would be the end of me. I put my hands on my belly, which seems to be growing larger by the day. I don't know why my hands go straight there, when I'm anxious. I suppose I'm thinking I must protect the child, somehow. "I've done things I'm not proud of, I'll admit that. But I'm no thief."

She cocked her head and raised an eyebrow at me, as though I were a child caught with her hand in the honey pot. "You see, Mr. Cork said—"

"You talked to him?" I felt my head begin to grow light and my heart pound.

"My father did. He thought he could make the scoundrel see what his obligations were towards you and …" Her eyes slipped down to my belly for a moment. "The child. But of course, it was no use. Not only did Mr. Cork profess uncertainty as to whether he was the father, but he also told some story about how you once worked for the Legrands and absconded with some silver. I'll tell you straight out that I was inclined to believe it. My intention was to reveal this sordid tale in the final number of the Observer, all of it." She pursed her lips. I clutched the edge of my chair. "But Father insisted that I first speak with you and give you a chance to defend yourself. He wouldn't even let me ask the Legrands what happened—although he pointed out that Miss Legrand was in the same room with you on several occasions and never appeared to take any notice of you. In any event, that is why I've come."

I swallowed hard and stood. And suddenly I felt a strange calm come over me, knowing that what I had most feared seemed about to happen. "I won't blame you if you don't believe me," I said. "There's no reason you should, after what I've done to you. But here's the God's honest truth: When I told Mr. Cork I was going to bear his child—and it's definitely his, I'll swear to that—he threatened to tell the Legrands that story about me taking the silver. And it's not true, not a word of it. That is, I did work there, for a few weeks, but I didn't steal anything. He just wanted to keep me from talking, because if that rich lady of his finds out about me and the child, she'll call off the wedding. He'd do anything to keep me from talking, and who knows what the Legrands will believe? They could have me clapped into prison, easy as you please. So you see, that's why I can't give his name to the authorities. I can't take the risk."

She looked at me uncertainly, like she was trying to make up her mind about who to believe, him or me. I imagine it was a difficult choice, since she disliked both of us so much. I didn't want to appear desperate, but I felt that there must be something I could say that would make her believe me. Only I didn't know what it could be.

"He said he would marry me, you know," I went on. "And I was fool enough to believe him. Otherwise I would never have …" I smoothed my apron over my belly. "I know I did wrong. It was a foolish mistake—more, it was a sin. But he's just as guilty as I am, is what bothers me. And he's able to go on about his life, and marry his rich lady, just as though none of it ever happened. While me, I'm in the almshouse, wondering how I'll ever feed this baby. And wondering now if I'll find myself having the baby in jail."

I felt the tears coming, I couldn't help it. They were genuine, even if not everything I'd told her was the absolute truth. I had to turn away from her, as I didn't want to give her the satisfaction of seeing me cry. "It's the women that always suffer, I suppose. It's our disgrace, and our burden. While *they* fly off, free as birds. But I won't trouble you further, Ma'am. I've told you the truth, that's all I can do. Now you must do with me as you will. Anyway, I suppose I deserve to suffer, like that Clara in your book."

I started to make my way to the door, quick before my tears overtook me completely. But my skirts caught on the edge of Mr. Farker's desk and it made me stumble. I almost fell to the floor, but I felt a hand catch me and steady me. Her hand, I realized.

"You've read *Clara D'Albe*?" she said, once I'd regained my balance. I nodded, still not looking at her, my cheeks wet. She sounded as though she wouldn't have thought someone like me capable of reading a whole book. There had been copies of it lying about the house, and I guess she never noticed when I borrowed one and took it to my room, wanting to see what all the fuss was about.

"And what did you think of it?"

That was odd, I thought, her caring what I thought. But I reckon if you write a book, or even translate one, you're curious to know what anyone thinks of it.

"It seemed very true to life," I told her. "I could understand how she felt, loving someone she couldn't have. And doing … what she did."

I'd liked *Adelaide* better, or what I'd read of it, but I thought it best not to add that. Anyway, I couldn't see the point in standing here talking about novels, when what little hopes I'd had for the future were just about ended, so I told her good day and started to make my way again towards the door. But she called me back.

"Tell me, Margaret, why is it you didn't find some other work, once you … left us? Surely you could have saved some money, for when the baby comes?"

I hardly knew where to begin explaining it all to her. It was like trying to get James to understand what real life is like, when you don't have a fancy house and heaps of money to draw on. I certainly wasn't going to tell her about the night I put on Alice's pink frock and one of her feathered hats and went down to Oakum Bay, and how as soon as a sailor approached me, fat and drunk and leering, I went running off as though I was being chased by a mad dog. So I told her I'd tried slop work, but that the season was over and the work had dried up. "And I couldn't go back into service," I added, "not without a reference."

"No, I suppose not." She was silent for a moment, and I thought she was done. But just before I turned away from her she spoke again. "But haven't you got somewhere you could go? Isn't there someone who might take you in?"

I shook my head and tried to keep the anger from my voice. "If I had, I wouldn't be here, would I?" I only wanted to get away from her now. I started for the door.

"No one?" Her voice was like a pin jabbing into my flesh. "A brother, perhaps?"

I stopped and took in a sharp breath. It was almost as if she knew. But how could she?

"I did have a brother. That is, I suppose I still do. Only I don't know that he'd want to see me, let alone take me in."

"Why ever not? Surely, if he knew your situation—"

"He had a terrible argument, years ago, with my father. And I took my father's side, you see."

"But—no, stay just a moment! Perhaps his quarrel was only with your father, not with you. Perhaps he's been thinking of you, all these years, and wondering what has become of you. For all you know he'd welcome the chance to see you."

I could feel the tears coming on again. Like before, it seemed she knew more than she should, somehow. Only this time she seemed to know what was in my head, even in my heart. Many is the time I've thought of John and wondered if perhaps he was thinking of me. We were close, once. One day when I was small he'd taken a stick and beat back a wild dog that looked ready to eat me alive. And he used to lift me over the creek on our farm, so I wouldn't wet my shoes or the hem of my dress. I realized that was the sunny bank I'd been thinking about since that camp meeting, the one Alice had spoken of — the bank of that very creek. I'd imagined sitting on it with Papa and Mama and Fanny and John as well, only of course in my mind the sunny bank was somewhere in Heaven. But suddenly I saw John and me and the child that was still in my belly, sitting on the bank of our old creek all together, laughing and singing, like we were a family.

And then I thought: no, it was impossible. Not after all the ugliness, and what he'd done to Papa, turning him out of his own farm. Papa would never allow us to even speak his name. Fanny didn't mind, she'd only been a baby when we left and hardly remembered John. But sometimes I'd forget and say something about him, and Father would give me the darkest of looks.

"You mustn't feel you'd be betraying your father, you know, if you were to make amends with your brother," I heard Mrs. A say. And I wondered yet again: how did she know? "If you still love him, that's between him and you, and no one else. He's all you have, now, your brother. And a brother is a very precious thing."

It sounded familiar, that phrase. And then I remembered: I'd said something very much like it to Polly, only about mothers. I put my hands to my temples and rubbed them, trying to think clearly. If John still loved me, if I could go back to the farm and live with him, and raise the child there …

"I don't know," I said. "My brother is a very religious person, or he was. I don't know what he'd think about my situation. I'd be afraid to tell him."

Mrs. A was silent for a moment. I looked at her, and she seemed to be thinking hard — thinking about how to help me, it seemed. I couldn't understand. Why would she want to do that?

"We could tell him you were married," she began, slowly, "and that your husband died. He had a fever. Or perhaps it was an accident, at work. A brick, perhaps, or a load of them. They fell on his head." She was speaking faster now. I thought of what Polly had said, about her making up stories. "In any event, we could tell him you're a respectable widow."

I had to laugh at that, a little. But why was she saying "we"? What was her part in any of this?

"I'll write to him," she said, as if to answer the question I hadn't asked, "on your behalf. I'll vouch for you, as your employer.

And I'll ask him if he could find it in his heart to take you in and save you from this distress. This misfortune."

I could only stare for a moment. "Then you're not going to put anything in the paper? About me and Mr. Cork?"

She smiled a bit, but she wasn't looking at me. It seemed she was smiling at herself. "No, I suppose I'm not. I don't suppose it would accomplish much, really, would it? It certainly wouldn't add to anyone's happiness, not even mine. It would only engender more misery, and we have quite enough of that already. I'll put something in about Mr. Cork — he deserves one last riposte, at least — but nothing about you, never fear."

I thanked her and told her it was very good of her. I tried not to show my surprise too much, as I thought it might make her suspect I didn't deserve to be helped. "You can send the letter to the McKenzie farm, near Bel Air," I said. "That's all the address I have, but I imagine it will reach him, if he's still there. And now I'd best be getting to the oakum shed, as they'll be wondering where I've wandered off to. And I suppose Mr. Parker will want his office back." I was far from eager to get back to work, but I felt so much lighter now, with the kindness and hope she'd given me, for whatever reason, that the prospect hardly bothered me at all.

And then she said something I never would have expected, something even more puzzling and surprising than what she'd already told me.

"No," she said, "you'll go and get your things and come with me. There's no need for you to stay in this ..." She looked about and shuddered, though Mr. Parker's office was quite the nicest room in the place. "This den of horrors. You'll stay with us until your brother comes to fetch you. In your old room."

I was staring again, and I fear my mouth was open like an idiot's. I thought I must have misheard her. But no, she said it again, impatient like — "Go on, get your things!" And now I ran, before she had the time to change her mind. What might happen if my brother didn't answer the letter — or if he said he didn't want me — was something I preferred not to think about. It seemed that Mrs. A felt sure he'd be glad to hear from me, and I could only pray she was right.

From the Observer, December 26, 1807:

DOCTOR CRAWFORD'S THEORY,
And an application of it to the treatment of diseases.

As I am very desirous to bring this subject to such a conclusion as to give it some appearance of a finished work, I determined to appropriate a portion of the present number to its completion.

I have experienced the common fate of all who have hazarded innovation; I have been loaded with obloquy, and represented as committing the lives of my fellow creatures to the issue of doubtful experiments.

To those who carefully read what I have advanced on the present subject, I shall not appear inconsistent in believing that a development of the causes of disease will lessen the miseries of the human race because I have alleged that premature death was necessary to the conservation of our species. I have supposed that if the cause of our maladies comes to be in any degree adequately disclosed, much clearer views of management will be adopted than can have hitherto existed. If such should be the happy result, I shall not have labored in vain; I shall not have, in the course of more than fifteen years, often wasted the midnight lamp fruitlessly, nor sacrificed the best worldly prospects for an imaginary good; although deferred, I shall be in the end gratified by a sure reward.

J.C.

BEATRICE IRONSIDE'S BUDGET.

Gentle readers, language fails in doing justice to the deep sense I entertain of your countless merits. I therefore give and bequeath the task of celebrating your praises to the enlightened panegyrists you possess in the Companion, the Critic, the Spectacles, and Moonshine. As for me, hapless Beatrice, a sad office awaits me – the ghost of poor Benjamin Bickerstaff has been wandering on this side of the Styx, and yester-night *with visage pale and grim, his rosy smile of* self-complacence *vanished, the doleful wight appeared before me! O Mistress Beatrice, Mistress Beatrice, cried he, Charon refused to waft me to those shores where dwell my tutelary divinities Conceit and Folly, whom you know when here I so faithfully served.*

Therefore in pity to the shade of him who, when in this world, so fondly cherished me, *I go to give peace to his ghost. For no sooner is his hour of penance over than his soul is to pass into the body of that noble Bird consecrated to Folly, called in* Greek *(once his favorite tongue) a* ken — *in vulgar English, a goose — and his high employment is to be standing at the gate of his divinities and cackling loud at every passenger whom he beholds bending his steps towards the temple of wisdom. To the kind task I go, and therefore bid you the eternal adieu of*

BEATRICE IRONSIDE.

Chapter Twenty-nine: Eliza

I spent much of the morning posted by the window, or at least
on the alert for the sound of wheels pulling up to our door. For
though John McKenzie had said he would come, I think Margaret
and I both still entertained some doubt. We exchanged glances
throughout the early afternoon, and I saw her peering anxiously
at the clock in the library as often as I did. What would become
of her should he not keep his word was a subject I pushed from
my mind. We haven't the money to keep her on here, with a
child; nor, I confess, did I relish the thought of having the gossips
speculate about the morals of my housemaid as well as my own.
But I knew I could never bring myself to send her back to that
Stygian bog of an almshouse, its tortures sufficient to rival those
Dante imagined for his Inferno—I've grown too fond of the girl
for that.

Yes, fond of her! Never in my wildest imaginings would I
have predicted such a turn of events. There was a time, not so
long ago, when I saw her as a villainous conspirator in the destruction of my happiness. Now she seems to me one who trusted
too blindly and was betrayed, far more a victim than a schemer—
a victim of James Cork, just as I have been. I know better than to
believe she is entirely innocent, and yet, as Father said, who has
not made mistakes in their youth? Must we be condemned to suffer for eternity for them?

I suppose my change of heart began that day I overheard her
praising me to Polly, although I wasn't aware of it at the time. I
realized as the memory kept entering my mind that she had no
reason to say anything kind about me after I'd thrown her out,

nothing to gain — for she had no idea I was listening. And in the three weeks she's been back with us, it's as though I've begun to see her through a new pair of eyes, all the little foibles that used to irritate me now transformed into charms. Well, not quite all. Her manners could still use some polishing, and I think she'll never have the temperament for service; a request that she clear the table or light the fire is still apt to produce a put-upon sigh and only reluctant compliance. But she's so loving and skillful with Polly it makes up for a multitude of sins. Her child, when it comes into the world, will be fortunate to have such a mother.

And Polly has taken great pride in showing off her skills in reading and writing to Margaret. It's astonishing how much progress she made, once I began making up little stories for her to read, and then having her write stories of her own to read to me. Madame Lacombe has agreed to take her on as a half-day pupil next month, as she's become so accomplished. I suppose I didn't give Margaret enough credit for allowing the child to exercise her imagination; I had no idea it could be harnessed to such useful purposes. The child could use more work on her numbers, but for the time being I've allowed the two of them, her and Margaret, to spend hours together making their drawings — and even to receive instruction from an expert.

It was Polly's idea that Mr. Godefroy should give her drawing lessons, and she was quite insistent about it. I was hesitant at first, of course, but I knew that Mr. Godefroy could use the bit of money it would bring him, and Polly was so eager to see him again. I was too, of course, but all that had transpired between us had put me into such a state of embarrassment and confusion that I couldn't bring myself to ask him, and I had Father make the arrangements. When he arrived and saw that Polly had already acquired some skill in drafting, he asked with whom so young a child had been studying. "It was Margaret!" Polly declared.

Margaret was then produced, along with some of her drawings, and Mr. Godefroy now exclaimed over *her* talent and ability. "If I didn't know your situation," he exclaimed, "I would say you must have had a teacher of some skill."

"Well, my mother taught me a few things, when I was a child. But in fact …" Margaret had turned bright red and looked from him to me and then at the floor. "I won't lie to you, sir, though I'm not sure you'll like the answer. It was Mr. Guy!"

We were all stunned into silence for a moment, and then we all burst out laughing. Mr. Godefroy declared that they would all draw together — he and Polly and Margaret — and that he warranted there were a few things he might learn about drawing portraits from Margaret, as she appeared to have a gift for it.

He has been here four times now, but I've barely been able to bring myself to speak to him. I imagine he expects an answer of some kind to his declaration that he wishes to make me his wife, but I remain seized by the paralysis that struck me once I realized that neither Father nor the law would prevent me from shedding my old husband and acquiring a new one — that the decision was mine. I steal glances at Mr. Godefroy and a part of me yearns to be by his side, to have him hold me in his arms. When he arrives or departs and kisses my hand, it is all I can do to stay upright. And yet I cannot act, cannot bring myself to speak. And as he has made it clear that the first move must be mine, we have kept one another at a polite but exceedingly awkward distance.

Although Father has tried to engage me in conversation on the subject, I have told him I would prefer not to discuss it. Perhaps my present state is less than entirely happy, but it is familiar, and now that Polly is well I have told myself I must not ask for more, for who knows whether change will bring good or ill. And these past few weeks, with Margaret here to tend to Polly, I have begun to work again — not on submissions for any of the periodical papers, as I have had done with them and their foolish vendettas. But I have secretly begun writing the novel I have had in my mind these last several months, about a woman who marries unwisely and is abandoned by her scoundrel of a husband, leaving her with a young child. It is pure delight to escape from my present world into one of my imagining, even if it is one that bears some resemblance to my own. I have my plot and my characters to absorb me, I have told myself, and it is far less dangerous to stir up emotions on paper than to stir them in one's heart, or in that of another — for it is easier to direct the course of a novel than the course of one's life.

Indeed, I even managed to write a few sentences of the novel this morning, wresting some few minutes of concentration from my hours of vigilant watching for signs of Mr. McKenzie, when, towards eleven o'clock, there came a knock at the door. We all hurried to the front hall from our different corners of the house —

myself from the sitting room, Father from the library, and Margaret, with Polly in tow, breathlessly running up the stairs from the kitchen. Nearly colliding, we smiled at one another in nervous anticipation.

"Go on, Margaret," I coaxed. "You open the door."

But she said she couldn't, and begged me to do it. I thought of all the times I'd had to open the front door myself, cursing the fact that we hadn't the sort of servants who would bestir themselves at a knock, and wondering what my visitors would think when they found *me* standing there—especially if one of the visitors happened to be Betsy. I could only laugh at Margaret now, just inches from the door but frozen in fear, and say that of course I would be the one to open the door if she wished.

He stood there on the top step, a large man with a ruddy complexion and hair the same coppery color as Margaret's, looking as frightened as she did. Behind him was a cart pulled by a sturdy if inelegant steed, the sort more accustomed to farm work than the clatter and bustle of a city street. Indeed, it seemed that the horse might be the most frightened creature of all in this scene.

"Won't you come in, Mr. McKenzie?" I said, and introduced him to Father. "And here is ..." I turned around, but Margaret had disappeared. I looked at Polly, who pointed silently to the closed door of the library. What was wrong with the girl, I wondered? After all I'd done to bring this plan to fruition, all I knew that she hoped for, why would she run off at this juncture, just when she should be poised to seize her happiness and her future?

"Father," I said, thinking as quickly as I could, "won't you take Mr. McKenzie into the sitting room while I fetch Margaret? And Polly, run down to the kitchen and ask Mrs. Morris to bring up some refreshment for us."

As soon as Father and Mr. McKenzie were safely behind the door of the sitting room I slipped into the library, where I found Margaret collapsed in a chair, her face in her hands. "Whatever is the matter?" I said, and I fear there was some sharpness in my tone.

She looked up, her eyes red and her cheeks streaked with tears. "I'm sorry, I don't know what's come over me," she said. "I do appreciate what you've done, finding John, and having him agree to take me. But." She swallowed. "Couldn't I just stay here? I'll make myself useful, I swear I will. And the baby won't eat much, and I'll keep it quiet, I promise."

"Now, Margaret." I perched on the arm of the chair where she sat and put a steadying hand on her shoulder. "You know that's simply not possible. And we decided it was better for you this way, remember? Out in the country, where the air is clean? Where you might find a new life—even, perhaps, find a husband, who could be a father to your child? And you've told me you don't want to spend your life in service. This is your chance for something better."

She nodded, but the tears continued to roll from her eyes. "Yes, but what if I don't like it out there, on the farm? What if John and I don't get on well together? What if he finds out I never had a husband? I keep trying to remember what you told him killed my husband—I don't know whether it was a load of bricks or a fall from a platform. What if I say the wrong thing and John gets suspicious? He does have a temper, you know. It may not be perfect here, but at least it's familiar."

"I can't promise you things will be better if you go," I said, taking one of her hands in mine. The cuts in her hands from the almshouse had healed now, and though they'll never be mistaken for the hands of a lady, at least they weren't painful to look at. "But there are few rewards that come without some risk. And Mr. McKenzie is your family, all the family you have now. Remember what he said in his letter, that he has often thought of you these past five years and hoped that you were safe and well? And how eager he said he was to see you again, and to provide for you and the child? We have no reason to doubt his sincerity. And he's here now, having come all this way for you. He's waiting. The least you can do is see him. And it was a fall that killed your husband—he was working on the steeple of Mr. Godefroy's church. That's all you need to remember."

"But." She removed her hand from my grasp and stretched it towards me. "John will be expecting a ring, if I've been married. And I haven't got one. He'll know it's a lie!"

"That's a simple problem to solve," I said, twisting and pulling at the gold band on my own finger until I wrested it free. "Here, take this."

She stared at it, her eyes wide, as though I were offering her a diamond tiara. "Oh, I couldn't. Not *your* ring. Are you sure?"

"Quite sure. It hasn't done me any good, Lord knows. It might as well serve some useful purpose."

She took it from me carefully, as though it might break, and slipped it on her finger, where it fit as though it had been made for her. I rubbed at the indentation the ring had left on my hand, an unnatural narrowing, now the only physical reminder that I was legally bound to a man I loathed. Even that would soon fade, I thought, my finger filling out to match the others.

Margaret took a moment to admire the ring, holding it to the light so it shone, then took a breath and squared her shoulders. "All right, then," she said. "Let's go."

When we opened the door to the sitting room, Mr. McKenzie bolted up from his chair and put down his teacup with a clatter — the thin china had looked distinctly out of place in his meaty hand, and seemed far more at its ease on the table. The two of them, brother and sister, only stared at one another for a long moment, and I held my breath, fearing that all this had been a mistake, that angry words might have passed between them that could not be forgotten, no matter how long ago they'd been spoken.

But then he held out his arms, wide, and in a choked voice, said only: "Maggie!" And Margaret went running to him and embraced him with such fervor that I knew all would be well for her, at last. I couldn't help but think of Thomas, of course, and how I should most likely never again share an embrace such as this with a brother, never hear his voice calling my name. I glanced at Father and saw that he was gazing at me, his brow knit in such a way that I suspected his thoughts ran along the same lines.

The next hour or more was spent in conversation, Mr. McKenzie exclaiming over Margaret's collection of drawings. "They're as good as Mama's, they are, or better," he declared, and I saw Margaret beam. "Do you think you could do a drawing of me and my wife, and our little girl?"

"You have a wife?" This was obviously a piece of intelligence with which Margaret was unfamiliar. "And a daughter?"

"That we do. She's two years old, and her name is Abigail."

Margaret pressed her lips together, and it looked as though she might cry again.

"Our mother's name," he explained to Father and me.

"Of course I'll do your portraits," Margaret said softly, "and in pastels, not just charcoal." She turned to me, seeming to have regained her composure. "Did you know Mr. Godefroy has given me a going-away present of a set of pastels? And he's taught me how to use them."

"No, I didn't know that," I said, feeling my face flush at the mention of the name. It was a present I suspected he could ill afford—no doubt it had consumed all the money we'd paid him for the lessons, if not more. "How very kind of him."

"I don't know you'll have much time for all that," Mr. McKenzie went on. "There's always more to do on the farm than we have the time for, and we'll need an extra pair of hands." He looked thoughtful for a moment. "It's too bad, you know. There was a man came through our parts two or three year ago, offering to do portraits, and he had more business than he could handle. He made a nice little pile of money, and he wasn't near as good as you, Maggie."

Margaret brushed some hair from her eyes and cocked her head at her brother. "What do you mean, then, that it's too bad? Maybe some of those people would pay *me* to do their portraits."

Mr. McKenzie drew his head back. "A woman? I don't see the farmers I know paying a female for that sort of thing."

"How ridiculous!" I heard myself exclaim. "If the portrait is good it's worth good money no matter who painted it. You can tell those farmers, Mr. McKenzie, that in France there have been several women artists of great renown, some of whom have even been admitted to the *Académie*—although I don't suppose that will mean much to them."

I saw Margaret regarding me with a smile of wonderment and delight, as though she couldn't quite believe she was hearing these words from my lips—though I can't imagine why she should be so surprised. Perhaps she was merely surprised to hear that there were female artists who had met with success. I confess that I myself had been unaware of the fact until Mr. Godefroy had told me of Madame Guiard and Madame Vigeé-Lebrun and some others.

Mr. McKenzie shrugged. "If Maggie can find anyone willing to pay her for drawing them, she's welcome to do it as far as I'm concerned," he said. "We can always use a bit of cash."

Then he announced that they must take their leave if they were to reach the farm before dark, and there ensued a flurry of bringing parcels down from Margaret's room to the cart, and promises to Polly that she could soon come and visit. Margaret made a present to us of three portraits of Polly that she'd done, including the one that Father had shown me that day of the child's recovery. But she assured us that she had plenty of others to remember Polly by, until such time as they met again.

Father and Mr. McKenzie were loading parcels in the cart, and Polly watching them, so that for a moment Margaret and I found ourselves alone. She turned to me with an urgent look and seemed about to speak, but not a sound emerged.

"What is it, Margaret? There's no need to thank me, really. It gives me great pleasure to see you going off to what appears to be a bright future."

"No, it's not that. That is—I *am* grateful, more grateful than I can tell you. But ..." She looked out to the street through the open door. Father and Mr. McKenzie were patting the last of the parcels into place on the cart and ensuring that they were secure, and Polly was skipping about in the street next to them, her distress at Margaret's departure nearly forgotten in all the excitement. Margaret returned her gaze to me and her words came out in a rush.

"I hope you won't think I'm speaking out of turn, Ma'am, but there's something I have to say. You've done so much for me, I'm thinking maybe there's something I can do for you." She swallowed and took a breath. "It's Mr. Godefroy. Polly asked him, the other day, if he would be her father, you see. And he smiled that sad smile of his and said he'd like nothing better, but that it was very complicated. But I don't see why it should be. It's clear to me he loves Polly, and she loves him. But more than that, I can see that he loves you. And I think you love him too, even if you don't know it. And I don't see why you should be miserable, when you could be happy. You could be a family."

I blinked and shook my head, amazed. I don't know what I had expected, but it wasn't this. "But Margaret! I can't ... You know I have a husband."

She held up her ring—my ring—and gave me an impish smile. "Do you? You conjured up a husband for me. Surely you could conjure one away for yourself, if you tried."

I had to laugh at that. Father and Mr. McKenzie were coming up the walk now, and Mr. McKenzie was loudly saying his thanks and regretting that they had to leave, which was clearly meant to be a signal to Margaret that there must be no further delay. But Polly had thrown herself against Margaret's skirts and was clinging to them for dear life.

At length Margaret knelt down and whispered something in Polly's ear, then gave the child a gentle push in my direction. And Polly came to me and wrapped her short arms around my skirts instead. I reached down and stroked her hair.

Margaret started down the steps, but when she reached the bottom she turned and looked at me one last time. "Promise me," she said in a sort of whisper, but one that carried clearly. "Promise me you'll try!"

And I nodded and smiled at her, a tear spilling from my eye. "I will," I murmured, holding Polly a little tighter. Then stronger and louder, so Margaret could hear: "I will!"

Epilogue

R eader, she married him. That is: Eliza Anderson, who was a real person, really did marry Maximilian Godefroy, another real person, in 1808, the year after many of the events described in this novel took place.

Much of this book is fiction, and several characters are entirely invented, most notably Margaret McKenzie. But many others are real — not only Eliza Anderson and Maximilian Godefroy, but also Eliza's father Dr. John Crawford, Elizabeth Patterson Bonaparte (known as Betsy), Elizabeth Caton (sometimes known as Betsey, but here, to avoid confusion, referred to as Bess), Francis Guy, William Groombridge, and even Mr. Webster (whose first name is lost to history, but whose first two initials were "W.H."). While James Cork is fictional, there was a real person who used the pen name Benjamin Bickerstaff. I chose to give him the name James Cork after seeing that someone had written "Jas. Cork" next to the name "Benjamin Bickerstaff" in a copy of the Companion, the predecessor of the Observer.

The Observer was a real publication, and excerpts from it (along with excerpts from other publications of the time) are reproduced in the novel with minor editing and some excisions. I used what facts I could glean from these publications, and from letters and other sources, to help provide the outline for my fictional story.

My journey to writing this book began in 2005, when I went to an exhibit of Gilbert Stuart portraits at the National Gallery in Washington. One, a triple portrait of a breathtakingly beautiful woman, nearly made me catch my breath. The subject, I discovered, was Elizabeth Patterson Bonaparte, known as Betsy, who I'd never heard of despite having grown up in Baltimore, where she's relatively well known. My curiosity piqued by an anecdote that was posted next to the portrait (which described how, in 1804, Betsy had appeared at a Washington party wearing such a skimpy dress that she'd caused a scandal), I began to do some research.

In the first of the twenty boxes of Betsy's correspondence at the Maryland Historical Society I came across three letters from a friend of hers, Eliza Anderson, all dating from 1808. These letters were so engaging that I began investigating the woman who had written them, and what I found was so intriguing that I gradually abandoned the idea of writing a novel about Betsy and decided to focus on Eliza instead.

One thing I discovered was that Eliza Anderson was one of the first women in the United States to edit a magazine — perhaps *the* first. The only woman I've been able to find who preceded her was an anonymous "Lady" who "compiled" a publication called the Humming Bird in 1798. It appears to have been a more modest affair than the Observer, which ran an unusually large number of original articles (as opposed to reprints from other publications), and which lasted an entire year, longer than most weekly periodicals of the day (only two issues of the Humming Bird are extant, the debut issue in April and another in June). And, like the compiler of the Humming Bird, nearly all female editors of the 19th century presided over magazines specifically targeted at women. Eliza, in contrast, clearly intended the Observer to appeal to a general readership.

During the same year she edited the Observer — 1807 — Eliza also really did translate two books from French into English: *Claire d'Albe* by Sophie Cottin (now available in a scholarly modern edition with an introduction that describes it as containing "what may be the first depiction of female orgasm in polite fiction," a passage that Eliza largely omitted from her translation); and Maximilian Godefroy's memorial on military fortifications. In addition to writing the memorial, Godefroy really did design a neo-Gothic church for what was then St. Mary's College (now St. Mary's Seminary), perhaps the first structure in the Gothic style built in North America, and one that still stands in downtown Baltimore.

In order to marry Godefroy, Eliza needed to obtain a divorce from her errant husband, no easy task in the early 19th century. Even though he had abandoned her and her daughter years before, Eliza had to prove his infidelity—"not an affair," as she remarked drily in a letter to Betsy Bonaparte in August of 1808, "to which men usually call witnesses." Finding that her lawyers weren't exerting themselves sufficiently, she resolved to journey alone up the Hudson to Albany—the last address she had for Henry Anderson—becoming one of the first passengers to travel by steamship. In an age when females rarely traveled alone, such an undertaking must have been remarkable.

In the novel I've speculated that there was gossip regarding Eliza and Godefroy in 1807, but certainly by 1808 there was talk about the couple. Eliza wrote to Betsy in June of that year, while in New Jersey seeking her divorce, "As for what the town says of me, and much I hear they say, I care not. ... Why should I be at the trouble of getting a divorce and overcoming the difficulties that attended getting the means to do it if I had already sacrificed honor?" (Why Eliza traveled to New Jersey to secure a divorce is not clear.)

When Eliza arrived in Albany, she was appalled to discover Henry Anderson working as a fisherman and, as she wrote to Betsy, "associating cheerfully with servants" (she was in fact something of an elitist). But, after a week or so, she was able to return with the evidence she needed, the names of one of Eliza's former housemaids and of a doctor in Baltimore. The doctor's role in the infidelity is unclear, but he may have performed an abortion on the housemaid or delivered her child. Apparently this evidence was sufficient, because on December 29, 1808, Eliza Anderson and Maximilian Godefroy were married. (Betsy, no democrat herself, annotated Eliza's letter of August 1808 with the remark, "She divorced her vulgar husband and married Godefroy.")

Godefroy went on to enjoy some success as an architect in Baltimore. Among other things, he designed the striking neoclassical First Unitarian Church, which still stands, and the Battle Monument commemorating the War of 1812, which not only still stands but also appears on the official seal of the City of Baltimore. But financial success eluded him, especially after a falling out with his friend Benjamin Latrobe in 1816, and the Godefroys lived hand-to-mouth. In 1817, Edward Patterson wrote to his sister

Betsy that the couple was "almost in a state of starvation." He also told her, "our friend [Eliza] Godefroy has behaved so badly of late that we have all determined to give her up. She made her appearance at two or three soirées so much intoxicated that the hostesses were obliged to put her to bed." Edward predicted that the Godefroys would soon have to leave Baltimore because they had "made themselves so many enemies."

Eliza's own letters from this period tell a somewhat different story, suggesting that the family's troubles stemmed from misunderstandings and lack of appreciation for Godefroy's talents. Still, it's clear they were in dire straits. Dr. Crawford had died in 1813, leaving many debts (although it appears the family was allowed to stay on in the house after he died), and Godefroy failed to get some of the commissions he applied for, including the design of Baltimore's Washington Monument. In 1817 Eliza lamented to Betsy, "It is not enough to live like the birds of the air, unknowing today where the food of tomorrow is to come from, but one's soul must be perpetually wounded in its best and noblest feelings." By 1819 the couple had decided to try their luck in England, where Eliza had relatives.

Shortly after they embarked, tragedy struck: Eliza's 19-year-old daughter, also named Eliza but nicknamed Polly—who had been described in an 1812 letter written by Latrobe as "not well attended to" and "sickly"—contracted yellow fever and died, despite her mother's desperate efforts to find help. (The story is recounted in a detailed article that appeared in the Baltimore Federal Gazette of September 27, 1819, and which may have been written by Eliza herself.) Heartbroken, her mother and stepfather resumed their voyage to England, where they spent the next seven years.

They had hoped that Godefroy could make a living there as an artist, and he did exhibit his drawing of the Battle of Pultowa at the Royal Academy in London in 1821. But the couple continued to struggle to make ends meet, and in 1827 they relocated to France, where Godefroy was able to obtain a pension for his military service. He was also hired as a government architect, first briefly for the city of Rennes and later for the Department of Mayenne, based in the town of Laval. But the position was ill paid and—in the eyes of both Eliza and presumably Godefroy himself—unworthy of his talents. In a letter to a friend in 1830,

Eliza wrote that often, "in contemplating the various productions of [her husband's] genius & in musing over his destiny," she had compared him to "a Corinthian capital, torn from its supporting column, and trodden under every careless foot." Pleading that he might be considered for an appointment as consul general to the United States, she referred to herself and Godefroy as "two footballs of fortune, so wrecked, so shattered by many a tempest."

As for Eliza's own career, I haven't been able to find any evidence that she wrote or translated anything after her remarkably prolific year in 1807. It's possible that she threw her energies into promoting her husband's career, albeit unsuccessfully. Or perhaps she did continue to write, but her writings either remained unpublished or have been lost to history. In 1832, a letter Godefroy wrote to a friend in Paris suggests that Eliza may have gone there to try to interest publishers or booksellers in something she had written.

Eliza died in Laval in 1839 at the age of 59, apparently in some degree of poverty and obscurity, taking with her to the grave a sense of injustice that her husband's talents hadn't received their proper due — and, having grown up more or less in the shadow of his masterpiece, the First Unitarian Church in Baltimore, I suspect that she was right. Three years before she died, Eliza lamented in a letter to a former student and friend of Godefroy's that she had seen "so much talent wrecked, so much genius thrown into such utter darkness, such high and noble honor doomed to such a lot."

But despite the couple's misfortunes, Eliza seems never to have regretted her choice of a husband. In 1830, after twenty-two years of marriage, she wrote that in all those years "no tear has ever filled my eyes, no pang has ever wrung my heart, which he occasioned or which he could avert — sorrows and bitter cares often pressed heavily upon me, but amidst them all, I have blessed that which I should otherwise have deprecated, the hour that gave me life, since I felt that all was redeemed by the consciousness of belonging to such a Being."

Acknowledgments

This book has been a number of years in gestation, and I owe debts to many who have guided and encouraged me along the way. My thanks to the staff at the Maryland Historical Society library, who always cheerfully responded to my questions, unearthed boxes of precious letters and other documents, and initiated me into the mysteries of their microfilm readers. Mary Jeske, editor of the Charles Carroll of Carrollton Papers, also provided valuable guidance and context.

I am also grateful to the Library of Congress. The breadth of its holdings never ceases to boggle my mind. I discovered, fairly late in my research, that every issue of the Observer was not only available there on microfilm, but actually downloadable onto a tiny flash drive, so that I could peruse the articles on my own computer at leisure. I cannot imagine how surprised Eliza Anderson would be by this development.

I have also benefited from the publication of several recent biographies of Betsy Bonaparte, which readers who are intrigued by this character may wish to consult: *Wondrous Beauty* by Carol Berkin; *Elizabeth Patterson Bonaparte: An American Aristocrat in the Early Republic*, by Charlene M. Boyer Lewis; and *Betsy Bonaparte* by Helen Jean Burn. And for those who want a strictly factual account of Eliza Anderson Godefroy's life, I have written one that was published in the Summer 2010 issue of the Maryland Historical Magazine, entitled "'What Manner of Woman Our Female Editor May Be': Eliza Crawford Anderson and the Baltimore Observer, 1806-1807."

Margaret McKenzie is a fictional character, but in creating the details of her life I was helped tremendously by *Scraping By: Wage*

Labor, Slavery, and Survival in Early Baltimore, by Seth Rockman, a careful and engaging work of scholarship.

Thanks as well to the friends who read early versions of the manuscript and urged me to keep going, even though I got side-tracked by other endeavors — most notably, in a turn of events that paralleled those in Eliza Anderson's life, becoming the editor of a blog that focuses on public education in Washington, D.C. While that experience certainly slowed the progress of the novel, it also gave me additional insights into the rewards and challenges Eliza faced some 200 years ago. The medium may have changed, but much else has not.

The largest debt of gratitude I owe to my husband. Like Eliza, I am fortunate to have found my soul mate, and I can say with her that "no tear has ever filled my eyes, no pang has ever wrung my heart, which he occasioned or which he could avert." We've also been lucky enough to share a lot of joy and laughter, not to mention two amazing children.

Praise for Natalie Wexler's previous books

A More Obedient Wife: A Novel of the Early Supreme Court

Bronze medal, historical fiction, Independent Publisher Book Awards

First place, Writer's Digest Self-Published Book Awards (Genre Fiction)

"Gripping" *The Bethlehem Press*

"Compelling" *Historical Novels Review Online*

"Riveting" *Midwest Book Review*

The Mother Daughter Show

"Amusing and perceptive" *Portland Book Review*

"Clever, witty, acutely observed social commentary" *Washington Independent Review of Books*

"Satirical fun and worthy insights" *Library Journal Xpress Reviews*

CPSIA information can be obtained at www.ICGtesting.com
Printed in the USA
BVOW05s1633300914

368851BV00001B/4/P